The Order of Nature

ISBN 10: 1775160009
ISBN 13: 9781775160007

To Mark,
Because everything else is commentary

Article 144: Unnatural offences

(1) Any person who—

a) has carnal knowledge of any person against the order of nature; or
b) has carnal knowledge of an animal; or
c) permits any person to have carnal knowledge of him or her against the order of nature;
is guilty of a felony, and is liable to imprisonment for a term of 14 years.

—Criminal Code of The Gambia

Prologue

SUNDAYS HAD A slower start. Unlike other days of the week, sunrise on Sundays gave way to stillness and silence. The city's low-rise buildings and narrow lanes stood frozen in sunlight. Street hawkers kept their carts covered longer. The markets opened later. Roads were mostly empty – the broken-down cars and vans that crowded the city streets kept off the road. There was a brief respite from the usual hum of horns and mufflers. Stereos that otherwise provided a soundtrack to daily life stayed off. Not many fishermen ventured out on Sunday mornings. Their small colorful boats dotted the blue and turquoise sea, stretching far off into the vast ocean. It was the most peaceful time of the week, and one that only a few took time to appreciate.

Usually, Thomas was one of the few. He'd get out of bed, put on his running shorts and sneakers, and head down towards the beach. He loved the emptiness of the small dirt streets between his home and the main road. Normally they were filled with men sitting in groups and small children playing with balls and rubber tires. Now only a few stray dogs rummaged through trash. Running down the deserted main road through Fajara, Thomas would pass one last row of palm trees before hitting the sand. It was at that moment when he normally stopped and ran on the spot for a short while, taking in the sight before him. There, under the canopy of palm leaves, he stared out from the white beach, sand still undisturbed, as it gave way to dancing crystals of light on the water.

But on this Sunday, Thomas skipped his run. Actually, he hadn't been running on a Sunday for some time. Sunday had started to take on a new meaning. It was his day off, and he spent it with Andrew. It was their day to wake up together, lazing around in bed until they felt like getting up. Later they would go out, not as a couple, but as two friends enjoying all the day had to offer. Their relationship was still a closely guarded secret, even from the friends and colleagues with whom they spent their time. But being together all day from start to finish was what mattered. They had all day to laugh together, to eat and drink together. It was the closest to normal they'd get.

Secrets can be burdensome companions, and Thomas and Andrew were never without theirs. The paranoia that subsided over time never quite vanished. They were always wondering if someone saw them coming back at night or leaving in the morning. Were they too loud? The curtains were always drawn before the sun went down. During the day there was concern that an affectionate look, a suppressed blush, or some other interpretable sign may be noticed. But there was something about how they'd been spending Sundays that disarmed their fears. Even if they couldn't hold hands, it was nice to be out.

Thomas always woke up first. Sleeping in was foreign to him. Growing up in a small house in the countryside with siblings and dogs running between the houses, mornings were never a quiet affair. Andrew, on the other hand, was the quintessential American college grad. He loved to sleep in, and Thomas was reluctant to disturb Andrew's sleeping. In those moments, lying awake waiting for Andrew, Thomas would replay the reel of their burgeoning romance trying to predict what might happen next.

A combination of brightness and heat woke Thomas up that day. The summer rains were approaching, with the heat and humidity at their peak. The air was stiff and heavy, leaving everyone a little sweaty. Making it more unpleasant, the fan wasn't working because the power had gone off, again. He turned to his side, opening his eyes just enough. Andrew was still sleeping, his breathing rising through the still air. Normally he'd have given Andrew a bit more time, but after work the day before, Thomas knew that if he stayed in bed awake he'd only think about the previous day's events and go crazy. He needed Sunday's distractions; he had to get out.

"Wake up," he said as he nudged himself up to Andrew. "Lazy boy, get out of bed."

"You're so annoying," Andrew mumbled.

"According to you, who sleeps through the morning leaving me alone," Thomas grinned.

Andrew turned his head and grinned back. "It's hot in here. Why isn't the fan on?"

"Why do you think?"

Andrew didn't have to ask. He'd been in the country long enough.

"I'm hot," said Andrew, turning to face Thomas. "Why can't the power stay on?" By now they were both lying on their sides, foreheads touching, speaking in that low morning voice when tiredness can mask as tenderness. "How'd you sleep?"

"Fine."

"Are you still pissed about last night?"

"Yes, but I'd rather not talk about it now. It was embarrassing enough having to deal with it then. I'll be fine."

"It's going to happen again. It wasn't the first time he punished you for spending time with foreigners. It won't be the last either."

They both knew this was true. Of all the hotel staff, Thomas had always been the friendliest with foreigners. Even though they weren't in on his secret, he felt a connection to them. If they did know they'd surely understand, unlike his own people. Most of the time his socializing with them didn't matter. But if he — for whatever reason — upset a guest, or worse, did something so right that he was publicly rewarded with an extra tip, his colleagues unleashed mockery and jealousy on him. Last night was one of those nights. So he had to work late, and miss the dinner he and Andrew planned to cook.

Andrew closed his eyes, leaned in, and gently kissed Thomas. "I'm sorry my people get you in trouble."

Thomas smiled. "You don't get me in trouble. I do it to myself." He leaned back in for another kiss. And then they lay there, in a still and silent embrace as their bodies woke up.

The fan started and broke the silence.

"Yesss," Andrew said, as he turned away from Thomas, throwing the sheets off to let the fan blow directly on him. He closed his eyes and took a deep breath, trying to relax and cool down. "It's so fucking hot."

Thomas leaned in to cuddle Andrew but he pushed him back. "I can't. It's *sooo* hot."

"Then let's go. I want to enjoy my day off," Thomas declared as he got out of bed and pushed the mosquito net off to the side. He stared down at the pile of clothes on the floor to figure out which were his, grabbed a t-shirt and boxers and put them on. Then he picked up Andrew's t-shirt and threw it at him and smiled. Andrew smiled back and sat up while wiping the light layer of sweat off his forehead.

"Okay, let's go," he said, as he put the t-shirt on.

They had breakfast – Thomas had toast with two boiled eggs and Andrew ate imported British muesli. They each had a mango, freshly picked from a tree in the yard. And Andrew made tea. They ate sitting on the oversized couch in the living room in front of the fan.

Thomas was still a bit unnerved from the night before. A group of female British tourists at the hotel remembered him fondly from a visit the year before. They spent quite a while chatting with him at the bar. After some time, they bought him a drink. Staff weren't allowed to drink on the premises so at first Thomas refused. But they were the only people at the bar and it was late in the evening. He relented.

That's when his boss appeared. The look he gave Thomas was enough to signal his displeasure and the women immediately started defending Thomas.

It was our fault. He refused and we kept persisting. He was only being a good employee. Really sir, please blame us. We apologize and it won't happen again.

Thomas's boss smiled politely, assuring them he understood. But later that night, when the women had gone back to their rooms, he reprimanded Thomas in front of the hotel manager. He called Thomas a *wannabe white*, which made the manager laugh. He told him he would have to work the next three Sundays without pay as punishment.

"Can he even make you do that?" asked Andrew.

"They can do whatever they want. There are no laws in this country for these things. If a boss says you have to do it, you do it."

"It's only three days, I guess."

"It's not the working."

"The comment?"

"Yes." Thomas turned his face away from Andrew, pausing for a second before looking back up. "It's fine. As long as I'm not fired they still pay me. I don't care what they think of me. And by the way, he's the wannabe white, not me. He's the one who always walks behind the tourists, laughing and agreeing with every stupid remark they make, or telling them how wonderful they look in those stupid khaki vests with all those pockets. Please!"

Andrew laughed. He owned no such vest.

After they ate Andrew walked into the second bedroom, picking up the blanket and frisbee left behind by his old roommate, Alex. They were two travel essentials Andrew had never thought to bring with him, but learned he couldn't do without.

Thomas stood by the front door ready to leave when he turned to Andrew in the doorway of the other bedroom. "I'll see you in a bit."

Andrew walked towards him, gently kissed his lips, looked at him, and said, "Okay."

It was their routine. They realized early on that it would appear suspicious if they always showed up to places together. So to keep the ruse going, they decided to arrive at least fifteen to twenty minutes apart. It was prudence meets paranoia.

When Thomas left, Andrew spent a few minutes cleaning up from the night before, picking their clothes up off the floor, neatly tying up the mosquito net over the bed, and doing the dishes in the sink. Then he looked at his watch and waited another five minutes before leaving.

After the long head start, Andrew hopped on his bicycle and made his way down to the beach. The dirt and sand on the roads were so thick that at times he struggled and had to walk his bike; the ground was parched this time of year. He stopped in at a bakery he liked to see if it had any fresh croissants; it didn't, and unless they were hot, the croissants weren't worth buying.

The afternoon at the beach was uneventful. Everyone was a bit sluggish because of the summer heat. A smaller crowd meant people dispersed more quickly, making it easier for Andrew and Thomas to wander discreetly up the almost-deserted beach. Even the locals were escaping the heat. They walked with their bikes slowly at the water's edge where the sand was hardest, mostly telling jokes and laughing at funny memories from the trip they took with Alex and his girlfriend Liv several weeks back. Sometimes when they laughed, their eyes inadvertently met and locked. The laughs then turned into shy, blushed smiles. Andrew always looked away first.

"What?" Thomas asked.

"Nothing," Andrew answered, looking back up and still smiling.

They walked this way past the few empty hotels on the northern stretch of the beach, past the wooden shack selling grilled fish and rice, and past a small group of kids playing soccer at the top of the beach who tried – but failed – to get their attention by repeatedly yelling *hi*. They kept walking as the sun started to set, tingeing their faces with the softer light of dusk.

Eventually, under the cover of darkness, they made their way back to Andrew's house. Not wanting to attract suspicion, they again arrived separately. Thomas locked the gate behind him, left his bike up against one of the mango trees and walked across the grass yard through the compound up to Andrew's little beige bungalow. The kitchen lights were on. When Thomas entered, quickly closing the door, Andrew was already in the kitchen, looking to see what they could make for dinner.

"We might have to eat pasta again."

They enjoyed cooking together. It made them feel normal. Not that cooking pasta was any great feat. Still, it was domestic. Normal couples were domestic.

Dinner was eaten inside where they wouldn't be seen. That and because a past outdoor experience proved eating saucy food in the dark was a bad idea. They mostly talked about Andrew's upcoming work week. He was supposed to spend three days at meetings with officials from the education ministry to talk about group learning strategies, an area he'd been singled out for. He was dreading it. Constant over-the-top introductions and greetings that went on forever, the overly ambitious presentations that rarely translated into concrete action, and the food. The food at these meetings was never very good.

"And because Mr. Jalloh is going to be there," referring to his principal, "I have to participate. He loves meetings. It's terrible."

Thomas took pleasure in these moments. It was Andrew's initiation into how things did or didn't get done in his country. "At least you'll have air conditioning."

"True."

At the school where Andrew worked, only Mr. Jalloh's office had air conditioning, and even it was broken most of the time.

When they finished eating, Thomas asked if they could lie outside for a bit before they cleaned up. Andrew was usually not one to leave a mess, but he felt lazy and agreed. He took the blanket out of his bag and they set it out on the grass. There was only a sliver of a moon out so the night sky was awash in silver specks of stars.

Lying on the ground, Thomas nestled his head up against Andrew's shoulder and his arm around Andrew's chest. But for the occasional car driving by on the main road, all they heard were crickets and each other. Thomas tested Andrew on the constellations, which he was getting better at. Stars didn't exist much in suburban Chicago and Andrew never knew much about them. But Thomas knew a lot. As a boy, he and his father would often fish on the River Gambia at night. Thomas was always awed by the night sky. His father didn't know the constellations' names, but like any good father who doesn't want to disappoint his son, he made things up. When Thomas was older and able to read, he found a book on the constellations, realizing most of what he and his father labeled was wrong or didn't even exist. Still, for some of them he ignored their real names and preferred the make believe explanation. It gave him something from that period of his life to hold on to.

After a while, when Andrew dozed off, Thomas heard the sound of a car he thought was getting a bit close. There was a small path off the main road that cars would sometimes use to get to the dirt road that ran adjacent to the house. At first Thomas assumed this was the case. With the noise growing louder, he realized there was more than one car. Headlights could be seen through the cracks of the gate bouncing up and down as the cars navigated the bumpy path. They should have turned away by then to get to the other road, but they were still headed straight for the gate. Thomas stood up and took a big gulp as the sound and lights drew nearer. His sudden movement woke Andrew who only had a few seconds to process the lights and noise before three cars stopped outside the compound.

Part One

I

It was nearly dusk when Andrew walked off the plane in Banjul. He looked around at the empty tarmac. Theirs was the only plane. A fire truck sat nearby, but from the looks of it, Andrew wasn't sure it was working. The terminal building was worn and crowded. Women wore shiny colorful dresses with big matching headdresses. Many of the men wore long shirts that resembled pajamas. People gesticulated wildly and spoke loudly, often yelling across the arrivals hall at people who appeared to be strangers. Everyone seemed to be sweating. Andrew noticed he was one of only a handful of white people. Realizing this, his eyes scanning the crowd, Andrew was struck that for the first time in his life, *he* was the minority.

There were only two immigration officials working the long line. Andrew had heard stories about foreigners landing in Africa and having to bribe immigration officials. He worried this would happen to him, but entered without any fuss.

Exiting the terminal, Andrew faced a throng of unfamiliar faces waiting to pick up arriving passengers. Pressing himself between the hordes of people, Andrew wearily pushed his luggage through a crowd reluctant to part ways for it, accidentally rubbing it against a disgruntled-looking man, his "excuse me" to no avail. Making his way past, he spotted his name on a piece of paper, held by a middle-aged woman. She dressed in Western clothing, her hair in a pony-tail, carrying a distinctly large handbag, and with sunglasses atop her forehead. She smiled at him as he walked over and extended her hand. "Hi Andrew, I'm Haddy. Welcome to The Gambia!"

"Thanks."

"Long journey?"

"Yeah, it was."

"Then let's go to the car," Haddy said before she turned to a man and instructed him to bring Andrew's bags. "It will take us about forty-five minutes to reach your house. You must be tired. Are you hungry?"

"I'm okay."

Stepping towards the parking lot, Andrew watched cars dashing frantically towards any open space as newly arrived passengers load-ed their baggage. Horns sounded at a dizzying pace. Police officers blew whistles to control traffic. The sun, though setting, still radi-ated heat. Staring down at him was a giant billboard advertising the country's beaches, with a picture of a smiling man in white clothing who Andrew knew was the country's president. "WELCOME TO THE GAMBIA – THE SMILING COAST," it said.

Andrew could barely hear Haddy as they walked through the crowd. Besides the noise and commotion around him, Haddy also had an accent. Not too thick, but enough that Andrew, being tired, had to concentrate on what she was saying. He didn't understand everything, but was too embarrassed to ask her to repeat herself. She introduced him to the driver but he didn't catch his name.

They got into the car and left the airport with the windows down. There wasn't any air conditioning and the car quickly filled with heavy, humid air. Andrew reached for his seatbelt only to discover there wasn't one.

Staring through the windows of the other cars leaving the airport, Andrew saw the continuation of the same animated conversations that filled the arrivals hall and parking lot. People passed mobile phones and treats back and forth between one another. The women's headdresses were as high as the roofs of the cars. Watching these scenes go by, his excitement building as it sunk in that he had finally arrived, Andrew's head filled with his parents' reactions when he first told them he was going to Gambia.

"You're going *where*?!" his mother asked from the other end of the phone. "Zambia?"

"No. Gambia," Andrew corrected. "It's in West Africa, a small country. It's actually called *The* Gambia."

"You can't be serious. You're not actually going to Africa. You have teacher's college this fall! And you've never been anywhere like that!"

"Where's this coming from?" his father asked. "It's pretty out of the blue, son."

He hated being called son.

"But *why*, Andrew?" His mother sounded desperate to know.

For too many years he'd lived their lives. It's not that it was a bad life – an upper-middle class, WASP upbringing in a Chicago suburb had its perks. He had things. They vacationed at nice resorts in the Caribbean. College was paid for. His parents didn't intrude into his personal life, mostly because emotional insight was neither of their strengths. But, they still loved and cared for him and wanted him to have a good life. From the outside, his upbringing was enviable.

"I just don't understand why you need to go so far away. To *Africa*," his mother said, pronouncing Africa with a blend of shock, fear, and distaste. "I won't be able to sleep for a whole year! You're not running away from us are you, Andrew?"

"No, Mom. I'm not."

It was a half-truth. Andrew told himself he wasn't as much running away as giving himself much-needed space. He was outgrowing the world his parents created for him. When he discovered his placement was in a country with hostile views on homosexuality, he was only slightly deterred. It certainly wasn't ideal. But the year was never about coming to terms with himself as a gay person. He could handle being in the closet. He just needed to get away.

"Mom, Dad. I'll be fine." He tried not to sound exasperated. "I'm going to email you a few things. Why don't you read them and we can talk again tomorrow, okay? You'll see what a great opportunity this is for me."

"Okay, son," his Dad said. "Bye-bye." He hung up the phone.

Son. It was a relationship of congratulatory pats on the back and handshakes goodbye.

As the car veered onto the road from the airport, the distance between Andrew and his parents hit him. Reminding himself why he left in the first place, he exhaled and sat back, determined to prove he made the right decision.

"You have the house to yourself for now," Haddy said as she turned to face him. "Your roommate Alex is upcountry on a trip. He should be back by the weekend. But you'll learn in Gambia that what should be and what is are not always the same. So better to say he'll be back in a few days." She spoke with a disarming smile. Haddy's phone rang, interrupting her, and for the first time Andrew clearly heard Wolof, the predominant local language.

Haddy's conversation kept going and at some point during the phone call Andrew tuned out. He sat and stared out the window. It was a two-lane road without any neat end to the pavement on either side. It just sort of fell off unevenly into the dirt. There were no sidewalks either. Instead, people walked on the edge of the road or the dirt next to it, which didn't provide much more of a buffer. They shared the road with cars Andrew couldn't believe still functioned. Some looked like they'd been put back together in a scrap metal yard. Speeding past rusted, white mini-vans, he noticed young men hanging off open side doors who appeared to be yelling out to the street. Each glimpse inside a van revealed the same image of bodies tightly packed together, one nearly indistinguishable from the next.

There were also goats, lots of them. Ropes tied some to trees or poles, but others roamed freely. The male ones with huge balls made Andrew laugh to himself.

The road was lined with shops – many looked like convenience stores. Some were in proper buildings. Others were in shacks with a light bulb hanging from a string. The colors of their painted signs were faded, the text was often uneven. An endless line of men sat outside on chairs or benches. Some drank out of bottles, some gathered around small televisions, and some did both.

Traffic increased and they slowed down in an area filled with mechanics and car repair shops. The shops' equipment spilled onto the deep, brownish red earth by the roadside. They had no formal garages and men and boys of all ages were working there. Loud Afro hip-hop blared in the background. Andrew was struck by the number of young men and boys working – in shirts, tank tops, or bare-chested – covered with dirt and grease. They all had the same lean bodies and defined muscles. Their white eyes popped out from deep-black complexions. As he met their eyes from his window they stared back at him. He mistook their looks of exhaustion and curiosity for suspicion and unfriendliness. The stares unsettled him. Instinctively he went to close the window but stopped himself. Haddy and the driver weren't fazed at all.

A few of the repair shops had small fires going in steel drums. They all had small tables with rows of old bottles, filled with a strange yellowish liquid.

"What's in those bottles?"

"Foo-el," answered Haddy. It took Andrew a second to get past her accent. *Fuel*.

"Wow. I've never seen it sold like that before."

"We also have proper fuel stations. But this is the old fashioned way." Haddy turned around. Her face was soft and her smile was warm. "You will see and experience lots of things here that you haven't before. Have you been to Gambia or Africa before?"

"No."

"I hope you will love it. We will soon be at your home. The house is not far from our office or the school where you are working. But don't worry about that now. Tomorrow morning at nine the car will come to pick you up. It will bring you to the office and we'll go over everything. Tonight you must be very tired."

He was. Andrew barely slept on the plane, making it two nights in a row. He started taking deep inhales as he struggled to keep his eyes from closing.

Andrew awoke to knocking at the front door. Rubbing his eyes, he peeled himself up slowly from the mattress, unsticking his sweaty face from the pillow. He looked around, only to discover his vision was obstructed. White mesh hung over his bed. *Right, the mosquito net.* The breeze of the fan blowing from the corner of the room reached him but brought little relief. The knocking continued while he took an extra second to regain his bearings before he pushed the net up from the floor to let himself out from his bed.

"Andrew?" called out a voice from the door.

"Coming, I'll be right there," he yelled back. He got out of bed realizing he was still dressed in his t-shirt and pants from the night before, and walked to the front door where Haddy waited for him. He squinted as the light flooded the room.

"You're alive!" she exclaimed while walking in. "You fell asleep in the car last night. We woke you up when we got here. You were barely awake walking into the house. Do you remember?"

"Yeah. Sort of."

"Okay, well as long as you rested. Today we'll get you settled." She spoke and moved in a hurried fashion that he found slightly disorienting.

He stood in a small living room too crowded with furniture, seeing his house in daylight for the first time. An oversized, brown couch and sitting chair with felt-like material that looked like a velvet knockoff. The walls and floors were mostly a faded tan color. Behind Haddy, outside, he could see an older woman walking through a yard with a bucket. Unlike Haddy, who dressed in jeans, this woman was more traditionally dressed. She was walking around the base of a tree picking things up from the ground and placing them in her bucket. Suddenly, Andrew realized Haddy was talking to him.

"...I think this is a good schedule for today."

"Uh, yeah."

Haddy turned and also noticed the woman in the yard, called out to her in Wolof and turned to Andrew. "This is your maid, Isatou. She lives next door and we've been using her for some time now in this house. She's quite familiar with everything you will need."

"I have a *maid*?" Andrew asked as he wondered to himself what he might need.

"Of course! You need a maid. Isatou will do all your cleaning and laundry. And if you want her to cook for you just ask her and she will."

Isatou timidly walked to the front door, stood in the entranceway, but didn't come in. Her face was mature but her skin was smooth, camouflaging her age – somewhere between forty and fifty? She wore what looked like a long skirt wrapped around her, a plain, loose-fitting t-shirt, and a green headdress. Haddy introduced them. Andrew wasn't sure if he should shake her hand or not, so he just waved from across the living room.

"I'm Andrew."

"Hi. Nice to meet you. My name is Isatou." She spoke slowly and deliberately, in a much heavier accent than Haddy.

"If you have trouble understanding each other," Haddy said, "you can always bring one of Isatou's daughters over. Their English is better. Right Isatou?"

"Yes."

Haddy quickly followed up in Wolof, laughing as she spoke to Isatou, who only smiled and nodded in response.

"Okay?" Haddy asked, turning to Andrew.

"Yes, sounds great."

After a short silence Haddy gazed at Isatou, who gently waved goodbye and went back to gather her bucket.

"What's she picking up?" Andrew asked Haddy.

"Mangoes."

Oh yeah, Andrew recalled, remembering his info packet mentioned the mango trees outside.

Haddy let Andrew know she'd come back in a few hours to pick him up and get him sorted with some paperwork at the office. In the meantime, he could unpack and settle in. There should be some food in the kitchen, but just in case she brought him some bread, jam, and bananas. The house didn't have hot water, but it was so hot outside that the water in the pipes was warm enough to keep showers pleasant.

"Okay," Andrew said, hoping he hid his disappointment. *No hot water?*

"Isatou only stopped by to get some mangoes – she normally helps herself. If you need her she's in the compound next door," Haddy added, picking up her purse to leave.

Andrew didn't know what a compound meant. Did he live in a compound?

"See you soon. Enjoy your new home!" she said before walking outside, leaving the front door open.

With Haddy gone, Andrew just stood there, alone. He looked around at his strange surroundings suspiciously.

He stepped outside to survey the grassy yard. The solid black gate was imposing, and nearly double his height. On either side, thick walls obstructed Andrew's view to the outside. Turning his gaze to the yard, he realized that he hadn't seen mango trees before. They were large and incredibly lush. The branches extended wide revealing too many green and red mangoes hanging between the leaves to count, with many more on the ground. A clothesline with bed sheets hung between two trees. In the middle, a lone standpipe rested against the front of the house; owing to a rusted spout, its working order was doubtful.

Walking over to the gate, he peered through a crack, discovering his house was just off a main road. Female voices carried up from behind him. When he turned to see an empty yard and the jutting walls that enclosed it, he realized it must have been coming from Isatou's compound.

Andrew looked at his watch and saw it was still on Chicago time. He thought about his family back home. They were probably sleeping.

Back in the house, Andrew peeked into the cramped and nearly empty kitchen. Alex's room was the same as his, but with clothes strewn on the bed and floor, and his closet left open. Andrew had an aversion to mess.

He lugged his suitcases into his room and unpacked, ordering everything. While unpacking, Andrew noticed how silent it was. Normally at home he or his sister Lindsay would have music or a television on. He thought about calling her but didn't have a working phone. He thought of emailing but didn't have internet access either. Standing above his half-empty suitcase, Andrew's mind returned to the drive from the airport and how he'd been unsettled; it looked stranger, more foreign than he expected. Growing anxious, he examined the unfamiliar bed, the beige wall with chipped paint around the window. Not wanting his mind to fill with unhelpful thoughts, he refocused on unpacking and wondered when Haddy would come back.

When he finished, he had nowhere to go and no one to speak to. The table next to his bed was empty save for the journal his sister gave him. Deciding to give it a try, he picked it up and took it to the front stoop of the house, sat for a second, and started to write.

Haddy eventually returned and brought him to their small office where he completed the requisite paperwork. He also got a SIM card to get his phone working, and the internet for his computer, both of which made him feel less far away from home. Haddy also said she'd heard from Alex, who was coming back early and should arrive home by the evening. Before leaving, Andrew used one of the office computers to write an email to his family.

Dear Mom, Dad, and Linds,

Just wanted to let you all know that I've arrived safely. The flights were long. I was picked up at the airport just like they said. The airport was literally one big room basically and we were the only plane there. Apparently it gets more crowded when tourists start arriving, which happens later in the fall. I slept well last night — so well that I first fell asleep in the car to my new house. The house is nice, and mom don't worry — it's tidy, and we have a maid to keep it clean. Haven't met the person I live with yet, but am supposed to later today. Gotta go now but wanted to let you know I'm safe and I'll call you soon. I have a phone number. It's 220-354-5338. I don't know if you need to dial anything special first though.

Love,
Andrew

There was more he wanted to say but didn't. He thought of writing a separate email to his sister admitting his apprehensions about the move but didn't do that either. What had he expected, really? He remembered why he was there, put on a brave face, and pressed send.

Alex came home shortly after Haddy dropped Andrew off. He was unshaven and wearing comfortable clothing well-suited to the climate. He projected the aura of someone completely at ease, which made Andrew instantly feel more relaxed. The confidence, or maybe it was normalcy, that Alex projected was reassuring.

"Hey! You must be Andrew. I'm Alex." He extended his hand and smiled, revealing noticeably white teeth. He had messy brown hair and was of average height and build, especially when standing next to Andrew.

Andrew was tall and thin. Some mistook his thinness for lankiness, but it was more that he was lean. His jaw was quite pronounced, giving his face a certain stature and presence. He was handsome, with dirty-blond hair, blue eyes, and eyebrows disproportionately bushy for a face otherwise largely unable to grow hair. Even though he was never really good at sports, he had the body of an athlete, resembling someone who did long-distance running or played basketball and soccer.

"Hi, nice to meet you."

"When did you arrive? Today?"

"No. Yesterday. In the evening."

"Oh great. Welcome, I'm sure it's all a bit disorienting. I remember when I got here." He paused, smirking. "Where are you from?"

"Chicago. Well, just outside it. You?"

"Miami. Did you just graduate? Where'd you go to college?"

"In Illinois. You?"

"Georgetown. But I graduated last year. I was in South Africa for six months and then came to Gambia in January."

"Oh, cool. What were you doing in South Africa?"

"Same deal, an internship in development. It was great, South Africa's awesome. But I studied development aid and wanted to be in a place a bit more off the grid."

"And?"

"Let's just say, this is more the type of place I had in mind."

"It's that bad here?" Andrew asked, immediately second-guessing his choice of words, worried it made him sound insensitive or ignorant.

"It's not bad. It's... it's a unique environment. You'll see. The people are amazing. Don't get me wrong. I'm loving it and have made great friends here. But it has its... well, interesting side. You'll learn and discover a lot. Plenty of conversations to be had over beers. Did Haddy take you to your placement today?"

"No, she said we'd go to the school tomorrow."

"They're mostly the same – the school placements, I mean." Alex started to walk towards his bedroom before turning back. "Oh, did you meet Isatou yet?"

"Yeah, this morning."

"She's great. Her daughters are nice too. She'll try to get you to marry one so you can take her back to the U.S."

"For real?"

"Totally serious," he said. "Watch out!"

In the evening, Alex's girlfriend Liv came by. Andrew liked having people around who were familiar. Liv was from the UK, and he discovered there were enough similarities between them that she also counted as familiar. Her and Alex's knowledge of the country and daily life was also reassuring. Earlier in the day, Haddy suggested a few nearby restaurants Andrew could go to for lunch. He went to one of them but was surprised to discover it only served local food. Andrew didn't yet know any of the local dishes. When the woman at the counter offered Andrew yassa, domoda, or benachin, he was left staring back into the pearly-white smile of an obese woman who was clearly amused by Andrew's bewilderment. He picked domoda because she told him it was the only dish they had ready and that he should "try, because you like it." He did, sort of, but other than knowing it was chicken, he didn't fully know what he was eating.

"It's a peanut sauce," Liv interjected. "But I prefer yassa. It's chicken or fish cooked with tomatoes and onions. It's not as heavy."

Alex and Liv also said they would introduce him to a group of expats who hung out together on most weekends. They would take him tomorrow to meet them. Americans and Brits made up the biggest nationalities.

"Mostly Brits, though," Alex said.

The next day, Alex and Liv took Andrew to one of the country's five-star resorts on the beach. He stepped into a different world. The lobby was white marble and stucco. Bouquets of flowers lined the tables. Everything smelled so fresh. Walking through the resort, the staff called him *Sir*. There was a rectangular pool with perfectly clear water. Lounge chairs with cushy, white mattresses surrounded it. There was a bar in the corner where some people were drinking. They were laughing with the young bartender. Andrew noticed how every patron was white.

Alex walked over to a small group of people on the deck by the pool. He introduced them to Andrew and like the other night with Liv, the same first-encounter questions were asked of Andrew and the same answers were given. *Chicago. Just graduated. Teacher's college. I wanted to try something different before going back to school. Older sister, Lindsay. No girlfriend.*

For the rest of the day, Andrew was back with people he felt he could relate to. In the back of his mind he asked himself if this was why he was in Africa – to spend time at fancy pools with more white people – but he reminded himself this wasn't his every day. And, he just arrived.

As the new arrival in the group, most people were interested in talking to Andrew, giving their perspectives on what he might expect. Regina, an older British woman in the country for her second year, was critical of the local population.

"They're lazy," she professed midway through their conversation.

"Don't be so negative to the new guy," someone with a Scottish-sounding accent chimed in, turning towards Andrew. "It's merely a different way of living. Don't let the old grump turn you off. I'm Nathan, by the way," he said while extending out his hand. "Nice to meet you..."

"Andrew."

"Nice to meet you, Andrew."

Some people spoke about local politics, and others offered newcomer advice, like where to get the best imported groceries or where to travel. "You *must* go upriver," a young woman named Emma instructed. Andrew sat patiently through all of this, holding his head up attentively as people took turns speaking to him. He sat up on his lounge chair and quietly listened, quickly forgetting peoples' names, but still nodding politely, injecting the occasional *wow* or *interesting* to show he was still paying attention. At some point, when no one was talking to him, he took off his shirt, lay down, and started listening to music.

Alex asked if he wanted a beer. They walked over to the bar at the other side of the pool and each ordered one. Alex explained that he wasn't a regular at the hotel and preferred going to the beach where the locals hung out.

"Sometimes it's nice to come here to relax. But I try not to make a habit of it."

On Sunday, like all Sundays, there was a locals-versus-expats soccer game that Andrew should join. "It's a better environment than being here. A bit more genuine, and a lot less posh, to use a word I learned from Liv. And it's also a fun way to meet people."

"Cool," Andrew said. "Sounds great."

Their beers arrived and Alex paid and thanked the bartender. Walking from the bar, Andrew turned back to get another look at him. He was wiping a glass clean with a napkin when he looked up, his eyes meeting Andrew's. Andrew instantly and nervously turned back away and kept walking with Alex.

2

THE NEXT DAY Andrew visited the school where he would be volunteering. It was a dilapidated building at best. Its pale walls had been bleached by the sun and assaulted by years of dust, rain, and neglect. Most of the classroom windows were open cut-outs to the outside. Long wooden desks had been picked at and were missing pieces. The uneven blackboards were dusted with past lessons that didn't completely erase. Without students it looked like a deserted building, a ghost from a previous era.

The principal, Mr. Jalloh, was middle-aged. He had closely cropped hair and narrow, thick-rimmed glasses that made his large face appear even bigger. He wore one of the traditional long shirts Andrew first saw at the airport. This one, light blue, was a little different. It extended outwards around the bottom and pointed to the front, falling at an angle off his protruding belly. At first he appeared to forget who Andrew was and looked puzzled when his secretary brought him into his office. After she reminded him that Andrew was the new international volunteer, he greeted him warmly, revealing a wide, welcoming smile. His hands were huge but surprisingly soft, and his handshake was far less firm than Andrew expected from a man of his size.

"Ah yes, of course, of course! Andrew. How are you?" His voice leapt out, filling the room with a thundering timbre.

"I'm good, thank you, how are you?" Andrew said, speaking in a much more reserved tone.

"I am very fine, thank you. It is our pleasure to have you here. Have you been to The Gambia before or is it your first time?"

"It's my first time. My first time in Africa," he added.

"Ah wonderful, wonderful. I believe you will like it very much here." He spoke with confidence and enthusiasm.

"I think so," Andrew agreed.

"And if I remember correctly, you are about to begin your teacher's college in America, right?"

"That's right."

"I'm sure you'll do an excellent job here. You can take some of what you learn back to America with you," he said.

"I hope so."

"Are you married?"

Andrew, somewhat unsettled, answered that he wasn't.

"Eh! Why not?" Mr. Jalloh responded jokingly.

Andrew didn't know how to respond to the unexpected line of questioning. It was in stark contrast to the safe subjects he'd stuck to with Alex and Liv. Maybe it was a cultural thing.

"I guess you are still young to be married in America. I myself have two wives," Mr. Jalloh proudly proclaimed.

Andrew was taken aback despite knowing polygamy was legal in Gambia. Men were permitted to marry up to four wives, a custom rooted in its Muslim traditions.

"Never mind," Mr. Jalloh announced. "Let me introduce you to our school."

The school wasn't much more than a long hallway with different classrooms branching off it. The students would only start to arrive in a month. Mr. Jalloh finished the tour in the schoolyard – dirt and a few trees, next to which some of the school's teachers had come to find shade. They all introduced themselves to Andrew and started asking him questions about his life back in the United States, his experiences in college, and then on subjects he couldn't answer.

"What are the biggest crops the U.S. produces?" He didn't know. *Wheat maybe?*

"How does snow feel?" *Um*, he'd never had to think about it before. *It can be fluffy or hard? And wet.*

Mr. Jalloh, squinting very curiously through his glasses, with his mouth partially opened, turned to Andrew. "Tell us, Andrew. Why are Americans always going so crazy over homosexuals? Why do you make a such a fuss about those people?"

Those people, he thought. It wasn't how he said it, or that it came out of nowhere. Mr. Jalloh asked the question as candidly as all the other questions. It was the words he chose. Andrew looked around at the half-dozen faces fixed upon him. They all were intent on hearing his answer. About to open his mouth, he froze. He had no answer. A sinking feeling overcame him as he tried to come up with a generic response.

"Well, Mr. Jalloh," he spoke slowly, before pausing to organize his answer. "In the U.S. laws require equality, and those laws also apply to homosexuals." He was careful not to label himself as one who agreed, and couldn't believe he was using the term homosexuals. "It's been decided," he continued, removing himself from the decision, "that homosexuals are no different than anyone else, really."

There was a nervous pause.

"I think," Mr. Jalloh proclaimed as he looked at his colleagues to garner their support, "I think your country is too concerned with people like this. It is very unnatural." The other teachers nodded in approval. "Thankfully in this country we have a very strong president who does not tolerate this type of abnormality. I hope we will stay this way, Inshallah," he added.

Andrew swallowed. He wasn't sure what he was supposed to say.

"Let them all stay in America," one of the teachers snickered before adding a sentence in Wolof, making the whole group laugh. Andrew stood motionless. His eyes scanned the small crowd as their laughter and smiles faded.

For the rest of the day, Andrew was quieter and more reserved than usual. He wondered if he made a mistake. Maybe he was better off at home trying to come to terms with himself. Why did he think accepting a placement in a country with widespread anti-gay sentiment was ever a good idea? This was his punishment for making a rash decision.

Andrew didn't have a wealth of gay experiences to fall back on for reassurance. He had only been with someone once, earlier that year during spring break. A group of his friends went to Mexico for the week. He shared a room with another male friend of his. They weren't the best of friends, but were close enough and nothing about them sharing a room was awkward.

The all-inclusive was overrun with loud college kids stuffing themselves with burgers, fries, and watered-down margaritas. They shifted between the pool and beach, only breaking for lunch. Some nights, the local resorts would throw combined parties that turned into an orgy of booze, drugs, and, well, orgies. On those nights, there was always at least one group of friends Andrew could find to dance with or talk to who weren't busy trying to get laid. The friend he roomed with was normally in the group too.

Most nights he and his friend got back to the room drunk and passed out. On the second last night of their trip, Andrew walked into the room and fell onto his bed, lying flat on his stomach, his head buried in the pillow. Instead of walking to his own bed, his friend fell on Andrew's. Drunk and stunned, Andrew froze and couldn't look up. He thought it was a mistake that within a second his friend would figure out. But his friend didn't get up. Andrew's heart started to beat faster as he tried to discern whether his friend was just too drunk or if something else was happening.

Uncertain, Andrew slowly opened his eyes and lifted his head up off the pillow. Turning to face his friend, he saw he was looking directly at him. His friend didn't say anything, and instead brought his face to Andrew's and kissed him quickly at first. When Andrew didn't resist, he kissed him some more. Pulling back from Andrew, he sat up. Andrew, excited and confident, sat up towards him, put his hand on the back of his head and pulled his friend back into him. Andrew felt a hand going up his shirt and pressing into his chest. They took off each other's shirts, kept kissing and fell back down together. Andrew loved the feeling of their bodies pressed against each other.

Andrew had never known how his first experience with a man would be, or who it would be with. He certainly didn't picture it unfolding this way, especially with a friend he assumed, and probably still assumed, was straight. Andrew always imagined it would be sweet and romantic. This was not. But he wasn't thinking about any of that now. On his bed, he was too busy letting himself be guided by a desire that until then was hidden deep in his closet. Having someone's hand pressed tightly against his chest, slowly moving down, excited Andrew in a way he didn't think possible. He gasped when his friend held him.

When they finished, Andrew was breathing heavily. They were both lying there silently in the dark room, naked. It didn't take long before Andrew was as confused as when they first started. After a short while his friend stumbled into the bathroom to clean himself off. Andrew followed. They made brief eye contact in the mirror before Andrew's friend looked away. It was a look that might have contained a hint of shame or regret – Andrew couldn't quite tell as they stood there, sharing an awkward silence.

That night, Andrew barely slept. At some point not long before the sun started to rise, he began to doze off. By the time he woke up the next morning, his friend was already gone.

The two of them never spoke about what happened. When they were back at school the awkwardness continued, which left Andrew feeling confused and disappointed. By the end of the year, they only saw each other when out with mutual friends. A moment that had been Andrew's most liberating quickly pushed him deeper into the closet.

Andrew retreated from the schoolyard into the teacher's room to fill in forms from Haddy when Mr. Jalloh walked in. He spoke loudly and quickly on his mobile phone. At first Andrew thought he was angry, but when Mr. Jalloh let out a laugh so loud it nearly shook the room, he realized this was simply how Mr. Jalloh spoke. His face was still frozen in smile as Andrew turned back to his forms. The only words in Mr. Jalloh's conversation Andrew understood came at the end. They were "Inshallah," followed by, "okay, I will see you then. Goodbye." After that Andrew felt a hand of giant proportions squeezing into his shoulder.

"So this is where you will come when the children are too much for you," Mr. Jalloh joked. "Hopefully it will not be too often."

Andrew looked up and nodded at Mr. Jalloh. His amused expression was caricature-sized. It was friendly and inviting, and as Mr. Jalloh towered over him, Andrew tried to reconcile this man with the one from outside. Taking his hand off Andrew's shoulder, Mr. Jalloh reached down to the forms, pushed around the sheets of paper and leafed through them.

"What are these? The forms from Haddy?"

"Yes."

"So many questions," Mr. Jalloh said, flipping through the numerous pages. "Everyone is always so careful with *toubabs*," he giggled.

Andrew had heard the word a few times now. Alex told him it meant white person.

"Ah, do not worry," Mr. Jalloh said, as he put the forms down and placed his hand on Andrew's back. "If there is anything you need, or things we can do to help you, you must ask us. In The Gambia, there is no problem we cannot fix!"

That evening, Andrew walked up to the gate of their compound and saw Isatou was leaving with a basket of his clothes.

"Washing," she said.

"Thank you."

Closing the heavy gate felt like putting up a barrier between him and reality. Whatever existed on the outside would stay on the other side. Alex had already shown that their house would be somewhere he felt safe and comfortable. He picked up some mangoes off the ground and walked inside, sat on the couch, and took out his journal.

> *Interesting day. Met Mr. Jalloh. Seems everyone at the school hates gay people. WTF.*
>
> *In other news, interesting curriculum reform work to be done. Jalloh is excited about having me on board. Said having a white teacher should make the students more serious. I don't fully know what that means. Nice roommate. He seems more comfortable here than I do, but he's also been here longer. No need to be dramatic, this is what I wanted. People stare. I try to smile back but at times it freaks me out a bit. Kids are really cute and mostly yell hello when I walk by. I don't miss home so much. I should tell Lindsay soon. The food's been okay.*

For all the anticipation of excitement and adventure, routine defined Andrew's Gambian life. Isatou became a regular fixture in the morning. As Andrew woke up she'd already be hanging laundry in his yard or sweeping. On a number of mornings Isatou's daughter Awa would accompany her. She had her mother's shy smile and mostly kept in the background, collecting Andrew and Alex's clothes for washing. Awa was in secondary school, but Alex told Andrew he rarely saw her out of the compound and wondered whether she was actually enrolled. Isatou's other daughters rarely came by. Apparently a young man lived with them too, a cousin or nephew, Alex thought.

"I've only seen him once."

Andrew's mornings were always rushed – he still slept like he did in college, so he never had much time to talk with Isatou and Awa before having to run off to work. He went in to school each morning for eight thirty and spoke with Mr. Jalloh for half an hour, sitting in his nondescript office cluttered with files, listening to Mr. Jalloh's curriculum concerns. Mr. Jalloh believed the teaching methods prescribed by the government were not engaging enough. He tasked Andrew with coming up with new ones in the hopes of improving student performance.

"Never mind that you haven't started teacher's college," Mr. Jalloh shot back as soon as Andrew questioned his qualification for such a responsibility. "You have been admitted to an American teacher's college, and you certainly remember proper teaching skills from when you were a student. Sharing this perspective is invaluable to our success." Mr. Jalloh often spoke in a grandiose manner. Over time Andrew realized Mr. Jalloh was of a generation that deferred, on some level, to the presumed expertise of a foreigner without a basis for doing so. Alex called it Empire-lite.

Mr. Jalloh watched Andrew's confidence grow over the first weeks. He took more initiative talking to teachers, proving he was serious. As time passed, he proposed more and more ideas to Mr. Jalloh to re-engage students and make certain aspects of teaching less formulaic.

"If your ideas work here, and I am sure they will, you must stay with us longer than one year. You will fix all our schools and take for yourself a pretty Gambian wife," Mr. Jalloh said laughing. Andrew let out a nervous laugh to equal Mr. Jalloh's.

"Maybe."

"Maybe you will be like me and marry more than one wife," he bellowed, unable to hide his amusement. "That would make people in your country think you have gone mad! But you would be an authentic Gambian."

"I would be," Andrew answered, smiling politely while averting his eyes to the bulky computer in the corner of Mr. Jalloh's office that never seemed to be turned on.

Conversations referencing the need for Andrew to take a Gambian wife became commonplace.

"I don't see you with a girlfriend," one of his coworkers pointed out one day after school.

He became skilled at politely laughing them off and changing the subject. After each one of these entreaties from Mr. Jalloh or another teacher, he wondered if Gambians were this forward with each other or if it was because he was foreign. Either way, he quickly came to view it as innocuous. They were trying to be friendly.

Personal space isn't so much of a thing here. I get at least one comment a day, said as a joke, about why I don't have a girlfriend. Even though it's a joke they do want to know and it's strange. I want to tell them why. I want them to know that I'm different, but the same. I want to point out to Mr. Jalloh that I'm not judging him for having two wives. They all like me. I wonder what would happen if I said it. It would be a huge shock, that's for sure. Probably not a good idea. Let's start with Lindsay. And Alex.

Lindsay was a year older than Andrew and had spent more time than him pushing the family envelope, however gently. She inherited the athletic genes and the parental admiration. She was often attending sports tournaments in high school and college. Lindsay also had a steady boyfriend since the tenth grade. These features made her more curious and independent than Andrew. And also more confident.

Fiercely protective of her little brother, Lindsay had always been close with Andrew. At college – they went to the same one, though they occupied different social circles – she always invited him to parties. She regularly checked in on him. Except for one, there were no secrets between them. Andrew didn't doubt that she'd have no issues accepting him. But for a reason he could never figure out, he was never able to tell her. Lindsay's interventions were instrumental in helping their parents accept his decision to go abroad, and the frustration of hiding his secret from the person who always had his back kept growing. He'd resolved to tell her before leaving for Gambia, but when the two of them were out for dinner before he left, he chickened out.

On the morning Andrew left home, Lindsay walked into his room holding a shopping bag. He was sitting on his perfectly made bed looking out the window.

"You look like crap," she teased him.

"I didn't sleep."

Lindsay looked around the room. For the past four years Andrew had barely used it, and it had the sterile feel of a room that was once lived in. The desk was wiped clean. His bookshelf was perfectly in order. A newly framed college diploma hung on the wall. On his bedside table was a frame that held a picture of their entire family at Lindsay's graduation. In a sharp break with tradition, they had all decided to make silly faces. The result was actually quite a funny picture that always made Andrew laugh. Lindsay noticed that the frame was now empty. She thought to say something but didn't. Instead, she handed Andrew the shopping bag.

"Here. It's nothing big. Just some things to keep you busy on the plane, and some snacks in case you get hungry."

"Thanks."

"You look nervous," she said.

Smiling at her, he asked if she was nervous for him.

"A little, obviously. It's a big step. But we both know it's the right one. Don't worry," she added stepping closer to him, "it's going to be awesome. A great adventure."

"I know. I'm excited."

"Good. I'm secretly jealous. I can't wait to see pictures."

Andrew stood to meet her as she walked up to him. They hugged. It was a quick hug. One that felt constrained, almost superficial.

Lindsay would've been proud to see her younger brother settling into his new life. It wasn't only the excitement of living in Gambia. Andrew also relished how different his social world was from home. His new friends were unlike many of the people he'd left behind. When they asked probing questions they did so not to gossip but because they took a real interest in him. In the beginning, he was guarded in his responses. But he quickly shed some of his suspicions and opened up more.

For the first time, he sensed that he wasn't being judged. He found himself spending less time worrying what others might be thinking about him. When they went to the beach on the weekends, he didn't feel bad for sitting out most of the soccer games at first. As weeks advanced, however, he was pressured into joining the game. To his surprise though, no one cared about his poor skills. Even Simon, a British volunteer and talented player who took the game more seriously than others, wasn't fazed when Andrew kicked the ball into the sea.

"Beginner's luck," he teased.

Before long, Andrew became a regular player. It was fun.

This carefree life became the antidote to his anxiety. He was less rigid and became more comfortable. His obsessive application of insect repellant waned. White t-shirts found themselves in the same pile as colored ones. In social settings he smiled more. He relaxed more. He was even better in markets.

Andrew's first trip to a local market had been overwhelming. All the stalls were crowded close together. Each vendor called out to him as he passed by.

"Hey, *toubab*, what do you want to buy? Some mangoes? Papaya?"

Scanning from table to table, Andrew was inundated with nearly identical colorful fruits and vegetables spread out, bananas dangled from strings tied between umbrellas. The stands all had the same items. How was he supposed to choose? Looking down at the aisles in front of him, he grew weary of how crowded they were. The women, with children strapped to their backs, or holding large rubber basins overflowing with goods, left little room for him to pass as they haggled with the many vendors.

He started to feel himself sweating in the humidity when he decided to stop venturing further into the market and try his luck at whichever stall was closest. He asked for a few bananas and oranges. The price sounded high, but the woman at the table assured him.

"It is a fair price. Very juicy oranges."

Andrew had no point of reference, so he handed her his money, which she placed in a plastic bag filled with crumply looking bills.

That night he showed Alex what he had bought. Alex asked what it all cost.

"250 dalasis. She said the oranges were expensive because they're from South Africa."

"Ouch. You got ripped off."

"Really?"

"Yeah."

That was then. Now, Andrew marched confidently deep into the market stalls, pushing his way through, undeterred by the crowds and heat. He haggled with vendors.

"No *toubab* prices," he would say. "I want Gambian price. Give me the Gambian price."

He even impressed himself.

The only occurrence that kept him slightly unnerved was at the hotel pool. It was the bartender, the same one who all the tourists seemed to get along with so well. Andrew noticed him the first time he was there. He had a presence. He was confident behind his bar.

He also seemed to like watching Andrew. The bartender's eyes and subtle closed-mouth smile followed him each time he walked up to and from the bar. When Andrew was sitting with other expats, sometimes he could feel the bartender's eyes on him. Not knowing who he was, or anything about him, Andrew wondered why he kept looking at him. Maybe somewhere else it would have been more obvious. Here though – at the hotel pool in a completely foreign culture, where he was extra careful to repress any of those feelings – it never occurred to Andrew that the bartender might be seeking to attract his attention, hopeful they'd come to know one another.

3

THOMAS HAD BEEN working at the hotel for over a year. He started out as a cleaner by the pool. He was charming and attentive. Guests liked him. When families arrived he made sure to ask the children their names, managed to remember them, and always snuck maraschino cherries into their drinks. He could always tell when people needed an extra hand gathering up their belongings at the end of the day.

His affability with guests led to conversations about their experiences at the hotel. He discovered people loved proffering opinions and suggestions on everything. There was little he could do about the speed of the restaurant, or the Wi-Fi, but he could see about fixing their drinks. One of the more common criticisms Thomas heard in his early days working by the pool was how the drink menu was too plain and boring for a hotel that tried to be as plush as it did. Its cocktail menu lacked imagination; the margaritas were never consistent.

"We are a Muslim country," he once explained to a friendly Finnish couple who took issue with the poorly-crafted mojitos and too-sweet daiquiris. "Not many people here drink alcohol, so maybe this is why they do not know how to make them properly."

As he got tired of giving the same explanation, he asked for suggestions on how to improve the drinks. After a few weeks, when his boss saw how Thomas's drinks were popular with guests, Thomas became the new bartender.

He was young, only nineteen, and came from one of the country's smaller villages upriver from the capital. It was a community of thatched roofs, red mud trails, wandering chickens, and a simplicity since disappeared from most other places on earth. It was also one of the few Christian villages, with a small church occupying a central piece of land. Its center was surrounded by fields for subsistence farming that turned a lush green during rainy seasons. Many of the men fished on the river. Women sat on short stools outside homes frying all sorts of foods. There was one primary school, still without the windows or floors the government had long promised to install. It made for a challenging learning environment during the rains.

To Thomas, the village represented the best and worst of his country. It provided a warmth and hospitality rarely on display in the city, but one often coupled with ignorance to life outside its small existence. It was at once nurturing and suffocating.

Tourists were always curious about where Thomas came from. Fully aware they weren't seeking an indictment, he kept his answer to what he thought they wanted to hear.

"It's very small, tiny. You can reach it by road or from the river," he told a group of tourists one late afternoon. "You grow up running around from house to house. Even those who aren't your family take care of you. Everyone is friends with one another. And it's a very beautiful place."

"You were lucky to grow up there," one of them observed.

"Yes."

Invariably there were predictable follow-up questions. *What else did you do in the village?* Not wanting to let on that he spent much of his time alone, Thomas kept to his happy history and spoke about evenings and nights fishing with his father, gazing up at the stars, and learning about the different constellations.

"We had a small dugout boat, made of wood. Or sometimes we sat on the edge of the river to do our fishing."

It sounds amazing, was a common response.

He left the village in search of more economic opportunity, he told them, landing a job at a restaurant when he first arrived in the capital. Eventually, thanks to his strong English skills, he got his job with the hotel. He started working by the pool, cleaning up after guests, clearing their towels or dirty dishes. It wasn't glamorous like he'd hoped, but it was dependable. Also, the grounds were pretty. He felt calm there, protected – it didn't look like the Gambia he knew. For this reason, he was especially happy to hear one day that his boss wanted to talk to him, *about something good.* At the end of his shift, Thomas went to meet his boss in the office behind the front desk.

"Come in," he said, looking up from a pile of guest registration forms. "Rules," he huffed, dejectedly pushing the papers aside. Thomas was doing a good job. "You are a good worker, and the guests like you." He was being promoted to bartender. "It is clear you are more skilled at the job than Patrick."

Thomas blushed, tried not to appear boastful, quietly responding, *thank you, sir.* Not only was Thomas getting a new job, a better job, but it came with a raise – five more dalasis an hour. Things were starting to look up.

It was a story of positive upward mobility. And he always spoke kindly of the village when people asked if he missed his home. He didn't want to sully anyone's imagination. *It is a beautiful place. Calm and quiet. But that type of life isn't for everyone.* Those in Andrew's circle believed Thomas was becoming one of the country's success stories. Absent from his story was any mention of vitriol, the bigotry, or his early struggles in Banjul. He withheld all the stories about the loneliness and solitude of his existence, his community of one.

As far back as Thomas remembered, he was uninterested in girls. It never registered with him to be attracted to them. At first he didn't realize this made him any different from the other children growing up around him. It was just who he was, and he took it to be normal. He didn't know precisely when, but at some point approaching his teens, when he better understood the basics of life, he noticed more people talking about how one day he would have to marry.

"Don't learn from your brother," his mother instructed him when he was around thirteen, making reference to Thomas's oldest brother, Sheriff, who'd by then finished secondary school. They stood in the kitchen and she watched through the window as her oldest son took some treats from a few girls passing by outside. He was sitting in a plastic chair with some friends when they walked by.

"Give me those sweets," he demanded, before reaching his arm out.

"He is not nice to those girls," his mother told him. "He does not respect them the way he should. When you take a girlfriend and wife, you should be more soft around her. Your brother is too stern and he puts himself above them."

But I don't want to take a girlfriend or a wife.

Entering his early teens, as talk of girls and marriages became more commonplace, Thomas began to appreciate that he was different. And he knew enough to know he wasn't different in a good way. There was no label for what he was, if he *was* something. In their small village, no one spoke about gays or lesbians. But from his observations of how boys went off with girls, and the village's collective insistence on boys marrying girls, he knew his growing desires were pushing him up against the established way of life. There was so much talk about a person's future in this respect. It didn't seem like a future for him, at least the future he wanted, was possible.

As his self-awareness grew, he struggled to find ways to cope. He couldn't think of anyone to turn to for help. His parents, he feared, wouldn't understand. They wouldn't want to understand. There were no other relatives or teachers he could think of approaching, either. As far as he could tell, no one else in the village was like him. It was his secret. At some point during this time, he learned there was a word for him. He was a homosexual, or gay. Apparently, he wasn't the only one after all. With this knowledge came another piece of information: being gay was a sin.

Most of what Thomas learned came from the pastor at their church, who began pontificating on homosexuality with greater frequency. At first he tried not to let it get to him. Ironically, the pastor's words sometimes gave him a little optimism. Living isolated and shut off from much of the world around him, it was only through these sermons that Thomas learned homosexuals could form relationships, and even in some instances, families. It was something he never fully thought possible and it was this discovery that sparked a fast-growing urge within him. He wanted what the pastor was telling him mustn't be permitted. He wanted to have someone too.

Thomas's urge grew in tandem with the pastor's obsession with homosexuality. Initially, Thomas was mostly puzzled. He couldn't understand the pastor's fixation. It all seemed for naught. No one spoke of anyone being gay in the village and Thomas detected no homosexual army waiting to invade. In fact, it was clear to him that it was he who was most threatened. With the pastor's obsession taking greater hold within the congregation – meaning most of the village – and disdain and disgust towards homosexuality became the norm, Thomas felt that it was he himself who was being denounced and vilified by his entire community. It was then that he finally began to wonder how much longer he might be able to take it.

His only problem was that he had nowhere else to go. The entire family was still in the village. Of his two older brothers, one was now married and embraced his role as the patriarchal head of his family, socializing with the village men while his wife did most of the farming and all the cooking. Sheriff, who was single and entrepreneurial, would be the first in their family to leave the village for Banjul. Thomas knew he couldn't run away with his brother. He needed a clean start. If he left, he would have to go alone.

Not all church services demonized gays, but when they did, their pastor spared nothing. Thomas's last Sunday in the village was one of those mornings, the hyperbolic hysteria on full display.

"...And watch your children. Lock their bedroom doors at night, because you know who lurks when you are unsuspecting. I do not need to tell you that the gays will come when you least suspect it, take your children and recruit them into their cult of sickness and evil.

"We must always stay alert! Our future as proud Christians, as proud *African* Christians, depends on it. We want a future where our savior Jesus Christ and his teachings will reign. This cannot happen in a world controlled by the conniving gays."

Thomas looked around as the pastor spoke. It was his father's face he would remember the most. Thomas's father was one of the more relaxed men in the village, at times he played the role of the joker. He rarely got angry. He made one feel at ease. It was for this precise reason that Thomas remembered his father's face so vividly. As the pastor spoke, as he cursed the homosexual, Thomas's father displayed a sense of conviction he had seldom seen before. His father, who never got worked up over anything, was now swaying violently back and forth with the pastor's words.

"So join me, my brothers and sisters! Join me in building a world that leaves no place for these people. Let us build a future free of these sinners. Let us work together to make sure the African-Christian purity is never diluted. AMEN!"

"AMEN!"

It was a deafening chorus. Everyone took part, Thomas's parents, his brothers, all his extended family, neighbors, and people he only barely knew.

It was the final straw. Thomas couldn't take the feeling of slow suffocation any longer. Two days later, on a sunny and peaceful morning when he was just sixteen, Thomas told his family he was leaving for the capital. Although he was a strong student, he was dropping out of school in favor of finding work.

"I will be able to make money for the family and send it back home, so you can buy more land," he told his parents in an attempt to persuade them. It was the only way he thought they'd agree to the move.

After his parents talked between themselves for a short while, Thomas's father came to see him. "Fine. You can go."

For the first time in his life, he'd be alone. The prospect was frightening and liberating. The next day he left on the back of a motorbike with his few belongings in his knapsack.

For all the successes of his new, city life, Thomas still kept mostly to himself outside of work. He lied to his brother saying he lived with friends, and was grateful Sheriff never pressed him on it, seeming equally content to live separate lives. The one exception to Thomas's solitude, his only friend, was Suleiman. A few years older, more mature, Suleiman was the caring big brother Thomas never had. When Thomas was new to the city and working as a waiter in a restaurant, he befriended Suleiman, who often ate there. Over time they grew close and when Suleiman learned Thomas slept in the back of the restaurant he insisted Thomas stay with him.

Suleiman came from an upper-class family. His father was a top bureaucrat in the finance ministry and curried favor with the government. Suleiman excelled in school and because of his father's privileged position, earned a scholarship to study journalism in South Africa. He returned to Gambia and immediately landed a job as a reporter at a prominent newspaper. He started covering municipal issues, but was promoted to writing on national affairs, including crime and security. While the paper was very supportive of the government, he wasn't. His time in South Africa gave him perspective on some of the country's challenges, which he blamed the government for. He lamented the apathy he saw around him and wished others would break its paralysis. Still, he knew his boundaries and the rules he had to play by if he was going to stay out of trouble. Suleiman decided to toe the line in order to unravel it.

Because of Suleiman's professional success, and for helping him adjust to his new life, Thomas always looked up to Suleiman and felt completely free around him. But he never came out to him. The societal taboo against men discussing their feelings meant neither Thomas nor Suleiman ever brought up the discussion.

In the back of Thomas's mind, he suspected Suleiman might have figured it out. During his year in South Africa he'd been exposed to gay culture in ways most Gambians had not. Thomas may not have fed into traditional stereotypes, but he shied from the mention of women or talk of a family in his future. He was relieved it didn't affect their friendship. Even so, Thomas was still too nervous to say something. He had a good friend and a place to stay.

Once Thomas began working at the hotel they saw each other less. Still, Suleiman occasionally dropped by for a drink. Many times he used the opportunity to gently express his frustration with some new governmental development he didn't like. Thomas, disconnected from politics, was the one person with whom Suleiman felt comfortable ragging on the government without having to worry his opinions might land him in trouble.

So one evening, when Suleiman sat down at Thomas's empty bar, there was nothing immediately unusual about their banter. But quickly, Suleiman's face turned serious. He told Thomas he'd spent the past two days looking into rumors that the government and police force were starting to crack down on people suspected of being gay or lesbian.

Thomas froze. "What does that mean?"

"I don't know. No one knows. First off, who is suspected to be gay or lesbian? How does one even get on such a list – I have no idea. But what I've heard is that they want to use this issue to bring people together. To promote what they say are national and African values, whatever that means. Food prices are rising and I guess they need to find a new distraction. They go after the easy targets."

Thomas didn't know what to say. He tried to busy himself behind the bar.

"Thomas."

"Yes," he said as he looked up at his friend.

"Please be careful."

Hesitantly, Thomas nodded. He thought about saying something but no words came to him. He felt vulnerable. Although he grew to trust Suleiman, he felt uncomfortable confirming his secret. It was obvious now that Suleiman knew, but it was another thing for him to *know*.

"You know as well as I do, this place can be unpredictable. That's all I'm saying. I don't want something to happen to you. And please don't worry. You don't have to say anything or be concerned. I didn't come here to scare you or force you to have a conversation you don't want to have. But you're my close friend and I don't want to see anything happen to you."

Suleiman paused and offered Thomas a sympathetic smile, hoping to reassure him. "Maybe one day our world won't be so upside down."

"Wouldn't that be something," Thomas muttered stoically.

"It would be."

And with that, Suleiman stood up, said goodbye, and left Thomas standing alone at the empty bar.

4

ANDREW STEPPED OUT of the pool. It was later in the afternoon when most people had started going home. He walked to his belongings, picked up his towel, and started to dry himself off. He rubbed the towel on his hair, covering his face. As he moved the towel down his body, out of the corner of his eye he felt someone looking at him. It was the bartender, again, standing and staring at Andrew, completely still. Unlike other times, Andrew didn't break away, pretending not to notice or that their eyes were merely passing each other by accident. Instead, this time, he looked back at him. The bartender also didn't look away. In fact, once he caught Andrew's eyes, he looked deeper.

Andrew's heart began beating faster. He debated looking down or smiling but couldn't do either so he kept looking across the pool at the bartender whose name he still did not know. If people around him were moving or talking, Andrew didn't notice. The only thing he could make out was that the bartender moved his lips enough for Andrew to see him smiling. Andrew, without thinking, did the same. He then subconsciously snapped himself out of his trance, went back to drying himself, hurriedly leaving the pool area.

During his trip home, and all that evening, Andrew didn't say much. He lay in bed at night wondering if what he thought had happened actually happened. He was pretty sure it did, which intimidated him, but even more, as he pored over it, it excited him. He was sure he wasn't reading too much into it. It wasn't only a look. The past few weeks, all the little looks, it started to make sense. Why did it take so long for him to notice?

The week crawled by. Time at school dragged on and evenings lingered. All Andrew wanted was for the weekend to arrive so he could go back to the hotel to ensure he wasn't imagining things. He did manage to casually ask Alex if he knew the bartender's name.

"Who? Thomas?"

Thomas. Andrew had never been overtly attracted to black men before, but he also wasn't *un*attracted to them. Many of his friends at university quickly wrote off whole racial or ethnic groups. He had his preferences, if he was being honest, but kept an open enough mind that at times he even surprised himself. And from what he saw, Thomas was cute. He had a friendly face and good body. But much more importantly, it was something about how they looked at each other. Andrew hadn't done that before, with anyone.

More eye contact followed the next Sunday. Andrew walked up to the hotel from the beach and tried his best to pretend not to be looking for Thomas. Thomas was less guarded about his intentions. As soon as he saw Andrew he came out from behind the bar and started to put drink menus on the surrounding tables. He looked up at Andrew and smiled. Cautiously, Andrew smiled back.

They played this game for the rest of the day. There was a shared synchronicity between them – each time one of them looked up, the other followed suit. Andrew debated walking up and asking for a drink but was too embarrassed. He'd blushed the last time they smiled at each other and hesitated to approach Thomas with so many people still around to watch them.

He saw Thomas was very handsome that day. Like many Gambians, his hair was short. He had a gentle and inviting smile. He wasn't tall enough to be noticed, so he moved about slowly and deliberately, almost floating, holding his head and chest high in a way that drew people to notice him. Not in a show-offy kind of way, but in an *I'm here* kind of way. In the absence of actual conversation, Thomas spoke with body language. He wore a tight-fitting t-shirt that hugged a defined chest and flat stomach. Small but distinct arm muscles unobtrusively pushed through the sleeves. The t-shirt was tucked into black jeans that hugged the entire lower half of his body. He was young. Andrew guessed he was a few years younger, probably around twenty.

In the afternoon, when Andrew was sitting with only Liv and Alex, Thomas walked over.

"Good afternoon," he said, standing next to Andrew, choosing proximity over eye contact. Alex and Liv each ordered a beer. When it came time to take Andrew's order Thomas turned his head down towards him, letting off a slight smirk. "And you?"

"I'll also have a beer," answered Andrew, who couldn't help but smile as Thomas walked away.

That evening Andrew made dinner with Alex and Liv, but quickly said goodnight, closing the door to his room. He went to Skype with his sister. The conversation he was about to have was years in the making and had played out in his head so many times. The only difference was that now he was more confident and less scared about himself. He'd said barely a sentence to Thomas, who he didn't know at all, but he felt different. He felt free to have a crush. And strangely enough, here of all places where the law forbade it, he started thinking there was a place, a space he could carve out and inhabit the same way as everyone else. As excited as he was, he knew this was just the tease of infatuation. But that was enough.

"Linds?"

"Hey! How's it going? What are you doing now?"

"It's good thanks. I'm getting ready for bed. What's happening at home?"

"Honestly? Not much. I keep trying to keep track of things you're missing, but it's all been the same. How's school? Did Jalloh find a third wife yet?"

"No, but he keeps suggesting I pick up a Gambian wife." Andrew felt himself tensing up. Lindsay always made a joke about Mr. Jalloh's wives and Andrew planned to use it to shift the conversation.

"Are you thinking about it?"

"Not really," he said, before jumping in again before she could reply. "Lindsay, I'm gay."

He just said it, rushing, throwing it out there, barely thinking and processing what he said, as if knowing that if he took his time, the doubt that was never far from his mind might take over. There was more to say too; years of thoughts and secrets were waiting, piled high behind a dam ready to give way. He gave her less than a second to respond but could see on his computer screen that her mouth was still. Her face at least looked sympathetic, as he'd expected, so the brother who had never been overly emotional continued to unleash himself.

"I've wanted to tell you forever. I don't know why I waited so long, and until a time when we're so far away. I thought about doing it so many times, but I don't know, something always came up. I promised myself I'd tell you at dinner before I left, but I chickened out then too.

"Maybe the distance finally made it easier, I don't know. Maybe I was scared? Not about how you'd react, but about having to admit it to myself – to actually have to say the words out loud and not be able to take it back. You're the first person I've told this to. And I don't want to pretend anymore. I can't."

He kept looking at her as he spoke into his computer. "I'm sorry to spring this on you all of a sudden. I know it's not what you expected now. I can't. Well maybe I could. But I don't want to. I don't want to pretend. I don't want to lie. I mean I've known all along but being here is helping me see. There's this whole world, and I don't want to keep shutting myself out from it."

He spoke so fast he barely knew what he said – it was all pouring out. He also realized he hadn't let his sister get a word in as he stopped and looked closer at the video of Lindsay on his screen. She looked proud of him.

"Linds?"

"I love you Andrew," she said through heartfelt eyes. "That isn't going to ever change."

In that instant he was unshackled. The fear of an unknown life ahead, feelings of inadequacy, shame for being unable to fit in – feelings that had for years followed him everywhere he went, all became easier to cope with. Somehow, he felt he'd be okay. There were tears in his eyes.

"I'm sorry if I ever did anything to make you think you couldn't feel comfortable with me. And I'm sorry you had to go through this by yourself for so long."

Andrew smiled through his tears, amazed at his sister.

"You never did anything," he said trying to reassure her. "It was all in me. Something I didn't know how to deal with. A lot of the time I wished it would go away and I'd wake up one day and realize I'd made this big mistake. Like suddenly my life would become easy instead of dealing with this. People say college is this great place for personal growth..."

"Not the college we went to."

He paused to collect himself and his thoughts, sniffling and wiping his tears away.

"Mom and Dad will freak out. I don't know what to do about them."

"Nothing. There's no rush with you over there. One step at a time." Lindsay paused and her face showed concern. "Andrew, do you have a... a boyfriend there?"

"No. That'd be pretty messed up." His commentary came out automatically, by accident – the remnants of an older, guarded Andrew.

5

"You seem distracted."

Mr. Jalloh was staring through his glasses at Andrew. The two of them were sitting in his office for an end-of-week discussion. Mr. Jalloh was right, Andrew was distracted. This was the third time during their meeting he inadvertently tuned out.

"Sorry, Mr. Jalloh. I'm listening. And I agree with what you said."

It was Friday afternoon and the anticipation proved too strong to ignore. Andrew's step had been a bit lighter since telling his sister, but for most of the week he tried not to think too much about the start of what he thought might be a sort of liberation. As the prospect of the weekend approached, Andrew found it harder and harder not to think about Thomas and how he wanted to see him. His mind could focus on little else.

"If you agree with me, would you be willing to double your student load? It won't be for long, Inshallah, but it could be for some time." Mr. Jalloh stared back at Andrew, who knew two things – he hadn't been paying enough attention to know what Mr. Jalloh was talking about, and when a Gambian said something might take some time, they meant it.

Andrew loved the teaching he was doing, and his students were gravitating to him. Recently the cultural barriers began falling and a true mutual understanding and appreciation was forming. They paid more attention in class, doing their assignments, which were improving, and more frequently invited him to kick soccer balls with them outside the school. He started to get the sense that they actually liked him. The thought of doubling the number of students – why, he still wasn't exactly sure – seemed like it would frustrate some of the progress he'd made.

"As long as you don't think it would hurt my class dynamic."

"It will allow more of our students to benefit from your teaching and creative methods. It will be good for the school."

From the little Andrew knew of Mr. Jalloh, he knew he wasn't going to win this debate. He smiled and accepted the compliment, knowing there was no other option and it would probably bring their meeting to a close. "Sure."

Going home, Andrew took a different route. Instead of heading through the side streets, unpaved sand roads crisscrossing through quiet residential neighborhoods, he opted to head down the main road lined with shops that connected to the highway. He passed between men, women, and children who somewhat noticed him, and exchanged passing looks. With a deliberate pace, he walked around the groups of commuters huddled at the road's edge, waiting for their broken-down mini-vans or 7-7s, the converted taxi shuttles. Normally he would have peered into the few bakeries along the way to see if anything looked enticing, but this time he walked straight past them. He walked past where he should have turned off the main road too. Instead, Andrew kept going, to where the road ended and met the sand. He walked up to the edge of the beach, which was filling up with runners and walkers, found some shade, and sat down.

Andrew sat for a while, doodling in the sand with a stick, watching the people pass him by. He tried not to think about anything. But since not trying to think about anything most often means you really want to be thinking of something, Andrew's mind kept filling with thoughts. This went on for a while. At some point he asked himself what he was so afraid of. When most of the sand in front of him had been dug away, he brought himself to his feet and turned south, which was the opposite direction of home, and started walking.

The hotel pool area was almost empty. The rainy season had ended but it was still before the tourist season began in earnest. By the time Andrew arrived, the sun had mostly set. The white marble path leading from the beach up to the hotel's pool area was illuminated by pot lights in the ground reflecting up into the palm trees. He'd never observed it this way, so empty and dim. Walking up, he saw it as a tableau, and before stepping into it, he had one final opportunity to second guess himself. He did, paused for a brief moment, then continued.

Thomas was cleaning and organizing behind the bar when Andrew approached. The last guests at the pool were busy trying to get their children out of the water. Andrew stood motionless in front of one of the pot lights, keeping him largely in the dark. In his work clothes – pants, an untucked shirt, and a knapsack over his shoulder – he appeared out of place.

Just as the parents ushered their children away, Thomas turned around and saw the silhouette standing across from him, knowing instantly who it was. For a few seconds they both stood there, inadvertently re-enacting their look from the previous week. The distance between them was not bridging itself, and Andrew decided he had to make the first move. He would walk to the bar and buy a drink. Making his way towards Thomas, he was unsure of where to look.

"Hi."

"Hi."

Andrew had never dated, or seriously flirted with anyone for that matter. The words didn't come naturally to him. The shyness he spent the past months shedding started to reappear.

"I'm Andrew, by the way."

"I know. And I'm Thomas." Thomas's smirk hinted confidence.

For the past many weeks, it was probably more than a month by now, Thomas played his game with Andrew. Eye contact, smiles, nudging close to him when taking group orders. It wasn't solely to tease him. Thomas treaded a fine line and knew it. People were friendly, and at times entirely unassuming. Thomas needed to be sure before he took any risk that might leave him exposed and vulnerable.

Based on the crowd Andrew spent his time with, Thomas assumed he was in the country for an extended period of time. Offhand conversations with friendly patrons quickly confirmed this, which meant Thomas didn't have to rush. Andrew wasn't going anywhere and competition was unlikely to spring up.

Week in and week out, the routine would play itself out. Thomas would be extra friendly when Andrew and his friends visited the hotel. He found reasons to make repeat trips over – delivering menus, dropping off coasters, bringing the drinks two at a time instead of all at once on a tray. Sometimes he'd let an arm accidentally fall or rub up against Andrew's shoulder, always quick to pull it back in a nondescript way to dispel any suspicion that he was being deliberate, except to Andrew, who caught on quickly, and never objected. There were the smiles, subtle but unmistakable, to which Andrew always reciprocated. And each time Andrew left, they always managed to sneak a look at each other. That look became the most honest shared expression of their existence. It was a resigned and despondent look. It was a *maybe another time* look, when another time didn't necessarily mean tomorrow.

And so, when Thomas saw Andrew standing alone at a time when he had no reason to come to the hotel, he lit up. His efforts, his patience, had paid off. Another time meant now.

He watched Andrew slowly rest his knapsack on the ground, pull out a stool, and sit down.

"Can I get you something?"

"Uhh, sure. A beer. Thank you."

"My pleasure."

"Do you want to have one too?"

"I can't. We're not allowed while working."

They spoke like it was their first date.

Thomas asked Andrew what brought him to Gambia, how long he was planning to stay, and how he was finding it. He enjoyed talking to Americans. Most of the tourists who came to the country were from Europe and it was nice to meet someone from elsewhere. Andrew remarked that Thomas's home village must be a nice place.

"I've only seen a few of the villages along the river. They all sound pretty, with the river and forest."

"And the hippos you have to watch out for."

"Yeah, well... I guess not everything about them is ideal."

"No," Thomas sighed, "not everything."

A waiter from the restaurant walked over to drop off drink orders. Thomas saw Andrew shift his gaze away. His eyes looked like he was thinking. He didn't know how to respond. Better to keep the conversation simple, Thomas thought, at least for now.

As Thomas prepared the drinks, Andrew checked his watch.

"I should get going."

"I'm happy you came by."

"Me too."

"Will I be seeing you tomorrow?"

"I think so."

And with that, Andrew stood up, leaving his dalasis on the bar.

"Goodnight, Andrew," Thomas said with a mischievous smile.

"Goodnight," Andrew responded, before walking out through the lobby, propelled by excitement.

Over the next few weeks, Andrew returned to the hotel bar late on Friday afternoons. The conversations started out light. But when it became laborious to keep talking about the challenges and idiosyncrasies of Gambian living – Andrew not wanting to sound like a stuck-up Westerner and Thomas wanting to retain some pride for his homeland – the conversation became more personal.

Thomas spoke of his frustration growing up in such a small house in such a small village. He shared a bedroom with his two brothers and not much separated them from their parents. Everyone in the village knew everyone. Neighbors' doors were always open.

As he discovered more about himself, he wished he had places to retreat alone. He and his father spent hours fishing in boats or on the river's edge. Often they'd lose track of time and arrive home well after the time to eat when Thomas's mother would sarcastically but playfully berate them for always being off on their "adventures" – especially when they returned empty handed. She'd tease that they didn't truly appreciate all her work to cook a good meal while they were out having fun together and letting it get cold. While this went on, Thomas's father would position himself behind his wife, and try to make Thomas laugh with silly faces, only to increase his mother's frustration. She always caught on, turned around, and jokingly raised her hand to her husband as if to smack him.

"And then we would always all laugh," Thomas said through a wistful smile. "It's very frustrating to have people with whom you have such memories, who raised you, but then on the other hand, they do not even know you."

"And if they did know you?"

"Well, I had to come here..."

"Right."

"But I don't think about it. In this place it's not worth it to spend your time thinking those things." Thomas always had a gentle way of hinting when he no longer felt like answering questions.

"Right."

"What about you? Do you have parents?"

It was a strange question to Andrew, but he began to appreciate how different life in Gambia could be.

"Yes, I have parents. And a sister."

"How lovely! What are they like? Are you close with them?"

Andrew had been thinking about his family, especially his parents, quite a bit these days as he confronted becoming more comfortable with a life he was unsure they would understand or accept. Still, he tried to be less harsh on them than he had been at home. He couldn't tell if the distance changed his perspective, making him more sympathetic towards his parents, or if it made him forgetful. Without them hovering over him, he was in no rush to judge at that moment.

"My parents are, well, interesting. We're close, but probably not how you would define close. We don't talk so much, or have much in common. I don't know if that's anyone's fault. I don't think anyone sets out for it to be that way. We're just different. They were so mad at me when I told them I was coming here. If it wasn't for my sister, they wouldn't have let me come."

"Really?!?"

"Well, not exactly. Ultimately it was my choice, but they weren't happy. My parents, and I guess me until coming here, live a pretty sheltered life. They've never really faced challenge, or had to deal with difference. And I've started to realize a lot of who they are is because of that. But they mean well. They've always been kind to me, given me what I needed or wanted, and let me be," Andrew ended, cutting himself off.

Andrew looked up at Thomas. "Sorry, I'm rambling. I should shut up."

"No. I like getting to know you."

6

THOMAS'S BROTHER, SHERIFF, moved to Banjul shortly before he did, and started making his living working at a shop. His earnings were well beyond those of a regular shopkeeper, and he even had left-over funds to send to his family back home. They were initially suspicious, though ultimately grateful for the unexpected help. Eventually, Sheriff let on that he was making money as part of an auto-part smuggling ring bringing cheaper parts to the city from Senegal. Knowing his father was the unofficial village mechanic — being the person everyone went to in order to fix a broken motor-cycle — he began suggesting the rest of the family move to Banjul, where life would be easier. Their parents, John and Grace, always rejected his entreaties; they were content in the village, with Thomas and their other son still living with them. Life was peaceful on the river, the fish were still in abundance, and Grace didn't want to stop tending the family plot. "I don't want to be someone who can only get food in the market," she would tell him.

After Thomas left, Sheriff continued pressuring their parents, using Thomas's leaving as further incentive. It would be easy and comfortable; he had already done all the hard work for them. His home, he said, had room for both of them, and his other brother and wife if they chose to come. "And I have a generator," he told them. "Your lives won't depend on Nawec and always having to worry about cash power anymore." As enticing as escaping the woes of the country's power supply was, John and Grace stayed put.

On his way home from work one night, Thomas called Suleiman and asked if he wanted a visit. Thomas was feeling celebratory on account of meeting Andrew. Even if nothing had materialized, Thomas achieved what he wasn't sure was possible: he met someone. The irony of celebrating good news with a friend while keeping that news a secret wasn't lost on Thomas, but in the circumstances, he would take what he could get.

Their last celebratory evening was when Thomas got his promotion. He had used some of his tip money to buy a nice cake at the restaurant he previously worked at and where the two of them had met. It was then, while they indulged in cake and ice cream, that Thomas saw how generous Suleiman was, how lucky he was to have found him.

Thomas boasted to Suleiman how with higher wages and tips he'd be able to save more money and eventually move out. "Soon you won't have me taking up your space any longer."

"Don't say this," Suleiman said. "I want you to stay here. This is your home." Sometimes Thomas wondered why Suleiman was so giving.

The night after seeing Andrew, Thomas returned with another cake.

"You're always telling me I don't visit you enough. Now you cannot say such things, at least for a while."

Suleiman didn't question why Thomas visited when he arrived at his door holding a cake in a box. He frequently reminded Thomas it was important for them to keep in touch and appeared pleased that his friend took initiative.

"It is good of you to visit."

The feeling of too much icing eaten too quickly was settling in their stomachs when Thomas's phone rang. It was his father, but it was unusually late for him to be calling. Suleiman pretended to busy himself to give Thomas privacy.

When Thomas hung up the phone he was silent, his eyes and furrowed brow signaling a mind flush with thoughts.

"What is it?" Suleiman asked him.

"My parents," he answered hesitantly. "They're moving to Banjul, to live with my brother," he continued, speaking slowly, digesting the news himself. "My other brother is staying, but my parents... they're coming here. And they think I should also move there, with them."

Thomas had never told Suleiman the real reason he left his family and village behind. The desire for more opportunity was sensible enough that Suleiman never questioned Thomas's motivations. Still, the infrequency with which Thomas spoke about his family suggested there was more to Thomas's relationship with them, with his home, than he let on.

"But Banjul is farther from the hotel," Suleiman said. "It would take you so much more time going to and from work. Your life would be much more hectic."

Suleiman was right. It was also the most practical and banal excuse Thomas could think of without having to address the unspoken.

"Yes. Yes, you're right," Thomas said excitedly to Suleiman, realizing he had a valid reason to refuse.

When Thomas called his father the next day and explained how driving from Banjul to Serrekunda every morning, and back again at night, could add an hour each way to his commute, his father reluctantly understood.

"But you must visit us," he told his son. "After all, we will be very near to you."

"I know, father. I will visit. Of course I will."

That night, Thomas lay awake, unable to fall asleep. With his non-acclimatized parents living with him, Sheriff would again have the opportunity to demonstrate his skillfulness, navigating his family through life in the big city. He would be the expert, the guide, the model. The contrast between how Thomas and Sheriff lived would exacerbate the childhood tension that never seemed to evaporate from their relationship. He could hear his parents speaking. *Why isn't Thomas more like his brother?*

The space he worked so hard to carve out for himself would be squeezed.

Thomas's father would fall easily into Sheriff's orbit. John never went to school. He was a self-taught man who could fish, farm, and fix things. And he'd done well enough by that. He believed that life isn't easy and requires hard work and discipline, and Thomas knew his father would be impressed by the life Sheriff had built, the material things he acquired that ostensibly certified his success. *You just need to work more like your brother, Thomas.*

With the family living apart for the past couple of years, conversations placing Thomas's difference in the spotlight became infrequent. Lying awake in bed at night, growing increasingly anxious and restless, Thomas knew that was about to change. Heightening his anxiety was the thought that he risked putting into focus how different he was, at a time when things were starting to fall into place.

Andrew was surprised at how quickly he was falling for Thomas. But even with his feelings, he knew he couldn't be the one to make the first move. First, there was the practical. There was nowhere the two of them could be alone. Andrew still hadn't said anything to Alex, though he planned on it. Second, Andrew was scared. So much was unknown, and Andrew didn't like the unknown. As much as he desperately wanted to move things forward, the prospect of figuring out how had overwhelmed him. So he was content to let Thomas take the lead.

It was their fifth Friday. Andrew took a shared taxi to the hotel instead of walking along the beach. He would walk down to the beach almost automatically when he left school earlier in the afternoon. These Friday dates became his favorite part of the week. But this time he stopped himself when he turned to start his walk towards the hotel. The nerves were getting to him. He knew sooner or later he and Thomas would have to confront what existed between them – the good and the bad – and he wasn't sure he was ready. None of this had been in his plan. Upon arriving at the beach, he pulled his journal out of his knapsack, sat in the sand, and tried to make sense of the jumbles of thoughts slinging back and forth in his head.

This might be a big mistake. I don't know what I'm doing. I'm most definitely not thinking. Or maybe I am. No one would tell me this is a smart thing to do. But isn't that the point – that this is the time where I listen to me? I don't think it's dangerous. I've spent enough time in this country to know there's a lot of talk and not a lot of action – nothing will happen and it's easy to keep something quiet. Alex won't care and Isatou is really the only other person who comes to our compound. And Awa. But neither of them would say anything if they ever saw anything, which they won't.

It's not hard to figure this place out. Sure, people aren't accepting, but hold on anyways. I'm not starting up with anyone. This is about two people, starting to like each other, in private. No harm should come of that. And, nothing's happened, and I can't see how anything would anyway. For the first time, I am clear on things and that's what I find so confusing. No one knows how anything ends. But that doesn't mean you don't start.

While Andrew sat alone on the beach that Friday night and tried to make sense of everything, Thomas stood behind the bar, waiting for the approaching silhouette. Other male hotel guests flirted with Thomas before – the brazenness of some amazed him. But it was precisely that attribute that led Thomas not to trust them. From the start they assumed they could have Thomas, but they never took any time to try and talk to him, to actually know him. Only Andrew took a real interest in him. It was the first time a courtship developed on equal footing. Physical attraction brought them close, but something deeper drew them even closer.

Wondering what having a real connection was like caused many sleepless nights for Thomas. In his parents' village, and in the capital, he would lie awake and try to imagine what it might feel like to see someone and smile at him. Would it be excitement? Happiness? Maybe it was a feeling of finally being at ease.

He never took the step of imagining himself living out such a connection with someone else. He never saw himself in someone else's arms. Lying there awake, wondering, he never closed his eyes to pretend. He was too aware of his reality to let himself be fooled and disappointed. Better to wonder instead of dream. Dreams provided escapes, but rarely possibilities. So what was the point?

Now though, there was starting to be a point.

It was getting dark and Andrew was still sitting on the sand. Lost in his own indecisiveness, he sat absent-minded staring into the distance, overpowered by lethargy. For weeks now, all he'd done was sort out rationally what he was feeling and experiencing. So now, he didn't want to think about it anymore. His journal lay open in front of him. He paid no attention to its pages slowly being flipped over by the wind.

Eventually, and without his consent, his mind wandered back to the coming out conversation he had with Lindsay. Besides saying how happy she was for him, and that she still loved him, she also told him she really hoped he'd find someone special.

"Andrew, when you get home you deserve to find someone *amaaazing.*"

When you get home.

It wasn't a warning against romance while he was away. It was meant to be completely innocuous. Lindsay wasn't with him. She wouldn't understand.

He got up, shook off the sand, walked up towards the road, and got in a 7-7 heading south, away from his home.

Andrew had been getting pretty good at making small talk in 7-7s. He enjoyed learning about fellow passengers. It offered a window into daily living and each person brought a different story or perspective, making each ride down the same road different. But this time Andrew got in and sat silently, pressed against the side of the car. He quickly nodded at the woman sitting in the middle, turned away, and with an expressionless face stared out of the open window. Lights blurred past him.

He sat still, but inside his mind and heart were racing. Images from his past flashed before him. Boyfriends and girlfriends he watched walking into classes holding hands, couples in restaurants and movies – moments he never experienced. He saw the taunting looks he got from summer coworkers. His attempts to suppress a reaction when minding his own business only to overhear someone call someone else a fag. He started recounting all the lies he told to friends, to family, and to himself. Everything that made him question himself was rising back to the surface now, thrown in his face by the wind as he sat there more determined than ever for it to blow past.

"You're going to find someone great. I know it." Lindsay promised him.

What if I don't? It was a question he asked himself for as long as he could remember. *What if I can't?* A lump in his throat surfaced. He knew the feeling. It had been there before, many times.

The 7-7 pushed ahead down the darkened road, clunking along as it found some potholes and missed others. Andrew noticed none of it and paid no attention when it stopped to drop off and pick up new passengers. He just kept sitting and staring out – a tall boy pressed into a small back corner.

The car slowed as they neared the stretch of hotels. Up ahead was a police checkpoint. These weren't unusual at night, especially around the hotels. It was an attempt to deter drunk drivers. Normally Andrew thought nothing of them. But tonight's was enough to jolt him out of his trance. His heart shifted from a thump to a pound as he felt the palms of his hands turn clammy.

With the wind gone, the warm stale air of the taxi enveloped him. The tacky lights on the car's stereo system jumped out in different colors. The seat leather was torn and suddenly felt dirty, as did the shopping bags belonging to the woman next to him resting on his legs that he now noticed and pulled away from. Wires hung from under the steering wheel. The flashing lights from the stereo soon joined with those atop police cars. The driver had yet to lower the Afro-pop playing from the speakers and it was still too loud. The DJ's voice talked over the song – they frequently did that and Andrew didn't understand this desire to ruin the music. It was all becoming too much.

The 7-7 inched forward, not letting in enough air to calm his now heavy breathing.

He closed his eyes and exhaled.

He was squeezed against the door of a barely functioning car in a far-flung part of the world next to people he did not know and who would never understand him. Maybe this brief reprieve was all he needed to confront life with the confidence that had always been missing. Approaching the checkpoint, he started to feel something he hadn't felt since arriving, vulnerable. He sank deeper into his seat. Through the flashing lights he saw his family and missed them. The home he hadn't lived in for years and hadn't wanted to return to all of a sudden tugged at him. He thought about getting out of the car to head back to his house, hoping Alex and Liv would be there to give him the comfort of familiarity. But the driver, unaware of one of his passenger's growing unease, kept creeping forward.

When it was their turn at the checkpoint, the car approached cautiously. There were eight armed officers operating in teams of twos, on either side of the road. A pair approached and shined flashlights at the driver and all the passengers. Andrew grimaced in the brightness. They were all waved through. It took less than thirty seconds. The car picked up speed and a refreshing wind hit Andrew's face as they raced forward. He exhaled one last time before his breathing returned to normal. His nerves had stayed at the checkpoint and the wind no longer carried troubled memories, it carried clarity.

Fuck it.

Thomas sat on a concrete ledge next to the bar, looking at the pool lights through the water, trying to keep his legs still. There was no one at the pool or restaurant so he had nothing to do but wait for Andrew, who on every other Friday would have come and gone by now. Thomas began to worry he might not be coming. He chided himself for letting himself be fooled into thinking he could fall in love in this place. But at that moment someone appeared in the hallway from the lobby and started walking towards the pool. Thomas thought the person was holding a knapsack, which Andrew carried from work. Andrew stopped in the doorway when he got close enough to make eye contact with Thomas, who stood up and was now positioned behind the bar. Andrew slowly walked over, took his knapsack off his shoulder, rested it on the floor, and sat down on a bar stool. His chest pushed out with his breath.

"Hi."

"I was starting to think you weren't coming."

"I'm here."

They smiled.

"There's no one left. I can close the bar now," Thomas said. "Did you want to go for a walk?"

"Sure," Andrew answered, blushing. "I'd like that."

Part Two

7

MAYA MITCHELL WAS nearing the end of her posting in Gambia. After three years, the Consular Affairs Officer at the U.S. Embassy was ready for a change. The country was peripheral to U.S. interests and she felt out of the action. She spent most of her time helping Americans get medical treatment for malaria, or with small-scale aid programs that were largely symbolic. What bothered her most was being stymied with each and every project designed to effect positive change in the country. Maya joined the foreign service after 9/11 as an idealist. She believed in the promise of American power and the necessity for the United States to help solidify strong democracies and keep the world safer. She wasn't necessarily a Bushite, but she believed in freedom, thought it was worth fighting for, and that with the privilege of growing up free came a responsibility to help others achieve the same.

Gambia was her first posting, and after three years her idealism was starting to falter. There were limits to what the world's biggest superpower could do, even in the smallest of places. She came in with so many ideas – about how the U.S. government could work with students and journalists, lawyers and judges, to strengthen political freedoms and free expression curbed by the country's strong-arm government. She wanted the U.S. government to react more angrily when elections proved to be little more than a fig leaf for electing the same person over and over again. She hoped her government, and its embassy, would provide a platform for those activists who lacked one in an attempt to foster a fairer democracy where the rule of law existed in more than name only.

But none of that happened.

Instead, Maya watched as her government stood by as an observer. When journalists were fired or arrested for writing articles critical of the government, her embassy and the State Department remained silent. The same was true when judges routinely decided cases in the government's favor. The only time she could count on a statement being issued was on the country's independence day, when Washington would release a carefully crafted message congratulating Gambians on the occasion. Her hopes that diplomacy might be a tool for peaceful and constructive intervention were dashed. Maybe, she thought, if the country mattered more.

For the short time that remained, Maya planned to stay under the radar. Big change wasn't coming now or in the foreseeable future. She would do her job, and do it well, but that was it. After work, she wanted to enjoy herself and a carefree tropical life. It wasn't such a bad plan. That was until one afternoon when she was told a young British woman was waiting to see her.

Alex had finished his placement and moved back to the U.S., and Liv, afraid of going to the police, didn't know where else to turn.

A marine stood guard outside the embassy entrance.

"Do you have an appointment?"

"No. I'm here because I think a U.S. citizen has gone missing."

"Are you an American citizen, ma'am?"

"No, I'm British, but the American man is my friend. I've tried looking everywhere for him."

She was told to wait while the marine went into a booth and picked up a telephone. He returned, gave her a form to fill out, took her cellphone and passport, and sent her to a side entrance reserved for non-citizens. The waiting room was typical government and could've been anywhere in the world. There was cheap gray linoleum floor tiling, sterile white walls, and rows of plastic chairs bolted to the floor. The air conditioner was on too high, so Liv wrapped her arms around herself as the smiling faces of Barack Obama and Hilary Clinton looked down on her. She took a seat amidst the Gambians processing or hoping to process visa applications. She thought of Thomas and the night not too long ago when she let it slip that she'd suggested Alex look into how he might get asylum in the U.S. Thomas gave her the look of a hopeless optimist. It was a look she'd seen too often from him and many times made her regret whatever comment elicited it, as it was often a stark reminder of how different their lives truly were.

"I'll manage here," he said. "It's okay."

"I hope you're right."

Now, sitting in the embassy waiting room, Liv wondered if she could have been more insistent with Andrew, especially once Alex left and Andrew and Thomas had more time alone at the house. She looked at the Gambians sitting around her, blamed them for what she feared had happened to Thomas and Andrew, and grew angry at them. She sank further into the plastic chair, overcome by a feeling of helplessness. For the first time in her almost two years in the country, she wanted to go home.

After some time, a young, smartly dressed black woman approached her. Her appearance, together with her deliberate mannerisms, gave her away as an American embassy staffer.

"Ms. Holden?"

"Hi, yes."

"My name's Maya Mitchell. I'm the Consular Affairs Officer here at the embassy."

Maya led Liv into a windowless interview room with a desk and two chairs.

"Can I get you a drink?"

"No, thank you."

She took out a small notebook and pen as they sat down.

"You say you know of a missing American citizen?"

"Yes. Well, at least I think so. Andrew Turner."

"How long has he been in the country?"

"I don't know exactly. Almost a year?"

"How do you know him?"

"We're good friends. My boyfriend, who has since left the country, was his roommate."

"Would you say you know him well?"

"Relatively well. As well as any expat can come to know any other expat."

Maya smiled at Liv. Her answer displayed her maturity and thoughtfulness. It confirmed to Maya that she probably wasn't one of the paranoid over-worriers who often claimed their friends and relatives were missing or dead if they didn't show up to a restaurant at the designated time.

"When did you last see or speak with him?"

"It's been around a week. He didn't answer my calls or texts. And now his phone is off. I went to his work. They haven't seen or heard from him either."

"Has he done something like this before?"

"No."

"Do you have any reason to think something might have happened to him?"

"Maybe. He was in a relationship with a Gambian man."

Maya stopped writing and looked up at Liv. "He was?"

"Yes, for several months now."

"Have you gone to the police to report him as missing?"

"No."

"Was his relationship public knowledge?"

"No. Not that I know of. No. I would've known if it was."

"How long has it been going on for?"

"Oh, I don't know. Since sometime last fall."

Maya looked up again. "That long?"

"Yes, that long."

Their meeting was brief and finished shortly thereafter. Maya asked Liv if she'd been in touch with Andrew's family, which she had not.

"No. I've never been in touch with them before. I didn't want to worry them without being sure."

"Right, of course."

Maya asked Liv for a list of Andrew's friends in the country, where he worked, and where he spent most of his time. The last thing she asked was for a physical description and if Liv had a picture of him, one to complement the sterile passport photo she was about to look up.

Liv did her best to describe Andrew. "He's tall, a mix of lanky and slightly muscular." Laughing, she said, "He's definitely more imposing from afar." As for a picture, all she could provide was a photo from Andrew's Facebook, but the Marine had taken her phone. Maya led Liv down the hall to a room with a computer, where she downloaded a picture of Andrew for her.

"Thank you, Liv," Maya said, before confirming they had each other's contact information. "I'm going to start making some inquiries."

"Is it unusual for a foreign national to be arrested here without the authorities notifying the embassy?"

"It would not be in keeping with diplomatic protocol."

"Has it happened before?"

"A week would be a long time for an American citizen to be held here incommunicado."

And with that, they found themselves back at the entrance to the waiting room.

Maya extended her hand. "Thank you for coming in. And just to let you know, privacy laws can limit the information we can share, so don't be too concerned if you don't hear back from us," she spoke with the calm, reassuring voice of someone who'd had these conversations before. "If we need to be in touch with you, we will. Please call us though if you hear anything or get in touch with him."

"I will. Thank you," Liv said, as she turned to walk briskly with her head down past the rows of Gambians.

Maya had been in Gambia long enough to know it was unlikely that authorities would fail to inform the embassy if they arrested a U.S. citizen. But it was not unthinkable. Especially if the charges related to homosexuality. The country's government made it very clear that homosexuality was one of the few areas where the usual rule did not apply. A small number of foreign diplomats had quietly left the country over the past few years after rumors began to circulate that authorities would disregard diplomatic immunities in cases of suspected homosexual conduct.

Maya picked up the phone to call the directorate of the country's police services. In almost all instances she had a good and pleasant relationship with her Gambian counterparts. But now, a part of her thought that if Andrew was in fact arrested for issues relating to homosexuality, she might not get confirmation.

After exchanging the usual warm and enthusiastic greetings, Maya stated she was merely following up on a report that an American citizen may be missing, and whether the police had any information for the embassy. She deliberately did not insinuate that Andrew may have been arrested.

"When did this person allegedly go missing?" she was asked.

"It would have been within the past week."

There was a delay in his response. "I cannot confirm whether an American citizen has been taken into custody."

Maya seized on the deliberate ambiguity and pressed further. "Are you absolutely sure?"

"I can only confirm individuals were arrested recently for committing unnatural offenses, which as you know is against the criminal code, and as you also know, is an offense for which the Government of The Gambia has zero tolerance, and which has been publicly stated to be an offense for which the government pledges to deal with harshly."

"And is one of those arrested an American citizen? A Mister Andrew Turner?"

"I'm sorry, Maya, but I cannot share anymore. Once our investigation is complete and any individual is formally charged, all information will be available through the courts as is the ordinary practice."

There was little else Maya could extract from a usually verbose bureaucrat who had suddenly become frustratingly obstinate. Not wanting to give up so easily, she offered courteous reminders about diplomatic and consular protocol, expectations of reciprocity, and the rule of law. All of which fell on deaf ears.

"The Government of The Gambia has been clear and consistent in its position on these heinous offenses and those people who commit them."

Those people.

Maya knew any more attempts to extract information would be futile, so she hung up the phone and called someone she was certain would be able to discover what was actually happening if he didn't already know.

Maya and Suleiman shared a friendship and an unofficial working relationship. They had many friends in common and over time had grown close. One evening over drinks, Suleiman shared information he learned about a government program. Maya had found it particularly interesting and was surprised she hadn't heard it herself. It was nothing groundbreaking, but the information proved reliable in the end. Maya came to appreciate the limits of official government communication and realized it might be useful to at times take advantage of her friendship with Suleiman. His privileged position as a well-connected journalist in a small country sometimes proved the only way for her to get a straight answer.

Maya assumed her phone call to Suleiman would be nothing more than a routine off-the-record request for information. She was far more concerned with what her next steps would be if in fact Andrew had been taken into custody. It was the type of arrest no one wanted to deal with. Her efforts on behalf of someone accused of homosexual activity would cloud her relationships with almost every other local she interacted with, professionally and personally. There was no way the government, once it went public, was not going to do all it could to push its narrative of traditional African values standing up against the onslaught of the West's culture of immoral hedonism. Maya, who would be responsible for offering whatever consular assistance she could, would become a public face of that culture. She wanted her remaining months in Gambia to pass anonymously. Now she'd be working on a story at the center of the media and political worlds. It would be a huge headache for her at a time when she needed it least. She hoped Andrew had run away with his local boyfriend, or contracted malaria and was lying in a hospital bed somewhere.

Maya asked Suleiman if he knew of any Americans arrested in the past week, to which he said he didn't.

"None at all? None arrested quietly under the anti-gay laws?"

"What!? Where did you hear this?" Suleiman shot back.

"Nowhere. But a British girl came to see me this morning. Her friend, an American, hasn't been seen or heard from in about a week and she thinks he might be missing."

"The friend is gay?"

"Yes. And apparently he is dating a local man."

Suleiman's heart sank. He opened his mouth to ask a question but forgot what he was going to ask.

"Suleiman? Do you know something? Can you find out?"

"Let me try. I'll call you back," he said as he hung up abruptly.

Suleiman rushed out of a cafe where he was working and into a taxi and headed towards the hotel. If Thomas had been arrested and his phone was still on, he didn't want the police to see his contact showing up. It was still early in the day, but Thomas would have been at work by then.

In the taxi he tried to think of the last time he saw or spoke to his friend. He couldn't exactly remember. It had been some time, longer than usual.

At the hotel, he briskly made his way through the lobby out back to the pool. Behind the bar was a man with his back turned to him. He was much taller than Thomas. When he eventually turned around, Suleiman didn't recognize him. He found a waiter who looked familiar and inquired if Thomas was working that day and what time he might come in.

"Thomas hasn't been here for several days. Nobody has seen or heard from him. They were pretty angry at first."

"And now?"

"Confused. It's not like him."

"Has anyone called him?"

"They tried but didn't reach him."

It had to be true.

Suleiman thought about the likelihood that someone who mattered might know about his friendship with Thomas. Then he wondered if he shouldn't have been more insistent about him leaving the country. Then he wondered what they were doing to his friend. But he didn't wonder for long. He had a pretty good idea.

Suleiman sat down at a table near the pool. He ordered himself a juice. Even though they were being coy with Maya, no police officer would knowingly arrest an American and keep him detained without someone in the government being aware. A police officer or district commander would never hold an American without offering consular assistance unless those were his instructions. He knew exactly who he needed to call.

The official in the Justice Minister's office boasted and hid nothing. He was proud. "We arrested them several days ago. We are almost finished the investigation before charges are officially brought."

"When will it become public?"

"Any day now."

Suleiman said nothing. His source continued to brag that this would be a significant victory for the government, "and for the whole nation." Of course Suleiman must be happy too, the man suggested. He worked for the country's largest newspaper and this would be his story. "The Americans will be furious. But we have been very clear about these acts."

"Absolutely."

"You must be excited for your career. This will be good for you."

"I know," he muttered, before thanking his source for his time and information.

"It is my pleasure," he responded, adding how the government planned to turn this into a big story, with a lot of media attention. It would make up for the last, embarrassing attempt. The trial would be well publicized and the punishment, harsh. He spoke as if the whole thing was already planned out. Suleiman noticed his source was so eager to brag that it never occurred to him to ask how Suleiman found out.

"How were they discovered?"

"The American had a maid."

"Of course."

After hanging up the phone Suleiman took in a deep breath. He tilted his head back and let it hang for a while with his eyes closed. He thought about what was to come. His friend, who was most likely being abused by his jailers, would be paraded before the country as a pariah. Pastors and imams would call him a disease from which the country must be cured. His family would likely completely abandon him. He'd have no one.

But he wasn't only focused on Thomas and what this would mean for him, he also thought about himself.

Suleiman knew he would be expected to cover the trial. His reporting beat included law and order and this, especially because it involved an American, would be huge. And it would be unthinkable, and perhaps dangerous, for his coverage of the trial to support any position but the one advanced by the state in its crusade to purge homosexuality from African shores. He was scared and ashamed for when Thomas would see him next and hoped his friend would know that he too was trapped.

He exhaled, brought his head forward, and opened his eyes. It was a bright day. In front of him was the undisturbed water of an empty, perfectly tended swimming pool. The manicured grounds around it so peaceful and inviting. From the bottom of his eyes, Suleiman glanced at his phone on the table. It stared up at him. He had to call Maya back but chose to wait, just a few more minutes, so he could sit, savor the silence, and finish his juice.

Maya answered her phone right away.

"They're at the police headquarters, with Serious Crimes, both of them."

"How long have they been there?"

"I don't know. They were arrested Sunday night. They may have both been at the NIA first."

NIA. The National Intelligence Agency. She knew what that meant.

A flood of questions followed and Suleiman told her what he knew. *When would they be charged? What are the charges? Is there any actual evidence? Are they being held together? Do they know Andrew's an American? Does the prison population know what they're suspected of? Did he know why they never contacted the embassy? Who is the other man?*

"He is a close friend of mine."

Maya paused before responding incisively. "What? Seriously?"

"Yes, seriously. Thomas. I have known him for years. He stayed in my house for a while not long after he arrived in Banjul. He's from a smaller village on the river."

Maya was stunned.

"Maya, they're going to make an example out of them. Especially after the last try."

"I figured they would." A checklist of what she'd have to do next was growing in her head.

"Will you be able to help them?"

"Them?"

Her reaction hit Suleiman square in the face. For Maya and whatever resources the U.S. government would expend, there was no them, only Andrew.

"I mean, what if they are charged together? Then they would only need one lawyer right?"

"Perhaps." The list in Maya's head grew longer. She became short. "Suleiman, I need to go and speak to the Ambassador and we'll have to make some calls."

"Of course."

"Thank you for the information. You're reliable as always. I'll keep you as updated as I can about the situation and about your friend." Looking down at her scribbled notes she couldn't see his name written down anywhere. "What was his name again?"

"Thomas."

"Right, Thomas."

"How long have you known about Thomas and Andrew's relationship?"

"From the beginning."

8

SEVERAL MONTHS BEFORE, there was a text message on Suleiman's phone from Thomas.

can i c u?

Suleiman couldn't remember the last time he received a text from Thomas, let alone one asking for them to get together. Suleiman always initiated. Given the imbalance between them – Suleiman, the son of a high-level official and a promising young journalist, and Thomas, a lonely, poor village boy who'd been sleeping in the back of a restaurant – Thomas was always careful not to appear dependent or too needy as their friendship took hold. He was deeply appreciative of Suleiman for his kindness. He did not want to jeopardize it by taking advantage. He tried not to expect anything.

For his part, Suleiman wasn't entirely certain what drew him to Thomas, who was several years younger. They were from different worlds and lived different lives. Suleiman certainly knew plenty of other people who didn't share his fortunes. Still, there was something about Thomas that Suleiman liked. Contrasted with the ministry officials and their privileged children and those in the media playing the government's game, Thomas stood out to Suleiman for his sincerity and simplicity. He was warm. He was the type of disadvantaged person more fortunate people want to help – a nice guy trying his best to make it. Suleiman saw him as someone dealt a difficult hand who needed a little push. And he had the means to help.

Thomas had tried to say no when Suleiman invited him to move in with him. It was far too generous an offer for Thomas to accept.

"You're being foolish," Suleiman said, before adding he wouldn't have to pay anything. Thomas had to hide his tears.

The generosity, which Thomas didn't think he deserved, made him uncomfortable.

"Thomas, my flat is big enough. It's silly to have an empty room, and your living arrangements could certainly use an upgrade. Once you're able to move out on your own, you can. But until then, you need a proper place to sleep."

Suleiman's first reaction to the text message was that Thomas needed money. He always worried his friend might fall into financial trouble. Between low wages and job insecurity, Thomas had a small margin to work with.

They met later in the morning near the hotel at a roadside restaurant, which was mostly empty owing to the early hour. Thomas waited at a table in the back, dressed for work and sitting on a white plastic chair looking around anxiously. A bottle of Fanta sat full with a straw poking out. As soon as he sent the text message he started second-guessing himself. He knew Suleiman could be trusted and would be sympathetic to his situation. Still, he was nervous. Thomas had never confided in anyone before.

Seeing Suleiman's wide smile as he approached reassured Thomas. He eagerly hugged his friend, holding the tight embrace a second longer in an attempt to signal this was not a regular greeting.

"My friend, it's been too long," Suleiman said while still holding onto Thomas's shoulders.

"I know. You must be keeping busy. How is work?"

"*Ahhh.* It is too hectic." Suleiman proceeded to tell Thomas about some of the stories he'd worked on since his last visit to the hotel, back when he came to warn him about rumored crackdowns against gays and lesbians – something Suleiman worried might have overstepped the limits of their friendship, even if it hadn't pressed Thomas to admit anything. The rumor hadn't amounted to anything he could discover as of yet. Instead, his focus over the past months had been on new government anti-corruption efforts. A special investigator was appointed by the president to look into corrupt practices of senior bureaucrats.

"Your father?"

"No, no. My father is fine. As clean as they come. And he knows how to play the game to stay onside. It's the others who run afoul. Many of his friends."

Suleiman paused, realizing it was Thomas who wanted to meet.

"Sorry! I know you didn't ask to meet me so we could talk about politics."

"It's okay. I don't know where to start what I have to say."

It was true.

In debating how he would tell his friend, Thomas went back and forth on whether he should start from the beginning or the end. While he was sure Suleiman could be counted on, there was still some risk in disclosing everything about Andrew, especially since Andrew hadn't been consulted. But that was the most exciting part. Merely coming out to Suleiman only affirmed a truth that long went unspoken between them, cutting short the story without its happy ending.

"I met someone," Thomas began. He scrutinized a silent and still Suleiman for reactions as he spoke. "His name is Andrew. We've been becoming friendly for many months now. But last night it became something more."

Suleiman didn't immediately react and the usual look of concerned desperation radiating from his eyes now put Thomas on edge. He tried to project confidence, hiding his fear so Suleiman wouldn't see him as weak or vulnerable. "I don't want to make you uncomfortable or anything."

"You're not," Suleiman answered, shaking his head quickly to dispel any doubt. "I'm happy for you. I don't judge you," he said without much emotion. "People must be free to live their lives the way they choose."

Suleiman's matter-of-fact reaction didn't bother Thomas. Anything more would have been contrived. Even though Suleiman had studied in South Africa, the safest spot on the continent for a gay person, Thomas knew he probably still didn't fully comprehend homosexuality. But a lack of understanding was vastly preferable to the alternative. Even his suggestion that Thomas chose to live this way didn't bother him – it was a level of ignorance he could accept. If someone from his own background accepted him, he couldn't be infected by a foreign disease as so many other people would want to believe. Suleiman's support affirmed that he wasn't some pariah. He was who he was. Maybe there was a place for him.

"How did you meet him?" Suleiman inquired gently.

Thomas told him everything. How one day while working at the bar as usual and minding his own business he noticed someone. He wasn't looking to find someone, and certainly wasn't looking to find a guest of the hotel, but it was one of those unexpected moments to which you have no choice but to respond.

"The moments that change things," added Suleiman.

"Yes! Exactly." He appreciated that his friend understood.

"I admire your patience. Myself, I don't think I would have been able to wait so long before speaking to Andrew. Well, not Andrew," he clarified awkwardly. They laughed together, bringing their friendship back into focus. "Where is he from?"

"He's American. White, American," Thomas qualified.

Suleiman nodded and Thomas had a hard time interpreting it. He spent so much time around foreigners, the fact that he now found himself with a white foreigner shouldn't have been a shock.

"You have enough in common?" Suleiman asked.

"Yes. This was something I worried about. But I guess in a way it's like you and me. Sometimes people don't have much in common. For whatever reason, they are able to move past all their differences to find common things to share. From being around so many Americans, especially the Peace Corps ones, many of the things he speaks about, or the slang he uses, I have heard before."

"Does he understand about you? About where you come from?"

"Maybe a bit. He's learning."

Thomas didn't want to bore his friend with too many details but wanted to take advantage of this opportunity to finally share his life with someone. He gave an abridged version of the months of flirting and conversations between him and Andrew. He mentioned Friday nights and how they came to know each other, and contrasted the intimacy of Friday nights with their public meetings when Andrew would show up at the pool with expat friends on weekends.

"Those are tougher. We must pretend."

"You said last night it became more than you just being friends."

"Yes," Thomas answered, and for the first time smiled in a way that freely showed off his excitement. "We kissed," he said proudly.

"I'm happy for you," said Suleiman.

"Thank you," Thomas answered with a school boy's grin.

"And thank you for trusting me. I'm glad you feel comfortable enough to."

"I do. There's no one else, though."

"It's not surprising. You know how things are here. Thomas, please be careful."

"I know. We know."

9

WALKING UP FROM the beach, Andrew's heart was pounding as if he'd just run a marathon. He was overwhelmed by thoughts and emotions flying through his head quicker than he could keep track. He was ecstatic and nervous, relieved and tense all at the same time. Above all, he was in a bit of disbelief. Yes, it actually happened. And *it* had so many meanings.

It was late when he arrived home and he assumed Alex, and Liv if she was there, would be sleeping. He tried to keep quiet, but he desperately wanted to share the news with someone, so he tried to make just enough accidental noise to wake them up. When his shuffles failed, he walked into his room and sat still on his bed in the dark. He tried at first to block out everything crossing his mind so he could take in the moment. He wanted to sit there, pleased and proud of himself. But the moment didn't last. There was his family. They weren't the type to share in this milestone. Even Lindsay. Would she understand? And then on top of it all was Thomas. He wasn't who he'd pictured himself with. But that mattered less and less, if at all, since they'd first met. He was sweet and kind, and Andrew had fallen for him.

He took out his journal thinking it might be helpful to try and make sense of everything by writing it down. But when he opened to the next blank page and held out the pen, he froze. He wanted to express so much yet no words came to him. Finally, after several minutes of mental false starts he wrote the only thing that came to him.

I did it, finally. We kissed. Holy shit.

He then lay down exhausted and fell asleep.

When the sunlight finally woke him up he didn't immediately get out of bed. Instead, he lay there to make sure that what he thought happened the night before actually did. He turned to the table by his bedside. His journal was there with the pen still inside. He opened to the page it was on, looked at what he wrote the night before, smiled to himself, and closed the book.

Alex and Liv were eating breakfast and watching something on Alex's laptop when Andrew finally opened his door. Emerging into the sunlit living room wearing only pajama pants, Andrew's face scrunched up at the brightness as if biting into a lemon. Alex's expression suggested an immediate acknowledgment that Andrew seemed dazed after coming in late from somewhere, but that Alex wasn't also about to pry.

Andrew took the three steps to the chair in the living room deliberately and slowly, building the anticipation. Sitting down, he placed his hands on both legs and exhaled as if his joints were sore, looked down at the floor letting his neck hang as if still tired, before eventually looking up, eyes wide open, ready to make his announcement.

"I kissed someone last night."

Alex and Liv both tried to play it cool.

"That's great," Alex responded nonchalantly. "Who was it?"

"The bartender. Thomas."

"Wow."

"Yeah."

"How?" asked Liv.

"I dunno. It just kind of happened."

"Out of nowhere?"

"No, I kind of expected it. We've been hanging out at the bar every Friday night for the past few months. Well, I've been hanging out. He's been working."

"Wow," Alex said again, smiling but shaking his head. "Good for you!"

"Yes, great," added Liv less convincingly, eliciting a discreet look from Alex telling her to do better. "Are you happy about it?"

"Oh for sure. He's a really nice guy," Andrew said before pausing, his face turning quizzical. "Wait, did you guys know?" He didn't know what his preferred answer was. If they answered yes, did it mean he gave off a vibe – something he'd long tried to hide? Alex's facial expression formed somewhere between blank and sympathetic, oblivious to what Andrew was trying to get at with his question. Liv, on the other hand, seemed to get it. She leaned forward as if to begin answering.

At that exact moment the gate to their compound opened. The loud creaking jolted all of them. The only other person with a key was Isatou, and though she wasn't paid to come on weekends, she occasionally did to collect mangoes or use their clothes line. Sometimes she came inside to pick up their laundry. They sat in silence as Isatou walked up towards their front door, like children hiding something from an approaching adult. She was startled to see the three of them sitting there, all looking right at her direction as if they were expecting her.

"Good morning," she said.

"Good morning, Isatou," said Alex. "How are you?"

"I am fine," she answered before turning her warm face towards Liv, whom she not-so-secretly liked the most. "Hi Liv, how are you?"

"I am good, Isatou, thank you."

Isatou and Liv carried on with some small talk for a bit. Andrew and Alex sat looking at each other and waiting to return to the conversation. When Isatou walked into Alex's bedroom to get his clothes, they all turned to one another with the shared realization they couldn't carry on their conversation until she left.

"What's the plan for today?" asked Alex.

"I don't know," said Andrew. "Maybe we'll all go to the hotel?" he suggested sheepishly.

Isatou left with the laundry in a basket, bidding them all a good day.

Andrew broke the silence after the compound gate shut behind her. "I should have told you both a while ago. I meant to. I just didn't get around to it."

"Don't worry about it," answered Alex. "It's whatever you're most comfortable with. I don't think there's a right or wrong way to go about it."

"Thanks."

"So," Alex enthusiastically interjected, "you've been spending time together for a couple of months?"

"Yeah!"

"And this happened at the hotel last night?"

"No, on the beach, near the turn off for Fajara. We walked along the beach after he got off work."

"You know," Alex said grinningly, "once you go black..."

"Alex!" Liv exclaimed as she hit him.

Andrew laughed. The lightheartedness, or rather, the nonchalance of Alex's reaction, was exactly what he'd needed.

"And who made the first move?" he asked with the same grin. Liv smacked him once more.

"What?!" Alex shot back at her with a stunned look of innocence. He wasn't being inappropriate.

Still giggling, Andrew answered. "He did. I've always been the shy one." He stopped to think, laughing again, quietly. He was talking in their direction, but not directly at them.

"It's funny. The first time I went to talk to him, I had no idea what to say. I showed up one Friday after work without having any clue what I was doing. I mean, I didn't know him. Only his name. We made eye contact the week before. But not regular eye contact. Like the noticing you kind of eye contact. But that was it. Somehow I showed up there the next week alone. Me, of all people. I'd never done something like that before. I had thought of it a lot. I wanted to. There were lots of times I probably should have gone up to someone. Maybe this time would've been less daunting if I hadn't been so scared or nervous before. Maybe I wouldn't be here now. I don't know. Whatever, it's just something I never did."

Andrew, realizing he was unloading, looked over at Alex and Liv for a hint that he was going too far. Their expressions suggested the opposite. They wanted to hear what he had to say.

"So what'd you do?" asked Alex.

"I just showed up. I stood there, across the pool from him. He was behind the bar. It was like the world froze. I think there was a family there or something. They were leaving, but I don't think either of us paid them any attention. It was only a few seconds. But we both just stood looking at one another. It was one of those looks, where you know something but you're not exactly sure what. And you don't see or focus on anything else. It all just stopped in front of me.

"I'm not trying to be crazy, or in love or anything. It was like a connection look. But there was depth to it.

"I walked over to the bar, which is the only thing I ever initiated between us, well, besides showing up, and we started talking. I went back the next week, and the week after that, and then kept going back. And he was always there. It became pretty clear we were headed in this direction. We get along really well and have great conversations. He's sweet."

He reflected to himself, replaying a highlight reel in his mind before proclaiming with certainty, "I'm really happy when I'm with him." He looked over at Alex and Liv again and paused. All three of them were wearing subtle smiles. His eyes turned down before he looked up again.

"It's brought up a whole host of things for me to think about. There's my family back home, and that this isn't exactly the best place to start experimenting. It's a lot to process. So yesterday, instead of heading over right from work, I stopped to think. I don't know if I was scared. Maybe it was just nerves. Maybe it's normal? I don't know – it's all new to me. I wondered if I could go through with it. And what would happen after? You know?"

"Yes, I know," Liv replied, nodding. Considering that Liv always struck Andrew as the most mature in their small group, he was especially encouraged by her reaction. He was being introspective for the first time, and she appeared genuinely impressed. "There's no crystal ball," she added.

"Exactly!" Andrew responded. "But when is there ever going to be a crystal ball?" he asked rhetorically. "So I don't know what will happen next. But until now," he nodded, "I'm happy. You know the feeling, when you meet someone and you just want to see them all the time. Like in between being with someone it's almost like you're filling the time just to get to see them again?"

Alex smiled at his roommate with real affection, and in it Andrew saw the reassurance he'd long wanted and needed. There was nothing more Alex needed to say.

"That's what it's becoming," finished Andrew.

"That's great," said Alex.

Liv projected less enthusiasm. "Did anyone see you?"

Alex and Andrew both appeared taken aback. Her question was a downer.

"What?" she asked defensively. "Don't misunderstand me, Andrew. Of course I'm thrilled for you. You only deserve happiness and I, we, support you fully. But," she said as she softened her voice to be more emphatic, "this isn't America."

"I know. We know," he said, his voice quieter, dispirited by Liv's reality check. "No one saw us. And at the hotel I'm just another white expat looking for a break from the outside. No one thinks anything of the visits. Thomas would've said so otherwise. And we spoke last night about the importance of discretion."

"That's good. I never doubted you. It's just, you know, we're not in America," she repeated.

"I know. Thanks."

"So when are we going?!" asked Alex.

"Where?" responded Andrew.

"The hotel..."

Andrew smiled. "This afternoon, I hope."

They finished off the conversation shortly thereafter. Liv asked Andrew if his family knew that he and Thomas were becoming friendly. It was her way of prying into his life, code for *do they know about you?* His answer was abridged and sanitized.

No, my family doesn't know. He told them that besides them, only his sister knew he was gay, but he didn't think she'd understand about Thomas.

"I want to tell her, but I'm not sure she'd get it. And anyway, there's no need or rush to say anything now." Walking towards the kitchen he stopped, looking back at them. "Maybe soon."

When they were ready to set off in the early afternoon, Andrew took out his phone to text Thomas letting him know they were on their way. He looked puzzled as he scrolled through his contacts.

"What?" asked Alex.

"I don't have his number," Andrew confessed.

"I guess we'll surprise him."

There was an awkwardness to the afternoon. They arrived and met friends in the lobby before making their way through to the back. Convention prohibited Andrew from immediately acknowledging

Thomas, let alone going over to say hi. It took all of his mental energy to stop his neck from turning to the left towards the bar. As he entered the pool area he saw other friends of his that he needed to greet as he walked and settled in. He said hello hurriedly before shifting his glance over only to discover Thomas too was preoccupied with work obligations, pouring drinks for a large group of children, and probably hadn't seen him. It took almost a minute before their eyes met through the crowd. They smirked barely and briefly at one another before turning away.

With Thomas busy behind the bar and Andrew in the middle of expat social circles, there was little time for even subtle games. Andrew had his book with him but found it hard to concentrate. He'd pick it up only to stare at the same page while his mind wandered to try and figure out how he could talk to Thomas. The answer, which he knew, was that right then, in the afternoon with the pool crowded, he couldn't. Besides seeing one another, they might as well have been in different places.

"I can't even talk to him," Andrew whispered over to Alex while they lay out in the sun. "I smiled while ordering a beer, that was all."

"I don't know," Alex answered confusedly. "I think this is something that can only happen in private."

"Yeah," Andrew responded knowingly.

"Bring him to our place sometime."

"Really?"

"Why not?"

"I don't know if we're there yet, but yeah, maybe."

"Where does he live?"

"Somewhere in Serrekunda."

"Not somewhere you two want to be spotted."

"Nope."

As Andrew lay there, surrounded by friends, all he wanted was to pick up from the night before. But he was stuck. He tried to swim to pass the time but quickly got bored.

After about two hours had passed, Andrew's disappointment was clear.

"Let's go," he told Alex.

"Are you sure?"

"Yeah."

While they gathered their belongings, Alex reached into his bag, taking out a pen, and then into his wallet, pulling out a twenty dalasi note. He handed them both to Andrew, who didn't understand.

"For Thomas. Give him your number."

"Ooohhhh. Smart."

Andrew scribbled his number on the money and walked over to the bar. He thanked Thomas for the drinks and said *see you next time*. He handed him the dalasis and used his eyes to show that there was writing on it. Thomas acknowledged Andrew's hint and took the bill, which he put right into his pocket.

"See you next time."

IO

THE SMELLS HIT Thomas walking up the stairs to Sheriff's apartment. It was his mother's cooking – onions and tomatoes in the frying pan. The smell of fried fish lingered. She must be making benachin. Inhaling the familiar scents of his childhood, Thomas felt a little bit calmer as he pictured his mother standing in their old kitchen.

Thomas was nervous riding the minibus from Serrekunda to Banjul for their first family feast. Since leaving his village behind, he wasn't living with the cloud of suspicion or expectation following him wherever he went. Free from the lurking, curious eyes of family and neighbors, he relished the anonymity of being on his own. Even though he might not have fully taken advantage of it, it was still liberating. Now, part of that was slipping away. The fact that Andrew was slowly entering his life only complicated things more, heightening his need for privacy.

Approaching the front door, Thomas instinctively went to knock, but caught himself.

Just walk in. This is your family.

He opened the door and stepped in through a thick wall of heat and steam brought about by a long day of cooking. Having only been at Sheriff's apartment a handful of times, it now looked far more familiar than he expected. A worn-out *choka* board was set up on the table. There was a blanket strewn over the sofa, sewn together into a patchwork of yellows and reds. A grainy sepia photograph hung on the wall above, a young couple, not smiling, standing erect with a puzzled gaze, staring out at nothing, looking frozen in time in their crisp formalwear. Turning towards the second bedroom, he peered into an open closet where bright green and blue bazin dresses, intricately patterned and put together, hung. Then, turning towards the noises coming from the kitchen, Thomas saw the figure of a woman bustling about between pots and frying pans. It was then, facing his mother's back, looking at a sight he'd seen so many times before, that Thomas realized – in some respect, he was back at home.

Footsteps approached from behind, up the stairs. Thomas turned to see that he'd forgotten to close the door behind him.

"Brother!" Sheriff exclaimed as he walked in with Thomas's father, John. Each carried a bag with some fruits and vegetables. Striding towards his little brother, Sheriff, whose thick gold chain hung freely around his neck, raised his free hand high, revealing a large, shiny watch, and slapped Thomas's back. "It is good to have you here with us. Like old times, together as a family."

The force with which Sheriff slapped Thomas's back unnerved him and he reacted tepidly to his brother's welcome. Thomas watched Sheriff's expression change. His face displayed his brother's more deviant side. Thomas had seen this sinister expression countless times before, too many times.

"Right, brother?" Sheriff insisted, somewhat sternly, but still with the façade of excitement. "All of us together in Banjul!"

"Of course," Thomas answered, standing motionless. "Hello, Father. Here, let me take that for you."

"Nonsense! If I could move a whole house to Banjul, I can carry some bananas and onions. Just because I live in a city doesn't mean I have to become lazy."

As Thomas's father made his way towards the kitchen, his mother, Grace, turned to face them. Her eyes found Thomas's and they stood looking at each other. Her smile was endearing, the way a mother looks at her youngest child, the one she had to watch out for a little bit more.

"My child," she said to him.

"Hello Mother," he responded softly.

Before she could speak again, John was thrusting onions into her hands.

"Here, this is what they had at that market. I don't know from choosing them. It was much easier pulling them out of the ground."

"Because you always grew onions," Grace teased. "Your father is not yet adjusted to our new home, with all its concrete. But do not worry, he will adapt. Right, John?"

"Of course," his father said, oblivious to his wife's mockery.

"Come, Thomas," his mother beckoned. "You can come and help me in the kitchen if you wish. The food is nearly ready."

"Sure."

Throughout his childhood, Grace had been Thomas's protector. Something he came to know with time. It wasn't always easy being Sheriff's younger brother. Brash and bombastic, he was assertive and demanding. Their relationship was never close, or particularly friendly. Sheriff always preferred for Thomas to learn the hard way, like he had.

As he started doing better at school than Sheriff, Thomas, who was never skilled at fixing things, began noticing his bicycle chain breaking more frequently, or door hinges coming off in the bedroom he shared with his brother. Each time Thomas failed to fix something, Sheriff was always there, able and boasting that not all of life's lessons and skills could be learned at school. When Thomas learned from his parents how Sheriff made his money in Banjul, it didn't surprise him at all. Smuggling and trading in the black market suited Sheriff's personality.

Now, in his brother's living room, he could feel that his mother once again sensed Thomas's vulnerability and sought to bring him closer to her. When they were children she tried to be subtle. Sometimes at night, pretending to sleep, he heard her scolding Sheriff or telling John not to be so tough on him.

Sheriff, I know you are the one who broke his bike. I know you want to make him to be tough like you. But not everyone is like you. Remember that.

It brought Thomas a measure of comfort knowing his mother stood up for him. Still, each time she did so, it was a reminder that he didn't conform to their expectations. *Not everyone is like you* meant *not everyone is tough; not every man is strong like a man should be.*

As he held out dishes for his mother to heap the benachin and yassa into, John and Sheriff were sitting at the table, speaking about different work opportunities – refurbished stereo systems, a special tint cutting machine brought in from Senegal. Sheriff emphasized to his father that in Banjul, minivans, not motorbikes, proved the most lucrative vehicle to service.

"Like the kind Thomas takes from Serrekunda. Tell him, brother, that the road is filled with minibuses more than motorbikes."

"It's true," Thomas said.

He and his mother brought the food to the table. Besides bena-chin and yassa, there was another plate of rice, a loaf of bread, and, strangely, a plate of fresh cucumbers and tomatoes.

"I saw it in a restaurant," Grace said. "I thought we would try it since we live in the city."

There were also bottles of Julbrew and soda. Between all the food and drink and the plates and glasses, there was barely any room. They all reached quickly for the food, building heaping piles on their plates. Sheriff grabbed two bottles of beer, handing one to his father and keeping the other for himself. Before taking his first drink he turned to Thomas.

"Did you want a beer, brother? Do you drink them?"

On its surface, Sheriff's face was expressionless, benign. Underneath, however, Thomas pictured his brother beaming. With his heart starting to beat faster, his nerves rising, he calmly finished the food in his mouth before answering.

"I do drink, sometimes. But now I do not feel like it. Thank you, Sheriff." He reached for a soda.

The table felt small and overcrowded, especially as Sheriff's presence loomed large, sucking up the air around them. He and John kept speaking about work, leaving Thomas to his plate of food.

Thomas could see his mother watching him as her eyes moved back and forth from her husband and elder son back to him. There was nothing she could do. Sheriff commanded the conversation. John, as Thomas predicted, saw Sheriff as the expert.

"Sometimes, there is too much work," Sheriff proclaimed. "We have a hard time finding good people, people we can trust to do the work good."

Well, Thomas thought to himself. *Do the work well.*

"I don't understand why you don't come and work with your brother," John announced. "Can't you hear him? He says he needs good people to help him. You should help your brother, and in the process, you will get a good job."

The inviting indifference on Sheriff's face intimated he and his father had spoken about this before, or at least Sheriff hinted at this, subtly planting the prospect in his father's head. It was an idea with Sheriff's influence all over it. Just like at home, it honed in on Sheriff's success and Thomas's struggle, Sheriff's strength and Thomas's weakness.

Thomas could barely betray his emotions. He tried desperately to tame what he felt was an expression of frustration. When he didn't immediately react, his father kept speaking as Thomas grew angry towards Sheriff.

"Why are you working in that hotel? All day working and doing things for *toubabs.* Your brother is working to help Gambian people. He has no *toubab* customers."

"John!" Grace interjected. She looked unimpressed as her husband lectured on.

Turning to his wife, John continued: "But our son can work with his brother, make more money so he can live comfortably. Why should he have to worry about picking up chicken bones after people who don't know him or understand him. He should work with his family."

Thomas's parents looked at each other and then at him. His father's eyes conveyed earnestness. He thought he was being a good father, helping his son who he felt might be going astray. Thomas wanted to tell him he didn't pick up chicken bones. He was a bartender, promoted because of skill and affability. That, however, only scratched the surface. On a deeper level, Thomas wished his family knew that he was far further from them than they could imagine. He wished he could tell them this, if only so they'd leave him alone. It was impossible, though. How do you communicate such things? How do you reveal secrets to people for whom the truth can be anathema?

Thomas sat silently, thinking to himself how he could never tell them why, now especially, he had to keep working at the hotel. He could not tell them how one day not that long ago, while Thomas was at work, a boy came. Well, not a boy, a young man. He had this smile, the kind of smile that when directed at you, you felt its warmth. It was real and gentle and reassuring – one that could make worries momentarily disappear. It's what won Thomas over before he even knew this young man's name. He wanted someone to smile at him that way.

That young man kept returning to the hotel. With each week their connection grew, until finally, only the other week, the two of them cemented it. Thomas didn't know what would happen next. All he knew was that the young man, Andrew was his name, would come back to the hotel the next week, and hopefully the week after that, and for many more weeks. Because of this, Thomas couldn't go to work with his brother. He needed to be at the hotel when Andrew returned. He needed to make sure Andrew saw him, that he didn't wonder where he disappeared to, and if he would ever come back.

Looking across a small table that suddenly started to seem smaller, Thomas caught his brother staring at him.

"What?" Sheriff proclaimed brashly. "You don't want to come work with your big brother?" His tone was suggestive, confirming to Thomas his brother knew he didn't want to work with him. Sheriff sensed his discomfort, and was trying to make him more uncomfortable. "Together like when we were younger. And there is space for you here. So you don't have to live in Serrekunda."

The three of them were now looking at him. Thomas's hands were under the table, on top of his knees. He felt his palms sweating.

"It is a kind offer, Sheriff. But I should decline, at least for now." He rushed the last part in. A peace offering. "They are good to me where I work. They respect me and tell me I do a good job, and I like working there. It is a pretty place, very peaceful. I don't want anyone to be angry, or to not understand." He spoke softly, but with resolve. "I'm trying something different now. Tourism is an important industry. There is opportunity in it. I should like to keep trying, for now."

Though he often projected a sense of obliviousness, Mr. Jalloh had been particularly warm and welcoming to Andrew. They spent the first few months working in very close quarters before the students arrived. Andrew observed an over-worked and under-resourced man who had every excuse to complain but rarely did. Through it all, with an almost constant look of bewilderment projecting through his narrow glasses, he never failed to ensure that Andrew had settled comfortably.

It took some time for him to finally get organized, but eventually Mr. Jalloh had Andrew over for a promised Gambian feast.

"It's time to fatten you up!" he jovially proclaimed. "Otherwise your parents will think food in The Gambia is not delicious."

Andrew was not sure what to expect. He was curious to see Mr. Jalloh outside of school. What did his home look like, how was he with his wives? Mr. Jalloh greeted him with his usual excited smile. He was dressed in a smart-looking orange and brown dashiki Andrew hadn't seen him wear before. He was also barefoot. Led quickly through the courtyard into the home, they went straight into the kitchen. The weak air conditioning was overpowered by all the heat from the cooking and Andrew was confronted with smells he did not recognize. A saucepan sizzled as Andrew tried peering at the food being prepared, trying to detect something familiar. Two women in aprons, standing over large pots cooking on the stove, turned to greet him. He stood face to face with both of Mr. Jalloh's wives. Unsure of how to act, he tried desperately to look at both equally after smiling at them in the order they were introduced. Everyone laughed when Andrew asked how many people were coming to eat all the food.

"No, it will be just us. I told my wives our new volunteer is coming and he does not know authentic Gambian food yet. They have both been working all day to make sure you can try everything, and at least two kinds. There are dishes from all of West Africa that we have prepared for you. We have beef domoda and chicken domoda. There is fish yassa and chicken yassa. The benachin is also chicken and fish. And we have made pepeh for you."

Andrew was becoming more familiar with various Gambian dishes. Peanut-based domoda and tomato-based yassa were his favorites. But pepeh was one he never tried. Even Alex wasn't sure what was in it. It was some type of stew with cow feet and pepper. It wasn't one of the dishes he rushed to try.

Much to Andrew's pleasant surprise, his polygamous dinner company turned out to be less intimidating than he thought, and certainly less intimidating than the stew, which he dutifully tasted and did his best to finish. It was strange how normal Andrew found a polygamous arrangement to be. Maybe it was because Mr. Jalloh and his wives treated it as normal, which disarmed him. He still felt it wrong and probably exploitative, but... everyone had been so nice and welcoming.

That night Andrew saw a different side of Mr. Jalloh. Gone was the worry of the workday and the school that would never run properly. Instead, Mr. Jalloh – determined to provide Andrew with a proper and authentic introduction to a Gambian home – projected a sense of pride. He eagerly showed Andrew his home, however modest it may have been. Each dish had to be prepared just right. No ingredient or expense was spared. The generosity of the evening was not lost on Andrew.

"You must tell your parents that you are well looked after here. That in The Gambia they feed you well," Mr. Jalloh said as his wives cleared the food.

"They would be very appreciative of that. And relieved to hear it."

As he left the house, carrying several bags of food to take home, Mr. Jalloh stood in the doorway and asked Andrew if he was enjoying himself.

"It must be a big change for you, from America to here for the first time."

"Yeah, it's certainly been a big change. But a good one. I like it a lot so far."

Mr. Jalloh's smile widened to a size Andrew hadn't seen before. "That makes me very happy. You see, there are so many misunderstandings about life here. It is not some scary place. You see how beautiful it is, and how it is a friendly welcoming place. We are happy to welcome everyone!"

"I know. It's been great."

II

ALEX AND LIV were heading off to dinner. As usual, they invited Andrew to join. He told them he felt like staying home. He was tired, which was true. The real reason, though, was that he needed to figure out what, if anything, he was going to tell Lindsay. She understood Andrew's need for reassurance. But he wasn't sure she'd get Thomas. He wasn't sure she'd even want to if she could.

His relationship with his sister had grown more solid over the past months. As Andrew opened up to her, she also opened up to him. They spoke about her relationship challenges, frustration with family and friends, and a growing jealousy of Andrew's adventurous escape.

"Maybe I should've done something like that."

Lindsay should've been excited to hear her brother was falling for Thomas. She'd heard so much about his loneliness, about years of school where so many people around him were either coupled or hooking up, and how he had none of that. She knew the one thing crucial to giving him confidence and assurance was to find someone, so he could experience all that brought. And more fundamentally, to believe that those experiences were possible for him.

He was sitting on his bed under the mosquito net with the fan blowing on him, its white noise disturbing an otherwise tranquil night. He'd been sitting motionless, staring into space for nearly half an hour before he opened his computer and logged into Skype, resolved to tell his sister. She was online.

After exchanging greetings, he asked if their parents were home.

"No, they're out for dinner. What's up?"

"I've got a little crush here," he started, not wanting to throw it all out at once.

Lindsay's face became excited. "Who!"

"His name's Thomas."

"How did you meet him?"

"At the hotel we hang at on weekends." Her excited expression began to fade in the short while it took him to answer as she remembered where exactly her brother was.

"And what's he doing in the country?"

"He lives here."

She looked puzzled. "He moved there?"

"No, he was born here."

She didn't understand. "What do you mean?"

"He's Gambian."

Andrew saw his sister's face. Either she was trying desperately to keep her facial expressions neutral or the screen froze.

"Linds?"

"Yeah."

"You there?"

"Yeah. I just wasn't expecting that."

"I know. Neither was I, actually."

"Andrew, are you sure this is smart?" She expressed herself in the form of a question, but her opinion was clear.

"What do you mean?" he asked, attempting to feign innocence.

"How safe can this be? I've been reading more about where you are since you came out. You're not at home, where even if some people might not like it, they'll ignore it, or you can stay out of their way. Some pretty disturbing things have been said by the government, by the president even!"

She was angry, in a protective kind of way. "You're not asking for trouble? And how do you know he can be trusted, that he's not off telling someone who's going to tell someone who's going to tell someone?"

"*Because*, Linds, he has the same interest as I do in making sure this stays a secret."

"What's his name, again?" she asked dismissively.

"Thomas," Andrew answered, angry he had to remind her.

"What's his past like? How much do you know about him? I mean, how do you know he doesn't have..." she stopped herself.

"How do you know he doesn't have what?" Andrew asked. His tone was calm but firm. He knew what she meant to ask, but wanted to hear her actually ask it.

"Andrew. You know I didn't mean that."

"Mean what?" he questioned her. "AIDS? Is that what you meant to ask?"

"Andrew, I didn't mean it that way. You know I'm not that person."

"Then why'd you ask the question?"

Lindsay paused before she answered, her accusatory expression faded as Andrew continued staring straight at her. He hoped his disappointment and anger pierced through the screen. "Because I'm scared something might happen to you. Because you're my only brother and you're somewhere I don't understand, somewhere where I can't help you if you get into trouble, and somewhere where a lot of fucked up shit happens. And whether that gets exaggerated here or not, or I'm reading the wrong stuff, fucked up shit happens in Africa, and it seems to happen a lot."

Fucked up shit happens in Africa. He was unimpressed with her profundity. But there was something to her candor. He thought how a year earlier he probably would've said the same thing.

"What if something happens?" she said, throwing up her arms. "It's not like you can just call me and I'll come bail you out."

He wanted to still be angry at her. But she was being honest with him and reacted the way she did because he sprung something on her so unexpected. He hated making trouble.

"I know. We're being really cautious. So far I only really see him on Friday nights. I'm either sitting at a bar while he's working or we walk up an empty beach to a place where no one hangs out."

"That doesn't sound like much of a relationship."

"It's what we can do, I guess. And that should reassure you that we're being safe."

Neither spoke. Their silence was awkward but neither could think of what to say.

"Does anyone there know about this?"

"Alex, and his girlfriend, Liv."

"And you trust them?"

"I do," he answered in a deliberately calm manner. He was exasperated, subtly hinting his disappointment towards her suspicion and second-guessing.

"He's nice to you?" she asked, trying to shift the tone.

"Yes," Andrew blushed. "He's very nice to me."

"Okay," she said, exhaling. He knew it was her way of calling a truce, of ending a disagreement with no foreseeable resolution. "That's good. We'll talk about this more later. I have to go and get ready. I'm meeting friends soon."

"Okay," he said, not knowing how else to respond to her abrupt end to their conversation, uncomfortable with how things were being left between them.

"I'm sorry if I overreacted, but Andrew, please be careful."

"I will."

"Okay. Bye."

"Bye."

The call ended and he was left sitting on his bed, holding his knees to his chest. His sister's contact went offline.

Andrew left his computer on his bed and walked towards the kitchen when he noticed his cellphone, which he'd left in the living room, was blinking. He unlocked it and saw he had a text message.

hi. how r u? its thomas

He sat down on the couch and wrote back. *im good thx, deliberately leaving out the conversation with Lindsay. how are you?*

Andrew was waiting for a reply when Alex walked in alone after dinner.

"I was thinking, does Thomas play soccer?"

The question, out of nowhere, puzzled Andrew. "Umm, I don't know. Maybe?"

"We should bring him out one Sunday, to play with everyone. There are enough locals that come, so it wouldn't be awkward or random. It could bring you together somewhere besides the hotel."

"Do you really think it would be safe?"

"I don't see why not."

"What does Liv think?" Andrew asked, making clear he knew she was the more cautious one.

Alex smiled. "By the end of dinner she also thought it would be a good idea."

"Hmm. Okay."

Thomas responded right away to Andrew's invitation.

I'm supposed to go and visit my family in Banjul. But it's okay. I will see them another time. Thx for inviting me.

12

THE GROUP OCCUPIED a stretch of sand near a nondescript beach hut restaurant. Bicycles rested on top of each other at the bases of palm trees. People gathered around the restaurant's lounge chairs set up on the sand. Julbrew beers and soda bottles crowded the tables. Music blasted from speakers. Children ran up and down the beach kicking the soccer ball before the adults stepped in to take over. The atmosphere was lively and happy. A few people waded into the warm, gentle water, talking about local politics or foreign sports. Everyone knew pretty much everyone.

Andrew arrived with Alex and Liv around midday, before Thomas. Alex mentioned to some people that he'd invited Thomas to the game. Most people were a little surprised, but no one thought anything of it. The game had evolved over the years and people were always free to invite friends and colleagues, and local newcomers were especially encouraged. Alex figured since everyone saw him so often on Saturdays, it would be nice to include him in something social. *Nice idea*, said most.

Thomas arrived just before the game started. He wore white shorts and a red Manchester United jersey that he was proud to own. Andrew was happy for him when he saw it. It took Thomas a long time to save up for it. Thomas told him stories of how popular Premier League games were when he was growing up. In his final years in the village, Manchester United had gone on a roll, winning three championships in a row.

"Some of my happiest moments at home," he once told Andrew, "were when many of us in the village would gather in front of a television to watch a game. They were the best and most natural distractions."

Thomas's knowledge of soccer made Andrew slightly self-conscious. Earlier in the day he jokingly warned him in a text, *don't judge me, I'm not very good :-)*. Thomas promised not to and claimed he wasn't good either – a claim Andrew found hard to believe purely on account of Thomas's physique. His suspicion proved correct. Thomas was very good, at least by Andrew's standards, meaning he could run without overstepping the ball or kick and pass it on target. He even almost scored. Both of them spent the game checking each other out. Andrew regularly appeared in a bathing suit at the hotel pool, but Thomas was always in his uniform – the same white t-shirt and black pants. By mid-game, Thomas, like many of the other players, was shirtless and Andrew saw what he'd only been able to try and picture in his mind. He was impressed by Thomas's defined abs.

They didn't say much to each other besides *hey*. It was their first public outing and neither wanted to attract any untoward attention. So, in addition to playing, they each spent the game suppressing the urge to smile, or to walk up to one another and have a conversation. After Thomas almost scored a goal, Andrew took one step towards him, excited to tease him about his claim of not being very good before he remembered he probably shouldn't. After the play, Thomas scanned the group to see if Andrew noticed, but Andrew had already turned away.

One of the attractions to Sunday football was how everyone mixed so seamlessly. Andrew himself was welcomed despite his lack of skill. He wanted him and Thomas to be able to be like everyone else there — friends. But as soon as he saw him he tensed up. There was an uneasy dynamic between them.

Only as the game ended did they manage to sneak up to one another.

"When you leave, walk slowly up the beach to Bakau," Thomas whispered. "I'll come after you."

"Okay," said Andrew.

"Do people stay around for long now?"

"Some, but I'll walk up soon."

"Okay."

Andrew was uneasy with this short back and forth. They were sneaking around in public for the first time, planning a clandestine rendezvous. The idea compounded his unease.

Five minutes after Andrew began his slow, solitary walk up the beach he sensed someone behind him. Turning around, he saw Thomas jogging, still shirtless, holding his shoes and shirt in one hand and phone in another. Andrew's immediate reaction wasn't to smile but instead to quickly look around. They were alone. The path from Fajara to Bakau wasn't a popular stretch of beach. Devoid of hotels and restaurants, it was mostly empty, especially as evening set in.

"Hey!" Andrew said, smiling as Thomas sidled up next to him.

"Hi," he said, catching his breath. "That was fun. Thanks for telling me to come."

"Yeah, no problem." Andrew felt like there was still something artificial, or uncomfortable about how they were talking with one another. Removed from their usual cocoon, they were less sure of themselves, at least he was.

"Have you spoken to Alex?" Thomas inquired.

"Yeah, I did. And to Liv. They were both good about it, like I expected. And they can be trusted."

Thomas didn't doubt that. There was never a discussion about when Andrew was going to confide in them, but it was clear from their conversations that both knew it was coming. "I also told someone."

What? Andrew didn't quite believe him.

"Don't worry. It's okay."

But Andrew was worried. Based on their conversations it didn't appear as if Thomas had many people to confide in. He'd mentioned Suleiman, but not by name, when he told Andrew about how he spent his early days in the city. *We keep in touch from time to time,* Thomas had said.

"His name is Suleiman, he's the person who took me in when I moved here." Thomas tried to be uplifting with his tone, but Andrew felt exposed and a little betrayed.

"I should have asked you first."

They had both stopped walking by this point. Andrew knew he shouldn't be upset, or feel betrayed. It was unfair to ask Thomas to keep this a secret when he shared it with others. But a part of him, which he tried to suppress, trusted Alex and Liv more than whoever Thomas told. He knew he was being illogical, or worse, but he couldn't help it, so he tried to hide it.

"It's okay, really."

"I'll introduce you two."

They stood on the sand looking at one another, and the silence between them heightened the awkwardness. For the first time, Andrew struggled with what to say next. Normally their conversation came so easily. It was even less natural than their first meeting. The afternoon threw them off their equilibrium. They felt encumbered to be out in the open, despite the unsuspecting and friendly crowd.

Standing alone and silently on the beach, they stood face to face, confronting a realization that shouldn't have come as a surprise: it wasn't going to be easy. Thomas was desperately afraid that Andrew might get scared off by the challenges ahead and wanted to reassure him. He reached out and put his hand on Andrew's arms, which were folded across his chest.

"How's this going to work?" Andrew asked.

"I don't know," Thomas answered truthfully. "Maybe it is better to try in private at first. To avoid situations that would make us uncomfortable."

Andrew, mistaking the sounds of the tide for something else, quickly turned his head from side to side, seeing they were still alone. "Yeah," he said.

"It's not fair, but it's what we can do."

"Yeah."

Thomas took Andrew's hand and they kept walking up the darkening and empty beach. He told Andrew they weren't unlike young couples back in his village, who were forced to sneak around so parents and older relatives wouldn't catch them. It was their induction into coupledom.

"And it's better than nothing," added Thomas while squeezing Andrew's hand and swinging their arms, lightening the mood.

Andrew agreed. He squeezed back, but after a minute he let go. It wasn't completely dark yet.

That night Andrew wanted to try and fix things with his sister. He and Lindsay had never been in a real fight before. He didn't think they were in one now, but she certainly wasn't happy with him, and perhaps was even angry. He thought she was being unfair and closed-minded when all he wanted was for her to be happy for him. The thought didn't sit well, especially after how his afternoon and evening turned out with everything seeming more complicated. He wanted her to help him sort through things, but when he opened his Skype account Lindsay was offline. After sitting on his bed for a while thinking about what he should do, he reached over to his journal on the bedside table, opened to the next blank page, and started to write.

Andrew and Thomas didn't speak for a few days following the weekend. Andrew worried that Thomas was worried that Andrew might be upset for his confiding in Suleiman. Andrew didn't know what to do, which befuddled Alex.

"Just invite him over!" It was almost an instruction.

"Okay, I guess." Andrew seemed surprised it could be so easy.

"One night when he's done work. That way no one will see him."

He sent Thomas a text, who wrote back right away, accepting the invitation.

how about Thursday
k. can i bring suleiman? then u can meet him
sure

Before they both left for work on Thursday, Alex suggested Isatou could make a big portion of chicken yassa for everyone.

"Don't you think she'd ask who's coming over?"

It was a valid question. Alex hadn't thought of it. "Umm, yeah. We could say I'm having people from work over. But better not. At least this time."

So instead of yassa, Andrew got crisps, as potato chips were known in Gambia, another holdover from the days of empire. Not surprisingly, he'd spent most of the day worried that the evening would, like Sunday, end up awkward. He was wrong.

Suleiman proved tremendously reassuring. He was soft spoken and genuine and walked into the house with a warm smile. *It's so nice to meet you, Andrew*, he said as Andrew extended his hand, only for Suleiman to walk past it and hug him. It instantly allayed any of Andrew's remaining apprehension over the secret being shared.

They sat in the living room and Andrew caught Thomas surveying the home.

"Is it what you expected?" he asked.

"Actually, I thought it would be bigger. It is nice still, simple."

"We're not the kind of people who stay at your hotel," Andrew teased. He could see Thomas was pleased by this, so teased again, "not all of us are so fancy, you know."

When Thomas sat next to Andrew on the couch he nestled up to him, leaning into his shoulder. At first, Andrew recoiled discreetly. But after he looked around the room, he saw that no one seemed to flinch and that he was with friends. He then wedged himself slightly behind Thomas, bringing them even closer.

It was like many of the conversations Andrew had with people he met for the first time. Suleiman displayed his journalistic inquisitiveness, grilling Andrew and Alex about their experiences in the country, if for anything, to confirm they were positive.

"If you need something you can always call me."

The questions Alex and Suleiman asked of each other provided an opportunity to deflect the conversation away from Andrew and Thomas's burgeoning romance. It was a relief for Andrew, who worried the evening would turn to a serious discussion about a gay relationship in Gambia. Instead, Alex and Suleiman were both happy to relive some of their South African memories. Even though Suleiman had been in Johannesburg and Alex far away in the Western Cape, it turns out both had been hiking in the east of the country, in the Drakensberg mountains.

"It's beautiful, no?" Suleiman said. "I'd never seen such big mountains. Here is only flat. It was amazing to get to travel there." He turned to Thomas and quickly said some sentences in Wolof. From his gesticulating, using his arms to illustrate tall mountains, it was clear he was trying to impress upon Thomas the height of the mountains.

"Did you visit Lesotho?" Alex asked.

"No, did you?"

"Just crossed in to get a stamp and say I've been to a country entirely landlocked by another one," Alex boasted.

Suleiman chuckled. "The white man's passport."

"Were you able to see other parts of the country?" Alex asked.

"No, I only managed one trip. During their holiday periods I had an internship with *The Sowetan*, it kept me very busy. I loved working there."

"And you didn't want to stay on?"

"I would have loved to. It is a very exciting newspaper to work at." He turned from Alex to face the rest of the room and began to explain. "The paper started under Apartheid in Soweto, the township, and today has grown into a large national paper. It's much bigger than anything we have here. In fact, it's probably read daily by more people than in the whole of Gambia!"

"Why did you leave South Africa?" Andrew asked.

"This is home. I wanted to come back." It was a candid answer, as if staying in a more free and open society was never an option. "I wanted a great career, of course. But I also hope it can be meaningful." He seemed unconvinced by his own explanations. "It will take time, and in the end might prove futile, but I hope somehow my reporting has people questioning how things are run in this country. It can help lay a foundation for change."

"Do you see that happening?" Alex inquired.

"Not yet. Not soon."

"How did you two meet?" Alex asked. As Suleiman spoke about meeting Thomas in the restaurant, Andrew was struck by the difference between the two of them and wondered how two people that seemed so unlike might be friends. At home, so much of his life had been defined by socioeconomic status. He lived in a world where a waiter was a waiter.

"He helped me when I first arrived in Banjul," answered Thomas. "I had nowhere to stay and he took me in."

Alex appeared surprised by Thomas's answer. He knew little about Thomas's past. Andrew had told him almost nothing except that he came from a village upriver.

"What, you thought I was born a prosperous bartender?" he joked.

Without getting into too much detail, Thomas caught Alex up on his past. How he had an upbringing that was at once idyllic but also terribly cruel. That he lived surrounded by a large family he barely felt a part of. And that if he remained in his village forever, *I wasn't sure I could stay alive.* He told him about the morning he packed his possessions into a knapsack, hopped on the back of a motorbike and rode off without looking back. How he arrived in a city knowing not a soul. "And then I met him," he said, smiling at Suleiman.

"But it still took some time before I realized how desperate his situation was. I was just a restaurant patron. I didn't know he was sleeping in the back."

Thomas hunched his shoulders and lowered his head upon hearing Suleiman's word choice. Desperate sounded so severe.

"You were?"

Andrew sat quietly as the conversation unfolded. Seeing Thomas and Suleiman together, and how Thomas looked up to him – there was a deference Thomas showed when he spoke – made Andrew feel stupid for questioning Thomas's decision to confide in him.

"It was selfish of me," he quietly told Thomas as they walked in the darkness to the compound gate at the end of the night. Suleiman and Alex trailed behind, engrossed in a political conversation.

"Don't worry, it's okay. I get it," he answered softly. "Sometimes I forget you're not from here, and that it's still a different place for you."

13

Isatou was a regular fixture in Andrew and Alex's life. Arriving early in the morning, she sometimes came in while they were still home, to gather laundry or wash dishes, the latter of which they unsuccessfully tried to impress upon her was unnecessary. When she came by later in the day, mostly to drop something off, she'd have changed from her loose clothing and be done up in colorful, traditional dress. No matter what she wore, her hair was always wrapped up.

"I've never seen what her hair looks like," Alex said one day when they were speaking about her.

They didn't speak about her much, but when they did, it often revolved around what they thought she thought of them.

"I mean it must be weird," Andrew said. "To have these strangers show up with so much stuff, and a house to themselves, while she lives next door with her extended family in those cramped conditions. And she's not the least bit resentful about it."

She wasn't. In all the months Andrew had come to know her, Isatou had been nothing but warm and friendly towards him. Contrary to his initial suspicions, she didn't seem to judge or think much about him having a laptop, cellphone, and iPod all out on a table, with two pairs of shoes and a fancy backpack on the floor. In fact, his original view of Africa as a continent deprived of material goods quickly vanished when he saw many people had two cellphones, or at least two SIM cards, and dressed far more dapper than he ever did.

"Just don't be an asshole," offered up Alex, trying to assuage any lingering concerns Andrew might've still had. "You seem to be doing okay at that."

Conversations with Isatou were often limited by language barriers, but they were able to exchange pleasantries nonetheless. *How's your family? How is your day so far?* Isatou answered mostly the same, *they are fine* or *very good.* But on some days she followed with more details.

"Awa is at home now."

Andrew was never entirely sure how to respond when Awa came up. As Alex forewarned, Isatou had once suggested how Andrew might take Awa back to America with him. *So she can have good life.*

"But she has a good life here with you," Andrew responded awkwardly.

On the days Isatou brought Awa with her to help clean, she mostly kept quiet and close to her mother. Both Alex and Andrew tried to engage her in conversation but she proved supremely shy, perhaps embarrassed knowing her mother had offered her, however jokingly, to both of them at various points.

Isatou's comings and goings were one of the reasons Thomas was at first reluctant to spend much time at Andrew's.

"We Gambians do not understand much about privacy. It's in our nature to help ourselves in."

He was right.

It was a Sunday morning a couple of weeks after he and Thomas first kissed. Andrew had gone to bed late on Saturday, drunk after a night of charades at a friend's house. He somehow managed to get himself undressed and his mosquito net untied. It was hot when he went to bed and the power was off, so he fell asleep on top of his sheets, naked.

Normally this wouldn't have been a problem, but he forgot to close his bedroom door.

The compound's iron gate squeaked open but he was still dozing in and out and the noise didn't register with him.

"Not the kind of noise to jolt you out of bed, or at least I wasn't in the state where I was going to be jolted out of bed," he explained to Thomas.

Isatou let herself in, assuming he and Alex were either up or gone at such a late hour. She soon realized she was mistaken. Between the distance to his bed and the mosquito net veiling him there wasn't much to see, but it was still enough to send her into a quick freeze before she quickly and quietly fled off. Fortunately, he was lying on his stomach. The front door closed, followed by the squeak of the gate closing shortly after.

"I realized it was her just as she approached the entrance to my room," he told a giggling Thomas. "But I decided not to move. I thought if I was pretending to still be asleep we could avoid an awkward situation where we both knew she walked in on me like that."

"You see," exclaimed Thomas, "this is why I can never sleep over."

"No, things are fine now. She hasn't come back on a weekend, even to get mangoes. I guess I scared her," he said amusedly, wanting to appease his apprehension.

Despite Isatou's near-guaranteed absence on weekends, Thomas and Andrew still spent most of their time away from his house. Thomas's home was out of the question. First, even though he had a private entrance, he only had one room in a house of four. It was also in a dense residential neighborhood where there was no chance Andrew's coming and going could stay secret. So they were left to find their own seclusion. More often than not, they went to that spot on the beach between the Fajara cut off and the Bakau fish market. Away from any road, dotted by large rocks jutting out into the sea, the ground ascended high up behind them, forming a wall from where the land on top came to its end. It was the perfect location and was almost always deserted.

They tried to meet there at least one other night a week in addition to Fridays and Sundays, but sometimes life would get in the way. That, and they didn't want to press their luck. But each made a concerted effort never to miss a Friday. Andrew would show up at the bar after work and buy a drink. None of the hotel staff ever thought anything of it. He was just another expat coming to spend money on alcohol and they were happy to have his patronage. Shortly before Thomas closed up for the night, usually around nine or ten depending on how busy it was, Andrew would walk down to the beach and walk north, past two adjacent hotels to a small path leading up to the main road. After about fifteen or twenty minutes,

Thomas would appear. Covered by the night they would make their way up the beach, brushing against each other, and holding hands if there were no hotels or restaurants in sight. If anyone would pass them, it would only be the odd tourist, already a few drinks in.

These walks sometimes became a bit surreal to Andrew, serving as effective antidotes to the doubts regularly creeping into his mind about what he was embarking on. *It's worth it.*

One week after they arrived at their spot, Thomas started opening a backpack he was carrying, pulling out a plastic bag.

"What's that?" Andrew asked.

"Fish. For dinner."

"You've been carrying fish in your backpack?"

"I got them this morning, before work," he answered, smiling and holding up the bag, displaying it proudly as if he caught the fish himself. "We never eat together. Isn't that what normal couples do? You know, have food. Even though it is late."

It was sweet, Andrew thought. Certainly sweeter and more creative than anything he'd thought of or proposed.

"Come, we must find some small sticks for the fire."

They set off a bit further north, where the cliffs receded and the shrubs and trees returned to the beach. Thomas gathered small sticks and dead palm leaves and Andrew followed, doing the same. When they got back, Thomas set out the leaves and sticks in a small circle on the sand. They were as far back from the sea as one could be, with the rocks curving out and sheltering them on either side. He took out a lighter from his backpack and put it towards the kindling, lighting a small fire. Dispersed and faint sounds of the crackling wood interrupted the night's silence.

Thomas, sitting next to the fire, opened up the bag and removed two fish. He sprinkled some seasoning over them, put a stick through each of their mouths, and rested them on leaves at the base of the fire. Andrew stood curiously watching his every move.

"My father," Thomas said, in response to Andrew's gaze. "When I was a boy he taught me how to do this. He said I needed to know how just in case I was ever out on the river alone one night and couldn't make my way back. It was something most fathers taught their sons as they started getting older. Maybe he thought I would always be in the village.

"It's funny," he paused. "I only now realized how it's the first time I'm doing it without him. And I'm by the sea, not the river. And I'm not stranded and alone either," he said, turning his mouth into a big knowing smile.

"It's good you remember," Andrew said as he sat down next to him.

"What skills did your father teach you?" Thomas asked.

It was an interesting question, and not one he'd have thought to ask. Andrew had to think about how he would answer it.

"He taught me how to drive, and how to change a flat tire." He paused before grinning. "He used to get so mad at me. I would always hit the brakes too hard at first. He said I was giving him whiplash."

"And now?"

"I'm much better," he said, his grin still there.

Thomas looked down. Light hissing sounds emanated from the fish as smoke began rising off their skins. Small embers jumped out from the fire into the night. He picked up the sticks and turned the fish onto their other sides. Still looking into the fire, he asked Andrew if his father would be proud of him now. He knew Andrew hadn't yet come out to his parents, and was concerned about their reaction.

"But if he saw how you were happy. Would this be enough to make him proud of you?"

Andrew thought to himself for a moment. "I don't know.

"I want to think so. But, I don't know. Even though I have my doubts, deep down I always hope that between my sister's influence and him realizing that it's his son we're talking about, that eventually he'd come around." He stopped to think if there was more to say but there wasn't. "Would yours?" he asked softly. "And what's his name, I don't even know it."

"John," he said, looking up. "In our family many men are named after apostles."

For Thomas, it wasn't an answer he had to think about. He'd thought about it already for many years.

"No," he said shaking his head. "He would not be proud of me. He would say I am not his son. That this was not how he raised me. That I was not a good African, that I was not a good Christian." Looking up at Andrew with abandoned eyes he continued, "he would walk away from me, send me out, and turn away.

"I think he's brainwashed about this. Our president and the church. They make everyone so crazy. It's like they forget how we are humans too. Over the years, as they made more and more hysterical statements, and created this hatred, it's gotten into people's minds that it's okay to abandon us, to want to cast us away. It wasn't perfect before either, but at least you never had a president using homophobia to bring everyone else together."

"Have you ever heard him give a speech about it?"

"No. But even before he speaks I can tell you what he will say. He repeats himself. It's nothing new. It's not news anymore. People are so used to thinking about homosexuality as this terrible disease that they don't think twice when the president speaks that way. They've all been to church or their mosque. If their preacher says this comes from the Bible, that homosexuality is a sin that must be wiped away, how can it not be true? The president is only putting into action what the Bible commands us, or the Koran. So it makes it easier for people to cheer when they hear their president going after gays and lesbians.'

"When was the last time you went to church?" Andrew asked.

"Me, I haven't been to church since I left my village. I would need to be forced hard to go back into one. For me, they are torture. Even now, with my parents in Banjul, I don't go with them. They are very upset about it. I tell them that sometimes I go here, to a church in Serrekunda, or that I have to work. I don't know if they believe me, probably not, especially since I don't visit them as much on Sundays. At some point I know I will be forced to go. Thankfully they are still new to the church my brother takes them to, so they don't feel embarrassed I am not with them. But I don't like that I have to lie about it."

"What's so bad about them?" Andrew asked innocently. He had a sense they weren't welcoming to the idea of being gay, but his naïveté shielded him.

"I mean, I want to believe in this goodness they say they stand for. That there is this all mighty and powerful, loving God who watches over us. And then you sit there as a young boy in this holy place listening to the preacher, a man you are taught to respect and admire, a man you see your parents looking up to, and following his every word, who comes over to you after church and puts his hand on your head and calls you a good boy. But just before that you sat in his pew and listened to that man call you a disease. A maggot that has infected a healthy body. And all you can do is sit. You can't stand up and leave because everyone will see you, and then they will know, and where will you go? Nobody will help you. They all agree with the preacher. You are the disease. I tried not to listen, but even sometimes I could still hear."

He kept speaking as he prodded the fish to check if they were done. "And you can't change. You try, for many years once you realize you are this maggot he speaks of, you try so desperately not to be, but you can't change it. So you sit there, trapped in the church, in between your family and your community as your insides shake, crying out for God – not the preacher's god, not his god of vengeance, but the real God, the God of mercy, the God who created all of us – that's who you cry out for, that He may take you away to some place safe. But that God doesn't come. At least not here.

"No," he continued, "I will not go back to church. I don't think I ever could."

Andrew reached out and took Thomas's hand. So many of their previous conversations had only scratched the surface of what his life had been like in the village.

"When did you know you wanted to leave?"

"Maybe when I was around thirteen," Thomas answered, looking like he was thinking. "Maybe it slowly started when I knew I could not change that I started wanting to leave, to find someplace else. It was when I understood how for me being gay was not optional. But I was only a boy, and a boy doesn't want to easily accept that he doesn't have a future with his family in his home."

"I know," Andrew said, thinking about his own situation. Though saying it made him feel guilty, as if bringing his situation into the conversation trivialized Thomas's.

"And even you yourself had to leave too," Thomas offered up enthusiastically. "You also said you needed to find some place else to go. Even though America is filled with places to go," he teased.

"I wanted to combine mine with a little adventure. Make it less bleak."

"I'm happy you found your way to our difficult country."

"Me too."

When the fish was ready and cool enough to touch, Thomas showed Andrew how he could eat it with his hands. His fingers weren't as nimble as Thomas's in working around the bones, so he made a bigger mess. They laughed at his efforts, lightening the mood a bit. The fish itself was moist. Whatever the seasoning Thomas used was tasty, and not too spicy. The fire was all but gone, only a glow and simmering smoke, leaving just enough light as they sat there, backs pressed up against the earth wall, each resting their fish on a palm leaf, eating mostly in silence.

"It's really good," Andrew said as he licked his fingers.

"I'm glad you like it," Thomas said. He laughed to himself and thought for a minute before resting his head on Andrew's shoulder and looking out. "Maybe one day I will take you to meet my father and you can tell him that I did a good job."

Thomas was becoming a semi-regular fixture at Sunday football matches. As weeks wore on he and Andrew became more comfortable in public after growing accustomed to any awkwardness that came with their restrained public outings. They came to appreciate being out amidst others. They modified the expectations that flowed from being a couple and instead settled for friendship, the fun of activity, and for not having to look over one's shoulder. Thomas fit in well with the group. He was enthusiastic and appreciative to be there, and people liked him for that. He was very good at teasing people with the ball, faking them with his head and eyes while sending the ball downfield to other, open players. He was content letting others score and rarely did moves that might give the impression he was showing off.

After the game, he and Andrew both started staying for drinks. Andrew especially came to like when Thomas began telling stories of nightmarish guests at the hotel. He liked watching people smile and laugh as Thomas spoke. It reassured him to see people genuinely enjoy having him around. It meant he was making a smart decision.

They left the games separately. Sometimes Thomas left first, other times it was Andrew. The first to leave walked slowly, waiting for the other person to catch up. Just like on Fridays, they eventually found their way up the beach, pushing their bikes they rode to the games, before settling by the cove. These walks were more guarded – they began in daylight and the beach had yet to fully empty. To avoid garnering suspicion, on occasion one of them would bike up along the road and wait for the other at the spot. Sometimes whoever biked would stop for a bit of food – some fruits, or a bag of crisps. The other times they were empty handed. With work early the next day, school started at eight, they rarely went late into the night.

Walking up one Sunday evening, Thomas asked Andrew if he had spoken to his sister that weekend.

"No," he answered, shaking his head. "I don't remember when we last spoke. A week ago?"

It seemed to Andrew that for each step forward he and Thomas took together, he took one step back in his relationship with his sister.

"I thought she would come around. But she hasn't."

For Andrew, it became the biggest disappointment stemming from his relationship with Thomas. The person he'd been closest to in the years where her support mattered most was growing more and more distant.

"I tried explaining it to her – explaining us to her. She thinks I'm being reckless."

"Do you think she might feel you're drifting from her?"

Such introspective conversations made Andrew appreciate Thomas's insightfulness. The ease with which Thomas dissected emotions stood in stark contrast to how he generally avoided confronting them.

"Maybe. But that would make her a bit selfish, wouldn't it? She knew almost as much as I did how much I wanted to get away and have a completely different type of experience. And she supported me, and defended me to my parents. I mean, if this is how my experience is unfolding." He shrugged.

Thomas was silent as Andrew kept processing thoughts in his head.

"If I had a sibling who cared about me as much as you say Lindsay cares about you, I would try hard to work out our differences. I would want to."

"Of course. That's what I hope. But if she's not going to come around, if she can't be reasonable, it's not going to be so easy."

"I don't like how I'm making problems between you and her. It's not right."

Andrew saw an earnestness in Thomas's expression. It bordered on guilt.

"You haven't made any problems," he tried to reassure him. "I think this difference between us was always there. Now it's revealing itself." Andrew could see Thomas wasn't entirely convinced. "Don't worry. Her arguments aren't winning me over. *This* isn't changing," he proclaimed, playfully pushing at Thomas's shoulder.

"Good," Thomas said, smiling.

"Part of it is her lack of understanding from not being here. When you're back home you can't appreciate the context. Our images of Africa are so fucked up. But through my pictures and stories, she, and actually my parents, are starting to see past that. I'm still healthy, out of trouble, and there aren't any scars on my face from tripping in the jungle as I run away from animals or wild tribes."

They took a few steps in silence. Andrew started to say something but stopped himself. He wanted to be careful about what he was about to say. Thomas didn't know, but the last time Andrew and Lindsay spoke she asked him why he was setting himself up to be hurt. Between the country's laws and the fact that there was a finite timeline to whatever relationship was taking place, how did Andrew think it would end? *You're not bringing him home with you,* his sister said, *and you're not staying there forever.*

"Why can't it just be about now. And about me being happy?" he asked her.

"Because you're not thinking clearly, Andrew."

"I just wish she could be happy for me," he said taking Thomas's hand as they kept walking. "I mean, she might have a point, but who cares, right?"

"What do you mean she might have a point?" Thomas asked.

"That our situation isn't ideal. That this doesn't end with us together. That sooner or later, I have to go home."

It was nothing Thomas hadn't thought about himself on several occasions. Even still, he felt compelled to respond. "You could stay longer."

"Yeah," Andrew puffed dismissively.

They both retreated into their thoughts as they continued walking into the dimming light. Andrew watched Thomas struggle to contain his expression. The truth stung him, leaving Andrew regretful for having said anything.

"I'm sorry..."

"No," Thomas cut him off. "There's nothing to be sorry about. You are right," he spoke softly but resolutely. "It is still some months away, but you do have to leave."

As they kept walking, Thomas's comment was making Andrew think the opposite. No, he couldn't move to Gambia. Even he knew that much. But if he was finally happy in life and with himself, maybe he could stay a little longer to enjoy it. Why rush back and lose it all?

When they reached the cove, Andrew stayed standing as Thomas sat down.

"Why don't you come over now for a bit?"

"Where?"

"To my place."

"Really?"

"Yeah," he answered confidently, slowly nodding his head. "Only Alex and Liv will be there. It's dark. No one will see. I can go up ahead and text you to make sure things are clear. I'll leave the gate open for you."

"Okay."

"Great. We can go up from Bakau."

They pushed their bikes up towards the Bakau market, which was empty by then – just a smattering of cracked and worn wooden tables laid out on a concrete slab, lingering smells from the day's catch stuck in the cracks. A weak, buzzing streetlight hung overhead. Andrew said it would take him about ten minutes to bike home, and then he'd text Thomas to confirm everything was fine and that he should come. He pushed his bike forward and hopped on, only to stop, put his left foot back down on the pavement, and turn to face Thomas.

"It's not the worst idea, you know."

"What idea?"

"Staying."

Thomas smiled. Andrew smiled back for a second and then turned away.

While Thomas stood waiting, he took his phone out from his pocket. There was a text from his brother.

where are you hiding from us

A lump formed instantly in Thomas's throat. The message could've been a joke, or it could've been serious. There was no way for Thomas to know.

I'm sorry. I know I wanted to come c u today. Next Sunday. I promise.

Father wants to know if u will come 2 church

I can't in the morning. I'll come to visit in the afternoon, and stay for dinner.

14

ANDREW TRIED TO do as much research as he could into Gambia before he left the U.S. Information was scant, reflective of the country's minuscule size and economy. Beyond a few pieces about its bizarre president – who had little tolerance for political dissent and claimed he descended from a line of traditional healers that allowed him to cure AIDS – Gambia was almost non-existent. That is, except for *Roots*.

In the course of his research, Andrew sat at his desk one day in his dorm room, and googled "Gambia history slavery". He wondered whether Gambia was associated with the transatlantic slave trade like so many other African countries. It was. A small town in the country, Georgetown, contained a fort used in the slave trade. He made a note to visit it. Digging deeper into Gambia's association with slavery, Andrew also discovered an apparently well-known book written about an American family that traced its lineage to a slave, Kunta Kinte, who was brought over to America from Gambia in the 18th Century. Andrew googled "roots gambia". Several hits came up about a Roots Festival held each spring in Banjul. It was one of the biggest events in the capital, and Andrew wanted to see it.

This year's festival was on a Saturday, and many of Andrew's expat friends were going. Thomas couldn't go because of work. It may have proven too much anyway, as soccer on Sundays was so far the only time they'd been seen together in public. They also thought it might be unusual if Thomas joined in an outing like this and had not gone along with his friends. Maybe they were overthinking it, but better to be safe.

Andrew never saw the streets so busy. It felt like the whole country made its way to the city, packing the grandstands set up along the parade route. Striped red, blue, green, and white Gambian flags hung from every tree and post. Most people were wearing bright, traditional clothing. The men in their dashikis and the women wrapped in elaborate dresses and headdresses made out of bazin, the shiny polished cotton used to make nicer clothing that always appeared too hot for the climate. The sun beat down and produced an energy-sucking heat on the tightly packed crowd lining the streets. It wasn't long before everyone was gleaming, coated in sweat.

As with most large Gambian gatherings he'd been to, this was one of organized chaos. There was an order to the crowd and the layout that most others seemed to understand, he just couldn't decipher it. They kept walking along the side of the streets, swept up by the crowds, figuring they were headed somewhere. Small children snuck around Andrew's legs, parents nowhere he could see. He was glad he left his knapsack at home. He checked his watch; it was almost noon. The parade was scheduled to start at eleven, but they were told they'd be lucky if it started by one.

"Where are we going?" he asked Alex.

"I don't entirely know. Hopefully we get near the arch." The arch Alex referred to was the July 22 Arch, Gambia's Arc de Triomphe commemorating the president's coup over two decades earlier. "That's the central area."

The arch, like almost everything associated with the president, was larger than life. Its sun-washed columns towered over the main thoroughfare, far above anything around it. An unmistakable proclamation of strength whose purpose seemed split between a reminder of the past and a warning for the future. They finally made their way within sight of it just before one o'clock.

"Has the parade started?" Andrew asked a woman as he walked past her.

"Not yet. Maybe it will start soon," she responded, completely unfazed by the tardiness or the oppressive heat. "First the president will speak."

Andrew had never heard the president speak.

"Have you?" he asked Alex.

"Nope," he shrugged. "Have you?" he asked Liv.

"No."

They pushed their way to the front row only to discover they were within sight of the president's podium, a Gambian flag hanging behind it. He could see a white hat on a man diagonally behind the podium and assumed that was the president. Soldiers with automatic rifles stood at its corners. The Gambian national anthem played and suddenly everyone in the crowd stood still, singing loudly. There was something enviable about how Gambians sang their national anthem, Andrew thought. Far less bombastic than the Star Spangled Banner, but with an understated yet palpable sense of pride and commitment to their homeland.

Let justice guide our actions,
towards the common good,
and join our diverse peoples,
to prove man's brotherhood.

Silence followed the anthem. A few more armed soldiers spread out into the street between the podium and the crowd. When all was still, the white hat started to move closer to the podium. The president was tall. The flowing white robes, hat, and black sunglasses he wore made him appear larger and more imposing. In one hand he carried a ceremonial staff he always took with him.

His voice was markedly less accented than Andrew thought it would be. From his imposing appearance, he figured the president's voice would be intense and guttural, emanating from deep within his belly. Andrew was surprised to hear that it was actually a little high.

He began with the customary Gambian greetings Andrew had grown so used to, but moved quickly into his main theme – the Roots Festival was an important step in the reclamation of an African identity and culture that was *uprooted by colonialists, by racists*. It was true, Andrew knew. But it stung to hear it laced with such vitriol. The president was not trying to heal a wound. He was trying to deepen it.

"Africa, and The Gambia," he continued, "must stand tall and must stand proud. We have nothing to be ashamed of. It is the West who must atone for the sins it committed yesterday, and the sins it continues to commit today."

The crowd listened attentively as he continued. The list of transgressions was long, beginning with the slave trade and colonial carve up of the continent. It continued into the post-independence meddling by the West into the new states, *including the imposition of brutal dictators against the will of the African peoples.*

"The Roots Festival, and the celebration of our African and Gambian heritage," he proclaimed, "means we do not need the West to tell us how to grow. We do not need to keep swallowing their poison. Today they pretend we are all equal but do not stop with their lectures, with their arrogance towards those whom they consider inferior."

Andrew and Alex turned to each other and sighed. Andrew had learned a lot over the past three-quarters of a year about the West's involvement in Africa that he didn't know before. There were many valid grievances, for sure. It was just how the president was speaking. He was riling people up, extolling examples of injustice to further entrench the people's faith in him as their protector. And in the process, he seemed to be making them angry.

"And I want to speak directly to those in the West who have criticized The Gambia recently because we are defenders of African values." He paused before beginning again, speaking his next sentence slowly and clearly. "You are not welcome in The Gambia." The crowd burst into applause.

"We do not need your values – your immorality, your promiscuity, and your homosexuality. These are not welcome here. They are not welcome in The Gambia!"

It was like Andrew was kicked in the stomach. He assumed the president might say something along these lines, as he had on similar occasions in the past. But hearing him actually speak was different. It was hearing him while surrounded by thousands of people who agreed. Even though Andrew was with Alex, Liv, and some other friends, his thoughts were back under the tree in the schoolyard months earlier, when he first arrived and when Mr. Jalloh first brought up the question of homosexuality. He looked around at the unfamiliar faces in the crowd and each one projected the same sense of agreement as his fellow teachers did when Mr. Jalloh spoke negatively about gays. No one disapproved.

"Let us be clear. There is no room for these *criminals* in this country. If I find them, they will not be seen again."

Andrew jumped when he felt a hand on his back. It was Liv's. Her face was despondent. He appreciated her gesture, but still thought to himself, *easy for you*, before nudging himself away from her hand, not wanting to appear in need of sympathy at that moment.

"And no white man can save them!"

Andrew didn't actually hear the applause he witnessed taking place all around him. Instead, he raised his gaze up to the bright, blue sky, closed his eyes and let the sun hit his face while he breathed deeply. As the applause continued he thought about opening his eyes but didn't. He didn't want to see it. He didn't want to see men and women, young and old, smiling and clapping. He didn't want to see people who he liked and otherwise had tremendous respect and admiration for, turn away from him so sharply. His heart beating, palms clammy, he wanted to go home. Home home.

The speech continued, turning to a positive note. The president went on to declare Gambia was doing just fine and did not need saving. He went on to celebrate the numerous achievements and advancements his leadership had ushered in. *Leaps in development, greater prosperity, and the respect for the rights of all Gambian citizens by repudiating the intolerance that saw so many Kunta Kintes taken from these shores.*

"I want to thank the organizers of this year's Roots Festival for showing the true Gambian and African spirit. Thank you."

It was over.

In the applause, both Alex and Liv turned to their friend. Enveloped by the cheers of the crowd, he felt smaller.

Seconds later, loud drums drowned out all the noise. Guitars and bass followed. Then singing. The parade was beginning.

They stayed in their places watching the parade for the better part of an hour, facing the street and not speaking to one another. Alex and Liv occasionally turned to some of their other friends, but Andrew was positioned in a way that he didn't have to talk to anyone. He didn't even have to look at them, and he didn't. He simply stood, facing forward as floats streamed past him.

It was an endless celebration of different ethnic and tribal groups, and the full expanse of Gambian civil society. Traditional dancers danced their way through the streets in straw skirts, gyrating their whole bodies in a trance-like state. Men and women walked past in chains, slaves from another time. A women's literacy group marched behind their banner. School children in uniform. Musicians in marching bands blended new and old music and instruments filled the air with upbeat and rhythmic soundtracks that instinctively moved one's body. The lively crowd cheered for each passing group. It was as much a celebration of diversity as Andrew had ever seen in the country. The last banner they saw, carried by a group called the Gambian Historical Association, announced "WE ARE ALL GAMBIAN!"

Liv tapped Andrew on the shoulder. "Let's go," she said. "There's a VIP area up ahead. Some of my colleagues are there and said we can get in." She was smiling and casual.

When Andrew didn't immediately react, Alex gently slapped his back. "Come on," he said as a way to tell Andrew to put the speech behind him. It was an innocuous slap. And for precisely that reason, Andrew couldn't decide if Alex was being sensible or insensitive. Maybe Alex didn't quite get it.

They pushed through the crowds to get closer to the arch. The VIP area was covered and roped off but easily penetrable. All Liv had to do was namedrop her colleague, say they were together, and they were in.

As they entered, Andrew heard his name shouted so gregariously it could have only originated in one man's belly. He turned to his side.

"Mr. Jalloh!" he said as his face widened. They made their way towards one another, hands extended.

Of course Jalloh was there, he thought to himself. He'd never miss an opportunity to rub shoulders with anyone in a VIP section and always managed to get invitations to important events. He remembered that Mr. Jalloh had earlier insisted he attend the festival. It was an impressive and important commemoration of Gambian and African history. Putting the president's speech aside, he was right, and had reason to boast.

Mr. Jalloh was surprisingly well versed in *Roots* and the slave trade in general, and spent some time with his arm around Andrew talking to him about how some of the different groups that participated in the march were involved in educating Gambians about the West African slave trade. He said it was impressive to think a country could have its people plundered and then rebuild itself as The Gambia had.

It was nice for Andrew to see Mr. Jalloh proud about something. Normally he was stressed and overwhelmed, frustrated at teachers, students, parents, and ministry officials, with whom he shared a perennial and mutual dissatisfaction. He was someone Andrew felt sorry for: well intentioned, who for circumstances beyond his control seemed set up for failure. This was the first time he displayed his hopeful and upbeat side since Andrew was over for dinner.

"You must share with your family all that you saw today. How in Gambia we have taken a tragedy and used it to celebrate our diversity, and our commitment to a nation where everyone is free." As he spoke those last words, *where everyone is free*, with one arm still around Andrew, he stuck out his other arm and swept it across the sky, reinforcing that everyone in front of him was entitled to the freedom he spoke about.

"Of course I'll tell them. I'll tell them all about it."

"Good!" Mr. Jalloh proclaimed as he took his arm off Andrew and turned to face him. "And you must tell them how passionately our president spoke. About his commitment to building this free society."

Andrew must have looked startled, or puzzled, and failed to immediately react and assure Mr. Jalloh he would do just that. Mr. Jalloh sensed his apprehension.

"Don't be embarrassed because you are American. He wasn't speaking out against America. We love America here. But sometimes the country goes too far in trying to control everybody, and make everybody copy its customs." There was a pause before he continued. "Like with the gays."

Andrew still didn't react. He was nervous to even open his mouth. Afraid of what might come out.

"I know you don't like to hear it. You are too polite, Andrew. But even you must see how the president is right that they have no place here. This is not part of our culture. And America shouldn't make us try and give respect to such people. It's not in our nature."

It was not anger or fear, but disappointment and an overbearing sense of loneliness that was making it harder and harder for Andrew not to break down. He really liked Mr. Jalloh. In their many months together, Andrew grew to appreciate him. He personified a work ethic and commitment that had the potential to be a tipping point for the country. There was an apathy Andrew sensed among many working Gambians: they knew the lots were stacked against them so they did the bare minimum, took their pay, and went home to live quiet lives. It was easiest that way and he did not judge them for their begrudgingness. Invariably, pushing the envelope would have meant rubbing up against a government that cared more about preserving its own interests and entrenching its own power than advancing the interests and empowerment of others.

But Mr. Jalloh was different. Sure, he spent most of his time frustrated and exasperated, but he didn't give up. He kept pushing – students, teachers, and administrators. He wanted everyone to excel. *Education*, he would say, *is the only path forward*. And because Andrew adopted the same persistence as Mr. Jalloh – coming early and staying late to help his students, going above and beyond the basic lesson plans – he always took his side in disputes with students or other teachers. *Just look at the energy and creativity he has*, Andrew once overheard Mr. Jalloh saying to another teacher in response to that teacher's suggestion that Andrew might follow ministry lesson planning more closely. It was a suggestion Mr. Jalloh dismissed and later confided in Andrew he believed was motivated by resentment.

Besides his work ethic, Mr. Jalloh was kind. Though he never invited him back to his house, he often brought Andrew food prepared by one of his wives. *Especially for you.* He always made him try it in front of him. *Isn't it delicious?! I will tell them to make you more.* Sure enough, the next day, he always brought him more.

Not that he ever needed to, but if Andrew found himself in trouble or a misunderstanding, he knew Mr. Jalloh would be the first person to call.

So there he was. Standing under the canopy in the VIP section of the Roots Festival, celebrating the triumph of freedom, listening to one of the people he admired most in the country say that Andrew was a person unworthy of dignity.

"Andrew!" he exclaimed. He took his right arm and jovially smacked it against Andrew's left shoulder. "Enough of that for now. Today is for celebrating! Who are you here with? Where are your friends?"

Andrew saw Alex up ahead and pointed in that direction. "Over there," he said, his voice getting caught as he spoke, his throat still tight from listening to Mr. Jalloh speak.

"Very nice. I am going to speak to Pastor Gomez over there. Have you met him?"

"No."

"Oh. He is one of the most popular preachers in the country. Do you want to meet him now?"

"It's okay, thanks. I should get back to my friends."

"Of course. So I shall see you tomorrow at school." He said with a big smile, reaching back, this time more gently, towards Andrew's left arm and shoulder. "I'm glad you were here."

"Me too."

And with that Mr. Jalloh took off into the crowd leaving Andrew alone.

Before Andrew could take his first step, someone stepped in front of him with a wide smile.

"Andrew!"

Suleiman walked right up and hugged him, holding him tight and close in a genuine embrace. They had met a few times since he visited Andrew's house. Thomas wanted Suleiman and Andrew to become friends and spend more time together. So he arranged for Suleiman to come by the bar on a number of Friday evenings.

"It is good to see you here," he said. "This is an important event in the Gambian calendar. Did you see the parade?"

"I did."

"Did you find it impressive?"

"I did," he answered, trying to muster enough enthusiasm to sound convinced.

"You heard the president speak, didn't you?"

"Yes."

Suleiman sighed before looking around quickly. "I know it's hard, but try not to pay too much attention to it. It's merely talk; he wants to boost his popularity. Don't take it personally." Suleiman had never shared his concerns about the relationship with Andrew. Transparency was reserved for when he was alone with Thomas. Not knowing him all that well, he didn't think it was his place. Instead, he tried to be reassuring. And there was something reassuringly gentle in how Suleiman spoke. His big eyes heightened whatever emotion or point he was trying to convey. "You will be all right. Both of you."

"Yeah," he muttered, trying to believe it. "I hope."

"Where are your friends? Are you here with Alex?"

Andrew pointed to where they were.

"Great. Let me say hi. Let's go enjoy the rest of the afternoon."

They walked over to where Alex and Liv were talking to Liv's colleagues. Suleiman joined the group, introduced himself to those he didn't know, and fit right into the conversation. Someone was telling a funny story about their workplace. They all laughed.

15

THOMAS WAS OVER watching a movie with Andrew and Alex. Over time he started feeling more comfortable at their house. It helped normalize their relationship – sitting up against one another on a couch watching movies, talking without checking over their shoulders and lowering their voices if someone passed them by. It provided them a new normal. They'd cook together too. Thomas showed Andrew the few things he remembered from watching his mother as a child, and together they tried their best at making yassa and domoda. Thomas was frustrated he could never get it to taste like his mother's, but it impressed Andrew nonetheless. Spending time together like any other couple allowed them to connect in ways they couldn't before. Rushing to the stove to take the lid off an overflowing pot. Laughing after one of them slurped up spaghetti, sending sauce all over his shirt. Or being comfortable in front of one another during life's mundane routines, like getting dressed and putting away clothes.

It was always dark, or at least getting dark, by the time Thomas arrived, so there was never much concern of him being spotted. Isatou never came around after dark and Andrew always checked to make sure no one was within sight of the compound before Thomas appeared. If he stayed late at night, he hopped the gate when leaving to avoid its creaking when it was pushed open.

There had even been a few Saturday nights when Thomas slept over. The first time it happened was by accident. They were lying on Andrew's bed when they fell asleep. The next day Thomas woke up early before the sun had fully risen. He grew nervous and tense once he realized what had happened, having missed his chance at escape. But then he looked over and saw Andrew sleeping peacefully, his still face dimly lit by the light starting to piece through the curtains, and his chest rising rhythmically with each breath. A calm overtook Thomas in that moment. It was impossible to think there might be something not okay, that that wasn't where he was supposed to be. Thomas lay back down, nestling his head between Andrew's arm and chest, and fell back asleep.

On those Sunday mornings, which Thomas previously reserved for a weekly run along the beach, he and Andrew would laze around before making their way to join the group. Even though the streets on Sundays were generally quiet, leaving the compound in daylight was trickier. Andrew had to go out first to make sure the area was clear before Thomas slipped quickly out from the gate, walking towards the main road along the path like he'd always been there. He'd then walk to where he parked his bike, an isolated area close by. Even from there, Thomas never went straight to the beach. He always biked home first and put on his football outfit, conveniently allowing 'enough' time to elapse between when Andrew and Alex arrived and when he did. Eventually Thomas allowed himself to be persuaded to leave at least a pair of sport clothes in Andrew's room so he didn't waste time going home. They'd still arrive separately, but wouldn't it be easier this way?

"You don't think people might start noticing things?"

"What? That we have gone from arriving an hour apart to twenty or thirty minutes apart? No. I do not think people notice these things." And so Thomas, under the guise of his day off, started to spend more of his Sundays at the beach.

Alex got a text message just as they settled in to watch their movie that Sunday evening.

"Liv's coming over. She sounds pissed."

"Why?" Andrew asked.

"I dunno. She was at some thing her work colleagues invited her to. That's why she didn't play soccer today."

Fifteen minutes later, Liv burst into the living room letting her purse forcefully plop down onto the table. Her face was distressed. Alex was slow to pause the movie and Liv seized on that, standing deliberately right next to the television, staring at him, looking impatient and aggravated.

"Not a good event?" Alex asked with a smile, pausing the movie. He wasn't trying to be insensitive, but so many mass gatherings they'd both attended had been laborious – stuffy, non-air-conditioned halls, long winded speeches, mostly self-congratulatory, and short on concrete action. They were events that invited daydreaming while time seemed to go slower.

"No. It was not a good event," she answered affirmatively. She quickly looked over at Andrew and Thomas before turning her gaze back to Alex. "In fact it was very upsetting."

Liv worked with a women's cooperative that received microfinance loans to manufacture beauty products. She was a proud and militant feminist and believed her small efforts were part of a larger movement that could slowly undo Gambian patriarchy. She easily befriended most of her coworkers. They always invited her to their houses to meet their families.

Earlier in the week, a few of the women she worked with invited her to attend an interfaith dialogue event promoting tolerance and inclusiveness within Gambian society. The co-op was made of Muslim and Christian women and coworkers of both religions were going. She was happy to be invited – always impressed by the authenticity of religious coexistence in the country and the role women played in keeping it that way.

She met her colleagues at an Islamic center and mosque near the Serrekunda market, a bustling, if rougher area of town, where the streets were narrower on account of shops and shoppers spilling into them. The meeting was a cross-section of Gambian society made up of women and men and young and old. There were probably two hundred people present.

"It was fine for the beginning. What you'd expect at such a gathering. How the country is a model of religious and cultural understanding. All the different speakers thanking all the groups in attendance for being so committed to pluralism, blah blah, blah. You know how it is."

"We like to talk," injected Thomas jokingly but also a bit defensively. "But we are also much more patient listeners than people from the West."

"No, it's not that," Liv clarified. "That's true I mean, but that wasn't the problem today."

She continued to explain how after the first hour or so of speakers, the Imam of the host center got up to introduce a special guest, a Christian pastor in the country who started a new organization and was undertaking, in his words, *a holy mission*. The Imam said he hoped the whole community would come together to support the work of the pastor; it should be a joint effort between the country's Muslim and Christian groups.

By this point, no one in the small living room had any doubt as to where Liv was going with this. A lump was forming in Thomas's throat. He grew nervous for what Liv was about to say. Not because it made him uncomfortable – this was no surprise to him. It was Andrew. He wished he could shield and protect him from this side of his country. The Roots Festival should have been enough. He saw from Alex's expression that he also felt bad for Andrew. Someone who arrived with such innocence was so clearly losing it.

Liv went on to describe how a portly man of unimpressive proportions approached the stage. He wore an ill-fitting suit jacket that fell off his shoulders. It was either charcoal, or black and dusty. She couldn't tell. His tie was too short. He walked on stage clumsily and without coordination, while in his hand he clutched a crumpled mass of papers. When he looked up, however, she saw his face was very clear and distinguished. It revealed the type of contrast that made Liv do a double take to confirm that the head and body were connected to the same person. He was completely bald. The complexion of his dark skin made his cleanly-shaven face look soft and well cared for. He had a chin that was deliberately pointy, as if in protest of his round face. Inquisitive eyes peered out from behind circular glasses perfectly perched on his short nose. He had the aura of being part of the intelligentsia. His bottom lip curled downward, an accessory to a slightly open mouth permanently poised, ready to speak. "His name is Pastor Gomez."

He was from Gambia but spent the past many years abroad. Liv didn't remember all the details, but he studied and was trained with a Pan-African Evangelical Christian group. "I think they said he studied in Kenya? He worked in Uganda before returning to Gambia a few months ago."

As she started speaking, Thomas saw Andrew's face turn quizzical.

"Wait, I know that name," he interjected. "Jalloh introduced me to him at the parade. Jalloh knows him!"

"Well," Liv continued, "since returning from wherever, he started an organization called Pure Gambia. Its sole mission is to promote 'pure' Gambian values and Gambian families. He says the greatest threat to Gambia's future is that it will be undermined by a sinful and hedonistic valueless society, at the root of which he says is homosexuality and a homosexual takeover of Gambian morality." Turning to Thomas she added, mixing discomfort with disbelief, "He spoke with such conviction. It was frightening."

"Everyone hung on to his every word and intently followed the rise and fall of his cadence as he spoke. He was lyrical in his defense of the traditional family and how it must not fall 'to the homosexual agenda'. He pointed out that gay rights groups are becoming more common across Africa, and that South Africa's constitution guarantees equality for gays."

"'This,' he said, 'threatened the family structure throughout Africa,'" she reported to them. "He's using his organization to try and stop that from happening here."

"The family is the only structure that survived from the time of creation," Pastor Gomez told the crowd. "Kingdoms have fallen and kings have been slain. Great nations and civilizations have come and gone, their great creations and buildings leveled. But all through history, one thing has remained constant – no matter who rules and what great monuments are created, men and women have ultimately organized themselves around the family."

Growing bigger and bigger as he spoke, as if finally filling into his suit, Pastor Gomez pronounced that "today, for the first time in human history, the family is under attack. Our Bible, your Koran, is under attack. Homosexuals are being sent to infiltrate and destroy our families, and they will rot the foundation of what makes our Gambian and African societies great. No longer will we be a great nation of African Muslims and Christians. We will be a depraved nation, of no families, no faith, no freedom to be ourselves any longer. We will have all been perverted."

"And what was amazing," Liv exclaimed, a little too loud for the small living room, "was how no one seemed to disagree with him. Everyone's expression was the same – staring out to him with anticipation and agreement, wanting to take in more and more, as if he couldn't spew it out fast enough. Looking around, you'd think they were all raptured or something, that they were being programmed like robots to be sent out on a mission."

As Liv continued speaking and retelling the pastor's remarks, Thomas tuned out and found himself transported back to his village, into the church pews. He had seen the expressions she described – they were real. He didn't need her description of Pastor Gomez to picture the man she spoke of. The people in the crowd too were familiar. They were his parents and siblings. Neighbors and teachers.

"His goal now is to create a coalition of churches and mosques throughout the country to raise awareness about the dangers posed by what he called 'the homosexual agenda'."

Sitting on the couch and listening to Liv speak, Thomas realized he and Andrew were no longer holding hands. At some point they'd subconsciously come apart as each of them sat still and listened. Their faces were stoic, the worries and discomfort being unearthed within them stayed hidden.

"When Gomez finally finished, the Imam got back on stage with him and said how appreciative they were for his efforts. They stood ready to do everything they could to support him. He went on to thank the president, and said how everyone should appreciate that this was a country where the president understands the importance of this issue, and the danger posed by this 'evil'. He encouraged everyone in the crowd to speak to their imams or pastors about the work Pure Gambia was doing and to participate however they could. On the way out some of the volunteers were distributing pamphlets that were so vile and horrible in their descriptions I couldn't even take one."

"I'm sorry," offered Liv, looking longingly at both of them. "I didn't mean to upset you like this..."

"You don't have to be sorry," interrupted Thomas. "It's important to remember that our world is not equal outside this house. Especially when left to our religions and politicians."

As they all nodded, Thomas looked at Andrew. "Like the teachers at your school, who except for how they think on this issue are so nice."

"Exactly," he said. "And what about your colleagues?" Andrew asked Liv. "You always talk about them being so forward thinking. What was their reaction?"

"They agreed! The work Pastor Gomez is doing is extremely important they said. One of them told me we needed to do a better job at keeping our homosexuals away. It was horribly upsetting for me to hear them speak that way. They could tell I didn't agree, but I knew it wasn't the right time to confront them about it."

An uncomfortable silence followed.

"There was one more thing though," she said hesitantly. "Isatou was there."

"Our Isatou?" asked Alex.

"Yes. I'm almost positive she didn't see me. We arrived a little late and were at the back. She was closer to the front. But she was there. I don't know who she was with. It wasn't Awa or her other daughters."

Thomas grew visibly concerned. This wasn't a real reason to fear Isatou, but it meant he and Andrew weren't as protected as they may have thought. Looking at Andrew, he saw that he came to the same conclusion. His eyebrows raised slightly and his lips started to quiver as he tried his best not to reveal whatever was racing through his head. When he started shaking his leg restlessly, he tried to hold it down with his hand.

"Don't worry about her being there," Alex offered calmly. "It really makes no difference. She doesn't know anything and isn't going to. And her being there means nothing anyway. It was an event about religious tolerance. She's not signing up to be an informer, part of some neighborhood watch group." He reminded Andrew that sometimes she and her daughters cooked for their local mosque and probably heard about it that way.

"Right," said Andrew, trying to convince himself. "Right."

They didn't go back to the movie. Liv made tea and they spent some more time talking before each couple retired to their respective bedroom where Liv admitted to Alex that she was worried about Andrew.

"He may be in over his head."

"What do you mean?"

"Remember when he arrived? How he was quiet and timid."

"You called him lumpish," he reminded her.

"Yes. Lumpish Andrew."

"You think he'll go back to being that way."

"No," Liv answered. She wasn't worried he'd revert to his old self. It wasn't that. "It's that I don't think he's strong enough to carry on in this relationship as things keep heating up all around him."

"He's so happy though. You'd never know he used to be so quiet. And he really, *really* likes him. It's nice to see. Whenever we talk about it his face lights up. And when they're both here it's pretty amazing how natural they are together. I wouldn't have expected them to be as good together as they seem."

"Yes," she clarified. "I'm not ignoring that. And I can see it too. But don't you think he's riding this wave, and he's so caught up in the thrill of it he can't bring himself to stop, even though he knows it's dangerous? I mean, think of it," she continued, "he's so completely focused on Thomas that he can't see what's happening all around him."

"Well then, you certainly gave him a shock tonight."

"Right, but he can't handle shocks," she contended. "He's not programmed to be able to deal with them. And I'm nervous that at some point he's going to realize he's not in fact invisible or invincible, and when that realization arrives, he's going to panic and won't know what to do."

"They're really careful, Liv," Alex shot back. "We've seen how careful they are. I don't think they've ever done something I would've said not to. I know you worry about the whole thing more than I do. That's good though. Someone should worry."

"You don't see them when they're out alone together on the beach. We don't know what goes on."

Alex was both confused and put off by his girlfriend's insistence. "Sometimes I don't think you give them enough credit."

"And I think you give them too much credit. Did you ever have that talk with him you said you'd have, about being careful and making sure he knows what he's gotten into?"

"Yes, and it was awkward, exactly like I told you it would be. They're careful, and Andrew's happy. That's gotta matter!"

"It does, but you didn't see what I saw today. It's completely fucked up, Alex! If something happens, no one will come to his rescue. Or Thomas's."

His girlfriend's attempt at reason frustrated him. "It's not fair, Liv. They probably love each other. You want them to stop?"

"No one said this was fair."

The mood in Andrew's room was sad and serious. Andrew sat on the bed up against the wall, Thomas resting against him between his legs.

"Do you get used to it?" he asked Thomas. "I mean does it always sting just as much?"

"It stings more with time," he answered without taking a moment to think before he spoke. "As I grow up and can process it more, understand more and more what it all means, about how my own home sees me. It hurts much more. It drives you mad that this is the world you belong to. And you think you've pushed it away and are coping and then things like this happen, or you hear someone say something. I've realized I can't escape it."

"So why do you stay here?"

"Where should I go?"

Andrew had no answer. He hadn't thought about that before he asked the question and immediately felt guilty and regretted it. He forgot not everyone shared his luxury of being able to uproot oneself in the search for greater comfort and acceptance.

"A few months ago Suleiman came to see me. You and I had already met," Thomas said as he sat up and around to face Andrew, "but I can't remember how far along we were. He said to me he was worried things might be getting worse. But because of you I didn't want to listen to it. I didn't want to think there was something that might get in the way of us. And then he said something how maybe I should look to leave, and go someplace else."

"What did you say to him?" Andrew asked.

"That there was nowhere for me to go."

Andrew didn't respond.

"This is home. And even though it's so terrible, it's still not something that's easy to walk away from. I still want to believe there is goodness here, even if this may be foolish."

"Do you think there is?"

"I don't know. Now it's getting more difficult to think so. But I don't think I can give up on it. At least not yet."

16

THOMAS WOKE UP especially early with a sinking feeling. He was spending his Sunday morning with his brother and father, who were skipping out on church to organize new inventory at one of the warehouses Sheriff ran in Banjul. At first, Thomas tried to refuse, thanking Sheriff for the call and for wanting to help him out and involve him in his business. *But, as I said, I am happy working in tourism.* When his father intervened, grabbing Sheriff's phone, he pointed out how the work was being done on a Sunday, Thomas's day off.

"You will not have to miss work. It is only one morning to come and learn a bit about what your brother does. How can you say you want no part of something if you have never given it a chance? I will be with him. I hope you will join us," his father said, leaving him little choice in the matter.

"Fine, Father. I will join you."

Stepping off the minibus in Banjul, Thomas found himself in nearly-deserted streets he only barely knew. Low-rise buildings of worn concrete, paint faded or chipping off, and shuttered doors or garages were plastered with torn APRC posters lauding the president as the country's "Shining Light" and "Savior". Abandoned wooden carts cluttered the sidewalk outside the Albert Market. Dogs, worn down by the heat, and probably hungry, lay still in packs on the roadside. In the morning's emptiness, the paucity of activity in Banjul revealed the many cracks in its unkempt skeleton. The president's smiling face and the messages of propaganda looked all the more pathetic to Thomas. There was no light, no savior. Only empty promises, long-receded false hope. The city, like its residents, suffered at the hands of neglect.

Walking down the empty lane, narrow enough to keep out the light, Thomas could hear the commotion – metal tools hitting concrete, heavy boxes being dragged, tearing off tape. Nearing the open door, he could make out Sheriff firing off instructions.

"Move that one over there. Next to the spark plugs. Yes, yes. No. Here, I will help."

When he turned towards the inside he saw a mess of a room. The crowded concrete floor was littered with open boxes, packing paper spilling out, and closed boxes clumsily stacked waiting to fall over. Tools and auto parts, Thomas had no idea what any of them were, hung along the walls protruding out in a jumble of shapes and sizes. Light bulbs hung from the ceiling on wires. His father was unloading contents from a box onto a shelf. He was wearing what he always wore when he worked on motorcycles in the village – grease-stained brown trousers that were too big on him, his black belt, a short-sleeve white shirt, and sandals. Thomas could only see Sheriff's back, but saw he was smartly dressed. His clothing, with oversized prints and buckles, was what younger, more modern Gambians wore. Thomas saw he was holding a clipboard.

"Hello?" he offered, stepping cautiously into the shop.

"Aha! Brother, it is wonderful you have joined us!" Sheriff smiled broadly at him. It was welcoming and mischievous at the same time.

John also turned and smiled at him. His, there was no mistaking, was genuine. He wanted his son to feel comfortable and a part of Sheriff's business; it was something they could all bond over. "Why don't you come and help me with this. We need to empty these boxes of different parts. After we need to put some of them together. I will show you how."

Thomas and his father worked mostly in silence, with John showing Thomas what needed to be done — how to stack the parts and then how to assemble them. John was always a patient teacher. In the village he rarely got frustrated when Thomas or his brothers made mistakes or had trouble following. He displayed that same patience again as Thomas, clearly out of his element, fumbled with wrenches and screws.

"The nut," his father said gently. "You forgot to put on a nut. That's why it's not fitting properly." The softness of his father's voice, the lack of judgment in his expression, helped put Thomas at ease.

"Right. Thank you."

Thomas's phone dinged through the quiet. He took it out to see a text message from Andrew's number. *How's it going?* He put the phone back in his pocket without responding.

"Your friends are messaging you?" Sheriff's voice rumbled across the room.

"Yes," Thomas answered.

"That's good. It is important to have good friends in life. In Banjul I have made many friends," his brother boasted. "Good friends. We socialize often."

"That is good."

"What about you, Thomas? You have made good friends here? At your work? Ones you socialize with?"

"Yes, I have made a few friends. Not many, but I have made some."

"Very nice." There was a pause. He and Sheriff rarely carried on long or personal conversations. Just as Thomas turned away, Sheriff's deep voice pierced through the silence. "And women too?" His tone became more seriously inquisitive. "There are many beautiful women in Banjul. Father and I see them every day going to and from work. Not like back home, where everyone is worn from working in the fields and on the river. Here the women are delicate. Beautiful and smooth skin. They dress well, put nice makeup on. The women in Banjul have been very kind to your brother, even if I have not found the one to make my wife." He smiled like a braggart.

Even John chuckled. "I only ever knew your mother. But Sheriff tells me how times are different. How now there are more games to be played."

"And games to be won," Sheriff added. "And brother, I am winning at all the games."

Why must he ruin everything, Thomas thought to himself. The day was turning out much better than he expected, but now the lump in his throat was forming, the sinking feeling in his stomach returning, his hands becoming clammy.

"What about you, brother? How have Banjul's women been for you? I mean, at that fancy hotel you must be surrounded by beauties!"

When Thomas didn't immediately answer, still trying to formulate his words, Sheriff filled the void.

"Are you hiding any from us? You should share and save some for your brother," he laughed. Thomas felt disgusted and horrified. "Or have you not met any? It would be a pity if all this time here you have done nothing but work."

Turning to his father, Thomas saw that he saw nothing wrong in his brother's questions. His face bore the same curious look as Sheriff's.

"I haven't met anyone yet," he answered. "Maybe I will."

"Brother," Sheriff's voice grumbled, "this is not good. Do you want me to come to your hotel one day to show you how it is done, how you play a lady's game? Or maybe you need to come with me and my friends one evening. We can introduce you to many fine women. Would you like that?"

"Maybe," Thomas muttered, his heart pounding and mind racing.

"*Maybe?!*" his brother exclaimed. "That is not encouraging, Thomas. What's wrong with you? You don't want to have a wife?" Sheriff's eyes were piercing as he stared directly at Thomas, as if he was looking into him, seeing past the façade. "Every Gambian man is supposed to take a wife. Why are you any different? Something is wrong with you?"

Thomas was so unnerved that he had trouble fully paying attention to Sheriff. His mind kept telling him to keep calm and not make any expressions that might give anything away. He heard his brother ask if he was different and struggled to decipher his tone. Was he asking a question or being suggestive?

"No," Thomas said, his eyes breaking away from his brother, scanning the room around him, the foreign tools and parts hanging from the walls adding to the intimidation. "Of course I want to take a wife. I am young, though. I should work now to become successful first so I can properly support her."

"But if you have no experience, or wait too long before you show any interest, the women will not want you. Worse, people will start to wonder maybe you are not interested in women. That would be the end for you, brother, to have people saying maybe he does not want women. Is *that* what you want people to start saying about you? About someone in *our family*?" Sheriff's voice grew impatient.

"No, no. Never." Thomas was terrified of his brother now. He had never so much as hinted at broaching the subject of homosexuality. No one in their home had. It was so far from people's minds there was never any reason. That Sheriff now raised it stirred a new kind of fear in Thomas. *Does he know? Does he suspect anything?* He desperately wanted to be out of the shop, away from both of them, but he knew he couldn't leave.

"Then it is settled. You can come out with my friends one evening so I can introduce you to the women of Banjul. If you don't, I'll come to you at the hotel and make sure you talk to some of the beautiful women you see there."

"*Okay,*" he puffed emphatically, desperately hopeful it would end the conversation.

"I should come to the hotel?" Sheriff asked aggressively, clearly knowing what Thomas meant but seeking a more enthusiastic answer from his brother.

"No," Thomas said, trying not to sound scared or exasperated, "I will come out with your friends one night."

"Good," Sheriff answered, before turning back to his work.

Thomas too turned back, only to catch his father's glance. "You are lucky to have a brother who watches out for you like this."

He tried to smile just enough to appease his father.

After finishing work, the three of them were supposed to go back to Sheriff's to have lunch with Grace, but Thomas couldn't bear the thought of more time with his family. He imagined the four of them sitting around that small table, his mother invariably inquiring about their morning, what they did, what they spoke about. Surely, he thought to himself, either Sheriff or John would bring up Thomas and women and the whole conversation would happen again.

This time, however, there would be no stacked boxes to create artificial barriers between him and Sheriff, no tools in hand to distract their focus. They would all be sitting closely together, staring right at him, trapping him as they earnestly spoke about the importance of him quickly finding a wife. His mother would support Sheriff's plan. It was a prospect he couldn't endure. No, Thomas thought to himself, he couldn't go back for lunch. There was still a sufficient amount of work to be done before then. He hoped it wouldn't be obvious if after enough time elapsed he made up an excuse as to why he was going home. His father seemed to buy it. Sheriff, on the other hand, was suspicious.

"I hope I didn't upset you before, brother."

"No, you didn't," Thomas said, standing in the doorway, barely able to keep himself from breaking away.

"I am only looking out for your best interests."

"I know you are, Sheriff. And I thank you for that."

"As long as you know this."

"I do." With that, Thomas turned from his brother and walked speedily down the shaded alleyway until he emerged into the sunlight. The same discomforting streets of Banjul greeted him as they did in the morning. He made his way to where the minibuses departed, jumped into one half-full and sat, legs shaking impatiently, waiting for it to fill up so it could make the journey back home. It was then he remembered he hadn't written Andrew back.

It was fine. I'm coming back now. Hopefully I'll be able to see u tonight :-)

Andrew walked in earlier than Alex and Liv expected. They were sitting on the couch, eating roast chicken with chips and salad. Andrew's face had a look when he saw them, one which said he'd hoped to have entered undetected.

"What happened?" Alex asked. "Aren't you supposed to be with Thomas?"

"I was, but he canceled," Andrew answered, closing the door, clearly disappointed.

"Is everything alright?" Liv asked.

"Yeah. It's fine I guess." Andrew was speaking plainly, trying to imply he was holding back something significant. "He was with his family in Banjul. He was coming back early, but when his mother found out she called him and insisted he stay the afternoon. Now he says he can't get away. That it would be rude if he left them."

There was a silence. While Andrew paused to give Alex and Liv an opportunity to react, their expressions suggested they expected him to keep talking and get to the point.

"Oh," Liv said hesitantly. "Well that's okay. You can't argue with family. And, isn't it nice he's spending time with them?"

Andrew wasn't convinced.

"What, Andrew?" Liv continued. "You can't possibly be offended he's with his family. It's not like he said he doesn't want you two to be together again."

"No. You're right," he agreed. "But," he continued unexpectedly, "the more time he spends with them, the worse it could be for us. You don't know what they're like. They tease him for not having a girlfriend, actually make fun of him for thinking that working at the hotel is a smart idea, and want him to live with them, where he'd have to pretend all the time, like he did before, that he's someone he's not. They'd make him go to church with them. They'd make him find a girlfriend and get married. They'd ruin his life."

Liv rose, reaching for Andrew's hand. He let her have it, and she squeezed it. As she was about to speak, Andrew sniffled. He swallowed to try to hide it, but it was too late. His eyes were sad.

They stood together for a few more seconds, hands extended into one another's over the table covered with food. Alex sat still. These weren't the situations he excelled in. Then, unexpectedly, he blurted out, *it's okay, Andrew.* Andrew and Liv turned to Alex, letting their hands loose.

"It's not," Andrew responded assertively. "It's not okay, and it's not fair."

Andrew told Alex and Liv how Thomas told him that when he's with his family, he's scared he'll say or do something that makes them suspect him. *I wouldn't be their child any longer. I would become an outcast. Because the risk is so high, I have to be more than careful. One mistake — if I react the wrong way when they tell me I need to marry — that could be it.*

"What's *it*?" Alex asked. "You think his family would turn him in?"

"I asked the same question. He shrugged his shoulders at me, saying *in this country, it's not a chance anyone wants to take.*"

"It's so fucked up," Alex said. "Turning in your own family. How do you do that?"

The three of them looked at each other, no one volunteering to respond.

"I get it. I know, not everyone has the perfect accepting family. Case and point. We all have our shit," Andrew finally said. "Fine, life's not easy or fair. But *this* hard? *This* unfair? He *never* gets a break and the stakes are so high for him," he added, his voice quivering.

"And now he's there. They just sit in his brother's living room with Nigerian TV playing in the background. Every time a girl comes on either his father or brother makes a comment. Even his other brother's wife back in the village says she knows a girl he can meet. He's scared he won't be able to avoid it any longer and one Sunday they'll have her over too. So far he says work keeps him too busy."

"None of this makes the situation hopeless, though," Liv suggested. "You can't change where he was born and grew up. Maybe you can't solve all of his problems, or all of your problems. But, you can keep doing what you're doing, which is a lot in these circumstances when you think about it. He needs you. You're important to each other."

"Weren't you the one who told me not to do this?" he asked her, half joking.

She smiled at him.

"I still think you have to protect yourself. But, I do understand how important it is that you also, to the extent you can, protect him.

Maybe you can't always. Like tonight. There's a part of his world you can't be a part of. One you'll probably never be a part of. For me though, as hard as that would be, it would also be motivation for the world that you two share – how it should be that much more wonderful. At least in those moments, you can forget about all the terrible."

I know, Andrew said. He paused, glanced downwards at his feet and looked back up at Liv's empathetic gaze. "But that doesn't mean it still doesn't suck sometimes."

I know, she replied.

Andrew's phone rang, breaking the silence. He took it from his pocket and saw the number. It was Thomas. Nodding at Alex and Liv to let them know who it was, he answered.

"Hello," he said, walking into his room, his voice trailing off as he closed the door.

They didn't see each other that week.

Andrew and Mr. Jalloh worked into most evenings on a presentation the two of them were giving as part of an education ministry workshop the coming Friday. Originally, Mr. Jalloh was going to make the presentation with another colleague but decided that since Andrew only had a couple of months left in his placement, it might be a good opportunity for him to showcase what he had learned. He wanted Andrew to talk about how he formed such strong connections with the students, something Andrew didn't know how to explain. He'd just shown up in class and over time earned their respect. He didn't know how to describe disposition. Mr. Jalloh suggested he give examples of all the different group assignments Andrew assigned in class.

"Your students enjoyed the group work very much. I saw for myself how enthusiastic they were," he insisted. "So much of our focus has been on individual learning. But I think there is tremendous potential if we incorporate group work into our teaching. So I think you can talk about that and give examples."

The workshop took place on Friday at one of the larger schools in Banjul, which had been closed down for the day. It always amused Andrew how casual and last-minute schools could be about days off. He assumed the students were only told about it the previous afternoon.

Andrew began his presentation by addressing what he thought was one of the biggest challenges he faced in the classroom, the wildly divergent levels his students were at. He didn't want to teach at a level that left many behind, but nor did he want to teach at a level that left the top students bored. He decided group learning, where students of different levels were placed together and forced to collaborate, would be a way to move the class forward relatively consistently and inclusively. There was no grand pronouncement or passionate proclamation. No claim to be an expert. With an understated demeanor, he gave a number of examples of successful group projects his class undertook and explained why he thought they had been a success and were worth emulating. After speaking, he took some questions from interested teachers and administrators and then sat down to applause and a giant smile and handshake from a beaming Mr. Jalloh.

That evening, he went to see Thomas at the bar. He was looking forward to just sitting and relaxing. He didn't want to discuss the growing homophobia. Andrew ordered two rum and cokes, and Thomas was generous in pouring the rum.

"You trying to get me drunk?" Andrew asked.

Thomas giggled and Andrew looked around at the empty pool area – the pool, palm trees, neatly organized lounge chairs, the manicured plants that spilled out from the earth onto the walkways. None of it moved. Even the fountains had been turned off. The stillness of it all gave it the look of a photograph, a postcard. It almost looked pretend to him. It was spring, which marked the beginning of the end for the tourist season, so the hotel, which was never full to begin with, had quieted down. It would be some time before the sterility would be broken up again, and now for the first time the hotel seemed oddly out of place.

"It must be expensive to run this place outside of the tourist season," Andrew suggested.

"They reduce our wages."

"Really?"

"Yes, by twenty-five percent."

"That's ridiculous!"

"They keep it just above what we might make somewhere else so we don't leave for another job."

Thomas reached for the tip jar and held it out for Andrew. Both of them laughed.

"In America you have a minimum wage right?"

Andrew nodded.

"How much does it pay you an hour?"

Andrew's eyes widened in thought. His serving job at the country club paid him above minimum wage but he didn't know what it was. "I think it's a bit over seven dollars an hour."

"Seven dollars?" Andrew could see Thomas doing the conversion in his head. "Two hundred and fifty dalasis an hour," he proclaimed. "What a country," he concluded.

As he started to list some things he would buy if he were paid that amount – another pair of shoes, his own computer, a new mobile "and the DVDs of *24*," someone started walking through the hallway towards them.

Suleiman smiled and waved as he approached them, which Thomas reciprocated, but also managed to mutter under his breath to Andrew, "He only comes to see me now when there is trouble."

"What's that?" Suleiman asked pulling up his chair.

"I said you always come with uplifting news."

Suleiman smiled acknowledgingly. Thomas and Andrew waited nervously.

"What news do you bring now, Mr. Reporter?"

"I can't come and say hello?"

"You can, but you don't," he said as he popped the top off a bottle of Julbrew and handed it to his friend.

"On Sunday our newspaper is running an article on the front page claiming to expose a secret homosexual group that gathers at a secret location." Thomas and Andrew's expressions suggested they wanted to say something, but their mouths froze.

One of their reporters, he explained, had been given an anonymous tip explaining how on the first Monday of every month, in a house near the Senegambia strip not far from where they were, a small group of gays and lesbians gathered to discuss how they could advance gay and lesbian rights in Gambia. Apparently, the meetings had been going on for over a year and the activists communicated with other gay activist groups in Africa for help and advice. It didn't completely add up, but intrigued the editors enough to run the story. It would certainly sell copies.

"Is this true? Have either of you heard about this?"

They both shook their heads.

"We don't speak to anyone," Thomas added. "I do not know one other gay person."

"Our reporter was only able to get the name of the man who owns the house. His name and picture will be on the front page of the newspaper."

"What?!" Thomas exclaimed, before looking around, realizing he'd been too loud. "Do you realize what that will do to him?"

"Yes," Suleiman answered. "Thomas, I can't stop them. I'm only a reporter. I don't control the newspaper or what stories other reporters choose to follow."

"I know."

"There will probably be a police raid on the house. I hope the owner can get someplace safe in time."

"Can you warn him?" Andrew asked.

"No, I couldn't," Suleiman answered disappointingly.

"He would be putting himself at risk," Thomas clarified.

"Right," said Andrew. Thomas knew that asking Suleiman to take a risk to help this man was not fair. He wasn't sure he'd do it either. It might lead to him being exposed somehow.

"If the allegations are simply that this is a meeting group for gays and lesbians, I'm not sure how this breaks a law," Suleiman added, trying to reassure them both.

"When was this country ever so concerned about following the laws? You have written about our police and courts," Thomas shot back.

Suleiman was silent. He knew his friend was right. If they wanted, they would find a way to drum up charges against someone, or just detain them without any. It had all been done before.

"Do you think," Andrew began before pausing, afraid for the answer that might follow his question. "Do you think they'll start looking for more people? Besides those people in this group?"

"No." Suleiman was confident, taking a drink of his beer. "The government has no interest in using its resources to target gay people. Rumors from many months ago — when I came to warn Thomas, were just rumors. They're much happier bragging about it in speeches without having to follow up. Using it to build credibility with people."

"Right," Andrew replied.

Andrew left shortly thereafter. As soon as he was gone, Suleiman turned to his friend.

"Is everything okay with you two?"

"Yes, everything is perfect. That's the problem. We have this amazing relationship, this connection. We get along together so well. But the minute we step away from whatever protected place we're in, it's like a grenade goes off."

"But you're used to it, right? Unfortunately."

"Yes, but he's not. It's not his country. And I'm sure it can be strange enough on its own, without all this mess."

"Do you think he would say something if it was too much for him?"

"Maybe."

Suleiman asked Thomas if the pressure was too much for him to handle.

He answered right away since he'd thought about it before. "Sometimes. Most of the time no, because we do a good job of avoiding these situations. We do a good job at pretending. But other times, I worry a lot."

He continued and told Suleiman about Liv's experience that past Sunday and how hard it was for him to watch Andrew sit there and listen.

"He looked so frightened. It was worse because he is so innocent. He never asked for these troubles. It made me feel bad for him – he doesn't need this. He doesn't deserve it."

"Neither do you," Suleiman pointed out.

"I know, but now that bothers me less. I had a very hard time sleeping that night. I was thinking how in some way I'm responsible that he has to go through this."

"Do you question if you should keep going with it?"

"With what? The relationship?"

"Yes."

"It's a hard question," Thomas explained. "Maybe what we're doing does not make sense. We both know this. We've talked about it. But because something does not make sense, does this mean you don't do it? I can't speak for him. Only for me. And for me the reason is simple. I don't know that I will ever have another chance like this. You can always go and meet a girl, and be with her and find another if you don't like her or she doesn't like you. But I can't. And so finally, somehow, I found someone. Shouldn't I be able to enjoy that – even if this is how it is, even if I know it can't last?"

Suleiman hadn't thought of it that way before. Thomas wasn't asking for something unreasonable. He just wanted a chance. "I can't argue with that," he replied before looking at his watch. He said he was happy Thomas had this, and of course, he deserved it and more. "But look after yourself too."

17

ANDREW WAS SITTING eating breakfast with Alex, reporting Suleiman's news from the night before, when they heard the front gate creak open.

"It's Liv," Alex said, standing up. "We should get ready. Go and get this over with."

"Gamcel," Andrew sighed. "It's like a part of me dies each time I deal with them."

The three of them were off to Gamcel, their phone and internet service provider. The company released a new internet rocket stick it claimed was significantly faster than the ones they were using. Alex's placement was soon up, but Andrew and Liv were eager to take advantage of a faster, more reliable internet connection.

"It's funny how slow it's going to be to get faster service," Andrew joked.

Alex and Liv laughed.

"Alright boys. Saturday errands. Put shirts on," Liv ordered, ending breakfast.

They walked to the Gamcel building on Kairaba Avenue to discover that countless other Gambians were waiting to do the same thing. They walked upstairs to the waiting area, took a number a long way away from the one being served, and saw that all the chairs were taken. The staff – young Gambians in jeans and t-shirts – busied about behind the counter, serving clients of various ages, in an assortment of Western and traditional dress, who held out old-model laptops, multiple mobile phones, and USB rocket sticks all in need of service. Andrew recognized a Lebanese man who owned a restaurant he liked. The man refused to believe the employee had indeed fixed whatever wasn't working with his mobile.

I'm not getting all my SMS messages.

You will now, Sir.

Every time I come here you tell me this.

Sir, there was a problem with the account. It is fixed now, Inshallah.

Andrew loved the *Inshallas*. They were everywhere. *See you soon? Inshallah. Will the rain stop? Inshallah. Did you complete the assignment properly? Inshallah.*

The three of them parked themselves in a corner next to a young couple with a baby. They were engrossed in conversation. Andrew noticed they dressed, including the baby, in Western clothing. Each had an iPhone, which meant they had money. The baby had a bottle and some small toys that looked like they were purchased abroad. The man checked the time on his phone's screen and sighed.

"Do you want to go for the Indian buffet tonight?" Alex asked.

"Hmm. Yes, that would be nice," Liv answered. "Andrew? Did you fancy some curry?"

"Sure."

"I can't believe you never tried Indian food until you came to Gambia," she continued. "What kind of an upbringing did your parents give you in America?"

"A different one," he joked.

"I'll say."

Saikou says she's a dike.

The sentence went by so quickly Andrew wasn't sure he heard correctly. But from looking at Alex and Liv he could see that he did. Facing inward, towards each other, they kept quiet, all curious to overhear what the couple sitting next to them was saying.

"No way. I've known her my whole life. Your friend spends one evening with her at Lamin's party and convinces you she's a dike?!" The woman, whispering, sounded incredulous. "Tell Saikou he doesn't know what he's talking about. Tell him he's not to talk about her that way to anyone."

Andrew's back was to the couple, which was a good thing. They weren't able to see his eyes widening with equal measure of alarm and curiosity.

"I'm just telling you what he said. You know Saikou. He knows women. I don't think he'd lie or make a mistake like this."

"What makes him think such a thing? How can he be so sure? He can't be – he's never slept with her. Did she tell him, *oh sorry, Saikou I can't sleep with you because I'm lesbian?*"

"He said he just got the feeling. From how she was with him. I'm not saying it's true, but think about it. How many boys has she been with? You've said yourself she's your one friend who you never understood why she couldn't find a man. Maybe she doesn't want one."

Andrew saw Alex looking at him. He wondered if he could see his heart pounding out of his chest.

"Do you understand what you're saying, you and Saikou? Do you know what it means if you're right?"

There was a brief, crushing silence behind Andrew before the woman's voice started again.

"One of my closest friends?! If it's true, she probably tried so many times to come after me or another of our friends and we didn't realize. That *bitch*." She spoke the last word with such disgust.

"Saikou said you should try and trap her. Trick her into going with a woman and then force her to confess. She would have to change or else run."

"It would serve her right. She could never be around us again. And not around our child."

They look so normal, Andrew thought to himself, before he, without thinking, turned his gaze to the young couple. His eyes fixated on both of them in a way that made it clear he had been listening to their conversation and disapproved of what they were saying. As his head steadied itself, unable to break away from staring at them with an expression of moral opprobrium shooting out from his eyes, he felt Liv's hand tugging at his, trying to pull him back.

"Andrew," she whispered.

He heard her, but his head didn't turn back to her. He kept staring at the couple.

"What man? What is it?" the young man wanted to know. "Why do you keep looking at us that way?"

The harshness of the man's voice broke Andrew's stare. He looked away, nervously, back at Alex and Liv.

"Nothing. Sorry," he muttered.

"I don't think it's nothing," the man said.

"Enough," said the woman. "Leave him alone. He said it was nothing."

"It looked to me like he didn't like the way we were talking. Did you? Or didn't you." The man was still sitting, but he was sitting up straighter, extending his neck out, broadening his shoulders.

"Really man," Alex broke in, "it was nothing." Alex stepped forward, between Andrew and the man. "There's nothing. He stares all the time. I'm telling you, it was nothing."

Liv placed her hand discreetly on Andrew's back, which made him feel worse. In wanting, or thinking he wanted to confront this couple for their prejudice, all he did was create a situation that Alex had to fix with Liv comforting him.

"Maybe it was nothing," said the young man, relaxing back into his chair. "But I think your friend didn't like what we were saying. All you foreigners coming in here, thinking you know everything, how we need to live. But this," he said while pointing his index fingers to the ground, "this is Africa. We don't want your gays and your lesbians. Your diseases. And don't try to tell us we're backward because this is our culture. It's you who've been perverted. So don't try to tell us how to live. Don't come here to lecture me."

"Sure," Alex said. "Like I said, it was nothing."

Andrew felt cornered. Between the wall and the young couple, the only way to go was forward, towards the counter. He looked again at the young staff. They were the people who worked on the front lines of the country's development, in software, mobile technology. If there was going to be a group of people in the country more open minded it would be them. Now he wasn't so sure anymore. He stood looking at them wondering how many felt the same way as the couple next to him. How many young, modern, and connected Gambians refused to accept being gay wasn't an abomination?

Turning his back just enough to pull away from Liv's hand, Andrew quietly and without looking at Alex and Liv said *sorry*, before taking off, past the young couple, past the counter of Gamcel employees, down the stairs, and out the front door into the open air along a busy Kairaba Avenue. He breathed heavily looking left and right. Faces kept passing him by. In each one of them he saw a threat. A mother walked with her young child. He saw her eyes look at him before she looked down to her child. *Stay away from that man*, he imagined her saying. A middle aged man passed him by carrying several plastic bags. He lifted his head towards Andrew revealing a suspicious expression. The faces kept coming, passing him by on foot, through car windows. Each one, in slow motion, seemed to peer right into him. *I see you*, they kept saying, as he stood there alone, frightened and disoriented.

"Andrew!"

Turning back towards the Gamcel building, Andrew saw Alex and Liv walking hurriedly out the front door.

That night, when Andrew told Thomas what happened, he half expected him to be furious with him. He wondered if the risk of exposure and feelings of betrayal would be enough for Thomas to end the relationship.

"Now you're being silly," Thomas giggled as they lay in bed together. "You think you're so famous that everyone in this country knows who you are? That this stranger is going to somehow magically discover your identity, call the police, and now the police are outside your window listening to us? All because you looked at him?"

Andrew's face stayed serious. He knew Thomas was teasing. The notion was preposterous. Still, as irrational as his fears and anxiety were, he couldn't turn them off.

"What Suleiman said last night, about the arrest, and this secret society, that doesn't scare you?"

"Of course it does. There isn't much about this place that doesn't scare me sometimes," Thomas confessed. "This is why it's important to know what to be scared of, so that we don't *always* live in fear."

Andrew broke away from Thomas's arms, lying on his back, staring through the mosquito net at the ceiling, saying nothing.

"Okay. You shouldn't have done what you did today," Thomas offered assertively, making Andrew's stomach sink. "But it's done, and we're lucky it was minor. A lesson for the future."

"How do I know I won't do something stupid like that again? I didn't plan to do this. I just did it, knowing I shouldn't have. I couldn't control myself. Really, I mean, why should you just have to accept everything the way it is?" he asked, turning his head to face Thomas, whose face had the look of worry on it.

"Because this is the place I live in," he reminded him in a whisper. "And if after all this time, you think you can change it, maybe we do have a problem."

18

SULEIMAN'S NEWSPAPER PUBLISHED the article on the Monday, a day later than originally planned. When they didn't see it in the paper on Sunday, Thomas and Andrew naively thought the story wouldn't run, that somehow a source didn't turn out to be reliable, or better yet, someone's conscience got the better of them. Andrew's irrational side felt relieved. He feared this would spark a witch hunt that, after the Gamcel episode, would result in the couple coming forward to name him as a suspected gay person. In his mind he envisioned himself grabbing a backpack with his valuables, hopping in a taxi to make way for the ferry terminal to cross the river and flee to Senegal.

That morning, as with most Monday mornings, Andrew popped into Mr. Jalloh's cramped and disorganized office to check in with him before heading into his classroom. Like every other day, a pile of newspapers sat on Mr. Jalloh's desk. But on this day, at the top of the pile, Andrew saw a headline proclaiming, "SECRET GAY SOCIETY EXPOSED." Beneath it was a picture of an average looking Gambian home, which Andrew assumed was the home near Senegambia that apparently housed this secret society. Moving closer, he read the subtitle under the photograph, "Senegambia home where secret group plots to advance LGBT agenda".

"Amazing, isn't it?" Mr. Jalloh exclaimed as he watched Andrew discreetly glance at the article. "It reports how they have been operating for almost one year to find a way to change the Gambian legal system to favor the LGBT community." Mr. Jalloh struggled as he pronounced LGBT. It was evident this was his first time ever seeing and speaking the acronym, which he read out with a deliberate effort to not stumble. "It's a good thing they were discovered," he declared, "otherwise people might think we are turning into America." He chuckled giddily from his belly, amused by his own sense of humor.

Andrew abruptly changed topics without worrying about being too abrupt, and asked Mr. Jalloh if there was anything happening in the coming week he needed to know about.

"No, I don't think so. A normal week."

"Great," Andrew replied hurriedly. "Have a good day, Mr. Jalloh."

He was half out the door when he heard his name called out again. He stopped to clear the lump in his throat before turning to face Mr. Jalloh.

"Yes, Mr. Jalloh," he said anxiously.

Mr. Jalloh stared up from behind his desk, his eyes were surprised and his half-open mouth looked confused. He thought to himself for a moment as if to remember something he meant to tell Andrew. "I wanted to tell you that I have received excellent feedback about your presentation on Friday. The District Coordinator was extremely impressed and wants to have a task force over the summer to make group learning a bigger part of the curriculum."

Slow to process that he was being praised, Andrew looked back at Mr. Jalloh. "Oh, that's great. Thank you very much."

"He told me it's a shame you are returning to America this summer. I told him I agreed."

"Thanks, Mr. Jalloh," Andrew said before ducking back into the hallway, stopping to stand against the wall and collect himself for a second after dodging the bullet. Just then he felt a vibration in his pocket and took out his phone to see a text from Thomas. *its in the paper.*

> *i know. saw it in jallohs office. gtg to class. talk after work*
> *k. bye*
> *bye*

Thomas saw groups of staff members all huddled together around copies of the newspaper at the front desk and in the restaurant and wanted no part of it.

He left work early that evening for Andrew's. His hours had already been cut back, and during the week he could leave at seven if no one was at the bar. He walked through the lobby, second guessing how his colleagues looked at him as he strode past. He made his way out of the hotel and up to the road to catch a 7-7. The traffic barely moved. As they inched along the road, police lights flashed in the distance. It was too early for a nighttime checkpoint to be set up. There was probably an accident. The passenger sitting in the middle of the backseat let out a heavy sigh to signal her displeasure with the traffic. She was an older woman, too big for the small back seat, wearing a dress of green and blue patterns, with hexagonal glasses firmly fixed on her face, and a shiny black leather handbag on her lap.

"It is because of the gays," the driver said, making eye contact with her through his rear-view mirror. He'd been driving this route for many hours now and they were approaching the house where the gay society met. The police had been there all day, he explained, so had curious onlookers and sporadic protestors. "They had to call more police because people started throwing rocks at the house."

"And where are these people now?" the older woman demanded to know.

"Apparently they arrested this guy who owns the house early in the morning, before he had a chance to run away. But they don't know any other members of this society."

She let out a loud sound, an *umpf*, making her displeasure known – with the traffic delay or the activist ring, it was unclear.

The car kept inching forward to the flashing lights. Thomas felt the leg of the older woman pressing up against his. He felt himself perspiring under his shirt.

"Driver, let me go down here," he said. "I will walk." There was nothing unusual or suspect about the request.

The car stopped. Thomas opened the door, nearly falling into the dirt as the old woman's body spread out into his vacated seat. He stood tall and gulped down the evening's air as he fixed his bearings and then headed off, walking in the same direction the car drove towards.

As he neared the flashing lights, he saw heavily armed police officers standing on the road at an intersection. A small crowd, about fifty people, also stood on the road, looking. The police formed a barrier preventing them from turning onto a side street off the main road.

Thomas approached the commotion curiously and hesitantly, scared for what he might encounter. Visually, it proved to be anti-climactic. It was just a house. It looked like it did in the newspaper. It was two stories of beige stucco behind a red gate, which was open but blocked by a police jeep. A second-floor window in the front of the house was smashed. He asked a middle-aged man in the crowd if anything had happened lately.

"No, not since this morning when the police raided. They arrested the owner of the house. The head gay!" he proclaimed with approving enthusiasm.

Thomas, reluctant to engage the man any further, nodded and kept walking. His pace quickened as he fixed his gaze on the ground in front of him, paying no attention to the cars racing by next to him as they emerged from the slowdown. He looked at his watch. If he was going to Andrew's, he needed to get back into a 7-7. But instead of flagging one down, he took out his phone and sent off a text. *sorry, quite tired after today. gonna go home and rest. ttyl.*

As Thomas briskly walked away from the crowd of onlookers, he recalled one of his and Suleiman's recent conversations. They were sitting late at the bar one weeknight, long after Thomas's shift ended. Suleiman was trying to think of ways to keep Thomas out of harm's way. It was a struggle.

"Why don't you go back to America with Andrew? Claim asylum."

"And how do you suppose I do that? I have no money, no way of getting there. And besides, I could never do that to Andrew."

"Why? I thought you two said you loved each other."

"We do. But it's not so simple."

"Have you at least asked him?" Suleiman wanted to know.

"No. It wouldn't be fair to him. He has family. He has his life. I can't turn that upside-down." Thomas paused and looked down for a moment. Looking back up, he continued. "He hasn't offered."

"You can say something to him, find a way to bring it up."

"It's not something you bring up from nowhere, Suleiman. And also," he added, looking resolute, "I don't want to go. What would I do there? What could I do? This is where I live. I can manage."

"What's going to happen?"

"To us?"

"Sure, or to you."

"I don't know. I try not to think about it. Why can't I just enjoy this now? If I have to worry about the future, I can do this later."

Suleiman could sense his friend growing uncomfortable each time they had this discussion.

"Thomas, we can get you out of here."

"To where? America? Even you know you can't do that. Not with the people you know, and not with the people your father knows. Sometimes it's better not to promise at all."

"I never said America. To Senegal, and maybe Europe if we tried. In Senegal you'd at least be safer."

"I don't want to leave. At least not yet. Not while he's still here."

Suleiman knew when to stop pushing. "Fine. But keep your head down."

Andrew skipped going to the hotel bar that Friday. Friends of his and Alex's were meeting for drinks to watch the sunset and he decided to join. The plan was to meet Thomas on the beach by the hotel later, when he finished work, and they'd walk up to their spot together. It was their first time seeing each other since the article was published. Andrew's colleagues talked about it constantly. Coverage throughout the week expanded, focusing on the arrest of the house owner. No one knew what criminal offense he was charged with, but that didn't seem to bother people.

"As long as he is away somewhere. And can't try to infect the children," said one of the teachers at Andrew's school. Andrew wasn't entirely sure which stereotype his colleague was referencing. Was he concerned about children being infected with HIV or with homosexuality? "I hope they will catch the rest and do the same with them."

The fact that the police only arrested one person, with a whole group still said to be in hiding, created a pervasive sense of alarm among many Gambians. Fear was the only emotion that Andrew seemed to share with them these days.

That night Andrew and Thomas were nervous to see each other. Things had changed. People had been exposed. A man had been arrested. His friends, it was assumed, were in hiding or had run away somewhere. Both of them feared the calculus of their relationship would be different because of it.

Andrew stood alone waiting for Thomas. He was at the water's edge, holding his shoes, letting the wave's ripples gently massage his feet as they made their final push towards the land before receding back to sea. It was a warm and still night, the winter's cool long past. Andrew thought about all the different beaches in the world where he and Thomas could have been on when he heard Thomas speak from behind him.

"You're going to make me take my shoes off?"

Andrew turned slowly before walking to meet him. They made their way mostly in silence in an attempt to put off the conversation neither was particularly keen on having.

"How was work this week?" Andrew asked.

"It was fine," Thomas answered. "The same really. Not many guests."

"That's good, I guess."

"Yes. And your students? They behaved?"

"Yeah."

When they arrived at their spot it was empty as usual. Andrew began to sit as Thomas stepped out to the water, turning his head side to side on alert, staring out into the dark night.

"No one's here," Andrew said as he walked up, gently taking Thomas's hand into his. "There's no one out now. Let's sit down." He wasn't trying to be reckless, and he was secretly happy Thomas was being extra vigilant. But he also just wanted to relax, even if it meant letting his guard down, if only to ready himself for the conversation he knew they were about to have.

Thomas started. He said he thought they needed to be more careful. The whole population was consumed with who the other members of the LGBT group were. On television, radio, and in newspaper articles, everyone was speculating about who they might be, where they might be hiding, and who was supporting them. "And even though they say there were other gay groups in Africa supporting them, people are also very suspicious about support from the West."

Thomas worried in this climate of heightened suspicion, he and Andrew were at a bigger risk than before.

"Some person can see us walking together and decide they don't like how we look. They could report us to the police and that would be it. You could be this Westerner bringing homosexuality, or at least coming to support our gay-rights groups."

Andrew questioned how realistic something like that actually was. "It seems far fetched to me. You said yourself, about my little screw-up, that we needed to separate the real threats from fake ones."

"You're right. And maybe some months ago I would agree with you. Back then I also would question someone who said that this was a country where your neighbors would turn you into the police. But now I'm not so sure."

"Apparently the organization Liv was talking about, Pure Gambia, has a sign in front of the house."

"I've seen it. I pass it on my way to and from work. It says in big black letters, KEEP OUR COUNTRY PURE. Underneath it says PURE GAMBIA – AN ORGANIZATION OF CONCERNED CITIZENS."

"So we'll be more careful," Andrew announced resolutely. "But I don't know how we can be more careful. We're only in public twice a week – on Fridays I'm sitting at the bar like a customer and on Sundays we play soccer. We've agreed there's nothing risky about that. Unless you've changed your mind."

"I don't think we should come back here," Thomas said, looking around at their surroundings. Andrew's face turned surprised. "At least not at night, when it's dark and us being here is more suspicious. Wandering along after playing football is one thing, but like this, I don't think it's smart when everyone is so alarmed."

"Okay," Andrew said. Thomas's seriousness was making him nervous. Maybe he himself had become less aware of what was around him.

Thomas looked at Andrew through long eyes before apologizing. "I'm sorry I have put you into this mess." It was the first time Andrew saw him looking sad.

"You didn't," he said before thinking to himself for a second. "And it's not a mess," he wanted to believe. "At least not between us."

Andrew, seeing how distressed Thomas was, thought to reassure him. Impulsively, he decided to tell him something he hadn't been planning on telling him yet, because it wasn't for sure. "I asked Mr. Jalloh about staying another year."

Thomas didn't immediately react. His face wore no emotion as he processed what Andrew had just disclosed.

"He was very happy to hear I was thinking about it. He said I was doing a great job and the school would certainly take me back. But he wanted to speak to Haddy at the placement organization about maybe finding me a role with more responsibility, for at least part of the time, on things like curriculum development for more than just one school."

With Thomas still slow to react, it didn't take much for Andrew to sense how surprised he was. "You weren't expecting this were you?"

"No. Not at all," he said, still keeping his emotions in check while they sorted themselves out.

Andrew wasn't sure he was going to stay. He explained that regardless of what happened, he had to go home over the summer and see his family. It was the only way he could pull it off. But the thought of moving home permanently frightened him.

"I just wouldn't want to be alone like that. I've done it before already. I don't need to do it again." He liked being there. "With you."

When Thomas's reaction didn't manifest into outward exuberance, Andrew grew suspicious. "What's wrong?"

"Nothing's wrong. Honestly, I'm thrilled." He said, though still not showing it. "Nothing would make me happier. In fact, I don't know if I've ever felt this lucky. I don't want you to go, and the thought of being alone isn't one I want to think about either," he said through a guarded expression. "But if you stay, then what?"

"What do you mean then what?"

"You will again stay for another year? Or you will go home then? And when you come back after the summer, if things are worse than they are now?"

Andrew hadn't thought about any of that. Nor did he particularly want to. At least not then.

"For the past while I started to prepare my mind for us to say goodbye. As difficult as that may be to think about, I think, at least for me, it's important. When we're together it is the greatest thing I can ask for. But that's also why I have to keep in my mind that you will leave one day. Because if I don't, when you do leave – and you will," Thomas paused, "it would be too difficult for me to handle if it came out of nowhere."

Andrew nodded slowly to demonstrate he was paying attention, while he thought about what Thomas was saying, what it all meant.

"You can't stay here forever can you?" Thomas asked gently. "Okay, so maybe you will stay a little bit longer, but still, you have to leave, right? And I have to remain behind. Maybe this is being too negative? I'm not sure."

Andrew's face turned blank.

"What if something happens to you?" Thomas asked.

"What about if something happened to *you*?" Andrew shot back defensively. It bothered him how Thomas felt he needed to protect him, as if he wasn't able to on his own.

"This is my country, Andrew. It's my life, and I have no choice but to continue trying to live it the way I can in this place. I can't get on a plane and fly away someplace safe. But you can," he said earnestly. "You don't have to be trapped in this craziness. And if you stay, because of me, and something should happen to you when you could be safe at home in America, I'm not sure I would ever forgive myself for it."

He stared up at Andrew and his face looked strained and torn. His eyes welled up. Andrew saw him look out towards the sea to hide them from him while he brought his knees to his chest and his chin to his knees for a moment, as if to steady himself and stop himself from crying.

Andrew reached over and took Thomas's hand but still said nothing. Their hands fit perfectly into each other's. Both their heads were rested up against the earth and faced out. Shimmering waves rocked in and out, illuminated by the moonlight. The sound of them crashing into the sand carried directly towards the two of them, and together with the wind, disturbed the otherwise silent night. Andrew was listening intently, trying to find words to say next when Thomas spoke.

"I love you, Andrew."

"I love you too."

It was late when Andrew got home. He and Thomas continued sitting for some time before they each started dozing off and realized it was time to go before they fell asleep. He was hyper and tingly as he tiptoed into his dark house and made his way quietly to his room. He shut the door and fell onto his bed. On the one hand, he and Thomas had resolved nothing. On the other, he thought to himself, didn't they just resolve everything?

He knew he wouldn't be able to fall asleep as he was, so he opened his computer and logged into Skype. Lindsay's mood with her brother ebbed and flowed with time. Some of their conversations were normal, as they'd been before Thomas entered the picture. She was again his big sister. He was the little brother. They joked about their parents and friends, coworkers, and whatever stupid story was in the news. He told her about adventures he was having – day or overnight trips to different parts of the country. She was jealous he spotted hippos on a boat trip up the River Gambia.

"Go to the zoo," he suggested snarkily.

He treaded a fine line during those conversations. Andrew tried not to bring up Thomas. His sister didn't ask about him directly either, and only made a vague inquiry checking up that *things were going okay*, probably, he figured, because she didn't want to be rude. But there were certain times when she couldn't resist and followed up her question asking what he and Thomas had done together lately. The answer, and she knew this, was always the same. They'd spent Friday evening at the bar, Andrew pretending to be a patron, followed by a walk up the beach where they sat together for a while. On Sunday they spent a bit of time together at the beach, occasionally going for a swim before playing soccer and pretending to be friends. And then again they walked up the beach and sat alone against the rocks. If Thomas came by to watch a movie, he'd also tell her that.

Lindsay used the monotony of their relationship to advance her displeasure. She was happy Andrew was finally beginning to fall for someone, a feeling Andrew believed was genuine. But shouldn't the way they had to conduct themselves indicate that the relationship couldn't work? *What are you expecting?*

But Andrew didn't care anymore after that night. He was in love and he could think of no one he felt he needed to tell more than his sister. And despite whatever disapproval she harbored towards his relationship with Thomas, she'd want to hear it too.

He was right. It was as if she knew what he was going to say, and as soon as he started telling her he loved Thomas and that they'd said I love you to each other, she broke out into the big-sister smile.

"I know you don't approve, Linds," he said, wanting to mollify whatever inclination she might've had to interject.

"That doesn't mean I can't be happy for you, though," she said in a way that made Andrew feel like she was in the room with him instead of his screen.

"Thank you," he said.

"Who said it first?"

"He did."

"And how did it happen? Was this just today?"

"Yeah, it was just now. It was nothing crazy," he said. "We were sitting on the beach where we usually do, having a conversation. There was a pause. He told me he loved me. I said it back," he continued, omitting the tense build up. "There was no dramatic announcement or anything, just an affirmation really," he added, slightly fudging the story to better suit her. "It was a relief to finally get it out."

"I'm sure. It was quick, too! Jeff took over a year to tell me he loved me."

"You were younger."

"True."

"And, I don't know, I think we both kind of knew it. Things are kind of getting a bit intense maybe."

"But Andrew, it's May already." She hesitated. "You're supposed to come home at the end of July."

"I know."

"Are you?"

He must've paused for a second too long.

"You're thinking of staying," she said, as if she was piecing together a puzzle.

"I'm not sure. I might want to." He could see her expression changing.

"Andrew, you can't move to Gambia and marry him."

"We can't move to the States and get married either."

"Touché. But you know what I mean."

"I do."

Andrew was also excited to share what happened with Alex. But when he walked out of his bedroom the next morning before he could say anything, Alex asked him if he wanted to take a trip for a week.

"Where?"

"I think Sierra Leone. I was talking to Liv about it. Before I go back to the U.S. at the end of the month. It would be a fun last hurrah. They have beaches that are supposed to be gorgeous, nicer than here. We could go, find cheap places to stay. Eat seafood, swim, have a good time." He presented it like a no-brainer.

"Okay. Sure," Andrew answered without giving it a thought. "Count me in."

"Great. Do you want to invite Thomas?"

"What?"

"Yeah. Bring Thomas. It might be a good escape. I mentioned the idea to Liv. At first she didn't think it was a good one, obviously, but now she's cool with it." Alex saw Andrew's skepticism. "You don't have to bring him, but no one's suspecting anything – we'd be a group of four, two Americas, a Brit, and a Gambian. We can say we all work together. And none of the shit that goes on here goes on there."

As Alex spoke Andrew was thinking. He wasn't convinced it made total sense. But maybe it made just enough sense.

19

Andrew sent Thomas a text the next day.

Alex and Liv are going to Sierra Leone. Want to go with?

Thomas normally responded quickly to Andrew's texts, but after half an hour there was still no answer. Like Andrew, he was initially hard-pressed to imagine how traveling together in public might be a good idea. He didn't know anything about Sierra Leone and its attitudes towards homosexuality, but doubted that anywhere in West Africa would offer them a welcoming environment. When he lay in bed or daydreamed behind the bar and imagined them somewhere else, it was never in Africa. They were always somewhere far away, where he knew he'd never have to look back over his shoulder. But when was that ever going to happen? This might be their only break from the tiresome routine of masking their relationship. Thomas would finally be away from his family's reach, even though they'd have to come up with an excuse. Surely they could come up with something? He started warming to the idea. An hour after Andrew sent his text he got a reply.

Yes. I would :-)

Thomas told his boss a relative had fallen ill and he needed to return with his family to their village. It wasn't an uncommon occurrence. His boss didn't think twice about it and gave him the week off. Thomas decided it would be best not to tell his family at all that he was leaving. They would leave on a Monday and come back Saturday. He would be back in time to visit his family the next day if he needed. After a few days he would email his brother pretending his mobile was broken to explain any ignored messages. It was the most believable idea he could come up with.

They planned to spend their first night in Freetown, the capital city, before moving to some of the nearby beaches. Sierra Leone's beaches were unspoiled, devoid of Gambia's mass-packaged tourism. If anyone asked, they would tell the truth – the four of them had become close friends in Gambia and decided to travel together before Alex returned home. It was highly unlikely, they thought, anyone would suspect two of them were an interracial same-sex couple. The concept was too foreign to register with anyone who wasn't already suspicious. And they were right. For five days Andrew and Thomas would be just two people. No one would know them or pay them any attention. For the first time they were gifted with true anonymity and the privacy that came with it.

When the plane door opened in Freetown, Andrew turned across the aisle to Thomas, put his head back against the headrest and let off a subtle smile. He turned back to Alex and Liv, and smiled at them. Across the aisle, the moment hit Thomas even harder. It was, like so much in his life, bittersweet. Just like the teenage boy on the back of a motorbike leaving the mud-trailed village, Thomas's pursuit of love meant being someplace else. He wondered to himself how far he'd have to go one day to truly be free, and if he'd ever succeed in getting there.

The four of them made their way from the city's island airport to the mainland via ferry. As they approached land, the horizon revealed a stark change from the flatness and empty space of Gambia. They sailed over dark blue water towards a lush, green mountainside, at whose base sat a city of tightly packed buildings, roofs of corrugated iron seemingly stuck together into one. The anticipation and excitement built as they grew nearer.

In Freetown they navigated jam-packed streets — motorbikes, cars, vans, pedestrians, and vendors competed for limited space and blurred the line between street and sidewalk. Carts and trays of DVDs, sunglasses, and currency traders popped up everywhere, creating a zig-zag effect for those trying to get by. Music blared, like in Gambia it was local Afro hip hop, but here it competed with constant car horns enhancing an already dizzying pace of life. Together, it was all simultaneously disorienting, exhausting, and overwhelming. But for Thomas, it was also liberating. The pace and congestion of life on the streets swallowed them up and hid them.

Crawling through the Freetown traffic, Thomas was amazed at the differences between the Gambian capital and Freetown. The sheer volume got to him, never-ending cars made driving and crossing roads potentially treacherous. Making one's way on foot required strong shoulders to withstand the inevitable brush ups with people pushing through the other way. The buildings framing this picture were worn and pockmarked. Fifteen years after Sierra Leone's civil war ended, Freetown still bore the mark of fresh wounds. Selfishly, Thomas was relieved. As underdeveloped as he thought his home was, the chaos around him reassured him it was not as exceptional as he once believed.

They arrived at their small guesthouse without incident. The middle-aged woman behind the broken-down desk didn't flinch as she reached for a room key hanging from the wall before handing it to Thomas. The four of them walked up two flights of creaking stairs and parted ways down a narrow, poorly lit hallway. Thomas and Andrew found their room silently. Thomas opened the door and Andrew followed him in before he closed it, sliding the deadbolt through. The noise from the street, still present, slowly receded as they stood motionless, surveying pale and mismatched furnishings and upholstery, slightly dusty, giving the room a distinct smell of neglect. Andrew moved closer to Thomas and paused for a brief second before they embraced and fell on top of one another on one of the room's two beds.

"I'm so happy we're here."

"Me too."

If they were headed to Sierra Leone's beaches for quiet and seclusion, their night in Freetown made up for all the nights out in public that Gambia had deprived them from enjoying together. They planned to explore the slew of seaside bars popular with foreigners and locals alike and dressed up for the occasion. Andrew had never seen much of Thomas's wardrobe – his hotel uniform, beach clothes, and what little he wore around the house. But tonight, for Andrew, Thomas picked an outfit. He brought his best brown leather shoes that he polished before they left. He wore a pair of white jeans that hugged his thighs and butt just enough to make Andrew turn his head as he got dressed. He took out a yellow button-down shirt and put it on, leaving the bottom and top two buttons open. It fit him perfectly. At the bottom, where his shirt split apart, his belt buckle reflected in the light. While putting on a silver wristwatch he looked up at Andrew and smiled. He looked amazing.

The night was everything they wanted: an ordinary experience experienced extraordinarily. They arrived at a restaurant on the beach's edge and got a table for four on a patio under an umbrella. In the distance through the moonlight, you could see the surf crashing into the shore much more ferociously than it did in Gambia. The wind too was stronger and it gave the night a heightened sense of energy. The sky above was starlit. Colorful Christmas lights hung from the railings around connecting patio lanterns. The bar blasted last year's top 40.

They ordered beer, lobster, crab, and fresh snapper. And french fries.

"Cheers," Alex said, raising his beer to the middle of the table.

"Cheers," everyone followed.

It was the first time Andrew and Thomas had eaten together in public. At times during the meal they'd look at each other in acknowledgment. Neither had to say anything.

After dinner they made their way to an open air bar up the beach overflowing with patrons. Liv bought a round of drinks while the others went to stake out a table.

"What is it?" Thomas asked as she handed it to him.

"Just drink and enjoy," she said over the music, and then raised her glass up to him waiting for a clink. He obliged.

Andrew went to get another round as they sat at the table talking no differently than people seated at other tables. By the time

Alex came back with the third round, they ditched the table and found themselves on a dance floor, teeming with an enthusiastic crowd of young, well-groomed dancers. There were couples and big groups of all nationalities and ethnicities. Everyone seemed to blend into one. It was perfect.

They walked towards the dance floor as a group of four. For the first part of the night they danced mostly together. But there were also times when it was clear, at least to Alex and Liv, that Andrew and Thomas were dancing only with each other. Andrew wasn't a very good dancer. His body seemed incapable of moving on its own volition and he was overly reliant on waving one arm up and down while bending slightly at the knees. Thomas, however, was an excellent dancer, moving rhythmically in sync with each beat. The way he bent his knees, swayed his hips, and rolled his upper body – each separately or all together – gave the impression of someone perfectly comfortable and secure. Because his clothes were so fitted, you could see how his body curved and moved in perfect unison.

While Andrew struggled to keep up, he found himself fixated by Thomas. He'd never seen him that way, that loose. Alex and Liv also noticed. There was something in how he was moving, a satisfaction. It was more than just dancing. Normally restrained and subtle in his movement, he was now without any inhibition. He displayed a sense of pride they had never seen him display so fiercely. From the way he commanded their small portion of the dance floor they could see he knew it too. He alternated between looking at them with penetrating eye contact and a bright smile, and closing his eyes with a look of contentment, smiling seductively, at himself or at Andrew.

Under the clear night sky, Thomas moved in and out of the shadows amid the weak light from the patio lanterns that gently illuminated the dance floor. As the night wore on and the music enveloped him, and his shirt bonded more closely to his wet skin, he refused to grow tired. He kept dancing as each song brought a new opportunity for self-affirmation. Over time his regard for the others around him began to recede. He was overcome. By the music. By the place. By the experience. Each time he opened his eyes he saw Andrew, with Alex and Liv, dancing around him. Sometimes he saw their mouths move. But he could only hear the music. Somewhere else, transported by a feeling or a purpose that only he knew, he was a dancing silhouette. He stayed that way the whole night.

It was nearly three in the morning when they got back to the guesthouse. Through the darkness, they raced through Freetown's cracked and empty streets in a semi-functional taxi – a temperamental clutch, dashboard wiring system on full display, and missing side panels. Alex was in the front. Andrew sat in the back between Thomas and Liv. There wasn't much speaking and Thomas spent most of the ride looking out of the window as they drove along the coast and up into the deserted city center. At one point he looked over at Andrew and pushed his leg up against his, before turning back to face outside.

In bed that night, it was like Thomas kept dancing. Whatever was unleashed within him kept churning within his body, pushing it in ways he and Andrew hadn't experienced. Thomas let it overtake him, and could see and feel that Andrew did the same as they fell into one another, gliding off each other's sweat, moved to make sounds they made every effort to keep suppressed. Thomas was in complete control. With confidence and vigor he pushed Andrew away from him and pulled him back into him. His hands channeled all his strength, moving Andrew easily around on the bed, turning him from front to back. With each thrust and gyration, Thomas's muscles flexed more and more, bulging from beneath his skin. Each deep breath he took sucked up more of the room's warm, stale air. His sweat became thicker, falling in slow drips onto Andrew, who lay on his back. Thomas stood over him at the edge of the bed. His face turned up towards the ceiling as he closed his eyes. The intensity of his movements forced his eyes to close tighter and tighter, sending wrinkles across the side of his face from his eyes and up his brow as his nose inhaled whatever oxygen it could find.

His movements were so deliberate and hurried that they began to propel themselves on their own. He found himself moving without a sense of place, losing himself in the moment, and for the second time that night he had gone elsewhere. But this time there was no music, no full night sky or friendly breeze to uplift him. In the emptiness and silence of their room, it wasn't the same liberating release he experienced on the dance floor. It was a sad, embittered one. Life hadn't been fair to him and he wasn't going to take it anymore. Transported against his will, he saw scenes of his life and everyone and everything that should have prevented him from reaching this point. As each tableau flashed through his mind, visions of rejection and looks of revulsion, he grew more and more determined, ready and wanting the confrontation he'd always been too afraid to have. It was the confrontation where he proclaimed, *I am here, and this is who I am.* He wanted it more and more. He wanted it so badly that there, fucking his boyfriend in that unfamiliar hotel room in that unfamiliar country, for the first time in his life, he became defiant.

Andrew looked up at Thomas as he felt his hands digging into his hips in ways he'd not known. His body moved swiftly and intently, but his head was still. Andrew saw from Thomas's tightly scrunched face that he was concentrating forcefully on something else. He wasn't bothered. Andrew had sensed it was a night of conflicting emotions for Thomas. But as he lay on his back wanting to know what was going through his boyfriend's mind, he thought Thomas's eyes seemed moist, and he wasn't sure if the sweat streaming down his face was in fact sweat.

Thomas kept going, and the harder he went the more he looked to be fighting an urge to let his tears flow. But he wouldn't stop. He couldn't. He was fighting with himself against his past. The moment he stopped, the past would win. And he was resolute in his determination not to let that happen. Not any longer. Andrew reached up from his back to his hips where Thomas's hands were, as if to let him know that whatever it was, it was okay. He took Thomas's hands firmly in his and squeezed, forcing Thomas to loosen his grip as he acknowledged him and looked down. When Thomas opened his eyes and saw Andrew looking up at him he smiled the way one does when crying, acknowledging the contradiction. And it was in that moment, as Thomas smiled at the person he loved, and as that person looked back up into him with an expression that said, *it's okay*, that Thomas let go and was finally released.

When they woke up the next morning the weight of the night had lifted. Looking at each other, vision still fuzzy from sleep, they inched their heads closer together until their foreheads touched. They lay like that for a few minutes not saying anything, not needing to say anything, as the sunlight poked through the edges of the curtains and each took in the day's softer, fresher air.

20

THERE WERE SEVERAL beaches only a short drive from Freetown. All looked idyllic from the pictures. And with the dry season approaching its end, the number of tourists would be low. Their first stop was a beach called River Number 2. They hired a 4x4 to drive them from Freetown. The drive, on a road largely under construction and with potholes you could confuse for trenches, was, putting it mildly, unpleasant. The jeep lacked air conditioning and it was too hot to keep the windows up but too dusty to keep them down. Driving out from Freetown's hodgepodge of concrete, the land quickly gave way to the familiar contrast of reddish West-African earth and lush, deep green growing from within it. To their right they caught glimpses of the sea. To the left the earth rose up into the same hills and mountains they first saw from the ferry. When the jeep finally slowed and turned off into a flat dirt parking lot, there were no other vehicles.

"It's so empty," said Liv, hearing nothing but the wind and the sea.

"Not many tourists now. Most foreigners who work only come on weekends," said their driver. "No problem finding places to stay."

It was their own private paradise, and they couldn't believe their eyes. They walked from the car through a narrow path until it ended. Water of shifting shades of blue before them, delicate white sand to the left and right as far as the eye could see, and at their backs stood the tall palm trees keeping watch, the rolling green hills and mountains behind them.

They spent the next four days carefree – playing cards and frisbee, trying not to toss the frisbee too far into the sea, and collecting wood to build a fire at night. Everything else was taken care of for them. Their guesthouse even had its own lobster traps set up, and they all watched as Thomas repeatedly abandoned his fork to pry the meat out with his fingers. The first night the owner of the guesthouse insisted they all try the local palm wine, which they did. Alex said it tasted like something that would be illegal in the U.S. The guesthouse owner laughed at them the following morning as they sat nursing headaches from drinking too much of it.

Andrew and Thomas acted without any of the worries that hung over them each minute they spent on Gambia's beaches. They explored the beach, discovering its lagoon, swam, and just lay on the sand doing nothing. It was fun being unsupervised.

"Look at Thomas," Liv said to Alex and Andrew on their second day.

The two of them turned up from their card game. Thomas was running into the heavy surf head on, diving into its crescendo, floating up on his back to let the waves carry him to shore, and then doing it all again. Each time he hit the sand he did so with an excited expression on his face.

They all giggled each time he came crashing in with the waves. As his focus shifted from the waves, Thomas saw they were watching him. He wiped the salt and sand from his face before exclaiming. "You should all come and try it. There are no waves in Gambia where you can do this." He looked back out to the sea as another wave crashed at his feet before looking back at the three of them to re-emphasize his point, only to dart back into the water.

"You'll miss him," Liv said as Andrew sat and stared out, admiring.

"Huh," he remarked, snapping out of his stare.

"I said you'll miss him when you leave."

"I know," he said, before adding quickly, "but I think I might come back after the summer for another year."

"Really?" asked Alex.

"Yeah."

Andrew explained how he'd begun to appreciate the life he'd carved out for himself in Gambia. Just as he had spoken about it with his sister, he explained how comfortable he'd gotten with his job and the positive feedback he was getting from Mr. Jalloh. He said he could always reapply to teacher's college, and now with his experiences abroad, he wasn't worried about getting in. He also liked not having to think about coming out to his family and friends back home.

"It's not that I'm afraid to do it like I was before. It's more that I'm now comfortable being able to be who I am, and I don't feel like rushing back to have to confront and deal with that all over again," he shared.

But the real reason, he told them, was Thomas. "We love each other. And I don't want to leave him now. At least not yet."

"Have you told him?" Alex asked.

"Yeah. It didn't go like I planned, though."

"Why?"

"He's nervous for me. For us. That it's starting to get a bit more uncertain with the whole situation. The newspaper report and arrest really threw him off."

"Isn't that a good thing? You can't ignore what's been going on," Liv declared. "They arrested someone."

"You don't think I should stay?"

"I think you have to be very careful you don't become too comfortable."

"You didn't answer my question," he pressed her.

"It's not for me to answer. First off," she said, turning towards Alex and changing to a mocking tone, "*my* boyfriend's not staying, is he? Second, I'm not going to tell you what to do. But I will say that if you did stay, I would be concerned for your safety. It's becoming unpredictable. Is it really worth the risk?"

Andrew hated that question. He didn't think it had a right answer.

Liv spoke with such certainty. Andrew looked over to Alex. He wanted Alex to tell him that Liv was being her usual self, overly cautious and worried. But instead, and to his surprise, Alex let Andrew know he thought Liv was being sensible.

"Think of what could happen," he said.

"What could happen?" Thomas asked, standing over them, dripping wet, panting from his long fight with the ocean.

They all looked up at him with blank faces before Alex saved them.

"I told Liv I wanted to learn how they climb the palm trees to get the palm wine and she thought I was serious."

Thomas laughed and told Alex he wouldn't be able to climb five feet off the ground.

"And you would?" Alex challenged Thomas.

"It was never my idea."

Since most of their time was spent as a group or as couples, Andrew never did have a chance to finish his conversation with Alex and Liv. But he valued their opinions the most, probably even more than Thomas's on something like this. What bothered him was that they might be right. Thomas too. And his sister. All of them might be right. He still refused to concede it, but he couldn't ignore that everyone he trusted was skeptical. But for the rest of the trip, he tried to block it out of his mind.

The trip became one of those experiences that forever conjures up nostalgia. During their second night, it was discovered Thomas had never been buried in the sand, which Alex said was a rite of passage for any child who'd ever played on a beach. Thomas convinced them to hold off on doing it at that moment, but shortly after breakfast on day three, he obliged and lay down on the beach as the three of them took pleasure in covering him from neck to toe. When he was sufficiently covered and Alex found leaves to place on his private area, the three of them sat on top of him while the guesthouse owner took a picture. In the photo, everyone is laughing hysterically because as soon as they were all sitting Thomas said he needed to pee.

During the evenings, after they emerged from a short nap, they sat around sand-stained white plastic tables with bottles of Star, Sierra Leone's ubiquitous beer. Alex had brought speakers so they could listen to music, but they'd all become so enamored with the country's home grown music, a blend of R&B and hip hop constantly playing from the guesthouse kitchen, that the speakers never left his room. They spoke and drank late into the night and after dinner moved to the sand where they built a fire. Leaning back on their hands, faces illuminated by the crackling flames, they alternated between making fun of each other, telling random stories, or sitting silently, looking out or up. There was nothing amazing about any of it. They were just four people, three Westerners and one Gambian. No one saw anything wrong with it.

And so proceeded four days. Early on there was the idea of moving at some point to another beach, even more secluded and only reachable by a small dingy boat, but, contently lethargic, they all opted to stay put.

On the last morning, Andrew and Thomas took a walk together. They had to leave for Freetown after lunch to catch the ferry for the airport. Their steps had a lightness to them, infused with the placidity of their time away. But you could also mistake it for tiptoeing. As the minutes advanced, knowing their bags were packed and waiting to be whisked off to the airport, the apprehension started creeping back. The deserted beach before them was a natural facilitator for introspection, and each walked quietly.

They roamed far up from their guesthouse, which was no longer in sight, and reached a point where they could see nothing but the natural world. It was their own piece of *terra nullius*. Standing next to each other without touching, looking out into the sea, with Africa at their backs, Andrew went to speak but nothing came out. He sniffled and quickly wiped at the tear forming in his eye, hoping he hid it from Thomas.

"I don't know what to do," he said finally. "I've never been this confused."

The goodbye at the Banjul airport was strained and offered a difficult re-initiation into their new setting. Because they didn't want to be seen traveling together, from the minute they arrived at the gate to board their flight back to Gambia, Thomas became a stranger to the three of them. Andrew had given him enough dalasis to cover a taxi to a point where he could catch a minibus or 7-7 to get home. Thomas said it would be too unusual for him to arrive home in a taxi and he didn't want any of his neighbors growing suspicious. Andrew and Thomas kept turning to each other on the plane, but to be safe, did so in a way that could be confused with looking around for the sake of looking around. On the bus to the terminal in Banjul they stood next to each other but didn't speak. Thomas turned his mobile back on and saw three texts from his brother. They were all sent before Thomas had emailed him to say his phone had broken.

Coming Sunday?

??

Where r u?

He looked back up at Andrew, his eyes looking desperate as a sunken feeling took over his insides. The fairy tale was over.

The bus stopped abruptly, jolting Thomas as he reached for Andrew's arm to steady himself before quickly letting go and muttering *excuse me*. Once in the terminal building, they kept looking at each other in the immigration lines. But Thomas was in a line for Gambian nationals that moved much quicker, so he passed through before them. When he walked into the main hall he gave a quick glance back over his shoulder before disappearing into the terminal. Still in line, waiting with Alex and Liv, Andrew felt his phone vibrate in his pocket and took it out just enough to read the text.

I had a fun time with u. Everything will work out. You'll see :-)

Part Three

21

IT WAS DARK when Abdou finally arrived home. Thankfully he sat in the front seat of the 7-7 so the other passengers didn't have an opportunity to recognize him – something that was unfortunately happening with greater frequency. He kept close watch over his surroundings as he walked from the car into his neighborhood. Streets and walks that once brought the comfort of familiarity now made him tense. He'd never noticed how poorly lit they were; how many windows of parked cars he couldn't see into. Clutching his torn briefcase – he wasn't going to leave any important files at his unguarded office – he made his way briskly down the streets with his head down discreetly shifting his eyes, *left, up, right, left, up, right.* He swore the walk seemed to get longer and longer each night.

He sighed out as he arrived at his house and offered a *good evening, thank you* to the police officer begrudgingly keeping guard outside his gate. He only sought protection recently, one evening after he found the word TRAITOR painted on his home's front gate. After cleaning it off, he implored the authorities that he had two young children and was only seeking to uphold the country's constitutional guarantees of due process. Reluctantly, the police agreed to place a guard outside his home. None of the three officers who rotated the watch had been particularly friendly. It was obvious they didn't want to be there and resented the assignment. Still, he was grateful for their presence and hoped he made his appreciation known.

As the gate finally creaked closed and he retreated into the safety of his own compound, he looked around at his surroundings. One of his neighbors peered down at him through her window. Their eyes met briefly before he turned away and made for the front door.

Walking through the door, he could see his wife Manima cleaning in the kitchen. The house was quiet. Their children would have been asleep. The past several weeks he'd seen much less of them on account of his late hours. Manima turned to face him as he put his briefcase down on their sofa.

"How are you?" she asked, continuing to dry whatever was in her hands.

"I'm fine. How are you?"

"Fine."

"The children?"

"Sleeping."

He nodded and stood while savoring the luxury of time. It was night. Morning wasn't until tomorrow. He exhaled.

At the beginning of it all, Manima would have also asked how Thomas and Andrew were doing, but that wasn't a question that jumped from her lips as quickly. She cared about them, was incensed and embarrassed by the injustice of it all, and still prepared extra food for them when Abdou went to visit, but a part of her eagerly waited to put this all behind them and pick up the pieces and move on. Nervous and scared for her husband, she was secretly relieved the trial was finally starting.

The fallout from defending Thomas and Andrew put strains on their marriage. He discussed the case with Manima before agreeing to it and she never tried to convince him not to take it. Even so, they both knew that whatever happened, it would change things. From the minute word got out he was defending them he'd be labeled a gay sympathizer, or suspected of being gay himself. She would be pitied for being married to such a weak man, afraid to stand up for real values and African masculinity. Friends and neighbors would castigate her for standing by him. Their children too, at least the older one who was seven, would be taunted at school, probably at the instruction of the other children's parents. And then there was his law practice. How many of his clients would stay with him and risk whatever adverse consequences might befall their legal matters by being associated with a lawyer who defended gays? Abdou and Manima didn't need the attention. It would be impossible for the pressure not to get to them.

But can I really say no, Manima? It was rhetorical.

"Why you?" she asked him. "Or why don't you ask Ebrima to also join you?" she added. "That way you're not standing there alone."

"Ebrima wouldn't do it," Abdou responded while shaking his head. "He would be upset if I even asked him, that I would put him in a position where he would have to refuse me."

In the silence they could each see that the other was thinking.

"Most people who might do it would only do it at a very basic level. Enough only to go through the process," he told her.

"But others *would* do it, and some would do it properly... so why must it be you, Abdou?"

"Because I'm the one who's been asked, Manima," he said as they shared a look they'd shared so many times before. It was a look of trust, in each other.

"What should I tell our children if they ask why people are ridiculing their father?"

"That I am a good lawyer," he answered her matter-of-factly. Smiling mischievously, he added, "who hopes he's not making a stupid decision."

Manima smiled back, but it failed to hide the melancholy. "Just do your job, and do it well. But that's all. You have a family to take care of."

"I know."

Abdou had his picture in the newspaper and on television when it was disclosed he was representing them. THE GAYS' LAWYER ran one headline on a day he tried not to venture out in public.

When Thomas thanked him for spending so much time on their case *at the expense of all your other clients*, Abdou omitted the fact that he had more time to work on their case because most of his existing clients had left him. In relaying that his legal practice was strong, he also failed to mention that his law firm kicked him out once he took up the case. They supported his decision, they wanted him to know, but as the exodus of clients demonstrated, the reputational damage was just too great. *It would be best, for everyone, if you went your own way*, the senior partner told him, the same senior partner who had recruited and mentored him after his graduation. *This way you can focus more on these types of cases.*

As for his wife, besides being the laughing stock of the neighborhood, she was also taunted at work. As a manager for one of the country's telecom companies, Manima once held the respect of her colleagues and the admiration of her supervisors. Not any longer. She was the wife of *the gay lawyer.* How could they trust her? *She must support him.*

Gossiping eyes followed as she walked to her desk each morning, or with her children in the neighborhood. She told Abdou that other parents were telling their children to stay away from theirs. *It will pass, it will pass,* Abdou kept telling her. But it didn't pass.

Even with all the challenges – it became far more trying and taxing than either of them imagined – neither regretted it. He was doing the right thing. *They deserve to have their rights defended in court,* he insisted to her. *The whole legal profession has gone silent on this, the entire defense bar,* he lamented. Manima offered a more human perspective – it wasn't only about laws. *It's about the type of people we are as a country, about how we treat each other.*

"We made the right decision, Manima," he said to her that night, ready to face the uncertain road ahead.

"I know," she said. "Are you ready for tomorrow?" she asked him gently.

"As much as I can be." His answer confirmed that while he was confident in his decision to take the case, he was less confident about its outcome.

He sat down at the kitchen table slightly deflated. Manima put a plate of food in front of him and he began eating it without stopping to look at what it might be. She imagined it was the only thing he ate since leaving in the morning. She rubbed her hand on his back before sitting down.

"Are you sure you don't want me to be there tomorrow?"

"No," he said. "I don't want you there. It will be too uncomfortable if it's discovered that my wife is present," he spoke resolutely, before becoming more lighthearted, "and you must go to your job, Madam Breadwinner. After this is done I'll be on track for early retirement." Small humor was how he coped.

Manima knew there was a decent enough chance he was right.

"And how are they?" she asked after giving Abdou time to eat.

"Tired," he answered, scraping the last bits of rice from his plate.

"And their mental state?"

"I honestly don't know." They hadn't given up, he told her. And certainly neither had he. "But it's different from the first time I met them. The disbelief that this is happening is gone. They're very aware of what's going on and what it all means. There are no illusions. Both of them, I think, are realistic. And it's hard to see how each is coping with it or to even imagine that they can."

"Are they scared?"

He looked at her with an air of contemplation. Just a few hours earlier he asked them the same question.

Abdou usually shied away from inquiring about Andrew and Thomas's emotional states. Andrew noticed how Abdou focused his personal questions on the physical – had their mistreatment ended, were they hungry, did they have enough space in their respective cells? Did they have any medical concerns? But he didn't directly ask how they were feeling. It wasn't insensitive; it just took some getting used to. Andrew had to remind himself that Abdou was his lawyer, not his psychologist, and was probably ill-equipped to delve into the range of emotional issues he and Thomas were each confronting. Instead, Andrew began to see Abdou's concern for their well-being coming across through his work ethic and unwavering commitment to afford them a comprehensive defense.

But earlier that afternoon, sitting across a rusted metal table in an impossibly small and suffocating prison interview room, Abdou looked at his two clients. They had already been together for an hour to go over some final case details. All three of them knew that any chance to wrestle them out of their presumed fates rested with him. In that moment, Abdou paused, turning back to his notes before bringing his gaze up to them.

"Are you scared?"

The question caught Andrew off guard. The silence from Thomas suggested he felt the same. Neither of them said anything immediately. Andrew was thinking of how to answer. The past month had been horrible for him, hell. He knew the same went for Thomas. Separated almost instantly and only infrequently brought together outside of Abdou's visits, what scared him most was the thought of facing whatever was to come alone. He'd burned through so much of his strength already he wasn't sure he'd have enough left. On top of it, there was the fear that came from not being there for Thomas, of leaving the person he loved to fend for himself when he knew Thomas's experience had been so much more horrific. It's what scared him most of all – that Thomas wouldn't be able to handle it, and he wouldn't be there for him when it happened. But Andrew was too afraid to say it. He didn't want to use these moments to worry Thomas with things they already knew, and knew they couldn't change. Deliberately or not, Thomas seemed to have adopted the same approach. Andrew sensed some thoughts between them went unspoken.

"Of course," Andrew spoke first. "Who wouldn't be?"

Thomas's expression showed no sign of disagreement.

In the silence, Abdou appeared to be searching for words of comfort. None came out immediately when Thomas started speaking.

"The trick is not to let them see it. In here, with you, with each other, we can be scared. We can admit we are fearful of them and of what they might do to us. But tomorrow, when we face them, we cannot let them see it. Otherwise they will only see us as trembling before them, either in shame, to beg forgiveness, or because of the punishment we know is coming." Thomas remained calm as he spoke. "It's important they do not see that side. It's what they want to see, because if they do, it will be easier for them not to see how behind our trembling is a real person, no different than they are."

Abdou agreed with Thomas's suggestion, adding, "even if it is difficult, don't give them what they want."

He then turned to Andrew and asked if Maya had seen him that morning. She had. The Gambian government's position towards Andrew's status as an American was unsympathetic. It had denied him consular assistance for the first week of his detention until he was formally charged, and thereafter only allowed Maya to have intermittent access to check up on him. She hadn't been completely transparent about every detail concerning the embassy's efforts to get him released, but from what she had told him, he knew their efforts had not made much progress.

"And she'll be there tomorrow?"

"Yes. She said she'll be there every day."

"And she and your parents have each other's mobile numbers?"

"Yes. And you too?"

"Yes, I have their mobile numbers, and they called me this morning with their hotel contact after they landed. I've promised to call them after each day's hearing."

Andrew's parents were in Senegal, the country next door.

Maya followed Andrew's suggestion and got a hold of his father at work. It would afford his father more time to process what had happened before having to confront Andrew's mother, whose control over her emotions Andrew doubted. Maya expected Andrew's father to respond with shock and disbelief. It would have already been a sensory overload to find out Andrew was gay or that he was arrested in a foreign country. The fact that he was arrested *for* being gay proved, at first, too much. Andrew's father grew angry at Maya and accused her of making everything up.

"Who are you? And what kind of nonsense are you trying to get me to believe?" he demanded to know. His son wasn't gay, and what kind of a country criminalized that stuff anyway. He accused Maya of playing a practical joke on him and of not working for the U.S. government. "You're going to have to take your very unfunny lies somewhere else. I don't know what my son may or may not have done to you, but this isn't making any sense."

"Are you in front of a computer, sir?" she asked calmly. After he replied he was, she asked if he could search for the U.S. Embassy in Banjul's website. He did. She asked him if he wanted to call the phone number listed where she would be waiting for him. He did. When she answered his heart sank.

It still sounded ridiculous, though. Maybe it was a mix-up, something that would soon be clarified.

"I don't think this is going to go away quickly, sir."

"What the hell is having carnal knowledge against the, against the what?"

"The order of nature," Maya said, her tone businesslike.

"Is that even a real crime?"

"It is in The Gambia. And one they take very seriously, sir. It carries a maximum punishment of fourteen years in prison."

"Fourteen years?" he asked incredulously.

"Yes, I'm afraid. Andrew's not in a good situation."

He asked her what she was doing to help him as he did his best to focus on the fact that his son was locked up in some African prison. *If* in fact he turned out to be gay, they could worry about it later.

"We continue to monitor the situation to ensure he's being properly cared for by the authorities while also pressing for his release."

Andrew's father didn't appreciate the diplomatic cloak to her language. *"Is he okay and when will you get him out of there?"* he yelled into the phone.

It was the next answer that finally forced him to grasp the gravity of the situation. Maya told him that Andrew was physically fine, and that she and the embassy staff would ensure that it stayed that way. But as to the second question, "that's not so simple. In fact, with this government, we're going to have to approach it tactfully."

"When?" he wondered sternly. "A day or two?"

"I don't know. It could take a while."

While Andrew was not there to see what happened next, he cried gently as Maya told him. His father immediately called Lindsay and told her to meet him at home. He sat her and his wife down and plainly told them what had happened. Andrew, their Andrew, was apparently in a romantic relationship with a man in Gambia. The country had criminal laws against homosexuality, and they had been arrested and charged. When Andrew's mother, whose emotions did stay under control, looked confused, Lindsay immediately offered up confirmation.

"It's true. I knew about the relationship." Both her parents looked at her in disbelief.

"*Really, you knew?* And you didn't tell us?" their mother asked.

"Yes," she answered. "He wanted to tell you himself when he got back."

It didn't matter, their father said.

"Now's not the time to go down that road. We can talk about everything later. We have to go get him."

And that's what they tried to do.

Maya didn't discourage them from flying to Gambia. She knew better than to try and reason with parental love. It was only natural for them to want to be as close to Andrew as possible and see for themselves that he was okay, even if they weren't thinking through the situation enough to realize there was little, if anything, they could accomplish by being there. She did warn them, however, there was a chance they would be denied entry into the country.

"The government approaches anti-homosexuality laws seriously. I wouldn't put it past them to refuse entry to individuals they know are coming to somehow play a role contesting those laws."

She was right. When the three of them anxiously stepped off the plane in Banjul and went up to the immigration desk, trying to keep their anger in check, they were told they were not welcome in the country. The government, it appeared, had blacklisted their names. They were given no official explanation and were dealt with harshly by the staff at the airport before being put back on their plane, which was returning to Dakar. They stayed there in a hotel for five days, even trying to unsuccessfully cross into Gambia by land where they thought they'd have better luck. When they finally accepted being in Senegal wasn't ameliorating Andrew's situation, they flew home, followed Maya's suggestion, and began meeting with members of the government and media, whoever would see them. His parents, his same parents who had worked so hard their whole adult lives to cultivate a life and image for themselves different from what Andrew wanted for himself, were now on television screens and newspapers, and in offices and on the phone with anyone who would listen to them, demanding that their gay son arrested for being in a relationship with an African man be freed.

Knowing that the trial, its onset or conclusion, presented a slim chance of Andrew's release, they both flew back to Senegal the weekend before it was slated to begin. Senegal was the first stop back to the U.S. for most travelers leaving Gambia. If Andrew was let go, it was surely where he'd be sent. They wanted to be there if that happened.

"And did you finally reach my family?" Thomas asked Abdou. His voice was tentative, afraid of the answer.

"Not really."

"You weren't able to speak to anyone?"

Abdou looked hesitant. "I spoke to your brother, Sheriff," he said. "He wanted me to tell you it would be difficult for him and your parents to attend the trial. Work for everyone is very busy now."

"Is that what he told you? Exactly?" he asked, knowing Abdou was lying to him.

"Yes, that is what he told me," Abdou answered, not breaking his eyes from Thomas's. "He said they are monitoring events closely."

This much, Thomas assumed was true.

In actuality, Abdou had been much more persistent with Thomas's family than he let on. He tried calling John, Grace, and Sheriff. Upon introducing himself to John and Sheriff, they immediately made it known they wanted nothing to do with him or Thomas, and hung up. His father threatened Abdou if he called again.

Refusing to give up so easily, Abdou tracked down Sheriff, going to the area of town he worked in to seek him out. It was a narrow street, with wires crisscrossing overhead, siphoning power from paying buildings to the body shops, each demarcated with a hand-painted sign. The noises of buzzing tools filled the air; the street was strewn with rubbish. Walking past the rows of cluttered and greasy auto repair stalls, workers poorly protected – if at all – from the sparks their tools sent flying, he found a man sitting behind a desk with a stack of papers who bore a faint resemblance to Thomas. Abdou exchanged a warm greeting with this man, even calling him brother.

"Yes, how can I help you," Sheriff responded, looking up at the smartly dressed man before him.

When Abdou didn't immediately respond, Sheriff's brow furrowed, making Abdou nervous.

"Mister Sheriff," he said, "we spoke briefly on the phone. I am Abdou, Thomas's lawyer."

Sheriff rose from behind the desk. He was much taller and bigger than Abdou and extended out his broad shoulders, reinforcing his size. He checked and saw there was no one else near them.

"I said already I do not want to talk to you, and I have nothing to say to that man." Sheriff's tone was sarcastic when he called his brother a man. He chastised Abdou for defending him saying people like *that man* don't deserve any protection. Leaning over, placing his hands on the end of the desk, Sheriff brought his angry face closer to Abdou and stared at him sternly. Again he glanced from side to side. Leaning even closer to Abdou, he whispered fiercely. *You tell that sick man he's finished to us.*

Abdou swallowed deeply, nodded his head, said nothing, and backed away. He hurried down the narrow street, seeking to be out in the open, where the hostility was less suffocating. When the sunshine finally hit his face, he stopped and took it in for a second. He thought of his brother, and of his two children. Siblings.

"What about my mother?" Thomas asked Abdou. "Did you speak to my mother, Abdou? She also said she is not coming? Or has no message?"

Thomas's expression was pained. He knew his mother's predicament. First off, like his father and brother, Thomas had no illusions about what his mother's thoughts on homosexuality were. He also knew she would be powerless to try and influence John and Sheriff's disgust and disapproval, which he correctly predicted would lead to disownership. Still, if anyone was going to react differently, less harshly, it would be her. She had spent his whole childhood trying to protect him from life's harshness. Surely that maternal instinct, the shared bond of the strongest kind between mother and son, could not instantly and completely evaporate. A part of him refused to believe his mother could so easily shut her eyes and her mind to the fact that he was, after everything, still her son.

"I never spoke to her," Abdou said, his eyes projecting sympathy.

It was somewhat true. When Abdou called the shop where Grace worked as a seamstress, he expected her to hang up as soon as she learned who he was. Instead, Grace went silent, but she didn't hang up the phone. So Abdou spoke, assuming she was listening.

"I am your son Thomas's lawyer," he told her. "His situation is quite serious, as I'm sure you are aware. I have little hope this matter will resolve itself or disappear without going to trial, something you probably wish would not happen. For this I am sorry; I am sorry about what this has meant for your family. If I am being honest with you, it has also been difficult for me too, and also my family." He paused, waiting to see if she would say anything.

Silence.

"But, Mrs. Sow, it has not deterred me from doing my job, from providing Thomas with the defense he is entitled to under our laws. Even though now you might be confused, or angry with him for behaving how they say he has, let me assure you that just as any other Gambian, he deserves to have his case defended, and this is what I am doing.

"I know he is feeling quite alone. You don't have to now, but maybe, perchance, if you ever wanted to visit with him, or pass along a message or a package of sorts for him, I would facilitate this. It would make him feel less alone to know he is being thought of."

Abdou generally avoided getting overly personal with clients and their families. Worried he might be straying too far, and not wanting to take advantage of Grace's attention, he concluded his monologue.

"I do not know your son that well, Mrs. Sow. But I have come to know him a little bit." Abdou hesitated slightly. "Despite what he is accused of, he is still a good man, a decent person." He exhaled as if to signal he was finished. He heard a crackle on the other end of the phone before the line went dead.

Abdou looked across the table at Thomas. He moved his eyes and furrowed his brow. He looked like he was thinking of what to say.

"I did call your mother. She was silent. It was difficult for her to speak. I told her you are safe and that you are strong. That we are defending the charges vigorously. I believe this would have brought her some relief."

Thomas sighed. "Good."

Before getting up to leave his clients, Abdou reminded Thomas and Andrew about how the trial would unfold. It would last for five days. "Maybe six if there are delays, but they'll prefer to finish in one week." The state's case will take the first three days, the first morning for opening statements and then the witnesses for two days beginning the same afternoon. Abdou would start calling their witnesses on the afternoon of the third day. He would first begin with a short opening statement responding to the government's case.

"On the fifth day we will have closing submissions before the judge retires to deliberate." Deliberation, he said, was unpredictable.

"Sometimes only a few hours, other times several days." He told them he expected the courtroom would be packed. There would be many journalists from all across Africa, and even a few from the West and observers from NGOs. "We can thank our American friend for this," he said turning to Andrew.

As much as Thomas took comments like that as stinging reminders of his failure to protect Andrew, they were also welcome reminders that if it weren't for him, the trial risked being far more slanted. With all the attention it attracted, it had to conform to the country's highest legal protections for accused persons. "They don't want to be accused of any irregularities," Abdou told them.

By now the afternoon had dragged on. As most of the conversation was repetitious, Thomas started to fade. His mind lost focus as he withdrew from the conversation. It was all getting to be too much for him. He didn't want to return to his cell. He wished they could sit there, in silence, undisturbed. Maybe even, for a brief moment, he could close his eyes and pretend to be somewhere else.

When Thomas sensed Abdou was winding up, he exhaled to signal his relief that the conversation was ending. Abdou responded by closing his notebook and standing up, before reaching over the table and placing one hand on each of their shoulders. He squeezed each tightly.

"I'm sorry for what you've already endured up until now. But you must be brave," he said to them. "It will be a long and difficult week. Are you ready for it?" he asked them.

Andrew nodded but looked terrified.

The look on his face shook Thomas. He knew how terrifying this must be for Andrew and worried desperately he might not have the mental fortitude to endure. It's why despite having lost almost all hope, he did his best to project strength and confidence.

"Yes," Thomas said definitively. He looked over at Andrew, reached out to touch his hand before looking back up Abdou. "We can survive what comes next. We have already survived."

22

As ANDREW STOOD up, Thomas put his index finger over his mouth, signaling to be silent. The gate to the compound was locked from the inside. They could hear movement on the other side, but no voices. All the cars had shut off their engines. Thomas took Andrew's hand and they started walking backward, slowly, away from the gate towards the wall that separated Andrew's compound from Isatou's, all the while keeping their eyes fixed straight ahead. When the footsteps passed behind Isatou's wall, Andrew knew they were not going to get away from whoever was there.

Four uniformed police officers hopped the walls of the compound, two in the front and two in the back. They all pointed their guns at Thomas and Andrew. "Get to the ground!" they yelled.

One of the officers unlocked the gate and four more officers entered the compound. An officer barked at Andrew to stand up, which he did. He was instructed to accompany an officer inside the house to retrieve his passport. Standing, in the moment before he took his first step, Andrew turned his eyes to the faces of the men sent to arrest him. What stuck out most about them was how indistinguishable they were from any other Gambian. They didn't look evil or villainous. They were intimidating, but that was because they were sweating and holding guns. They appeared no different than those who he played soccer with on Sundays, shared classrooms with at school, or encountered in shops and restaurants.

A torrent of thoughts flooded Andrew's mind as he walked past Thomas to fetch his passport. Thomas was trapped. Andrew was an American citizen and the authorities knew it. Why would they be asking for his passport if it wasn't important? He thought they would deport him. The unfairness of his presumed privilege brought more pain than relief. At the prospect of being sent away, Andrew was overridden by guilt.

He came out from his house and hesitantly glanced down at Thomas, lying flat on the ground with four armed officers standing over him muttering in Wolof. One of the other officers who wasn't holding a gun reached out and took the passport. As soon as Andrew handed it over he felt that he abandoned Thomas and grew angry at himself. When the other officers lifted Thomas to his feet they stared at each other. Andrew's dejected expression was his way of saying *I'm sorry*. Thomas seemed to understand, and in return, Andrew read his expression as saying *don't be*.

"You are both to come with us," said the officer who acted like he was in charge. He spoke without emotion. He stopped briefly to look at the other officers before uttering a hurried *let's go*. The officers forcefully whisked them out of the compound, placing them into separate cars. As they looked helplessly and hopelessly at one another through the windows it occurred to Andrew the officer never in fact said they were arrested. *Maybe this will all be over soon*, he thought to himself. Maybe he was being deported. *But then what about Thomas?*

No one spoke to Andrew during the drive. They drove into the heart of Banjul to a midsized building he had never seen before. A sign hung over the entrance that said Gambia Police Headquarters. They pulled into the back parking lot while the vehicle carrying Thomas kept driving. Andrew tried to follow it with his eyes but it quickly disappeared. As it did, he began to panic, scanning his surroundings and feeling suddenly alone.

They led him through an entrance in the back with a small sign on the door announcing it was for the Serious Crimes Unit. Andrew had never heard of it before but knew enough to know it didn't sound good. An older looking officer appeared to be waiting for him. He wore a crisp navy blue uniform. One of the officers who accompanied Andrew handed over his passport, which the older officer leafed through before taking it behind a desk to a computer.

What Andrew noticed most about those first few minutes was the silence. No one had spoken to him. The room itself was nearly silent. Only a few officers and staff were present, shuffling behind desks with small stacks of paper. Light bulbs overhead hung loosely from fixtures. The walls were the pale tan color ubiquitous among the country's poorly maintained, aged buildings. It wasn't dilapidated per se, but close.

"Andrew Turner," said the older officer as he walked back towards Andrew. He held open Andrew's passport as if reading out his name from the page. He dragged out the last part of his surname, saying it more like *Turneerrrr* to add effect. Stopping right in front of him, he closed the passport and held it out to his side as one of the other officers grabbed it instantly. "The American homosexual."

Suddenly Andrew lost his bearings. The walls, the lights, the people behind the desk, they were all blocked by the stern-looking face of the older police officer staring right at him, holding him with his gaze. He tried to calm his breathing to appear less nervous.

"Come with me."

As Andrew was led down the corridor, the vehicle carrying Thomas pulled up to the headquarters of Gambia's National Intelligence Agency. He prayed as Andrew's car backed up first that they would drive off in different directions, that Andrew's car would make for the airport. It didn't. They drove off together, in the opposite direction from the airport. Despondent, Thomas sunk further into the seat. When he saw that his car didn't follow Andrew into the police headquarters, he presumed he was being taken to the NIA and was relieved Andrew wasn't going with him. The NIA was notorious for mistreating persons it detained, many of whom were held for long periods of time without ever being charged.

Nearing the building, Thomas's car slowed before the parking lot and turned on an adjoining street. As far as Thomas could see, it was completely deserted, frozen by the fluorescent streetlight. But when the car pulled to a stop he noticed several figures standing in a doorway of the building to his right. Their faces were covered in balaclavas and they wore all black. The only thing he could make out, thanks to the reflection from the streetlight, was a machete, tucked into the belt of one of them.

His car sat idle for a second. He inhaled a deep breath to try and keep his nerves at bay for what he presumed was to come. From ahead he saw headlights approaching. Just as he was able to see it was a jeep, a man opened his car door and dragged Thomas out, throwing him face down onto the street. The men, he couldn't see or tell how many of them there were, pounced on him and held his limbs down as someone tied a bag over his head.

Thomas was surprised by how little he resisted. As someone lifted him to his feet he could feel what he thought was the butt of a rifle being jabbed into his lower back, shocking him and sending him back down to the ground as those holding him by the arms let go. Falling blindly towards the pavement, he barely had time to place his hands out to stop his face from absorbing the fall. He was kicked several times in the gut and on his sides as he winced to himself and did all he could not to cry out. They lifted him once more after tying his hands together behind his back and threw him into a vehicle, which he presumed was the jeep because it felt higher up than the car, before driving off.

The noise from the vehicle was muffled by the bag over his head. He could hear himself breathing loudly. Because of how his hands were tied, he was leaning slightly forward and his body jerked wildly as the jeep raced ahead, bouncing up and down over Banjul's deserted, uneven streets. Every bump intensified the pain shooting through his body. With each slight movement, he had to clench his jaw and fists as tightly as he could to stay silent. There were men seated on either side of him, their bodies pressed together in the backseat; he was sure they could feel each time he grimaced through the pain.

Before his head was covered, Thomas quickly searched for but wasn't able to see any identifying insignia on the men who took him. As the jeep pressed on he imagined they were probably the rumored Black Boys, an unofficial police unit outside the official command structure who reported directly to the president. It was believed they were responsible for most instances of torture and abuse in the country. Placing a bag over a person's head was said to be how the sessions most commonly began.

Eventually, the jeep slowed down and came to a stop. The back-left door opened and the person sitting next to Thomas got out. All he heard was the silence.

"Get out," commanded the person sitting to his right.

Thomas carefully shuffled his tied and hooded self to the left when the person to his right pushed him fiercely and unexpectedly, causing his knees to buckle as he fell forward into the car seat. Still, no one made a sound. As he struggled up again he was pushed an-other time, but this time forcefully enough that he fell from the jeep onto the pavement, his shoulder and then head bearing the brunt of the fall. His arms instinctively tried to grab hold of his chest, where the pain was greatest, but they remained tied behind him. As the shock converged on him, the boots of the men began kicking him once more. He tried desperately to curl his body and use his legs to protect his exposed stomach, but with his hands tied behind his back he couldn't bring his legs up enough. Lying exposed on the pavement, the pain grew fierce. He'd never been in a fight before and had no idea what it felt like to be attacked, to have boot heels colliding with his rib cage, his head sent slinging from side to side as if his neck were on a spring. It was all happening so fast that he barely registered the torment he was in – his insides so sore and his ribs feeling so cracked that it occurred to him he was having trouble breathing. He tried to cry out but it was too hard. Instead he choked and coughed up his own blood into the bag covering his face, which made it stick to his chin.

The kicking stopped and Thomas was left stuck to the pavement, completely inert. All his senses had gone numb. He struggled to stay alert. The one thought he could process was that he was petrified for what might follow. After a while – it may have been five minutes or thirty minutes, he had no idea – he was lifted by his armpits and dragged forward. It felt like his skin was the only thing keeping his body in one piece. His head slumped forward and he wasn't entirely sure if his eyes were closed or if it was dark because of the bag over his head. Still no one spoke. A door in front of him opened and he was brought through it. The men carrying him let go of his armpits and he fell to the ground flat on his chest. It felt like cold concrete. He turned his head to his side and rested it against the floor, breathing slow, shallow breaths into the dark and bloodied bag, taking advantage of the reprieve.

Footsteps broke the silence as he sensed someone walking up to him.

"Thomas," the voice proclaimed. It sounded confident, almost amused. "Welcome to hell. No American can save you here."

American. Andrew. Thomas tried to lift himself up to his side. *Where was Andrew?* Was he okay? But he couldn't move. His whole body felt broken as he lay there flat with a man standing over him.

"You should know this is not a country kind to you people."

Thomas squinted through his eyes, wanting to see the face of the man who stood over him, but couldn't see through the bag. He wanted to confront, with a glare of disbelief, this man who decided how his country would act towards him. He wanted that man to have to meet his eyes as he spoke, to face his condemned.

Thomas's hands were untied and he was lifted to his feet. His arms were raised above him as his wrists were again tied, this time from ropes that must have been hanging from the ceiling. There was pressure as his arms and shoulders fought each other, his arms wanting to pull away from his body, his shoulder sockets refusing. His feet barely touched the floor. Someone cut his t-shirt from his body before his pants were pulled off, leaving him hanging in his underwear. A bucket of ice cold water was thrown on him and jolted him to attention. His senses became more alert while the shock of the cold numbed the stinging aches throughout his body. Suddenly he was doused with an equally hot bucket of water and cried out in agony. Three more cold buckets followed, leaving him shivering uncontrollably.

Hanging there in the dark, still not able to face his countrymen, he tilted his head back, as if to look up to the sky. Through tears of pain and fear he wanted to ask *why*. But no sound came.

The bag was removed from his head. His eyelids squinted and pupils grew smaller in anticipation of adjusting to the light, but the room proved almost completely dark. A small lamp in one of the corners provided the only source of light and his eyes widened to take as much in as possible. The room was bare. There were four men in front of him — three of the Black Boys, who still had their faces covered, and a fourth man wearing an NIA uniform. Thomas assumed he was the one who'd spoken to him. He sensed at least one more person, maybe two, behind him.

As soon as Thomas had enough time to take in his surroundings, the NIA officer spoke.

"There is no place for your kind here." Then the officer turned around and walked out of the room, leaving Thomas alone with the

Black Boys. The butt of a rifle hit him in the lower back. Another hit his head.

Thomas kept losing and regaining control over his thoughts as the Black Boys passed a wooden club, iron bar, and glass bottle between themselves and began to have their way with him. His aching and swollen fingers dug into the rope as one of the men pulled off Thomas's underpants and spread his legs with the club. As with the NIA officer, he tried to see through the masks of the Black Boys and into their eyes so they would first have to face him before they proceeded. But none would face him. Three of them just circled him slowly, holding their instruments. Once. Twice. Thrice.

He closed his eyes and clenched his jaw as tight as he could to send his mind away from his body when they forced the club into him. He saw Andrew over and over and over. He saw him the first time he came to the hotel. He wore a baseball cap, which Thomas later learned belonged to the Chicago Cubs, a black and white striped tank top and a gray bathing suit. His pasty skin gave him away instantly as new. He was cute right from the beginning. He saw Andrew as he sat quietly in groups of people talking, often choosing to mostly listen, nod, and smile. He'd always loved Andrew's smile. It was so simple and effortless. He briefly cried out as the iron bar went deeper inside of him and he was hit in the stomach with the club, but he stopped himself, not wanting to grant his torturers the pleasure of his pain. Instead, he went back to the third or fourth time Andrew had come by the hotel on a Friday night. He was getting up to leave. By then Thomas had enough confidence to ask what became the first spoken acknowledgment of their budding romance.

"All those people you come here with on Saturdays, where do they spend their Friday evenings? Is everyone together?" he asked him suggestively.

"A lot of people are together, yeah," Andrew answered.

"And you're okay to miss that," he followed up, hinting at a smile more with his eyes than with his lips. "It's fine for you to keep coming here even though your friends are somewhere else?"

Andrew, finally catching on, locked eyes with Thomas. "Yeah, it's okay," he said reassuringly. "I see them lots of other times. I don't need to be with them tonight."

The Black Boys slapped Thomas's face to force him to look at them. "Dirty boy," one of them taunted him, "look at me." Thomas raised his head towards the man. He could see beads of sweat forming around the man's eyelid. "You enjoy this, no? This is what you like."

Thomas looked away.

"How does your American do it to you?" another one asked. "He's not here to help you."

Even through their taunts, Thomas broke his mind away from the depravity. He met their cruel eyes with ones that were vapid and vacant, but not yet defeated. The visions that formed before him were not of the men violating him, they were of the times he lay in bed next to Andrew, watching him as he slept. He saw him lying there, oblivious to the shining sunlight, his body deep in rest, seemingly incapable of being disturbed, rising so peacefully with each breath. Those were the moments when Thomas felt luckiest. Against all the odds, *I won.*

But slowly he started to feel suffocated and felt himself drifting away from Andrew, who remained sleeping on the bed so innocently, unaware of what was happening to him, shielded from the wickedness of it all. He was being torn apart, and it was becoming unbearable. Thomas's torturers grew more determined and violent. In a final act of resistance, he tried to muster whatever strength he had left to think of the first time he'd been with Andrew. How gentle Andrew was, how tender. As they fumbled their way awkwardly and delicately the way new lovers do, Andrew kept asking, *Are you okay? Are you sure you're okay? Yes,* Thomas answered sincerely. *Yes.*

And that was when he couldn't hold on any longer. As Andrew's indispensable solace receded further and further away from him, when he could clutch onto it no more, he finally cried out with the savagery of a dying beast, his wail echoing into the dark and empty night. *Please stop,* he begged them. *Please stop. Please stop.*

Eventually they did, but on their terms. He was left hanging for some time, alive but robbed of his humanity, before someone returned to take him down. By that point he couldn't see anything so had no idea who the person was. A second person entered and the two of them dragged him through hallways and down stairs, dropping him in a small cell with nothing but a paper-thin mat and loose pants with a half-torn drawstring he quickly bled through.

23

"You can call me Officer Lamin," the older officer said to Andrew, pointing to a chair across a wooden table. As Officer Lamin closed the door, Andrew quickly scanned the room. Its stained walls closed in on him. Water damage in the low ceiling gave the impression that something could fall through at any moment. He fixed his gaze on a crack running diagonally across the length of one of the walls, originating from a small hole in a top corner. The chairs weren't entirely dissimilar to those at his school, wooden bottoms that curved downwards at the end by the legs, and a wooden half-back bolted to a metal rod up the length of the back. The wood, of course, was chipped and uneven and uncomfortable on his legs. He wished he was wearing long pants instead of shorts. The sound of Officer Lamin pulling his chair out rattled Andrew away from these mental distractions and returned him to his state of fear. *Shouldn't someone from the embassy be here by now, or a lawyer?* he thought to himself, assuming it would have been the usual practice.

"Do you know why you are here?" Officer Lamin's voice was mean-sounding and accusatory.

Andrew slightly and hesitantly shook his head. "No," he said, barely audible.

"Don't lie to me, Andrew."

Not looking any more confident than the last time, Andrew again shook his head in the same slight and hesitant manner. "I don't."

"Why are you lying," asked Officer Lamin, in a voice as calm as Andrew's but significantly more assertive.

Andrew could do nothing but sit and stare back at Officer Lamin. What was he supposed to say? *Yes?* What would happen if he admitted to knowing why he was there? And what if he kept saying no? At what point would it look ridiculous to keep denying. *But aren't you always supposed to keep silent? Isn't that what they say?*

The only thoughts Andrew could process were those confirming he didn't know what to do. That fear of being lost without the slightest of bearings to grab a hold of was rapidly metastasizing within him.

"Think about it. Think about it carefully," Officer Lamin said, betraying a sense of impatience. Then, standing up he took out a sheet of paper from a folder he'd brought with him into the room. "Maybe this will help," he said as he steadied the paper in front of Andrew before stepping away and opening the door. Andrew could hear the door being locked from the outside and the footsteps of Officer Lamin retreat down the hall as he was left alone in the room for what felt like an eternity. All he had was a solitary piece of paper and a growing sense of panic and dread. As the time kept ticking, disoriented and tired, Andrew began dozing off. He tried to fight it, focusing attentively on keeping his eyes open, afraid of what might happen to him if he wasn't awake. But his energy kept waning and he quickly reached a point where he could resist no more. He faded out and succumbed to exhaustion.

"Well, Andrew," bellowed Officer Lamin as he swung open the door, jolting Andrew awake. "Are you ready to stop lying?"

Andrew didn't answer. Before he'd drifted off to sleep, he resolved that he would demand to speak with someone at the embassy, or at least a lawyer. He must have rights, he decided. *They can't just keep me here like this.*

He swallowed and looked straight at Officer Lamin. "I'd like to speak with someone from the U.S. Embassy."

Officer Lamin's laugh was bewildering as he shook his head at Andrew before growing stern. "You think, Andrew," he barked at him, "that because you are an American you are going to get special treatment from us? Somehow we must act differently towards you? You are mistaken, young man." He reached down to the table and picked up the sheet of paper he left behind. "May I remind you," he said holding it up to him, "this is a law we take very seriously. There is no room in The Gambia for such bestiality. America may be filled with your types, but not here." He grew louder as he placed both hands on the table and brought his face up to Andrew's. "And you, Mr. Turner, broke the law."

He yelled out hastily into the corridor in Wolof. Almost immediately, two young police officers emerged. One was holding what only looked like brown material, which Officer Lamin hurriedly yanked from him.

"Here," he said holding it out to Andrew. "Take off your clothes and put these on."

Andrew didn't immediately react, especially since the three officers were still standing in front of him. Officer Lamin took his free hand and slammed the door shut with the other two officers still in the room before he turned back to Andrew and yelled.

"*Now!*"

He kept his boxers on, but still felt frightfully exposed as he changed in front of them, turning and bending to shield himself and maintain some privacy from their peering eyes.

When he finished changing, Officer Lamin looked at him and asked once more, "Do you know why you're here?"

Andrew thought hard before answering. He started to raise his chin, as if beginning to nod, only to pause when he detected Officer Lamin's expression turning satisfied as he anticipated Andrew's capitulation.

"Where's Thomas?" Andrew asked.

Officer Lamin huffed loudly and barked off orders in Wolof again. The two officers led Andrew out the door.

"He's nowhere you can help him," Officer Lamin said as Andrew was led past him, forcibly pulled down the hallway further from where he entered the night before.

The officers shoved Andrew into a cell. He stared down at a thin, torn mattress on the floor without any sheets. The cell was narrow, barely enough for Andrew to extend out his arms from wall to wall. It was cold, and he was alone.

Andrew heard footsteps coming down the hallway. These ones echoed differently from those of the guards who brought him food and let him use the toilet for the past seven days. They were more pronounced. As they got louder he could see why – they were from women's shoes. Maya walked quickly, like a professional with somewhere urgent to be. She had a folder in one hand and swung her other arm severely as if relying on it to propel her forward. Two guards trailed behind her.

This is it, Andrew thought.

She stopped right in front of him. She wore a U.S. Embassy ID around her neck.

"Andrew," she said. "My name's Maya Mitchell. I work for the U.S. Embassy here in Banjul."

"Hi," he responded with excited anticipation.

"Are you okay?" she asked. "I mean, are you hurt at all? You're not in any pain, you haven't been abused in any way."

"No."

"Okay, good. What about food. Are you being fed properly three times a day?"

"I get fed. I don't know if it counts as properly. It's disgusting."

"I think the standards here are different. Are you able to at least eat it? Are you going hungry?"

"No."

"What about medication? Do you take any regularly? Anything for malaria?"

"Yeah, I take Malarone. That's it."

"Do you have it here with you?"

"No."

"Okay, I'll make sure it's brought to you."

Her American accent made him homesick.

"And have they provided anything to you to help pass the time?"

"Some books," he answered, beginning to grow somewhat impatient with her check up.

"I see."

"Maya, what's happening?" he asked softly.

Maya turned to face the guards who stood closely behind her. "Can you move back and give us some space please, some privacy?" she asked, though she didn't speak like it was a question. They obliged.

"Of course. Sorry – I first wanted to make sure there was nothing pressing around your well-being." She closed her notepad and looked back up at him. "You're being detained for allegedly breaking the law prohibiting the commission of acts classified as unnatural offenses. Do you know what they mean by that?"

He nodded with a mix of embarrassment and disbelief.

"They are going to bring formal charges against you in the coming days. You'll have what's called an arraignment."

"A what?"

"An arraignment. The prosecution will announce the charges before the court. You can then admit to them or deny them. In America it would be like pleading guilty or not guilty."

"Don't I get a lawyer?" he asked her.

"Yes."

Before she could continue responding he had another question. "And where's Thomas?" he demanded.

"He's here, in one of the holding cells in this building. He was somewhere else until yesterday."

"Where?"

"I don't know for sure. Another law enforcement group."

"Is he also being charged?"

"Yes."

"The same charges?"

"I believe so."

"You *believe?*"

"Yes. Remember, Andrew, I don't have the same access to information about Thomas as I do for you."

He nodded contemplatively. "Is he also being held by himself?"

"No."

"Why not?"

"I don't know. I can only guess it's not normal protocol for a local citizen in detention."

Maya explained to Andrew he was being kept alone because the government did not want to risk something happening to an American citizen in their custody. For all the tough talk, it still wasn't something they'd want to deal with.

"Can I see him?"

"At the arraignment. You're being charged together."

"How come you only came today?" he asked, interrupting her. "What took so long?"

"We were only made aware of your detention today."

"Who told you?"

"A friend of yours came to report you as missing. Liv."

Of course Liv would've figured it out. It was good to be friends with someone who worries. Andrew thought of Liv and then Alex. What he would've done to be together in their living room right then.

Maya's face grew concerned and Andrew feared what she was about to tell him. "Andrew."

"Yeah?"

"It might be difficult to make a deal with the government that would have you removed from the country quickly. We're trying very hard, but it might take longer than you might want it to."

"But you think you'll be able to?"

"I want to remain optimistic."

The guards interrupted to say Maya's time was up. She protested that she was entitled to more time with him, but they said they had orders. She turned and looked back at Andrew. He was scared. He didn't want her to leave.

"Two minutes," she sternly told the guards, putting up her hand and holding out two fingers. Maya next asked Andrew for his parents' phone number so they could be reached.

"Can I speak with them?" Andrew asked.

"I don't think so," she answered apologetically. "They don't give prisoners the same rights here. I can try, but I'm afraid I can't force them to let you do that."

He thought of the shock his parents were about to endure. "Tell them I'm sorry," he asked Maya. He couldn't believe how after so many years of painful and painstaking discretion and secrecy, this was how his parents were going to find out – a phone call from a U.S. embassy employee telling them he'd been arrested.

"There's nothing for you to be sorry about, Andrew. Don't worry about things like that. It's most important for you to focus on staying strong."

The guards grew agitated and stepped forward.

"It hasn't been two minutes," she said sternly again, holding her whole hand up this time to stop them from coming closer.

Andrew was beat as she turned back to face him. He felt his eyes grow watery.

"Maya," he asked.

"Yes."

"Are you able to give Thomas a message?"

"I'm not allowed to see him, Andrew."

He nodded. *Of course.*

She had to go, she told him, because she had to phone his father and deal with a whole host of other procedural things she should have done already but didn't because she wanted to see him first. She was planning to come back tomorrow after confirming he had a lawyer.

"Will the lawyer be for Thomas too?" he asked her.

"Perhaps. We can look into that. People normally have their own, but it's been done here before."

She reached through the bars and put her hand on his face and kept it there for a few seconds before saying anything. "Hang in there, Andrew. We're doing everything we can." As she pulled her hand back and stepped away from him he felt helpless. He became panicky as her footsteps receded down the hallway.

"Maya!" he yelled out after her. He heard her footsteps stop.

"Yes, Andrew?"

He went to open his mouth but couldn't speak. If he did, he would have cried.

She walked back to him, where she reached out to his hand, holding it tight. "You need to be strong," she whispered. "I know it's hard, but please, do your best to be strong and we'll do our best to help you."

He nodded slowly. "Okay."

24

AFTER THREE DAYS of being kept on his own, food left once a day on his floor, a morning and evening trip to a pitiful toilet, Thomas was placed in a jeep and driven to the police headquarters building. He was fingerprinted, given a new uniform, and placed into a larger holding cell with ten other men, each existing as miserably as the next. None of them said much to each other, most wore tattered clothing. They were allowed outside once a day to wander in a small dirt yard, though no one had much energy, and many spent the time sitting in the shade up against the building's wall, weighed down by their experience and despondency. One morning, his fifth day in the holding cell, guards came for him.

"It's time to meet your lawyer," one of them said.

They brought him to a door and told him to go inside, wash, and change into a fresh set of pants that they handed to him. He obliged, and for the first time tried to gently clean away the crusted reminders of what befell him a week before.

Two guards had come to Andrew's cell and told him he had been given a lawyer that they were taking him to meet. His face signaled relief.

"When?"

"I don't know," a guard said. "They are bringing him. It shouldn't be long."

Andrew was brought to the police station's interview room to find Abdou pacing inside waiting for him. Once the guards closed the door and left them alone, Abdou extended out his hand to introduce himself. Andrew's first thought was that he looked young. The whole country was against him, the entire machinery of the government and justice system was being mobilized for his prosecution, and his lawyer looked like he was only a few years older than he was. *This is what I get*, he thought to himself. The second thing Andrew noticed was his voice. Introducing himself as *your lawyer, Abdou Bojang, should you choose my services*, Andrew was struck by how deep and authoritative his voice was. Perhaps it might compensate for his age. Either way, it made him sound serious and commanding.

The conversation followed the same pattern as the one with Maya. Abdou wanted to make sure Andrew wasn't being abused and was relatively well looked after.

"I will check up on the food," he said when Andrew complained it was mostly inedible. "But I expect I'll be told you're being fed what everyone else is fed, and I'm afraid I've been told by past clients it's not supposed to be very good, but you can exist off it."

"Have you had many other clients?" asked Andrew, trying to gauge how experienced Abdou was.

"I have. I have been practicing law now for three years." Abdou had meant the answer to placate whatever unease Andrew may have had, but it didn't.

Three years? Shit.

"All types of cases. Civil suits, family matters, and some criminal cases."

Some?

"Maya Mitchell has visited with you?"

"Yes."

"Good. She and I spoke by phone this morning. They should have immediately informed the embassy of your arrest. I will be raising this matter with the court."

Andrew gave a sort of shrug, looking lost in the technical points of law. He was unfamiliar with the workings of any criminal justice system, let alone Gambia's.

"Thomas should be here shortly," Abdou said, looking at the time on his phone.

Andrew's face lit up, instantly. "He's coming?" he asked excitedly.

"Yes," Abdou responded as he leafed through some papers, not looking at Andrew.

Andrew looked around the room as if it would make Thomas appear sooner. Realizing there was a third, empty chair around the small table, his heart began to race.

Abdou said he wanted to wait for Thomas to arrive before they had a substantive discussion – it was very important for both of them to have the exact same information if he was going to represent them, which the court said it would allow. To fill the time, he told Andrew he was lucky on account of his nationality.

"You're being detained in better conditions than most people."

Andrew found it hard to believe that he was getting special treatment. His cell was filthy. *The floor.* He couldn't imagine the last time it was washed. He tried never to touch it with his bare skin. Its walls stank of rot. If he needed to use the toilet between the two trips a day he was escorted on, there was a bucket in the corner of his cell and a smaller bucket of water. He was afraid of touching either. The thought of using them made him sick.

"You have your own cell," Abdou remarked. "This is very unusual. And during any of your conversations with the police, were you ever hit or threatened?"

"No."

"I'm sorry to say," Abdou told him, "I suspect Thomas's experience has been different from yours."

Andrew asked Abdou if there was any way for Thomas to be held where Andrew was and to receive similar treatment. "Because of me and us being arrested together?"

"I don't think so."

"What if I were to go to where he was?" he asked, trying to sound undaunted. He knew it was a bad idea but wanted to believe it wasn't.

Abdou didn't have to say anything. He just glanced at Andrew and shook his head.

The sound of the door being unlocked jolted Andrew. It sounded broken. When it opened, a body stood shackled in the entranceway. The person's top was stained and filthy. There were cuts across his face. His lip and one eye were swollen. He hunched forward, standing on unsteady legs, clearly needing to support himself on something, someone. Before Andrew could react, a guard walked in front and started to unshackle the man who looked nothing but helpless and hopeless, a body weak and defeated.

When the guard had taken off the shackles and left the room, Thomas lifted his face up to meet Andrew's eyes. He saw the blood drain from Andrew's face as his mouth dropped but no words came out. Just as quickly as their eyes locked, Thomas turned away, casting his gaze downward. Standing, in awful pain, short of breath from walking and now standing, he struggled to look at the face that for the past several days had been the only thing in which he found peace.

Thomas gulped in the air to help steady himself. Sensing how difficult it was for him to stand, Abdou jumped to his feet and led him by the arm to a chair like an elderly person. Thomas shuffled along the floor, moving a few inches with each step, his faced in a tightly-strained grimace. Desperate to not scare or worry Andrew, and embarrassed by his appearance, Thomas did his best to hide his pain, pretending to be brave.

It didn't work. When he finally sat down next to Andrew he looked up again, seeing Andrew's stricken face. Andrew's expression made it crystal clear to Thomas that his innocence – which Thomas loved – was gone. A young man who'd been unknowingly hanging on to boyhood had been forced to let go in the most horrible of ways. Thomas knew that even if he'd not been subjected to the same level of abuse, Andrew had been pulled down into the pit of his country's depravity, and was now face to face with its cruelty. It was a realization that shattered Thomas's heart into tiny pieces.

Thomas reached his arms out to Andrew, holding his hands open. Andrew reached back, his eyes filling with tears as Thomas squeezed his hands in his.

"What did they do to you," he asked with urgency. Turning to Abdou, panicky and shaky, he asked again, this time louder, with even more urgency. "What did they do to him?!?!"

Thomas squeezed Andrew's hands again, pulling him gently to look back. "What they did to me is done."

Andrew, realizing how terrified he was, for Thomas and for himself, pulled back from Thomas and, standing up while stepping back, uncharacteristically screamed. "FUUUCKK! What the fuck happened?! Where the fuck are we?"

Thomas watched Andrew lose it. *This can't be real; get us out of here.* His eyes moved frantically about the room, only to see four concrete walls with no way out. He looked as if he was about to collapse. Mustering all his strength, Thomas pressed his hands on the table to lift himself up. He wrapped his arms around Andrew, loosening his grip because it hurt his ribs, and whispered softly, over and over, *it's okay, we're going to be okay,* while Andrew stood there, weeping, uncontrollably.

It was only after Andrew calmed down that Abdou felt comfortable speaking.

"The positive news is that usually once lawyers become involved in a case, the mistreatment stops. What happened to Thomas was clearly terrible, but at least it is over."

"And you are okay?" Thomas asked, leaning back slightly to look Andrew in the face.

Andrew nodded. "Yes, I'm fine. They didn't touch me."

"Good," he answered, and pulled him close again. "It will stay that way. You are safe," Thomas said, stroking his back. "You are safe."

Andrew pulled back, turning and facing Abdou. "I'm sorry," he said.

"Don't," Abdou asserted. "You have nothing to apologize for. You have both been through much and are only now seeing one another for the first time. I expect this is difficult. But," he paused, "I am afraid this is not the end, there is a lot of work we need to do if you are truly going to be safe."

They looked at him while Abdou took a step forward, extending his hand out to Thomas.

"My name is Abdou Bojang, and if you agree to it, I'm your lawyer. I would like to start preparing a defense for both of you right away."

"Okay."

"Good, then let us begin. Please, we can sit down."

Much like Andrew, meeting Abdou did not immediately bring comfort to Thomas. All too aware – and significantly more so than Andrew – as to the gravity of their situation and how it would be presented to the rest of the country, he was immediately suspicious of any lawyer who would choose to represent them.

Abdou had prepared an answer to this question. Keeping it vague, he told them the case was brought to his attention by people who knew he had a strong commitment to upholding the rule of law and the basic rights of all people. He knew many in the legal community might not want to take the risks associated with defending persons accused of homosexuality, but for him, that was an impetus to defend them.

What he kept from them was the truth – that Abdou and Thomas shared a mutual friend who orchestrated the whole thing.

Suleiman called Abdou as soon as he got off the phone with Maya. Their fathers worked together at the Finance Ministry and they'd come to know each other well in secondary school. They remained close as their respective careers took off.

"You *have* to take it. Who else will?"

Abdou's first reaction was reluctance. Reasons not to take the case were numerous. He was a young lawyer, with a wife and small children to worry about and care for.

"This could jeopardize my whole career. You want I should lose everything?" he asked Suleiman.

"*They* have lost everything," retorted Suleiman.

Suleiman was right, and Abdou knew it. But that didn't make it any easier to take a losing case. For starters, what was Suleiman risking, or prepared to risk, to help his friend? Providing information to the U.S. Embassy and getting them a lawyer was one thing, but would *he* put himself on the line for his friend?

"I know you know this is wrong."

"I know," Abdou admitted.

Abdou didn't doubt he would take the case. He needed to first talk to Manima, but she would be supportive, even if reluctantly. The uncertainty of what would come was what unnerved him most.

It stayed with him as he walked into the police station to meet Thomas and Andrew for the first time. There was a trepidation to his step, a hesitancy as he handed over his identification and signed into the visitor log.

He had to be quick during their first meeting. After Andrew had calmed down, Abdou asked a few questions about each of their histories and how long they knew each other. He never did explicitly ask if they were in a relationship. "What exactly were you doing when the police arrested you?"

"We were in the yard of my compound," Andrew told him.

"And were you engaged in any type of activity that might contravene the laws?"

"No," Thomas exclaimed emphatically. "Not then."

Abdou gazed up from his notebook still in thought. "Better to just say no."

That was enough to get him started, Abdou announced. Papers needed filing with the court, formalities to officially register him as their legal representative. He also had to go back to his office and re-arrange other cases he had, postponing some matters as he expected this case to be expedited.

"Why?" Andrew inquired.

"The government won't want to waste any time. Moving quickly will let them take advantage of the publicity following the announcement of your arrest."

"When will that be?" Thomas asked.

"Later today, I've been told."

They both looked at each other.

"So much for not telling anyone," Andrew said lightheartedly, not knowing what else to say.

Thomas wasn't interested in Andrew's poor attempt at levity. He turned quizzically to Abdou. "Mr. Bojang?" he asked, looking concerned.

"Abdou," Abdou responded.

"Yes, Abdou. Tell me, exactly how did the police discover us?" It was a question on both of their minds the whole week. They'd each reconstructed as much of their relationship as possible and came to the same conclusion. They had been exceedingly cautious and had no idea who would have betrayed them.

He didn't know, he told them. When their arrest was formally announced it would come out, he imagined. He would have access to all of the state's evidence, so they would find out in due course.

"Patience, as challenging as it may be," he told them, "is crucial."

In the meantime, and until that point, Abdou began to explain how the arraignment proceedings would work. They would be led into the courtroom where Abdou would be waiting for them. The charges would be read out and they would be asked either to deny or admit to the charges.

"I assume you both want to deny the charges," he asked, to which they both nodded in response.

Following this, the court would address bail and scheduling the trial. Abdou was upfront and said he expected bail would be denied. "The government will move to deny bail on the grounds of Andrew's nationality and concerns that you will abscond."

"Abscond?" Thomas asked.

"Flee. They'll say because he's American he will run to the American embassy, which the Gambian police cannot enter. The court, I'm sure of it, will agree and deny bail." He told them he could fight it, and they could have a separate hearing on bail, but he was so sure they would lose that all it would do is prolong their pre-trial detention and delay getting to the actual trial.

"So, I'd like permission from both of you not to contest in the event the court denies bail."

They both nodded, clearly because he told them to and not because either had thought the matter through himself.

Abdou continued hurrying through his explanation of other formalities. That this would all take place before a magistrate and not a judge, but such a distinction mattered little. There was a chance, he added, the government would request, to prove how seriously they approached this case, to move the matter from a magistrate's court to the High Court, which they also needn't worry about. As he told them how often he would visit and his priorities going forward, he struggled to follow their expressions. It was hard to tell if they were focusing on anything. Abdou understood that little of what he now said was registering with either of them. The more in-depth he got into the specifics, and he wasn't getting in-depth at all, the blanker their faces became. Looking across the table at his clients, he saw through their stillness and silence that they appeared overwrought and small. Only a week into their ordeal, he worried about their ability to cope.

"You're fortunate," he said, hoping to soothe their anxieties. "Because of you, Andrew, and the attention it will bring to have a foreigner on trial, the government will be extra careful to ensure the trial proceeds fairly. There will be a lot of media attention and observers. They will not want to take any chances. So you mustn't be so put off."

Shrugged reactions suggested they appreciated his failed attempt to make them feel better, and an ominous mood descended over the room.

Abdou didn't want them leaving deflated. "We'll get through this," he added.

After the hearing he would be coming back for a detailed discussion about the case and apologized he couldn't stay to talk about it more then. But while he organized his briefcase, he said there was one more question.

"What about your mobile phones?" he asked, looking quizzically at them. "Text messages, pictures, you know, that kind of stuff."

"There's nothing," Thomas said quietly. "We always deleted text messages after we read them."

Abdou turned to Andrew, who nodded in agreement, before looking down to the floor.

"That is good," Abdou proclaimed, nodding. "Very good. Is there anything you can think of, either of you, that the police may have found when they searched your homes? Anything that might be incriminating and support their allegations?"

"They searched my house?!" Andrew asked incredulously, looking up at Abdou and Thomas.

"Of course they did," Abdou answered.

Andrew slumped his shoulders and rested his face on his hands at the news, understanding even more that this situation was not about to disappear. He thought to himself for a minute before suddenly looking up terrified, and turned to Thomas and then to Abdou. "I have a journal," he announced, not being able to close his mouth afterward.

Abdou took the news in stride. "Okay," he said calmly. Turning to Thomas he asked, "and you?"

Thomas, visibly troubled by Andrew's declaration – he didn't know he had a journal – shook his head. "No, nothing."

"Okay," Abdou said again. "Condoms?" he asked, hesitantly treading into the private. Thomas and Andrew gazed guiltily at each other before Andrew nodded. "Okay," he said once more. "That is important information."

As he took his briefcase in his hands, he implored both of them to stay strong. Turning to Thomas he added, "especially you, please," and in doing so he created an uncomfortable feeling between Thomas and Andrew. Thomas was embarrassed by the implication his situation was more precarious than Andrew's. He tried to shrug it off while Andrew turned to him with eyes that expressed urgent concern, mouthing silently, *are you okay?*

Yes, Thomas mouthed back dejectedly, but still wanting to be convincing.

"See you tomorrow," Abdou said, his deep voice breaking up their moment. He reached out and shook their hands before knocking on the door for a guard to come and open it.

If Thomas and Andrew thought they might have a moment of privacy once Abdou left, they were mistaken. As soon as the door opened, the same guards who brought each of them down appeared and they became fearful of looking at each other. They took Thomas out of the room first, pushing him to walk too quickly for someone in his state. When Andrew was led out, the hallway in front of him was already empty.

While Andrew and Thomas were being led down separate hallways, the government was finally going public with the arrest, just in time for the nightly news and talk shows. Their pictures were displayed on television screens throughout Gambia. Mobile phones across the country lit up with the news. Mr. Jalloh sat eating dinner with his family in disbelief. Liv was so bombarded with text messages from nearly everyone who knew her and Andrew that she stopped responding to them. Abdou worked late into the night keeping the radio on in his office. Thanks to the internet and social media, it didn't take long for the story to break internationally. Perspective depended on the news source, foreign or local: AMERICAN VOLUNTEER ARRESTED IN AFRICA FOR BEING GAY or POLICE ARREST AMERICAN VOLUNTEER WHO CAME

TO SPREAD HOMOSEXUALITY. When the head of the country's police force announced the arrest, he proclaimed it as a giant step forward in the country's defense of African values.

"Today," he declared, "The Gambia has acted on behalf of all African states and refused to accept foreign and alien cultural practices that have no place here." The state's case, he assured, was incontrovertible. After a tip from a neighbor who suspected illegal activity, the police had monitored the individuals and since taking them into custody had amassed the evidence needed to secure a conviction. As he closed his remarks, he looked up from his prepared text to face the cameras and journalists in the room. "And let me say to the people of The Gambia. I know, we all know, how seriously you view these crimes. Let me assure you we share those beliefs and have acted in a deliberate and calculated manner to ensure our efforts will be met with success. Justice will be swiftly delivered," he promised. "There will be no mercy."

Going to the courthouse for their hearing was the first time Andrew was made to wear handcuffs. They were cold and heavy, and it was intimidating to hear the buckles crackling as one of the guards tightened them on his wrists. His hands trapped in front of him, he walked unnaturally. Stepping out into the parking lot, Andrew was hit by sunshine and faced an open sky, an unexpected but welcomed respite. He looked up and closed his eyes, letting the warmth of the rays relax his body.

He was driven to a nearby building and led into a back entrance before being paraded into the courtroom with officers on either side, his hands still cuffed in front of him. Andrew was familiar with embarrassment, but on this day he learned the true meaning of humiliation. As he was led through the small and cramped court-room, whose smell immediately struck him – the smell of a room constantly filled with people whose scents lingered long after they were gone – Andrew for the first time in his life truly wanted to give up and disappear. He had no family, no friends, and except for a lawyer he did not yet know or trust, no allies. He only had Thomas, who was just as powerless as he, and they weren't even together at that point. It was only Andrew, walking in handcuffs, on display for curious onlookers to gawk at, for journalists to try and analyze, and for guards and police officers to stare at and suspect. Walking into the silent courtroom, he could hear and feel every-one's condemnation. It fell upon him unexpectedly, a weight that felt too great to bear.

When he reached the defendant's table, Abdou was there. He immediately leaned into Andrew. "When they bring Thomas through, try not to smile at him. Better to keep looking forward." He did as told. As Thomas was led to the same table, limping for-ward in pain, Andrew didn't once lift his face to him. In fact, when Thomas arrived next to Andrew, neither acknowledged the other. They just stood in silence.

The court was called to order and the magistrate was called in, Magistrate Colley, a woman. Andrew wasn't sure why, but he had figured it would be a man. For whatever reason the sight of a female magistrate put him slightly more at ease, a feeling quickly dispelled when they made eye contact. She looked impatiently at him like her mind was already made up.

It all happened very quickly. Each was called by name and stood up. The clerk of the court read out the charges, which they were asked to admit to or deny. Each did as planned.

After his turn, Andrew turned around and scanned the courtroom, looking for support. He found Maya standing in the back corner of the courtroom taking notes. She was looking down when Andrew's eyes passed her way and didn't see him. Liv, however, had her eyes firmly fixed on Andrew the whole time. She must've arrived after him and was seated diagonally behind him, positioned so he could easily turn his head to the side and see her. She was with two other friends of Andrew's, but his eyes locked immediately with hers. The look she gave him said everything and he swiftly turned away for fear he'd lose his composure. He turned his face to the ground and closed his eyes, wanting but unable to pay attention to the proceedings in front of him. He wondered what Thomas was thinking at that moment and wished he could ask him. He wondered what his family was thinking and wished they were with him. It was easier for him to focus on others because every time he tried to sort out what he was thinking, he grew exhausted from the onslaught of conflicting thoughts and emotions and gave up.

Looking back into the courtroom, Andrew saw Suleiman writing in his notepad. He was looking down, scribbling quickly, and didn't notice Andrew. Andrew turned his eyes back to Thomas only to see that Thomas was also observing his friend. Then, as if sensing the stares fixed upon him, Suleiman lifted his head from his notepad, his eyes meeting both of theirs. His expression was neutral, but Andrew thought he sensed a pang of guilt to it. Maybe he was reading too much into it. Shifting to face Thomas, Andrew saw that his expression was empty. By the time Andrew looked back at Suleiman, he had returned to scribbling notes on his pad. Andrew wondered what his article would say.

When Andrew brought his focus back to the proceedings, he could tell they were talking about bail. The prosecutor, as Abdou predicted, argued that bail should be denied.

"We cannot risk the chance that Mr. Turner will attempt to enter the U.S. Embassy or flee the country."

"And Mr. Sow?" Magistrate Colley inquired.

"Given his association with Mr. Turner, we feel he might try to leverage Mr. Turner's nationality and also attempt to abscond."

As if she'd been briefed by the prosecutor beforehand, Magistrate Colley agreed that the argument was persuasive. She asked Abdou if he had anything to say in response, to which he answered no.

Bail was denied. Also, as Abdou predicted, the trial was moved to the High Court as requested by the prosecution. The trial would begin on a Monday, in three and a half weeks. "Until then," Magistrate Colley proclaimed, "the accused will be remanded back to the custody of the state. This case is adjourned."

As Magistrate Colley excused herself, Abdou turned to Thomas and Andrew before they were whisked off. "I'll come to see you tomorrow. This was fine. Surprises are bad and today we had none. Don't worry."

Then on cue, four guards came to lead them away, paraded out as they'd been paraded in.

25

THOMAS AND ANDREW were taken to the remand wing of Mile 2 prison after their arraignment but were immediately separated and led in separate directions. Overcrowded and filthy, it was the country's largest and most notorious prison. Walking in, Andrew recoiled at the smell of unwashed bodies. He was led past rows of communal cells packed with desolate-looking men, many of whom had visible wounds. They all turned their gaze to him upon seeing a white man in a prisoner's uniform. *Is this where he'd be kept?* he asked himself frightfully. Fortunately for him, the answer was no, and he was again led down more hallways through a final door. Another short hallway followed. A lone, dying lightbulb hung from the ceiling. The rains hadn't arrived but the narrow concrete passageway soaked in the humidity, trapping whatever moisture it could. It smelled like mold. Two empty cells stood on either side at the end. He was placed in one – a small private cell, this time with only a mat on the floor instead of a mattress, and a small blanket. The floor was sticky and grimy, filthier than his cell before.

The barred door slammed closed with a jarring bang, echoing through the hollow space. Inspecting his cell, Andrew ran his fingers along the threatening scratches on the concrete walls, tracing the history of others who once occupied the lifeless room. He looked down at the floor and at the tattered sleeping mat and crumpled blanket — both most certainly infested with something. He sat down on his mat, buried his head in his hands, and without having to feign courage any longer, wept.

He'd regained his composure by the time Maya visited later in the afternoon. She wanted to let him know the U.S. government was continuing to do all it could on his behalf. The Ambassador had already made several phone calls and had a meeting scheduled with officials from the justice and foreign ministries.

"Do you think anything will happen?" he asked.

"We're hopeful, but we must be realistic. The government won't want to look like it caved to American pressure, so we need to approach this delicately, and probably with a little more patience than you might want."

She did bring some good news, though. "Your family is on a plane now. They're coming here."

"What?" he exclaimed, looking happy for the first time in over a week.

"They took the news as well as anyone could've in the circumstances. They bought tickets to Banjul right away. Their flight from Dakar arrives this evening."

"What?!" he repeated. "What happened? What did my father say? Please tell me everything," he asked her intently.

"I will," she replied. "But, first, before you get too excited, I want to tell you I'm not convinced they'll be allowed into the country."

"What do you mean?" he asked her, his expression forlorn.

She went on to explain how she thought the authorities would refuse entry to individuals who might be coming to advocate or voice support for persons accused of breaking the homosexuality laws.

"Oh," he said, not hiding his disappointment.

"But I wanted you to know that even with this possibility, your family still wanted to try. I'm going to the airport to meet their flight. Regardless of what happens, I'll let you know."

Maya returned several hours later, after having to convince the guards to let her in at night, only to tell Andrew that his family had been flown back to Dakar. They planned to find a hotel and liaise with the embassy there.

"Okay, thanks," he said to her softly. "Did you see them?"

"No. Your father called me from the immigration area."

He looked back at her with the same forlorn face.

"We have to take things as they come," she said.

He nodded without saying anything, but opened his eyes a bit wider to communicate that he knew. But after Maya left, for the second time that day, he sat down and cried.

Andrew was thankful the next morning when he was taken from his cell and led to an interview room where Thomas and Abdou waited for him. He was happy for the human interaction, which was in short supply in his prison cell. However, the news Abdou brought quickly unnerved him.

"*Isatou?!*" Andrew's face contorted every which way. "Impossible," he said, squinting his eyes, trying to see something he didn't believe existed. He turned to Thomas, whose calm demeanor suggested Abdou had already told him, or that he had less trouble believing Isatou would have given them up. "How did she know?" he demanded.

Abdou explained that Isatou's nephew had reported them. There were three Saturday mornings where this man saw Thomas leaving the house very early in the morning, before dawn, hopping over the gate. The man was on his way to prayers at the mosque. Thomas didn't have the look of a robber when he saw him the first time, and when he spotted him the second week he thought it was strange to see him leaving again so early in the morning.

It was then that this man remembered the shorts. A couple of months before, when Isatou was doing Alex and Andrew's laundry, she found a pair of sport shorts that resembled a pair her nephew had. Alex's and Andrew's shorts were loose and baggy, and various shades of khaki; this was the first time Isatou saw these black ones. Gambian men rarely wore shorts, except for exercise or playing sports, and even then, the shorts they did wear fell high above the knee, like those that were popular in North America in the 1980s. When Isatou saw the shorter shorts in the laundry she pointed out to her nephew that Alex or Andrew was finally starting to dress like a Gambian. Now that the nephew saw a Gambian sneak out of Andrew's compound early in the morning for the second week in a row, he wondered if the shorts belonged to this man.

On the following Saturday, Abdou continued, "he went out from the house early and walked along the outside wall of your house, to see if he could hear any commotion, maybe a robber who kept returning to steal things, but he couldn't hear anything. And then he positioned himself in the dark before five in the morning to see if Thomas would appear again, which he did. That day he told his aunt, your maid, what he thought was going on. He said he wanted to go to the police, but Isatou was reluctant. She worried about betraying you because she didn't believe it. He convinced her to go through your clothes. They found a number of items they didn't think belonged to you."

Andrew was irate and Thomas had to extend his arm out, as if to stop him from jumping up.

"After they found more of Thomas's clothes, the nephew wanted to go to the police right away, but Isatou still hesitated. Instead, she asked him to speak to the imam when he went for prayers to the mosque for advice. He did. This imam has gotten involved in some organization, Pure Gambia it's called. He spoke to the director, and they went to the police, who questioned Isatou and her nephew, who confirmed everything. That was two days before you were arrested. For the next two days, the police sat across the street from your house keeping watch. They watched Thomas leave early Saturday morning and come back alone later at night. Then they watched you both leave and return separately on Sunday before making the arrest. Just before they arrested you they went to your hotel, Thomas. They asked your boss if he recognized Andrew. When he said he came every week to sit at the bar with Thomas, they became convinced of everything."

Neither Andrew nor Thomas spoke. As calm as he tried to be on the outside, inside, Andrew was fuming. He wanted to lash out, at Isatou, her nephew, Pure Gambia, and, at himself. He asked himself how he could be so stupid, forgetting how meticulous they'd been to stay discreet. None of that mattered. *What the fuck was I thinking?*

He looked over at Thomas, who was shaking his head. It was Andrew who convinced him to leave some underwear and shirts in a drawer.

She doesn't go in drawers or cupboards. She takes the laundry off the floor and leaves it on my bed when it's done.

"They also went to your principal," Abdou said, flipping through his notes, "Mr. Jalloh."

The mention of Mr. Jalloh stung Andrew. The realization Mr. Jalloh knew about this made Andrew ashamed. He liked Mr. Jalloh. He wished they'd have left him out of it.

"He was apparently very surprised and defended your character, and your abilities as a teacher. He said he had seen no evidence you were a practicing homosexual."

Practicing homosexual. Jalloh always had a way with words.

"Now that you finally know how you both arrived here, you can begin to think of people who might be able to explain your story differently," Abdou suggested. He told them that as he continued to learn more about the government's case, he would keep returning with more questions and to talk about different strategies. He expected to obtain a copy of Andrew's journal, which he confirmed the police found, in the next day or so. That would certainly raise additional questions. In the meantime, he asked them, could they think of a list of people who could attest to how they spent their time together? "People who can say you behaved like friends."

"There aren't many," Andrew said. "We were always alone, or with Liv and Alex, and Alex is gone. Otherwise it was just the soccer games on Sundays, but no one there knew anything."

"I will want to talk to them," Abdou said. Andrew provided the names of people who played.

"I spoke to your parents," Abdou said, turning to Andrew and changing the subject. "They got my contact from Maya and called me from their hotel in Dakar."

"How are they?" Andrew asked eagerly. He couldn't believe his family was in Africa and would've given anything to see them there. He was proud of them for so many reasons and wanted to speak to them, especially if he couldn't see them.

"They are fine. They are concerned about you obviously. They are trying to arrange a phone call with you, and I think it will be granted shortly."

Andrew's face lit up and he looked over at Thomas to share his excitement. The disconnect of emotions between them only heightened their differences. Listening to Abdou talk about all the efforts Andrew's family was making on his behalf made him feel less abandoned. But until that moment he'd been ignorant to how that contrasted with the silence from Thomas's family and he tempered his expression accordingly.

"They have generously offered to pay my fees for the case. We spoke in detail about the case. They asked numerous questions and I explained exactly what the procedures are and what we can all expect. I promised to remain in regular contact with them."

"Thank you," Andrew said. He had many more questions he wanted to ask about them but restrained himself. He didn't want to upset Thomas when, all of a sudden, he felt a hand on his thigh under the table. He turned his face to Thomas, who smiled at him. It was his way of saying he was happy for him, not to feel guilty. Maybe it was the message his hand helped convey, but Andrew was struck by the amount of anxiety that could be alleviated by the touch of a hand. It made him wish they could be alone. As the weeks and interview sessions wore on they found themselves touching each other this way often. It was a way to reassure each other, but more importantly, it was a way to renew the fading connection and intimacy between them.

"If you'll excuse me," Abdou said, "I have some work I need to attend to."

"Of course," Thomas said.

Abdou was at his desk flipping through a copy of Andrew's journal when his phone rang. He didn't recognize the number or the voice of the woman with a British accent on the other end.

"Ah, yes, Liv." Her name was at the top of the list Thomas and Andrew gave him. "Thank you for reaching out to me," he said. "I was going to call you shortly. I'm sure you can imagine that you occupy an important place in this case."

"Yes," she said. That was the problem. Liv told Abdou she'd just been visited by the prosecution. The court had issued a subpoena to compel her attendance at trial as a witness. They told her they wanted her to testify about all the instances they presumed she observed Thomas and Andrew in the house. They wanted her to confirm she'd seen them go off into the bedroom and close the door.

"Abdou?"

"Yes," he answered.

"I saw them a lot, on many occasions," she explained with concern.

He was thinking about how detrimental her testimony would be.

"You have to help me," she pleaded. "There must be a way for me to get out of this." The prospect of providing incriminating evidence mortified her. "I tried to tell them I was sick. I don't know, I made it up on the spot. I said I hadn't been feeling well lately and would have to see how I felt at the trial. They knew I was lying and said the subpoena meant I *had* to testify."

"They're correct," he said. "I'm afraid you are required to go. We can work on how you say things, so it will be less harmful towards them."

"But it still won't be good?" she queried.

"No," he answered. "No, I don't think it can be good."

Tormented by the prospect of playing a role in their conviction, she asked Abdou what would happen if she left the country during the trial.

"I can't give you advice on that," he said. "I can't knowingly help you defy a court order. And besides, he added, because you're a foreigner, I'm sure they've attached a note to your immigration file. It will show up as soon as your passport is scanned at the airport. So even if you tried, you wouldn't be able to fly out of the country. And if you did somehow manage to get out, you certainly wouldn't be allowed back in."

"Okay," she replied, already scheming. He'd given her her answer. "Thank you."

"Let's find a time when you can come to the office and we can talk about everything."

"Sure," she said. "Of course."

Liv hung up the phone and went for a walk to think clearly before calling Alex to talk things over with him.

Do it, he said. *You have to.*

- ET w/ chais sched x 2
(on terrier)

S4

re is no affiliation between Capital One and these companies. Maps
 intended for navigation.

k guaranteed • May lose
rnment Agency

services are offered by the
, N.A. and Capital One, N.A.,

FDIC Member

Norton

EQUAL HOUSING LENDER

	Callie E. ...1849	$10.92
	Callie E. ...1849	-$10.91
	Callie E. ...1849	$36.15
	Callie E. ...1849	$6.61
	Callie E. ...1849	$28.57

The next morning before dawn, Liv slipped into the car of a driver she knew and trusted well. She carried her shoulder bag and a large backpacker's knapsack. She hadn't said where they were going and told him to first drive to the U.S. Embassy on Kairaba Avenue, where she quickly handed a sealed envelope to the guard in the guardhouse. On its front was written:

Attention Ms. Maya Mitchell

United States Embassy

Kairaba Avenue

Banjul, The Gambia

PRIVATE AND CONFIDENTIAL

She got back into the car and asked to be dropped off at the Banjul ferry terminal.

"You're going to Senegal?"

"Yes, only for a few days."

She arrived early, ensuring a place on the first ferry of the day. Standing alone among the masses waiting to cross, Liv kept her gaze fixed on the horizon as the rising sun calmly brought the northern riverbank into focus. Behind her, a man was speaking loudly on his phone and she resented him for disturbing an otherwise tranquil tableau. With the crowd growing, she braced herself for the inevitable crush of people looking to board. Stepping onto the ferry's rusted floor, a man pushed by her violently, knocking her knapsack from behind and sending her grabbing for the shoulders of an older woman in front of her.

"I'm sorry."

"Are you alright?"

"Yes, thank you."

Finding a corner, Liv squished herself aboard the overloaded and overworked ferry that shuttled people, cars, and goods north and south across the River Gambia. She leaned over the railing to escape the strong smell of petrol. The rumble of the engine rose, growing so loud it reverberated through the whole ferry. After a jolt forward they started the slow crossing, leaving a thick trail of black smoke rising up behind them. With the sounds of water splattering out from the ship's hull, Liv's mind turned to Thomas and Andrew.

Once on the other side of the river, she found a seat in a communal van that transported her to the country's northern land border crossing with Senegal.

There were no computers at this border. Instead, all records of comings and goings were kept, by both sides, in large ledger books. No official would scan Liv's passport. While crossing, the only question asked of her was from a guard on the Senegalese side.

"How long are you staying for?"

"About one week or so. I'm visiting friends."

And just like that, without telling anyone in the country, Liv was gone.

As Liv was stepping into Senegal, Maya was arriving at the embassy and found the envelope waiting for her.

Maya,

Please tell Andrew I couldn't stand the thought of doing something that might hurt them. Tell him we love him and that we better see him soon. Thank you.

-Liv

26

"YOUR FRIEND, LIV, she's gone," Abdou said on his next visit. "She fled the country two days ago."

Thomas and Andrew's faces looked confused. They weren't privy to each development associated with the trial. They hadn't known about her subpoena, or that she was being called as a witness.

"The prosecution intended to use her as a witness," Abdou explained. "They had the court issue a subpoena to compel her attendance at the trial even if she didn't want to. She worried her testimony would be harmful to you. Because of the subpoena, this was likely the only way for her not to testify."

"Did you help her get away?" Andrew asked.

"No, no," Abdou clarified. "I can't help with something like that. In fact, I told her she had to comply. Then two days ago I got a phone call from Maya. Liv left her a note but didn't say how she left or where she was going. She probably crossed by land into Senegal, undetected. They'll try to blame me or Maya for it, but our hands are clean."

Andrew was smiling, grateful for her friendship and her courage.

"Believe me," Abdou said, "it's better this way. From reading the journal I saw she was around for a lot. We won't miss her testimony."

"You got my journal?" Andrew asked.

"A copy, yes," he said, with a troubled look.

"How is it?" Thomas asked.

"It is not helpful, but not as harmful as I feared. There is only one reference to intimate relations and that is after you kissed the first time. But there is no other mention of sexual conduct in violation of the law, and I don't believe a kiss alone can be an unnatural offense, more intimate sexual activity would be needed. There are discussions about emotions we'd probably prefer weren't mentioned, but again, those are just feelings."

"But won't they say it's proof of a relationship?" Thomas asked.

"Yes," Abdou answered. "That's exactly what they will say. Still," Abdou contended, "in the absence of proof, it will be a greater leap for the court to come down with a guilty verdict. They can say you broke society's moral code, but that is not the same as breaking the criminal code."

Thomas looked back at him, unconvinced impressive wordplay would be enough to save them.

"This is why it's important," he continued, "for me to speak with as many people as possible who can attest to the fact that when they saw you together, you were not being intimate or behaving as expected for a romantic couple."

Related to this point, he told them, was an observation he wanted clarification on. "From your descriptions, Andrew, I get the impression that most of the time you and Thomas have been together was at night. Is this correct?"

"Yes," Andrew answered.

Abdou explained that finding examples of interactions in daylight would build a credible narrative for a friendship that took place in public. That would make it more difficult for the judge to convict them in the absence of concrete evidence of them breaking the law. "All these tales in the nighttime reinforce the idea you had something to hide."

"But we told you, besides playing soccer, it was always at night," Andrew said, looking concerned. They did have something to hide. "And even at night," he added, "we had to be careful."

The first Sunday evening that Andrew invited Thomas over was a nerve-racking experience. As soon as Andrew extended the invitation he grew restless and questioned if he had made an impulsive mistake. He rushed home on his bicycle breaking out into a sweat. As Andrew barged through the front door into the living room, Alex and Liv immediately sensed something was up.

"I invited Thomas over," he told them, expecting disapproving reactions from both.

"Great," Alex shrugged.

Even Liv didn't mind. "Did you want to watch a movie with us?"

"Are you sure it's okay?" Andrew asked. "It's not a risk?"

"Why would it be risky?" Alex replied. "Who's coming to supervise us?"

Their reactions were reassuring, but for the entire evening, Andrew's nerves were obvious. He went around the house making sure all the blinds were fully drawn. When it suddenly occurred to him that their shadows and silhouettes might still be seen, he asked about turning off the lights.

"Do you think you're being a little paranoid?" Alex asked him.
"I don't know."

Whether he was paranoid or not, each time Thomas came over, Andrew went through the same preparatory routine. If they were alone at night, he'd leave off almost all the lights inside, sometimes keeping on the kitchen light so they weren't in complete darkness.

"It was a relationship in darkness," Thomas explained. When they walked up along the beach at night they always separated when walking past the restaurants and hotels with patios. One of them would walk up ahead, the other followed a minute or two later. They would repeat this eleven times on every walk from the hotel until they reached their spot near Bakau.

Once, early on, they were walking past one of the more popular restaurants and Thomas went past first. Andrew followed but as the patio lighting illuminated his face he heard his name called out. He looked over and saw a table of people he knew. They waved at him and his body instinctively headed in their direction as he peered out into the darkness for Thomas. Andrew had trouble convincing them he had somewhere to be, and the conversation lingered as he refused to sit down. He began wondering if Thomas would still be waiting for him. When he finally got away he walked hurriedly into the darkness only to discover Thomas wasn't in sight. He scanned the dark horizon more carefully and saw him in the distance, sitting alone on the sand at the water's edge, letting his feet get wet. "Sorry," he said to him when he arrived. "I saw people I knew."

"It's okay," Thomas said, before getting up to continue walking.

Eventually, even they grew tired of the darkness. Since the time they made their fish by the fire, they continued to build small fires on the beach most Fridays and Sundays. They were never big, but they did the trick. Instead of two people meeting for a conversation, it felt more like a date. Gathering small amounts of wood and building the fire gave them an opportunity to do something together. One Sunday Andrew brought marshmallows to roast after noticing them unexpectedly in one of the higher-end grocery shops.

"You've never roasted marshmallows?" he asked with disbelief.

"No," Thomas answered, surprised Andrew was surprised.

"It's easy," Andrew said before finding a good roasting stick and piercing it with a marshmallow. When it was golden brown, but not yet burned, he pointed the stick in Thomas's direction. "Eat it," he said with a wide grin.

When it was Thomas's turn next, Andrew watched with anticipation as Thomas's marshmallow began browning and started to bubble.

"Ahhh!" Thomas exclaimed when it caught fire. Andrew laughed.

"It's not ruined," he said, before explaining he could pull off the top, burnt layer, and eat the gooey inside. "Like this."

They were always careful not to let the flames get too high – just letting them hover off the ground – unlike when they built their bonfires at night in Sierra Leone, when Thomas and Andrew kept piling the wood on higher and higher, like children discovering something for the first time. Alex and Liv watched with amusement as the two of them kept wanting to build the fires bigger until the flames shot well above Andrew, who was the tallest in the group. They kept going off to the tree line and coming back with bigger and bigger branches, throwing them atop the pile without regard for anything, watching the flames grow, illuminating their faces, smiling with amazement.

"And then there were my birthday candles," Thomas said, turning to Andrew.

"Oh yeah," he said as they both laughed. Abdou sat across from them, looking on, left out of the joke.

It was a Wednesday and they were meeting for Thomas's twentieth birthday. "He brought me this little cake, a small one from a nice place on Kairaba. He put twenty-one candles in it and said I had to blow them out quickly before anyone saw. So I blew them out and then he sang me happy birthday quietly."

Andrew finished the story as Thomas turned to him, remembering. "I forgot plates," he admitted, "and cutlery, so we had to eat with our hands in the dark."

Abdou smiled at them. "And when you made these small fires," he said, turning back to the matter at hand, "no one saw you?"

"Unless they saw from a distance and never came past us," Thomas said. "The fires were far back from the water so that the rocks curved and blocked them. You know how it is by Bakau?"

"Sure," Abdou nodded.

"And by the end, we stopped going there when the news broke about that house and the story about the gay society. And the last time we went, there was no fire."

"When you spent time with Alex and Liv, at your house," Abdou asked turning to Andrew, "how was that?"

"It was good," he answered.

"It was great," Thomas corrected. "When the four of us were together you would forget something was wrong. Not wrong, but that something about the picture wasn't supposed to be."

"We were just people, together."

"When we were alone, because of everything," Thomas added, "we spent so much time talking about this issue or that problem. When it was the four of us, we wanted to be normal, to be like them and try to have times where we could forget. Being with Alex and Liv, you know, watching them together made me feel like I was getting as close to normal as I could, because I was a part of it."

Andrew had never heard Thomas speak that way about those times. As he listened and watched Thomas express himself, he thought that that's exactly how he felt about them too.

In all their meetings, which were always held as a group, Abdou took diligent notes. He was exceedingly polite to both of them. He knew prison was a setting that thrived on robbing away one's dignity, so Abdou made every effort to treat Thomas and Andrew with respect. He always shook their hands and tried to be deferential when they spoke and not cut them off, even if what they were saying wasn't relevant. His disposition stood in contrast with that of the guards. If the guards were harsh as they barked their orders each day, Abdou was soft and hid whatever frustrations he may have been feeling.

Abdou was also sensitive to the conditions of their detention, always promising to try and find ways to improve them even as he expressed doubt he could succeed. "The worst is that they'll say no," he told them. He knew they were being kept in conditions most people would liken to squalor and that retaining one's hygiene was not easy. The food he brought them from home was deeply appreciated.

"You must thank your wife for us," Thomas said one afternoon, licking the domoda sauce from his fingers.

"Soon you will thank her yourself," Abdou responded. It was a kind and uplifting response. Even though everyone in the room knew it was probably a fantasy, they let themselves be misled for a minute.

Abdou tried to keep confident assertions to a minimum. Actually, he was more resolute than confident. But this was enough on its own to instill confidence in Thomas and Andrew. They observed his relentless determination to understand their story from every angle – to piece it together in the most advantageous way possible – and believed that Abdou was giving them the closest they could get to a proper defense. He picked up on each opportunity to highlight they were in fact just very close friends, who even if they were homosexuals, never took the next step to become lovers. Whenever he discovered a new example to illustrate this, he made the same assertive sound, an *mmhmm*, clearly satisfied with himself, before turning to his notepad to write it down. He even took his notes in a determined manner, his pen clasped firmly in his hand as he wrote with a look of deep concentration.

They were getting nearer to the trial and Andrew, at the end of one of their meetings, asked Abdou if he thought it was smart for them to admit to being gay. He reminded them that because they weren't going to testify they weren't required to admit to anything. But he looked at them and said, whether they admitted it or not, the evidence, namely Andrew's journal, was pretty decisive. "And on that matter," he said, "I'm afraid most people, including the judge, will have made up their minds."

"What do you think," Thomas asked cautiously, "about homosexuality?" Abdou and Andrew looked taken aback by the question. They hadn't veered into the personal like this before. "I know how Gambian men feel, including the progressive ones. So don't be ashamed, or maybe embarrassed is the better word. But I'm curious, after spending time with us, what you think about homosexuality."

"Honestly, I never thought much about it before I met both of you," he said, stalling for time as he thought how to answer the question. "And I don't want to be unprofessional and disclose personal opinions and biases that might undermine your confidence in me. But because I believe honesty is critical to trust, I'll share a little." He spoke in the formalistic way of many educated Gambians, a way of speaking that Andrew sometimes thought might be used to mask unpleasant or unnatural conversations. "What I will say is I've become good at distinguishing between homosexuality and homosexuals. And while I may not yet fully understand homosexuality, or be familiar with it, I have come to understand that... that one's confusion over homosexuality should not come at the expense of the rights of the homosexual. That is all to say that while I, and I believe many others in this country, become more acquainted with the idea of homosexuality and its existence within our communities, we shouldn't be taking out that confusion on the individual."

The looks on Thomas and Andrew's faces told him he wasn't being as eloquent as he wanted, nor had he convinced them he was a true ally.

"What I'm trying to say, and perhaps I am not being as clear as I want to be, is after having met and interacted with both of you, with homosexuals for the first time, I find it difficult to justify taking out... taking out," he appeared frustrated by his inability to articulate himself, and stopped himself and proclaimed, "Just because I don't understand, and for me it wouldn't be my first choice, it doesn't give me, or anyone the right to pass judgment on you. And certainly not criminal judgment."

He stopped to reflect on his answer and think if there was more he needed to say. Seeming content with himself, he turned to Thomas. "Is that a satisfactory answer? I hope it is, because it's the truth."

"It's very satisfactory," Thomas replied.

Abdou's visits grew shorter and less frequent in the lead-up to the trial. He spent most of his time at his office, crafting his arguments, preparing questions for the prosecution's growing list of witnesses, and speaking to Andrew's friends to try and shore up his case, which he knew – but didn't share with them – needed shoring up. When he did go and see them he had a list of questions that needed only short explanations.

"At Andrew's where did you park the bike? You said you hopped over the gate at night. You did this with a bicycle?"

"No," Thomas explained. The bike was always parked nearby, close to a fuel station but away from anywhere people could see. "It was in a mostly empty and abandoned area. I would park and walk to their house, and then walk back to pick it up."

"Okay. And this was your bike? You said you had little money to spend on things. How did you buy a bicycle?"

"My friend, Suleiman, the one I told you about who I lived with, he let me use his so I wouldn't have to spend money to get to work every day. When I moved out he insisted I take it. He wouldn't let me refuse."

"Aha. I see."

These sessions were the only events to break up the mundane waiting game before the trial. They interrupted the anxiety brought on by minds left with little to do but think as they waited and waited, wanting on some level just to get the trial over with and leave behind their uncertainty. Andrew had, for the time being, given up on Maya or the U.S. government's ability to free him. Even the guards taunted him, *they can't save you.* He equated the infrequency of Maya's visits with a lack of progress. The last he'd heard from her was that his family had returned home and were arranging various meetings on his behalf.

He was only given one phone call with them. It was after his second week in detention when Maya and Abdou came to tell him.

"Really?"

"Yes," Maya said. "Everything has been arranged. They've been given a phone number and will be calling in thirty minutes. They'll only let you speak for five minutes, though."

Five minutes? What do you say in five minutes?

Andrew was glad he only had a half-hour warning about the call. He wasn't sure he could've handled waiting longer. His heart was thumping like crazy as he waited. He tried to think of what he would tell them but had difficulty focusing and organizing his thoughts. He was also nervous for what they'd say, or didn't say, now that they knew about him.

Two guards led Andrew, along with Maya and Abdou, to a small office with a desk, chair, and telephone. Andrew was told to sit and the call would be dispatched through. He'd have privacy for the five minutes, but as soon as the five minutes were up a guard would come in and he'd have to hang up. Maya warned him the call would probably be recorded.

"Hello? Andrew?" It was his mother. The connection with the prison landline was poor and it made her sound faint and far away.

"Hi mom."

"Oh my goodness! Andrew! We're all here on speaker – your father, me, and Lindsay."

"Hi everyone." His eyes were welling up. "Where are you?" he asked, wanting to be able to picture them.

"In the kitchen," his mother answered.

He saw them sitting together at the wooden table. He wanted to be in the room with them.

"Andrew, are you okay?" his father asked.

"Yessss," he said, "I'm fine," before biting his lip to stop himself from crying.

"We're doing everything we can to get you home as quickly as possible," his father continued. "The people at the embassy and here at the State Department are being very helpful. Hopefully something will happen soon."

"Grant!" he heard his mother exclaim. "They said not to make him too optimistic," she continued in a hushed tone.

"Mom," Lindsay chimed in, "he can hear you."

Andrew smiled, knowing exactly what everyone's faces looked like on the other end at that moment.

"Hey, Linds," Andrew said tearfully. "Guess the secret's out," he added, his voice shaking slightly.

"Andrew, don't worry about any of that now. Everything is fine and we love you just the same." His father spoke quickly and assertively, in a manner that almost undermined the effect of his affirmation. "We've been speaking with your lawyer, Mr. Bojang. It's important for you to listen to what he has to say. He knows the system. We'll continue to work with the embassy and State Department to do what we can. If you're still there when the trial begins..."

If *you're* still there, Andrew heard, repeating it in his head.

"...back to Senegal so we can be close by," was all Andrew heard afterwards.

"Andrew?" his mother asked.

"Yes?"

She wanted to know if he was sleeping and eating okay. It was a mother's question, and he loved her for it.

He told her he was, and that sometimes Abdou brought food Manima made for them at home.

"*Oh*," she said, clearly choked up. "We have to thank her." Andrew knew she wasn't talking to him but to his father.

Talking over her parents, Lindsay asked if the conditions were clean.

"It's clean enough," he lied, not telling them that he wasn't sure how much longer he could endure the filth and stink all around him. "I'm allowed to wash every other day."

"Every other day?" his mother shot back, making him realize they probably didn't grasp the true nature of his conditions.

There was a knock at the door and a guard told Andrew he only had one minute left.

"Guys, I have to go," he said, barely able to get the words out of his mouth. "The time is running out." He was scared to say goodbye.

"Andrew, we love you," his sister said. "And we're going to see you soon."

There was a pause as everyone thought about what they wanted to say next.

"I'm hugging you as tight as I can," his mother said.

By the time Andrew's father told him he loved him, Andrew was inhaling a long breath through his nose that he held in an attempt to stop his tears. He gulped down the lump in his throat and closed his eyes tightly.

"I miss you guys," he said. "And I'm sorry about this."

He heard his mother saying his name as the guard approached and took the phone away from him.

As much as he yearned to speak to or see his family before the call, it proved destabilizing instead of bringing him comfort. It put him right in the middle of a tug of war that always ended in a draw.

The conversation reminded him that at his most vulnerable, his family still provided unyielding support — and that had to count for something. He dreamed of being together with them again, and with the family dynamic he'd always wanted. Their reunion, he told himself, would be the start of a new beginning. Andrew grew fixated on thinking of ways to run away and had wild visions of a team of Marines sent in to rescue him.

But invariably, each time he thought about his freedom, he wound up chiding himself. Everyone seemed to be working so hard to free him. But who, besides Abdou, was working to free Thomas? And really, what freedom could Abdou promise? To so many people in Andrew's corner, he was the full picture. But in Andrew's mind, he was only half of the picture. As the immediacy of the phone call with his family faded, the prospect of going home – of falling back into his own bed, waking up and looking around at the walls of his childhood room – did not bring the same comfort as thinking back to the times he spent with Thomas. When his cell went dark each night, he was transported back to all the nights they spent together, holding each other, content, surrounded by the same silence. He leaned up against the wall, resting his head on it, closing his eyes, and wanted to pretend it was Thomas, and that he was looking out into the sea.

Most of the time, his memories ended the same way, in defeat. He looked around and saw no beach. Above him were no stars. Maybe he had lost, and wishing for home was the next best thing. Or maybe giving up wasn't giving up. Maybe it didn't make him a selfish ass to hope to be deported, leaving Thomas behind to fend for himself. The circumstances had changed drastically, but on some level, isn't that what he always knew would eventually happen? It was hard to come up with an answer for what he was holding out for. The lack of an answer made Andrew feel like an even bigger asshole.

One day, as Thomas was left alone with his thoughts without word from Abdou about his family, he tried imagining how everything had played out at Sheriff's house and in the village. He tried to picture his parents' reaction. He knew they'd publicly disown him and make known their disapproval. But in their heart of hearts he was still their son. He wanted to believe there would be a pang of loyalty, or even guilt, that would follow them. He tried to picture the two of them talking at night in hushed tones in the privacy of their bedroom where no one would hear them. Would his mother or father prove to be the sympathetic one? Could their past be forgotten? He wondered if his father would completely sever off those years of fishing, all those nights on the river, only the two of them. How do you erase a memory?

It was just as Thomas began envisioning his parents' conversation that he was disturbed by one of the guards. Someone was there to see him. He was led to one of the interview rooms and told to wait for his visitor. Thomas had no idea who might be coming to visit him, but as soon as Suleiman walked in, Thomas was not surprised. When the door was closed behind him he looked over at Thomas.

"Are you okay?"

"I'm fine."

"Thomas? Are you actually okay?"

He looked across at his friend, feeling agitated. "What do you want me to say? I'm managing fine. Are you here as a friend or a journalist?" he asked suspiciously.

"Both. Because I'm a journalist I am able to come, but now that I'm here, I'm also your friend."

"Then you have come to do me a favor?" he asked with sarcastic impatience.

"In a way," he explained. He was granted ten minutes to ask questions for a story he was writing about the case. The police and government had at first refused, saying Thomas was under no obligation to answer any questions, but when Suleiman pressed them further and further and had his editor make some calls on his behalf, they relented, granted him access, and said he could try. "Because I don't want to lie, I'm going to ask you a few questions. You don't have to answer them. I will report how you maintained your right not to answer. But that's not the real reason why I'm here."

"So why did you come?" he asked. Thomas hated how the present forced him to wash over the past and all that Suleiman had done for him. He hated how easily he could be angry at someone who meant so much to him.

"I want you to consider changing your plea, to plead guilty. It's the only way they might be lenient with your sentence and not give you the maximum of fourteen years."

Thomas didn't immediately respond.

"Do you really want to spend fourteen years in this place? Your life will be over."

Thomas paused long enough for Suleiman's eyes to widen with anticipation for his answer. Turning his gaze away before speaking, a calm returned to Thomas. He looked back at his friend.

"You don't get it."

"What don't I get?"

"It's already over," he said in a low voice, almost a whisper.

"What do you mean?"

"Life. Whatever I had of it. It's finished. Walking down a street with the sun on my face and to feel at ease. To have a home.

Laughing. Being together in bed with the person you love and feeling protected. The relief that comes from knowing you're not alone, that life's most important piece has found its place. All of that, Suleiman, it's over. I'll never have it back. Even if one day I am released, it will be gone. There was a time when I thought that life was about being alive, that breathing was living. Luckily, I was able to discover how I was mistaken, how there is so much more to being alive. But that part of life, for me, is over now."

"Maybe there's a chance that if you get free, one day you will be able to start over?" Suleiman suggested, delicately.

"Start over as what?" he asked him. "Look, maybe something might happen. But I don't think so. Hope is important, but we must also be realistic mustn't we?" Though he continued to whisper, Thomas's voice became stronger. "Do you know what they say to me in here? The threats? The look on everyone's faces as they watch me? It's like they are wild animals waiting to pounce on their prey. And I never know when it will come, but I'm certain it will. Every night as I fall asleep. The guards. The other people in my cell. What they promise they'll do to me after the trial? Do you know what they *already* did to me?" he said in an excited whisper leaning across the table as Suleiman's face started to grow uncomfortable, registering what he thought Thomas meant. This shouldn't have surprised Suleiman, given his job. But everything personal is always experienced differently.

"Do you know how I sleep? However many men there are in my cell, there is always one sleeping mat missing. I sleep in the corner, like a dead rat, curled up. Do you know what they throw at me? What buckets they dump on me? And do you know what it's like to hear people laugh and cheer as this is done to you?

"I can show you the scars if you want to see them. Some scars though, you cannot see, they are in places you would not want to look.

"You don't understand," he said, regaining some calm. "The minute it was declared I was the homosexual, the one in love with the American boy, it was over for me. In here I'm nothing, not a man, not a human being. Maybe on the outside there was a place to hide, run away. But even that I doubt. And in here? That's not possible."

"What about the guards?"

"The guards?" he exclaimed in disbelief. "If they're not participating, they watch from the outside. Even the supervisors. I have no one, Suleiman. It's over. All I can hope for is that Andrew gets freed somehow, that the Americans can make enough pressure for him to be released."

"Are you giving up too soon?" Suleiman asked hesitantly.

"No," he answered confidently. "I didn't give up too soon. If I did, I wouldn't be here. Giving up in this country, for me, would mean not living. So I took a risk and got to live. I don't know if it was worth it. I don't know how you answer those questions. Maybe if I did I wouldn't be here right now. All I can tell you, Suleiman, is that what I got from what I did, I would have never gotten if I did not do it. And for a time it was more magnificent than I had ever imagined life could be. What's better? To live so you can be old, filled with regrets and bitterness, just to stay breathing? Maybe. No one can say. I chose one way. I refused to give up, and along the way discovered things I didn't know were possible. And now this is my fate."

When he sensed Suleiman was still incapable of speaking, that he had no real response to Thomas's sober assessment, Thomas spoke again. This time his expression and tone softened. The distress on Suleiman's face reminded him how much he did in fact mean to him. Thomas felt remorse for dismissing that. "You have been a good friend, Suleiman. Better than I could have ever asked for. Certainly better than I deserved. And it means a lot to see you here, trying to help. But seriously, there isn't anything you can do for me now."

Thomas could see Suleiman's face and understood that it was now he who needed to offer consolation. "Do you remember when you told me one time that maybe in the future our world wouldn't be so upside down?"

Suleiman nodded slightly at his friend.

"I remember it well. You had this look on your face that said to me you really hoped one day that would be the case, that his place will be less upside down. Well, it still is." Suleiman forced a smile. "You are a man with many abilities, certainly more than me. You must do what you're best at and write your articles to document the madness of this place, so one day people may grow so sick of reading it over and over, and they will wake up and demand change. And when that day comes, when this world is not so upside down, there will be evidence to pass judgment on the real criminals, the ones who have committed the real crimes. And if my story, and you writing articles about it, can maybe have a role in that, well that could be some satisfaction. Right?"

Suleiman tried to nod his head to show agreement but it refused to cooperate. His face was incapable of hiding his anguish.

With nothing left to say, Thomas shifted his tone. "Come, brother," he continued, "ask me your questions."

"It's okay," Suleiman said. "It's okay."

27

EXPECTING CROWDS AND traffic on the first day of the trial, the police brought Thomas and Andrew to the courthouse early. As a result, and to their surprise, they were kept together in a small holding cell in the back of the building until the trial began. It was the first time since their arrest that they were left alone. Well, not completely alone – a security camera hanging from the ceiling pointing in their direction served as an ominous warning against doing anything that could be perceived as incriminating. Still, they were the only two people in the room.

"I miss you," Andrew said, speaking to the ground.

"You too."

"Are you better?"

"I'm okay. They need me to look handsome for the American media," Thomas said, hinting a smile. "Has Maya brought you any news?" he asked. "What does she say is happening?"

"I haven't heard from her in a while. She said they're working on it. Whatever that means."

"Are they optimistic?"

"I dunno."

Thomas was looking right at Andrew, wanting to say something.

"What?" Andrew asked.

"Nothing," he answered, before continuing, "it's nice to be alone with you."

"This counts?"

"In a way," Thomas shrugged.

There was a discernable difference in their temperaments and Thomas was trying to lift Andrew up.

"I'm sorry," Andrew said, "I'm just..."

"You don't have to apologize," he said. Their eyes met, making the frustration apparent. Andrew sighed before looking away.

"Are you mad?" Thomas asked.

"Mad? At who?"

"I don't know. Anyone. Me?"

"Why would I be mad at you?"

"For getting you into this."

Andrew looked back up at Thomas and saw the concern on his face. He wasn't mad at Thomas. He *was* mad, furious in fact, at everything else, but not at Thomas. "You're like the only thing I'm *not* mad at right now. And," he added with a tiny smile, "don't take all the credit for this."

Thomas smiled back. "You have to promise me something," he said, his face turning serious again.

"What?" Andrew asked quietly, nervously.

"That if Maya comes to you to take you out of here, you won't think for half a second about it. That you'll go with her as fast as you can back to the U.S. It doesn't matter what. Sign whatever papers you have to sign. Say whatever you need to say about me. I don't care," he said, putting his hand out to stop Andrew from interrupting. It was clear he'd thought about this and needed to get it off his chest. "You can do so much more to help me from the outside. Even knowing that you're safe back in America will give me comfort. You have to promise me that whatever it takes, you'll do it and you'll go."

"This isn't your fault."

"It's not about fault or blame. I'm past that. In the beginning I blamed myself, but we all believe we're protected from these things. I don't think you and I behaved any differently than someone else would have. But that doesn't erase the fact that we're here now, and you could have a chance to get out. If you didn't do that because of how you feel about me, it's something I couldn't deal with. I would blame myself for it, and I don't want that to happen."

"Okay," said Andrew, uncomfortably and tersely, hoping to mollify him and move on to a new subject.

"*Promise me*," Thomas insisted.

"I do," Andrew said, widening his eyes as if to show he too was serious. "I promise. *I'll go*," he added, before turning to face the ground.

"Good," he answered, keeping his gaze fixed on Andrew, waiting for him to lift his face back up. When Andrew didn't, Thomas spoke again. "Andrew, what's wrong?"

"Nothing," he said, speaking to the floor.

"I know that's not true. You can tell me."

There was a pause before Andrew raised his head. His expression was different. Before, he tried to be reassuring in an effort to appease Thomas. Now, his face was tired and forsaken. "That's the problem. You're always trying to help me, or watch out for me, or take the blame. Every time something happens, your first reaction is always me. I've tried thinking of times when I've done the same for you, but can't."

"What?" Thomas exclaimed. "Andrew, you're being..."

Andrew didn't wait for Thomas to finish.

"Like, I still don't know what happened to you, what was actually done to you. And what's worse, in all this time, I haven't really asked. I don't know if it's because I'm scared to know. All I know is that my experience has probably been nothing compared to yours, but I haven't asked you, and you're always the one trying to look out for me."

"That's not true. I never thought once..."

"But it is true. And now, with this, if *I* have the chance to leave. What about you? Where will you go? Some nights I wonder why I didn't try to convince you to run away. How instead of me coming back for a year, why I never said we should leave together."

"Andrew, we both..."

They were jolted by the sound of the door swinging open. Four guards marched in and ordered them to their feet. Their unfinished conversation heightened their shared sense of helplessness as they were forced to stand silently, side-by-side, their arms out front as their handcuffs were placed on. Andrew watched as the silver buckles clamped tightly around Thomas's wrists. They were led upstairs to face an overflowing courtroom, with spectators forced to stand, lining the walls. They stood in the doorway, peering in.

It was bigger than the magistrate's court. The ceiling was higher, making it less suffocating. Before being led through, unexpectedly, the guards removed their handcuffs, letting them enter with their hands free. Looking into the room, they could both see Maya, who must've arrived early. She was seated in the second row, behind the defense table. Thomas tried to make out Suleiman but couldn't find him.

Something overcame Andrew as he stepped into the court-room, dulling his faculties. Even the sounds, spectators conversing waiting for court to be called into session, became muffled and dis-tant as he was led to the defendant's table. Abdou waited for them. He looked overwhelmed. His table was a mess of papers and differ-ent file folders. He rummaged between them, seemingly incapable of finding what he was searching for. His worn briefcase, fallen on the floor, had more papers spilling out. By contrast, the prosecutor's table was neat. The government's case was led by Mr. Touray, the country's chief prosecutor. He was tall and rail thin, with a stern and judgmental face, the product of a serious career that had no time for frivolities. He sat patiently behind a table organized into neat piles of papers and binders. Andrew counted at least five.

Unlike Magistrate Colley, the judge, when he entered, projected calm. He slowly made his way up to his seat. After he sat down he looked up and out into the courtroom, first at Mr. Touray's table and then at Abdou's. His expression was ordinary. His name was also Touray, an incredibly common surname in Gambia, and he had no relation to the prosecutor. Something about Justice Touray, who had a short and round figure, made him appear less intimidating than Mr. Touray. His face too. Andrew saw how his cheeks drooped from the side and fell from his face. They looked like they'd be smooth to touch. As Justice Touray took his time to arrange his notes, he did so with an expression exuding more curiosity than authority. Abdou had told them both that Justice Touray, one of the longest serving judges in the country, had a reputation for being fair. Seeing him in person made it easier for Andrew to believe.

Justice Touray was polite in welcoming everyone after the court registrar opened the trial. There was an air of business as usual when he asked for Andrew and Thomas to confirm their pleas, or change them if they so desired, which they did not. Everything about him in those first few moments suggested he wished to resist the hysteria that increasingly defined how the case was being portrayed outside the courtroom. Andrew had a hard time accepting it, but he found something about Justice Touray welcomingly reassuring.

By contrast, Mr. Touray delivered his opening statement in a harsh but measured tone, with an air of self-importance he derived from the occasion. He spoke from prepared notes but relied on them only periodically. His argument was simple and his words were to the point.

"Mr. Turner, a practicing homosexual, came to The Gambia knowing full well his lifestyle was in direct contravention of our laws. Nonetheless, he still came, determined to spread his unlawful lifestyle to the Gambian populace." But it was only when he met Thomas, Mr. Touray said, turning to draw Thomas into his severe gaze, that Andrew found a partner willing to participate in his perverse criminal activities. "Together, the two of them embarked on an illegal romance in direct contravention of criminal laws meant to ensure our society stays pure and remains consistent with our values.

"Andrew's illegal romantic partner, Thomas, wanted to run away from his Gambian life. He ran away from his family and came to Banjul. But in Banjul that wasn't enough, and he took employment at a place where he could come into contact with as many foreigners as possible in his desire to act upon his homosexual predilections."

Over the course of the trial, Mr. Touray promised, the prosecution would call various witnesses, persons who saw Andrew and Thomas together in private and public settings, who would testify they were engaged in what he called *romantic conduct of the most reprehensible kind*. The court mustn't forget what this conduct truly represents while the defense, he said, now turning his gaze to Abdou as if to challenge him, "parades individuals before the court who will ask us to disregard our laws and values. And if in the end the words of witnesses are still deemed insufficient, one of the accused himself has given us, in written form, all the necessary evidence to prove these two were in fact involved in a sexual relationship," he said, emphasizing *sexual* with disgust. "The same accused that, as a witness will attest, never had a girlfriend in The Gambia but still had condoms in his personal belongings.

"In the end, Your Honour, there will be no doubt the acts of the accused are in clear violation of the laws of this nation and of mankind."

It was surreal for Andrew to watch it begin. He and Thomas were actors in a play they never auditioned for. They were cast in their roles, forced to sit there and endure – helplessly unable to speak out against the theater unfolding all around them. It was debilitating to watch as Abdou, Mr. Touray, and Justice Touray took control over their fates. As Mr. Touray spoke, Andrew's anger and incredulity became hard to contain. He was horribly uncomfortable in his chair and kept subtly repositioning himself. Thomas kept discreetly looking at him, as if to try and calm him. At one point even Abdou caught on, turning to Andrew and asking with his eyes, *are you okay?*

Yes, Andrew nodded softly. But it was a blatant lie. Inside, he was squirming. *I can't believe this is actually-fucking-happening.*

The only witness scheduled for that day was Isatou's nephew, whose name, Momodou Jobarteh, Thomas and Andrew had only recently learned. Seeing him enter and walk up to the witness stand was the first time they ever saw the man responsible for what happened to them. Walking past them, Momodou turned his face towards the two of them but didn't react.

You, Thomas thought.

He seemed regular and lacked any distinguishing features. He was probably a few years older than Thomas, maybe around Andrew's age. He looked like a local, if there was such a look, wearing a shiny and colorful bazin dashiki, with a white-knitted taqiyah on his head. He swore his oath on the Quran, *Bismillah Rahman Rahim.* When Mr. Touray thanked him and asked him how he was, he replied, "*Alhamdu lillahi Rabbil 'alamin.*"

"Thank you, Mr. Jobarteh," Mr. Touray replied. He nodded, satisfied that Momodou had established his credentials as a pious man before the court.

His testimony was brief but unnerving. Mr. Touray used simple and direct questions. During the late spring and summer months when the days were longest, Momodou generally left for the mosque at five in the morning to recite the morning prayer, *Fajr.* Speaking in accented English, he told the court he was one of the main volunteers at the mosque, so he tried to arrive early on the days he attended. He confirmed that on early morning trips he usually encountered only a handful of other people on the streets, mostly men who were also on their way to prayers. He had been doing this since he was a teenager. He knew what the streets looked like in the dark.

"And during these trips to the mosque, did you ever encounter individuals you suspected were burglars?"

"Yes."

"Why did you suspect they were burglars?"

"From how they dressed, how they moved, and what they carried. A person doing a robbery tries to hide and go fast."

Thomas was the one who had to restrain himself most during Momodou's testimony. He knew the questions Mr. Touray was going to ask and was uninterested in the answers. Instead, he was trying to contain a burning desire to stand up and demand Momodou answer his own questions. If Momodou saw Thomas hop the gate, but didn't think he was a burglar, *Why was it any of your business?*

"And why didn't you think he was a burglar?"

"Because he acted like a regular person. He didn't carry anything. He dressed in normal clothing. He acted like a person going to begin the day, not in a hurry."

"How many times did you see him this way?"

"Three."

So, why did it matter to you? What did I ever do to you?

He told the story of the sport shorts in the laundry and concluded that upon seeing Thomas the second time, "I knew they must belong to this man."

So what? Why did it bother you so much? It was the same question Mr. Touray closed with.

"I know this behavior is wrong. It is prohibited by the Quran, and by the laws of this country. I needed to do my part." His answer, in contrast to his earlier ones, sounded rote and pre-programmed.

Abdou's cross-examination was very brief. Though he'd barely said a word the whole day, Abdou looked worn out. In contrast to Mr. Touray's crisp appearance, Abdou seemed hastily put together. His barrister's robes hung unnaturally from his broad shoulders; his sleeves were too long, making it more difficult for him to hold his notes. But just like when Andrew met him for the first time, as soon as he opened his mouth, letting his deep baritone fill the courtroom, he dispelled at least some of the doubt cast by his appearance.

In his questioning he merely wanted to confirm that Momodou had never seen Thomas and Andrew together, never heard them together, and never heard stories of them being together.

"No."

"And did you ever see, with your own eyes, Thomas inside the house located on the compound you claim you saw him emerging from?"

"No."

Abdou subtly nodded to Justice Touray signaling he was finished. Justice Touray adjourned for the day and announced that court would reconvene tomorrow. Abdou told Thomas and Andrew they would be taken to an interview room in the courthouse so he could speak to them briefly about tomorrow's witnesses. "And Andrew, Maya wants to speak to you too," he said, eliciting unexpected looks from both of them.

Maya's visit turned out to be disappointing. She had no news except to say she planned to update Andrew's parents on the case. They were following as much as they could from their hotel in Dakar, and she and Abdou promised to call after each day's proceedings. She also delivered messages of support they sent for Andrew, which he accepted with appreciation but also with haste, as Thomas looked on acutely aware that his family was nowhere. He looked away to give Andrew more freedom to react without having to worry about upsetting him. But as he tried to count the pockmarks on the wall, he felt a hand on his leg. He looked down and then at Andrew. Maya, too, saw what was happening and stopped. Thomas smiled appreciatively at Andrew in the brief silence.

Leaving, Maya told them that the embassy and State Department had one big idea, a new one not traditionally used, that she couldn't mention yet. They were going to try later in the week. *It's something that would be difficult to walk away from*, she told him.

"We'll see. Stay hopeful."

The session with Abdou was quick, a few clarifying questions before they were led out to the vehicles for the trip back to Mile 2. Only this time they weren't driving under the cover of the early morning. They saw the full extent of the fuss their trial created. The streets were packed. A huge crowd gathered outside the courtroom and there were too many signs to read, mostly deriding homosexuality, but one – <u>Thomas is not one of us</u> – stuck out. The number of news vans and journalists stretched for half a block. They could make out logos for CNN and BBC.

In Thomas's vehicle the guards turned to him, grinning. "You'll never escape this," one of them said. "No matter how far you try and run."

28

THAT NIGHT THOMAS drifted in and out of sleep. He thought back to how he'd dismissed Suleiman when he brought up the prospect of trying to flee and claim asylum somewhere. And what if Andrew had asked him to leave with him, would he have said yes? Could Andrew really have gotten him out? *Stop, this is not helpful.*

He awoke feeling entirely unrested and stepped forward out of his cell with trepidation; there was a more immediate concern. His supervisor, Mr. Bah, was scheduled to testify that day. Knowing the contempt Mr. Bah had towards him, especially when it concerned the favor he curried with foreigners, Thomas was dreading what he expected would be exaggerated testimony about witnessing his and Andrew's courtship. It was also the first time since the whole ordeal began that Thomas would be confronted by someone he knew.

Mr. Bah had a hard time containing his excitement throughout his testimony. Thinking that testifying on such an important matter made him a bigger person, Mr. Bah played up not only the substance of his answers, but his form, aggrandizing his voice and mannerisms to distract from his petite, overworked figure and small, beady eyes.

It was an onslaught. *Thomas loved foreigners... uninterested in his African brothers and sisters... He never quite fit in...*

Thomas listened to the indictment calmly. It didn't upset or anger him as much as he expected. In a sense, he thought to himself, Mr. Bah was right. Only the blame lay with him, not Thomas. *It is you, Mr. Bah, who pushed me away. You and all the others.* The part that did anger him, that infuriated him, was the blind self-righteousness, the hypocrisy of the accusations. As it began to sink in more and more, he struggled to put it out of his mind. He folded his hands over one another on the table to steady himself. When he sensed Andrew's gaze upon him, he turned to him and read Andrew's expression.

Try not to let it bother you. We both know it's not true.

What good does that do for us now? Thomas thought.

But when Mr. Bah went on to explain how Andrew regularly sat alone at the bar with Thomas, bringing him into a monologue of moral opprobrium, Thomas saw Andrew's body movements turning impatient, joining in his fury.

"Was there anything unique about Andrew's visits to the bar?" Mr. Touray asked.

"Yes."

"And what was that?"

"You could see how they..." Mr. Bah paused for effect. He was obviously well-rehearsed in how his testimony would go, and prepared for its climax. "You could see how they were in love."

A few disdainful gasps and whispers murmured throughout the courtroom as Mr. Bah proceeded to testify about how Thomas and Andrew behaved around one another. How they would reach across the bar and touch each other's hands or faces if they thought no one was looking, which was, at least the three of them knew, untrue. He also lied about how Andrew would sit at the bar, saying he often sat with his chin resting on his interlaced fingers.

"You know, like how the girls sit when they are dreaming about men," he said with ridicule.

As he spoke, Andrew was shocked at the flagrancy and shamelessness of his lies, as if the truth meant nothing. Thomas though, stuck in his seat, was past the point of feeling upset or betrayed. Instead, he grew embittered watching people he knew have no compunction for ruining his life with their lies. He thought he had outran them, but they caught up to him. And now they were pulling him down.

Two of the Gambian soccer players from the Sunday matches also testified how they perceived a different type of friendship between Thomas and Andrew.

"Not like the rest of us, who were normal friends," one of them said, without offering any specific example. "They weren't normal together."

Another noted that over time Thomas arrived earlier and earlier. "Before he would come just to play, but later he was there early, to spend time and not just for football."

Abdou's cross-examinations of all three were similar to that of Momodou the day before. Appearing tired, but managing to come across more comfortable in his clothes, he asked if any of the witnesses had ever seen Thomas or Andrew engage in the type of physical, sexual conduct prohibited by the law. He asked if there was any basis upon which they drew their conclusions, or if they concluded Thomas and Andrew engaged in the illegal acts solely on account of their subjective interpretations of their behavior, "which, I would like to point out, at the precise time you observed them, did not amount to a violation of the law."

His questions could be long-winded, but he still got the answer he wanted. *No.* No one had *actually* seen them break the law.

"But if you saw them, and saw what I saw about how they were together, you would agree that this is the only logical conclusion," implored Mr. Bah, trying to preserve his credibility.

It impressed Thomas to watch Adbou try valiantly to emphasize how none of the prosecution's witnesses ever saw Thomas and Andrew break the law. It felt nice to have someone stand up for him. Even so, he couldn't help but lose hope. The trial was a facade, a formality to be performed before the conviction everyone believed was coming came. A thick air of impatience hovered in the court as Abdou began his line of questioning. Everyone understood where he was going, but it was clear how little it mattered. Even Justice Touray, reluctant to appear biased, looked bored. *We know, Mr. Bojang – they didn't catch them in the act, but so what? What about everything else?*

They were just close friends didn't seem to be a convincing enough explanation.

Desperate for distractions, Thomas frequently scanned the courtroom. He quickly found Suleiman, always diligently taking notes, rarely looking up. They locked eyes on a few occasions. Suleiman consistently seemed uncomfortable and Thomas couldn't tell if it was because he was trying to maintain professionalism or if he felt guilty. During one of the breaks between witnesses, Thomas turned to Abdou and said he wanted to read copies of Suleiman's articles.

"He's the one who came to try and interview me in detention. I would like to see what he's writing."

"Sure," Abdou said quickly, pretending, like Thomas, that Suleiman was a stranger to him. "I will get you a copy." He spoke so quickly and failed to make a note of it that Thomas figured he'd forget. But during the next break he came back into the courtroom with a newspaper.

"Here," he said, placing it down in front of Thomas. "It's from yesterday."

GAYS ON TRIAL IN BANJUL read the headline. Beneath it was a picture of Thomas and Andrew that took up half of the page. It was, like so much else about the country's newspaper articles, sensationalistic. The subheading said it all. *U.S. and Gambian homosexual couple accused of undermining Gambian society, values. By Suleiman Darboe.* The article took up the bottom half of the page.

The trial of accused homosexuals, American Andrew Turner and Thomas Sow of Banjul, began today in the High Court of Banjul. The accused, appearing weak and forlorn, were led into the courtroom of Justice Touray for the first day of their five-day trial. The state's case is being handled by Chief Prosecutor Amadou Touray and the accused are represented by Abdou Bojang, a young barrister.

Global attention to the case is high due to Mr. Turner's American nationality. Journalists from several American media companies and the BBC were present.

Inside the courtroom it was clear there will be no special dispensation on account of Mr. Turner's citizenship. The government presented what it claims is evidence of a romantic relationship between the two men going back months. It suggested that Mr. Sow, who has a proclivity for foreigners, and Mr. Turner, purposefully acted in disregard of The Gambia's criminal laws to, as it was suggested in the courtroom, "challenge the very fabric of our way of life".

Many outside the courtroom agreed. "Let them rot in jail. We cannot have them here," said Awa Camara, a mother of four who came to show her support for the government. "We are standing up for our culture as Gambians." Another spectator, Musa Bittaye, proclaimed, "They want to make us impure, and live as sinners."

The silence from the country's legal and human rights community, who normally side with unpopular accused persons, underscored the condemnation and disapproval across Gambian society.

Others not attending the proceedings in Banjul, but also watching the trial closely, include the families of the accused. Mr. Turner's parents are in Dakar, trying to be as near to their son as possible after Gambian immigration authorities refused their entry into the country. Mr. Sow's family, some of whom live in Banjul and others in a village in the Mansakonko LGA, is hoping for the trial to come to a quick conclusion and for the maximum sentence to be handed down. "If Thomas is this homosexual, and we think now that he is," one of his brothers said, "he doesn't deserve his freedom and he's not a part of this family."

The trial is scheduled to last for the whole week, possibly more if witnesses require extra time. It will be

The Order of Nature

interesting to see what defense Mr. Bojang is able to put forward to disprove that the two were in fact lovers. His first foray into cross-examination was underwhelming and it does not bode well for the accused. With little evidence of a strong defense, and the prosecution confident, a verdict is not expected to take long.

Mr. Touray, the prosecutor, told this reporter that the prosecution has been working tirelessly. He said he intended to expose Misters Turner and Sow. "By the end of the trial no one will be able to look at these two men and think anything except that their very existence is, to borrow a phrase from our criminal code, against the order of nature."

Thomas had to temper his rage. His first instinct was to turn around and ask his friend why he betrayed him like this. *Appearing weak and forlorn? Little evidence of a strong defense? Was that necessary, Suleiman? And why couldn't Suleiman find anyone to speak in our defense? What happened to your plan? That your articles can help people see what's going on around them? Where is that in here?* Just as he was about to hold up the paper and turn to face Suleiman, he felt a hand on his wrist. It was Andrew, who'd read the article over Thomas's shoulder.

"Don't," he said. "What did you expect? He's only doing his job."

"He was my friend."

"He still is."

As court adjourned for another night, Abdou noticed Andrew was slow to get up. His face was stoic, impervious to the commotion all around him. It was distressing to see him like that.

337

"I will talk to Manima tonight and we will make you and Thomas some fresh domoda that I will bring to you tomorrow. The guards will let you eat it at the lunch break."

"Thanks," he said, expressionless, still seated, and seemingly unaware Thomas was being led away.

"Andrew, what's wrong?" Abdou asked, knowing it was a stupid question.

He looked up to Abdou, just as the guards, running out of patience, started walking towards him to take him from the courtroom.

"I just didn't think this is how it would turn out. That this would be my life."

Abdou didn't have a chance to respond before the guards took Andrew away, leading him through a side door and finally out of sight.

29

THAT NIGHT IN his cell Andrew was again alone with his thoughts. He hated thinking so much. It was all he did – think over and over, about the past, present, and future. And it was all so depressing and exhausting, but his thoughts became his only companion. He tried to transport himself away from them, to memories of happier times. But like so many other nights, his thoughts invariably led him back to the present and a growing heap of desolation and anxiety.

He tried sleeping longer, refusing his body's command to wake up. When that failed, and he grew uncomfortable on his mat, he faced the day with reluctance. It was the day of the trial he was dreading most, the one he felt most responsible for. The morning's witness was the police investigator who found his journal and he was being called to read certain entries. And though his use of the journal was highly erratic throughout the year – he could never quite get the hang of it – in retrospect, the times he did write in it now struck him as some of the most inopportune times to do so. The vindictiveness of his journal as the most definitive piece of evidence was almost too much to take.

Why did I ever write in it? I was such an idiot.

Mr. Touray exuded arrogance that morning. You could see it as he stood erect over the courtroom, surveying his surroundings. Calmly sitting down at his desk, he cast his eyes over Abdou, the young lawyer struggling to cope, furiously jotting down all sorts of notes for purposes unknown. The trial had been going well and today was the day, in his mind, when its fate should be sealed. There would be no doubt in the court's mind Thomas and Andrew were lovers, and guilty.

For added effect, or maybe it was genuine, the police officer came across as reluctant to read from the journal, as if its contents were so shocking and awful he was embarrassed to reveal them. The first entry he was asked to read was short.

I did it, finally. We kissed. Holy shit.

As Andrew lowered his face in embarrassment, Thomas tried to look over and reassure him. He had this sudden urge to kiss him right then and there. He wasn't seriously going to do it. But he wanted to show Andrew he needn't feel ashamed or regret for what he'd written. He hated how their personal memories were now being turned against them, used as proof of something to be spurned instead of celebrated. He wanted to tell Andrew not to let that happen. *Don't let them take them from us.*

The officer was asked to turn the page. "It is an entry," Mr. Touray explained, "written about a disagreement between Mr. Turner and his sister in America."

The officer read:

I don't understand why she has such a problem with it, with me being happy. You'd think after seeing me unhappy for so many years, or at least like she says, knowing I wasn't completely happy, that she'd finally be happy to see me like this. Instead she's being a bitch about it. It's kind of unfair actually. No one's judging the choices she makes. She gets to pick Jeff and because she's a girl and he's a guy no one cares. And if he was black and someone did care, they'd know it was wrong so they'd shut up about it. But because we're both guys, and he's from here, she has trouble accepting that. It's not what she envisioned for me, I guess. Well, she doesn't get to decide.

"Thank you," interrupted Mr. Touray. "That's enough. It seems Andrew's sister shares Gambia's disapproval of his lifestyle and he is angry because of it." His pithy conclusion, made without knowing Andrew and Lindsay's relationship, almost riled Andrew from his seat to correct the record. *It wasn't about me being gay. She didn't care about that. It was about me being gay here,* he thought to himself. *And it was rooted in love.*

Next, the officer read from the entry when Andrew admitted to being in love with Thomas. It was surprisingly early in their relationship — well before they admitted it to each other. But this wasn't a secret between them. After the relief of saying *I love you* subsided, the next time they found themselves walking alone they acknowledged how each of them felt that way for a long time already.

"When did you know?" Andrew asked.

"When I started sleeping again."

"What?"

"Remember I told you after we met I sometimes had trouble sleeping?"

"Yeah," Andrew said, remembering only vaguely.

"It was because I was in a state of disbelief about what was happening. I was too excited and I kept lying awake, distracted, thinking about my past but also looking into the future, our future. I was jumpy all the time, and in bed especially, because at night when you lie you have only your thoughts, and mine were too excited to let me sleep."

"So love put you to bed?" Andrew asked sarcastically.

Thomas laughed sweetly and teased Andrew with his eyes. He gave him a little shove on his arm. "It did. It relaxed me. Suddenly I realized that despite whatever surrounded us, everything was okay. Somehow it would work out. The most important thing was in order, and I could finally exhale and breathe out all the stresses. It brought peace to me. And it's when I began sleeping better." He looked over at Andrew, who seemed satisfied with the answer and then asked, "what about you?"

"It was at soccer."

He's the only person I really want to see there. And once he shows up, I wish the game would end already so we could leave together and be alone. Other things matter less now. They seem less important.

"Thank you again," said Mr. Touray stopping the officer.

Thomas found himself resisting more and more urges to turn to Andrew as he listened to the journal entries. *I felt that way, too,* he wanted to say. But with each passing entry, it became more difficult for them to face each other. These public reminders of what the relationship, and each other, had meant to them, made having it torn away from them all the more tragic and unbearable. It was the perfect encapsulation of the cruelty befalling them.

"And now," Mr. Touray continued, refusing Thomas or Andrew a desperately-needed break from it all, "if you'll please turn the page, to the entry for us."

Today is Thomas's birthday.

Andrew's jaw dropped. Even though they'd spoken about this with Abdou, he forgot about the entry.

We had cake on the beach. I remembered it was his birthday from an earlier conversation and he was surprised when I asked him how he planned to celebrate. He said probably nothing because no one knew it was his birthday, not even Suleiman. He was content to let his birthdays pass unacknowledged for the most part, except for his family calling. I said we should do something.

"What should we do?" Thomas asked Andrew across the bar.

"I dunno. Let me think of something."

In the end it wasn't anything grand. They met on the beach at night and Andrew brought the cake with fancy frosting and some candles. He thought to ask the staff at the store to write *Happy Birthday Thomas* on the cake but didn't in the end. Thomas would have to settle for frosted flowers. He also brought two birthday hats, the cone-shaped ones with pictures of balloons with HAPPY

BIRTHDAY!! written on them. He took them out of his bag to Thomas's laughter, before reaching across and putting one on Thomas's head and then on his own.

"Happy birthday!" he said with childlike enthusiasm.

Thomas, taken by Andrew's gesture, thanked him. "I haven't celebrated my birthday since coming to Banjul. My parents call me each year, but that's it. And now that they're here, I didn't want to be in Sheriff's living room, so I told them I was working late."

"Did you get presents when you were younger?"

"Of course!" he exclaimed. "And my mother used to make a feast of all my favorite foods. We'd have so many people coming to our house. I used to get many presents — toys, clothes. My brothers said I was the most spoiled child on my birthday. I don't know why, but it's true. My mother always planned a bigger party for mine. I think the others were jealous."

The highlight of the night for Andrew was watching Thomas close his eyes, make a wish, and blow out his candles. The setting was perfect — the two of them sitting alone on the beach, the wind and surf providing a soundtrack in the background. But mostly it was the look on Thomas's face in those few seconds when his eyes were closed. He was so calm and still, like nothing could disturb him. When he opened his eyes, before blowing out the candles, he turned to Andrew and smiled. It was a grateful smile. The candles glimmered and reflected off his face.

"Thank you for this," he said softly.

And then he blew out the candles. I asked what he wished for but he only smiled back and told me it was a secret, but that maybe one day

I'd find out. It was beautiful, but also terrible. Why should it have had to be like that? Why is everything about him done in secret? It made me sad for him, to see him alone with only me to celebrate. It made me hate this place for forcing people to have to live like this. Don't they understand what they're doing to him? Don't they care? They don't give a shit about people like him. Like us. But we didn't talk about any of that. We just ate the cake, with our fingers, smacking our lips for emphasis and making a mess with the icing, and silently hoping next year's birthday would be different. When we finished we threw the leftover cake into the water, for the fish.

It was a decision he wrestled with, but Abdou never shared the journal in its entirety with Thomas or Andrew. Andrew was familiar enough with it, and it wasn't necessary to get the information he needed from them to try and soften the blow it would cause at trial. He wanted to preserve as much of their strength and spirit as possible and decided that reading it in prison and having them see what it revealed wasn't what either of them needed to be concerned about. It was his problem now.

But he never truly appreciated how awful it would be hearing it in court until it actually happened.

Thomas shrank in his chair as the officer shared the intimacy and privacy of his birthday. That night had meant everything to him, and it was easy to guess what he had wished for. Listening to Andrew's version of it in their new circumstances, how determined he'd been to create a day where Thomas felt special, and loved, made it especially cruel. That it happened offered no silver lining, at least not then, not there. Seeing Thomas's defeated expression sent Andrew desperately seeking some measure of reassurance from Abdou. But Abdou's face, however sympathetic he tried to make it appear, didn't offer any. There was nothing he could do. It seemed all three of them knew it.

Mr. Touray instructed the officer to turn to one more entry.

"Just to leave no doubt with this court that Mr. Turner knew full well what he was doing when he embarked on his homosexual journey with Mr. Sow – that he was engaging in conduct he knew to be in direct violation of the country's laws, the following excerpt," he announced, "is from just before Mr. Turner made the decision to transition his relationship with Mr. Sow from one of friends to one of lovers. Please," he said to the officer, "if you can read for us."

This might be a big mistake. I don't know what I'm doing. I'm most definitely not thinking. Or maybe I am. No one would tell me this is a smart thing to do. But isn't that the point – that this is the time where I listen to me? I don't think it's dangerous. I've spent enough time in this country to know there's a lot of talk and not a lot of action – nothing will happen and it's easy to keep something quiet. Alex won't care and Isatou is really the only other person who comes to our compound. And Awa. But neither of them would say anything if they ever saw anything, which they won't.

It's not hard to figure this place out. Sure, people aren't accepting... No one knows how anything ends. But that doesn't mean you don't start.

"Thank you," Mr. Touray said. "That is all." And then he took his seat behind his table, not looking over at Abdou or Thomas or Andrew. No questions were asked of the officer, so Abdou had nothing to cross-examine him on. His attempts to deal with some of the journal entries would come through with his witnesses.

"Mr. Bojang," Justice Touray said after excusing the police officer, his voice cutting through the anticipation in the courtroom. "You may make your opening submissions if you wish, or you may proceed directly and call your first witness."

"Your Honour," Abdou said, rising from his chair. "The defense would like to adjourn until the morning to be able to better respond to some of the more recent developments."

The extra half day Abdou gained didn't bring much comfort. In fact, his concerns were exacerbated as soon as he stepped out of the courtroom.

"Mr. Bojang?" he heard called. Turning around he saw a man, he was big but looked small. He was clearly trying to avoid attracting much attention to himself. Leaning against a wall outside the courtroom, he motioned for Abdou to follow him to a more private area of the foyer before continuing. "Mr. Bojang, I am sorry to disturb you, I know you must be very busy..."

"Don't worry, Mr. Jalloh, for you I always have time. Are you ready for your testimony tomorrow? It is very important for Andrew and Thomas."

"Well... that is the thing, Mr. Bojang."

Mr. Jalloh was the main witness for the defense. He had agreed, after much coaxing, to testify on their behalf. It had taken Abdou a week of persistent, polite badgering to convince him, and only after he revealed to him his opinions on homosexuality.

"I don't like it either, Mr. Jalloh. Who would?" Abdou said to him, deliberate in his attempt to cast himself as someone Mr. Jalloh could understand. "But under our laws everyone has a right to a proper defense. Even these people, and we mustn't deny them that. And you've said yourself how much you admired Andrew as a volunteer in your school. He's supported you all year. He needs you now."

They had prepared for the testimony on three separate evenings. Mr. Jalloh always went to Abdou's office – he was too scared to do the sessions in his office for fear colleagues would discover what was going on. He told no one, not even his wives.

It was going to be simple. Abdou planned to ask whether Andrew was good at his job, to which Mr. Jalloh agreed that he was excellent, so good that he was working to get him a position within the education ministry next year. Also, his students liked and respected him, a feeling that was mutual. This would build up Andrew's character, something they both expected would have been called into question in the trial. Abdou wanted to re-humanize at least one of his clients.

But now that wouldn't happen.

"Mr. Jalloh," Abdou pleaded. "Please, you know how critical this is to their case. You backing out now will send a terrible message."

He couldn't, he explained. He was profoundly sorry, but since word had gotten out he was to be a witness on Thomas and Andrew's behalf he started sensing animosity from his colleagues. His wives too had become insolent. They criticized him for standing up for homosexuality without any regard for the consequences it would have on his home and family. And, though he knew he wasn't supposed to, he'd learned about the evidence the state put forward and was starting to believe it might be true.

"I can't, Mr. Bojang. I can't do it."

Abdou just stood there, struggling. "There's no one who will stand up for them."

It was a truth Mr. Jalloh would've preferred not to be reminded of. He was ashamed of himself for backing out, just not enough to change his mind. "Please tell Andrew I'm deeply sorry. I wanted to do everything I could to help him, but this is too much. I can't put myself and my family at risk like this. And especially if the allegations are true." He took Abdou's hand and clasped it in his giant, but soft, grip. "I'm sorry," he said one last time before he released Abdou's hand and walked off.

When Abdou turned around, Mr. Touray was exiting the courtroom. He tried to regain his composure as they caught each other's glances.

"Tomorrow is your day, Mr. Bojang," Mr. Touray said without breaking his stride. "Good luck."

Abdou needed a few more minutes to himself before stepping out from the courthouse into a barrage of cameras and microphones only for him to once again refuse to answer any questions, using his arms to protect his face from the thrusting hands of reporters as he tried to make his way back to his office.

He sat in his solitary office late into the night, until eventually it became morning. He pored over every note he took, from every person he spoke to, trying desperately to find an angle he missed or a piece of evidence he overlooked. His wife called him to make sure he was okay.

"Yes, Manima, I am fine. There are a few more things I need to do before I come home. You shouldn't wait up for me. I'll be home late."

"It's already late," she responded kindly.

"I know," he said. "I just need a little more time. I want to go over my materials again. How are the children?" he said after remembering to ask.

"They're fine. Sleeping. They miss you."

"Maybe when this is over we'll take them for a few days to your family in Cassamance. To have a bit of a break."

"That would be nice."

"Good. The guard is outside?"

"Yes."

"Good. Okay, I have to get back to this."

"Make sure to sleep, Abdou."

"I will."

He turned back to his notes and began to re-assess all he wrote down during the first three days of the trial, trying to discover any holes in the prosecution's case he'd yet to catch. He checked them against all the evidence and testimony he collected. Each page he flipped over, each pile he moved to the floor to make room for a new pile, only reinforced that there was nothing else; that he should go home to his wife. But he couldn't get the image of Thomas from earlier that day out of his mind. He'd never seen him like that before. To be so beaten and know it. And so it was that image that kept him awake tearing through the pages long after he should've gone to bed.

There was a sliver of light stretching across the horizon as he walked up to his home. The guard was sitting outside the gate as he approached. As he walked past him, nodding *good morning* and leaving the guard surprised to see him out at that hour, Abdou perked up his heavy shoulders and stretched out his slumping chin. He was done with always feeling and looking worn in front of everyone. Manima was sitting in the kitchen with a cup of tea when he entered.

"You're awake?"

"I couldn't sleep."

He walked over and sat down next to her. They savored the silence and sat quietly until Manima finally spoke.

"Here," she said, raising her chin to the pots on the stovetop, "I made food for you to take to them."

30

THE OPENING SUBMISSIONS Abdou planned were short. He intended to restate the position established by the previous witnesses – how no one so far had been able to point to a time or place where Thomas and Andrew were seen breaking the law. It was going to be largely technical: absent proof of the *actus reus* there could be no conviction. But when he stood up and looked around at the overflowing courtroom – piercing, judgmental glares from spectators, the impatient gaze of Mr. Touray, the sympathetic gaze of Justice Touray, who clearly understood Abdou's position, and finally the hopeless but thankful faces of Thomas and Andrew – Abdou had a change of heart. If he was to elicit even a measure of serious consideration for his arguments, he needed to display his local credibility. He couldn't merely be the deviants' lawyer.

"Your Honour." His voice rumbled, but he spoke in a measured tone, confidently and without looking at his notes. "We in The Gambia do not like homosexuals. We do not agree with homosexuality. Its ways are not our ways. Its values are not our values. We do not understand why anyone would choose such a path when there are so many indicators – religious, scientific, medical, and sociological – as to its harmful effects on the individual and on society. And as such, our laws are structured in a way to protect us from the harm we perceive that results from the homosexual, from the sodomite.

"But we are also a nation of laws. And our laws affirm all men are presumed innocent until proven guilty. That all men must be given the benefit of the doubt. We cannot compromise on those ideals. Not even in the most trying of circumstances."

Only when someone in the gallery coughed did Abdou realize how quiet the court was. His opening caught everyone off guard and the silent anticipation was as much curiosity for his words as it was curiosity towards him – who was this person willing to defend Thomas and Andrew?

"Regardless of what you think of Mr. Sow and Mr. Turner, if they are in fact homosexuals or not, you can judge them however you want according to your moral and religious codes. But here, here in the court, we can only judge them according to the law. And the law does not operate on a he-said-she-said basis. It does not convict people for heinous crimes because someone suspects how two people look at each other, what one person writes on a sheet of paper, or has in his bathroom. This is not how we judge our brothers and sisters in The Gambia."

He paused and turned to Thomas and Andrew before delivering his final challenge. The two of them wore grateful looks on their faces – they were the most surprised people in the court. Having spent hours with their lawyer, and having been told he intended to keep to black and white arguments about a lack of evidence, they did not expect this impassioned plea from him to suspend prejudice and follow reason.

Their faces each conveyed the same message to him. *You are making us proud. Thank you.*

"It is time for this court to break away from the world of passion and emotion. We do not condemn men simply because we disapprove of who they are, or who they might be. And that, Your Honour, is all we have seen so far in this case. We have heard it from people's words, seen it in their faces. They do not like these two men. But on its own, this is insufficient to condemn them. We will continue the trend started by the prosecution and bring forward witnesses who can attest that while Mr. Sow and Mr. Turner may have been seen together on several occasions, no one has ever seen them engage in behavior violating any criminal provision. This in and of itself must leave this court with at least a reasonable doubt as to their guilt and conclude they are in fact, not guilty," he declared emphatically.

"And now, if it may please the court, the defense calls its first witness."

It was a brilliant performance. One even Abdou was surprised by. He wanted to believe it would have an impact on the case, that at least it might be enough to let Justice Touray reconsider.

The remainder of the day, however, had less of an impact. By this point in the trial Andrew's state was growing more fragile. He didn't react well to the news that Mr. Jalloh had backed out. Mr. Jalloh agreeing to testify on his behalf had been one of the few instances of good news. He knew Mr. Jalloh disapproved of homosexuality, so he shouldn't have been *that* surprised. But Abdou had convinced Mr. Jalloh to put those feelings aside and focus on Andrew as a person, the person he respected and liked working with. He wasn't going to have to say anything that could be construed as approving of homosexuality.

"He was extremely apologetic," Abdou said, trying to appear confident. "I don't think it had anything to do with his view of you. He was scared, that's all."

Andrew scanned the courtroom to try and find Mr. Jalloh. He searched the crowd of spectators for one of those gregarious expressions Mr. Jalloh's face made each time he got excited about something. But the only faces he saw displayed the same hostile and disparaging expressions he'd been seeing for days. He tried to listen for his big bellowing laugh that could project itself over any amount of noise. But he heard only murmurs. Mr. Jalloh wasn't there.

Without Mr. Jalloh, the witness testimony was predictable but lackluster. True to form, both of the expat witnesses confirmed they had seen Thomas and Andrew together but added that the two of them gave no indication they were ever more than friends. They spoke matter-of-factly, if slightly apprehensively. Trying to hide the accent of empire, each of them said they expressed profound disbelief upon hearing the allegations that Thomas and Andrew were in a relationship.

While this was all Abdou could have asked for, Mr. Touray used it as further evidence of the relationship, arguing that the witnesses' perceptions of Thomas and Andrew were clearly clouded by their Western backgrounds. Through his questioning, he forced both to admit what Abdou was afraid they might admit, that they did not disapprove of homosexuality, confirming the suspicions of everyone in the courtroom and severely undermining their credibility.

"Can you say with absolute, one-hundred percent confidence, that your values and morality do not impact how you see the world, how you observe your surroundings?"

Neither could. *I think I'm an objective person, but no, I can't say so, at least with one-hundred percent certainty.*

"So all we know for sure is you frequently saw them together," Mr. Touray confirmed.

"And one last question," he said to each of them. "To your knowledge, did Andrew ever have a girlfriend in The Gambia?"

"No," they each answered, looking apologetically at Andrew.

By the time the second witness sat down and the day's proceedings had drawn to a close, Abdou looked somber and subdued as he bid his clients goodnight. He did what he could.

Each day of the trial he called Andrew's parents in Dakar as he rode back to his office. He always encouraged them to be hopeful, to know that the judge was fair, and that he would keep pressing forward with his case and the strategy he'd briefed them on. After today, Andrew's parents would want to know all the details, especially Mr. Jalloh's defense of Andrew's character. But Abdou, worn and angry — at everyone and at himself — didn't want to make the phone call. He wanted nothing more than to go back to how things were before he took this case. It was a feeling that made him feel even more dispirited.

Leaving the building and walking through a throng of reporters for what he hoped would be his second last time, Abdou spotted Suleiman standing at the edge of the road in front of the courthouse.

"Mr. Bojang, a question please," Suleiman said in a tone to attract his friend's attention and suggest it wasn't a standard journalist's request.

Abdou stopped for a second so his friend could see his face before he turned away, walking in the opposite direction as a few of the remaining spectators hurled insults at him.

31

ANDREW WASN'T SURE if he was already awake or if it was the footsteps that awoke him. He heard them from a distance. They were distinct, popping up from the concrete and sending out a more pronounced echo than the familiar sounds of the guards' boots. They continued advancing up the hallway towards the doorway of his empty cell block. His nerves ratcheted up several notches and his heart started to beat so loudly he thought he could hear it outside his body. His mind flashed back to taunting warnings from the guards. *One day, when you least expect it, someone will come to teach you a lesson.*

He didn't know what time it was, but it seemed too early for court. The trial had ended Friday afternoon and Abdou told Thomas and Andrew to expect the verdict some time on the weekend.

"Justice Touray will want to make it clear he is deliberating seriously," Abdou told them. "I'm sure the verdict won't be rendered immediately. Perhaps tomorrow, or the day after."

Since being returned to his cell, Andrew fell in and out of a fitful sleep for what felt like days, constantly waking but never feeling rested. There was nothing he could do but wait in the darkness. Alone, he'd never known silence to be so cruel.

Now, it was the breaking of that silence that made him fearful.

The door to his hallway unlocked and swung open. Several figures appeared, walking briskly. Standing and looking out to his left, he made out the silhouette of three guards in front, all shining flashlights into the darkness. Andrew frightfully jumped backward, placing himself as far from the door of his cell as possible, nervously awaiting the footsteps, which grew louder and louder. He hoped they would somehow keep walking past his cell.

They didn't.

Squinting and trying to block out one of the shining flashlights with his hands, barely able to make out the faces in front of him, he saw a woman standing at the head of the pack. He was too stunned and alarmed to think clearly and it took him several seconds to recognize Maya in the darkness. It took him several more seconds to realize he wasn't dreaming.

"Get the light out of his face," she ordered before taking a step closer towards him. "We have to go, Andrew," she said before motioning to a guard, who proceeded to open the door to Andrew's cell. She took clothes from the hands of another guard, *his clothes*, and handed them to him. "Here, change into these."

Confused, he barely moved.

"Can you give him some privacy, please," she said, turning to the guards, who backed away slightly. "Andrew," she spoke softly and kindly, "we reached an agreement late last night for your release. There's a flight to Dakar leaving shortly. You have a ticket on it, and then an onward ticket with your parents back home."

He stood for a moment in silence, thinking about what Maya had just said. "How?" he looked at her, wide-eyed and transfixed.

"You don't have to concern yourself with that right now. Suffice it to say we were able to leverage the existence of foreign assets held by the government and government personnel. The official agreement is confidential, so I can't give you any more information. What matters is that it's done. There's a release form waiting for you downstairs with your passport. It's time to get you home."

Home. Away from here, from this.

It was a scene that had played out in his head countless times. His rescue. How he might be plucked away from this nightmare. Over time though, he'd become more deflated and pessimistic about it ever materializing. By the end of the trial he figured he was trapped and started, however reluctantly, to accept that. Now she was telling him he was free.

But only he.

"What about Thomas?" he asked Maya, still holding his clothes, knowing but afraid of the answer.

"Andrew," she said sympathetically. He knew.

"What's going to happen to him?"

She paused, debating how forthright she wanted to be. "He'll probably be found guilty, like you would have been, and then sentenced."

He appreciated her candor, anything less and he would've known she wasn't being truthful. Still, getting the answer he expected didn't make it any easier to digest. Just a few days earlier Andrew was reeling at the feeling of being abandoned by Mr. Jalloh. The whole trial had been an illustration of a society turning its back on Thomas. Now Andrew was being asked to be that person and walk away.

"I'm just supposed to leave? Like that?" he asked her, his face starting to break.

"Leaving doesn't mean you have to abandon him. There's a lot you can do on his behalf from back home." She was right, he thought. Consolation, maybe.

She stepped aside so Andrew could see that Abdou was with her before continuing. "We've arranged for you to be able to say goodbye to him."

Andrew looked at Abdou, who had difficulty making eye contact with him, before turning back to Maya. He didn't have the energy to thank him and express his gratitude, which was profound. His mind was too worn out to think about so many things all at once.

"And that's it? I say goodbye and leave? Walk away and out the door and he stays inside?"

"I know how hard this might be."

"No," he stopped her, angrily. "You don't."

She apologized as his tears started to flow and he brushed them away, rubbing the dirt from his hands off onto his cheeks. She turned around as he changed to give him privacy, leaving the sounds of his sniffling to fill the hallway.

These pants are too big.

His tears were gone when he turned around to face her, not knowing what to do with his prison clothes.

"You can leave them in the cell. The guards will take care of them," she told him.

He dropped the clothes and watched them fall before turning his face back to hers. "You said you made the deal last night," he said to her with a puzzled expression. "What time is it now?"

"It's five-thirty in the morning," she answered, catching onto his question. "The government would only allow you to leave now as the agreement says you must go straight from here to the airport and onto the plane. We weren't allowed to bring you to the embassy or even to take you to your house to collect your things, which we'll arrange to have sent to you."

"Okay," he murmured. Even in his dreams he knew it would be hard to accept his freedom and leave Thomas behind. But in his dreams he was still able to balance his emotions, to accept this was truly the only way. At some level he could also rejoice, draw some comfort and relief. In reality, though, there was none of that. Andrew was feeling so terrible, so sick to his stomach, that he didn't think he even deserved any of that. He walked out from his cell heavily and hesitantly, as if his body couldn't make up its mind. What would he tell Thomas? *I'm getting out and you have to stay. But don't worry, I'll start a petition...* It sounded pathetic.

Thomas was waiting in the interview room. They had left him there in the dark without telling him why. When the guard turned on a light and opened the door, Andrew stood alone in the entranceway. He was wearing his own clothes. Thomas processed everything much quicker than Andrew had and immediately figured out what was happening.

"You're going home," he said with a big, loving smile. It was a genuine smile, one that in those circumstances only love could make possible.

Andrew's tears burst out from him and without any regard for the guards standing behind him, he threw himself into Thomas's arms and cried apologetically into his shoulder. *It's okay, it's okay,* Thomas kept saying to him, holding him for what he knew would be the last time. When Andrew regained some of his composure he lifted his head and faced Thomas.

"I'm so sorry," he whispered.

"You're keeping the promise you made. Don't be sorry. This is what I wanted."

Andrew smiled, before swallowing down some of his lingering emotions. He found Thomas's answer hard to believe.

One of the guards made a sound as if to hurry them up and they could hear Abdou demand they be given a few more minutes.

They were looking at each other in the silence, hoping it might suspend the time.

"Do you remember the night we danced? On the beach when we were walking, and heard that music playing?" Thomas asked quietly.

Andrew's face brightened and he nodded.

"It's one of my favorite memories. We were walking together and I stopped. You took a few steps ahead and then saw me standing there. When you figured out what I wanted, you had this amazingly tender look on your face that I can still picture. We'd never danced before. It wasn't big or grand, but it was intimate, it was ours. I think about it a lot and realize no matter where I am or what is happening, no one can take that away from me. So at night when I don't sleep, sometimes I close my eyes and I hear the music once more." As he finished the sentence, Thomas closed his eyes in front of Andrew and returned to his memory. His face projected satisfaction and peace of mind in a way it hadn't since their night of dancing in Freetown. For a moment, Thomas's upper body began to sway, slowly and rhythmically. "I can hear it still," he said, swaying softly with his eyes closed. Andrew had to listen closely but he could hear Thomas faintly humming the song's slow melody, seemingly having transposed himself out of the cruel prison interview room and back onto the beach, letting himself be soothed by its light breeze still blowing and the soft music still playing, seeing himself there, seeing both of them there, dancing.

Andrew looked down at his hand as he felt Thomas reach out and squeeze it. When he looked back up, Thomas was looking back at him with moist eyes.

"I'm going to be okay," he told him. They both knew it wasn't true, a lie they would let slip past. And then, before he was overtaken by the heartbreak and fear quickly consuming his insides, Thomas whispered to Andrew that he loved him. Andrew whispered it back, barely audible, struggling to move his lips. They squeezed each other's hands as tightly as they could.

"I'm going to get you out," Andrew told him. It was another lie they both thought, but one they wanted to desperately believe.

"Andrew?" Maya said nervously. "We have to go."

It was a straight drive down the Banjul-Serrekunda Highway to the airport. Andrew sat in the back of a U.S. Embassy jeep, with Maya and the driver in the front. Abdou was also in the back, behind the driver. Andrew didn't speak at all during the ride and was too exhausted to think about what was happening. It had all been so quick. With his head pressed up against the window, he was in a daze as they drove past places he saw only in a blur. The route from the prison to the airport didn't go through the area he lived in and where he spent most of his time, making much of what they passed unfamiliar. When he realized this, that he wouldn't have the chance to give everything one final look, he wasn't bothered – he couldn't think of any goodbye, with people or places, that he cared to have. He just wanted to go, and disappear. With the daylight bringing his surroundings into clearer focus, he grew anxious to be rid of it all.

As they kept driving, passing the same ramshackle shops and buildings that had unnerved him on that first drive from the airport, Andrew saw that everything was shuttered. The yellow-stained bottles of fuel were yet to be lined up on the roadside. The workers had yet to arrive for another day's work that would once again leave their bodies greasy and worn. It was quiet. The music that blared from shops and stands was not yet turned on. The road around them was almost empty. Even the trees and bushes were still. It all seemed so completely devoid of movement. And though it was early, when everything ought to have been still, seeing the morning frozen like that made Andrew remember all of a sudden. Of course, it was a Sunday.

Acknowledgements

The idea for this novel was inspired by periods of living and travelling in East and West Africa, in countries where homosexuality is illegal. It also followed a semester teaching law in India, less than a year after the Supreme Court affirmed India's criminalization of homosexual activity. During my travels, and at Toronto's World Pride in 2014, I had the fortune of meeting advocates from several of these and other countries. These advocates did not originally set out to lead movements or court challenges, but owing to circumstances in their societies, they have. It was never their dream to have their pictures in newspapers; they envisioned a life without threats to their safety.

Speaking with each of these individuals helped shape my outlook on the continuing struggle for LGBT rights. We can learn a great deal from their ideas and experiences. Their resilience and optimism deserves our support and admiration.

Writing a novel for the first time is a daunting task. I was fortunate to have a wide network of family and friends who were willing (and happy?) to take significant amounts of time to offer thoughts and insights over various drafts. Your comments made the finished product stronger and your encouragement provided critical reassurance. Most of all, the conversations we had about the book, as if it was a real book with real characters, were surreal experiences for me. And so, to the following, you have my gratitude and sincere thanks: Danny Auron, Marlon Danilewitz, Kristi Evelyn, Steven Friedman, Jon Katz and Lisa Lipschitz, Jill Lustig, Carol Moses, Ruth Panofsky, Bill Perry, Amy Rechtsman, Robbie Roth, and Spencer Shiffman.

Good neighbours in life are not to be overlooked, especially when one of them has a doctorate in English. Dr. Heidi Craig was gracious enough to act as my English editor, pointing out stylistic and grammatical faux pas I didn't know existed. Thank you.

My editor, John Paine, worked with me and pushed me to think in a more sophisticated way about how to take a good story and turn it into an interesting novel. Thank you for the challenge, and for assisting me as I strove to meet it.

I'd like to sincerely thank my family. To my in-laws, the Friedmans, though not all of you could commit to reading drafts in the tight timeframes I required, your support and curiosity throughout helped keep my determination going. To my brother, Robert, your glowing review of the first seven pages was one of the highlights of the drafting process; you could've stopped there. Thanks to you and Jaclyn for bookending this journey with unrivaled enthusiasm. To my dad and Nancy, you have always encouraged me to write, especially when I was just starting. Without that, I would not have had the confidence to undertake this project. My mom, Nurith Safir, spent years trying to impart to me one crucial piece of advice, "open your heart". I don't think I could've written this book the way I did had I not listened. Thank you.

While we're on the subject: Mark. On so many levels, this book would not exist without you. The time and energy that you put into it, acting as my editor and agent extraordinaire, made it far superior than I could have ever done on my own. Each time I saw you sitting at the computer, going line-by-line, and then pushing me to do better, I was amazed by your commitment and abilities. It's just one more reason I'm the luckiest guy to have found you. Hillel was right.

Last, a note about The Gambia. At first I questioned whether to set this novel in The Gambia or a fictional country. I was nervous about telling a story that would result in an overly negative image of the country and its people. Considering the warmth with which Gambians welcomed me and the fond memories I have of my time living and working there, this was a prospect that did not sit well. On the other hand, the truth is that in the past, the Gambian government has espoused some of the most hateful rhetoric towards LGBT individuals, a sentiment that found widespread support throughout the population. It was the reality of this contrast, a place simultaneously beautiful and cruel, that helped me grow comfortable with setting the novel there. In a way, that contrast makes it easier, for I would like to believe that a place that is capable of such beauty and generosity of spirit is ultimately incapable of forever seeing its brothers and sisters as anything but.